Praise

Best American Erotica 2007

"Curl up by yourself or read to your lover. Susie provides us with a cornucopia of sexy stories that are both hot and smart. Erotica for the thinking person!"
—Candida Royalle, erotic filmmaker and author of *How to Tell a Naked Man What to Do*

"Susie Bright just keeps 'em coming!"
—Kensington Ladies Erotica Society

"A multicultural, omni-sexual smorgasbord that ranges from raunchy to sweet, heartrending to hilarious. Who knew there was so much first-rate erotic prose out there today?"
—Laura Mirsky and Mark Rotenberg, *The Rotenberg Collection: Forbidden Erotica*

"Editor Extraordinaire Susie Bright is hard-wired into America's most decadent fantasies."
—Alison Tyler, editor of *A is for Amour, B is for Bondage, C is for Co-Eds,* and *D is for Dress-Up* (Pretty Things Press)

"This diverse and often thought-provoking collection contains something for every sensual or sexual taste."
—erotica author Lacey Alexander

OTHER TITLES BY SUSIE BRIGHT

The Best

AMERICAN
EROTICA
2007

edited by
SUSIE
BRIGHT

A Touchstone Book
Published by Simon & Schuster
New York   London   Toronto   Sydney

TOUCHSTONE
Rockefeller Center
1230 Avenue of the Americas
New York, NY 10020

Copyright acknowledgments are on pages 236–239

TOUCHSTONE and colophon are registered trademarks of Simon & Schuster, Inc.

For information about special discounts for bulk purchases, please contact Simon & Schuster Special Sales at 1-800-456-6798 or business@simonandschuster.com.

Designed by Jamie Kerner-Scott

Manufactured in the United States of America

10 9 8 7 6 5 4 3 2 1

ISBN-13: 978-0-7432-8962-7
ISBN-10:   0-7432-8962-5

This edition of *The Best American Erotica*
is dedicated to the memory of Octavia Butler

CONTENTS

INTRODUCTION

E NVY THE YOUNG. Their beauty, their incomparable strength, cannot be bottled, as dearly as their elders try to squeeze a facsimile out of a jar or a needle.

Youth—that petal before it uncurls, that curious morning dew—what enormous potential. Anything is possible because nothing has been tried. *Envy* them? We want to gobble them up—their very presence is an incitement, a rebuke to death. They are defiant.

But turn over the card. Power comes only with age, which elders have in spades.

You can't drive, you can't hold the keys, and you can't lay claim until you grow the fuck up. The very words "experienced lover" describe a life lived, adventures drawn upon.

Beauty and strength may open doors, but it's only wisdom that tells you how to cross the threshold.

When I was young, the phrase "generation gap" came into vogue. So did the thrilling insult of my old comrade Jack Weinberg: "Never trust anyone over thirty."

Those same baby boomers are rather testy these days, and trust no one. It's coming out in their erotica, as well as their children's.

The '60s generation, more than any before it, is outraged at the prospect of mortality and determined to beat it. No Olympian gods were ever so vain. They look at their offspring and feel a combination of possession, fury, and guilt. Love? Sure, of course. But I'm talking about the darker side of Zeus's parental ego, which among the boomer set is a constant battle with narcissism.

I speak from the cusp of boom/GenX. I've wobbled on both sides. I look at my daughter, and her beauty and vitality are so vivid I could faint. I want to lock her up—no, I mean, I want to *empower* her. Actually, no, I want to scare her shitless. Oh, let's be honest: *I'm* scared shitless. My generation has melted the polar ice caps, looted the bank, and my inheritance to her is what?

I can remember myself at sixteen so clearly. I wanted to know everything. I wanted to fuck everyone, especially the interesting, self-possessed grown-up types. I had one girlfriend, similarly inclined, who became lovers with the an older New Left patriarch. The fellow was twice her age, with thinning hair, and I was skeptical.

She shushed me. "He's great," she said. "I can wake him up in the middle of the night and ask any question, and he will always know the answer."

Her thirst for knowledge wasn't what impressed me. It was "the middle of the night" that was so seductive—those witching hours when only babies slumber.

When was the moment when our youth become aware of their charms, as well as their desperation? They seem younger now, although that could just be my mother talking. But look at our twenty-first-century culture. Every teenager knows the time to launch a career as a porn star is in the weeks following high school graduation. Celebrity journalism shows us that Hercules and Aphrodite will both be toppled in their early twenties without massive intervention. It's no wonder the commodification of good looks and muscles has wrought an erotic backlash.

Virginity. Authenticity. The natural pearl. These are what are idealized today, as well as commercialized beyond all recognition. Fake sex—titillation—is for sale; real sex is elusive and underground.

Take this state of affairs, couple it with a pox of unprecedented meddling in people's personal lives by the religious right, and the result is a toxic brew. Privacy, freedom, and nature are gasping for breath. Hypocrites alone have something to crow about.

In my fifteen years of editing *BAE*, I have never seen such a yowling, lustful, spitting breach between young and old.

Of course, such observations are taboo. Lower your voice! Young people aren't supposed to have a sexual bone in their bodies, right? And their elders, if they are immune to beauty and make all the rules, should be able to keep it in their pants. What a squawk.

There is so much guilt and fear about the obvious—that young people *d o* have hormones, and old people aren't altogether blind—that helpful discussion in the public sphere has shriveled. It is left to fiction for the truth to come out.

The truth looks like this: any conflict has the potential to become erotic. Such honesty might get complicated, tragic, or unpredictable. Eros is kissing cousins with aggravation.

The conscience of our society drives us to protect our young, to provide for them, to cheer and cherish their independence. But we wouldn't need any conscience if doing so wasn't a challenge, if it didn't demand sacrifice. The temptations include neglect, exploitation, and dependence.

Every one of those emotions came into play as I reviewed this year's erotica. As in each edition, there is a serendipity of issues among authors, a time capsule where writers who have nothing else in common find themselves buzzing on the same theme.

This year's tender spot is a brutal tug of war and lust between generations, in which tale after tale pits an attraction/ambivalence with youth on one side and their elders on the other:

> OCTAVIA BUTLER'S last novel, *Fledgling*, features a protagonist who appears to be a black girl-child who has barely survived a fire—but is, in fact, much older than even she knows.

> SHANNA GERMAIN'S story of a family camping trip shows a married couple who discover a unintended spark because of their grown daughter's romantic example.

> DANIEL DUANE'S novel, *A Mouth Like Yours*, traces a memory of a young woman who taunts her father and terrifies her boyfriend with her sexual independence.

> DENNIS COOPER, legendary in his work about young men hustlers, takes on the story of a teenage prostitute, whose death or myth is exhaustively debated by the men who hired him and perhaps killed him.

> JESSICA CUTLER'S memoir from *The Washingtonienne* is about a young woman who drags Washington's gray-haired elite down into a scandal pit, with nothing more than the crook of her pretty little finger.

ALICE ERIAN, the author of *Towelhead,* writes in the voice of a young Lebanese American teenager who, among other things, gets involved with a racist Gulf War soldier next door.

PEGGY MUNSON takes a walk, dyke-style, with Daddy and Baby, who play an erotic game of Rock, Paper, Scissors.

KATHRYN HARRISON'S novel *Envy* is about a psychiatrist who is seduced by one of his young clients, not without a bit of blackmail.

MARIE LYN BERNARD's story "What Happened to That Girl" is about a bunch of foster kids from the same home who unexpectedly reunite after their eighteenth birthdays, when one of them becomes a famous porn star.

IN TREBOR HEALEY'S "The Pancake Circus," a young man is attracted to an indifferent, handsome dishwasher his own age, who he discovers is on probation for sex crimes.

Finally, MATTHEW ADDISON, in his "Wish Girls," demonstrates one of the sweetest endings: a young man, nurtured by fembots, finally grows up and leaves them behind.

There are a few others in this collection that miraculously escaped the *Lolita* backlash. You'll find poker games, polyamory, kitchen grease, and other "dangerous games with competent people," as author Kim Wright puts it.

Of course Nabokov came to mind in my deliberations. Hence my little nickname for the culprits. Their generation-slashed stories made me want to revisit the history of what has been called the most exquisite novel in the English language.

Lolita was unique when when it came out in 1955. It wasn't reviewed anywhere, and sales were terrible.

But a year later, as publisher Maurice Girodias recalls, "Things started to happen—strange things indeed. Graham Greene mentioned *Lolita* as one of the the best books of the year. That provoked a demential reaction on the part of the editor of the *Daily Express* who accused Green and the *Times* of helping sell pornography of the lewdest variety . . . the overall result of that commotion was to create a great deal of interest in *Lolita* among partisans and detractors, an infinitesimal number of whom had read the book."

Nabokov has been afraid to publish his opus: after all, it was written in the voice of a cruel and remorseless pedophile who ruins quite a few lives, including his own, in the passion for his "nymphet." "Light of my life, fire of my loins, my sin, my soul, Lolita." I remember chanting that passage as a speech exercise in acting class; such was its legacy.

In Nabokov's heyday, postwar parents were about to send all their kids to college for the first time. It was a prosperous, middle-class expansion, it was America *Über Alles*. It was also the tremorous beginning of a beat/rock/art renaissance that would rip the covers off a variety of things Mommy and Daddy would rather not talk about.

It was a different time from today's tableau: quality education out of reach, class polarization, Bush fiddling while Rome melts. Yet it shares the same vibe of false consciousness—the pretty parade of fake news, fake sex, fake confidence—that can never cover up the bubbling pitch.

And so, to strip myself bare, I have to admit there is one story missing from my collection this year. The finest erotic book I read the past twelve months was the English translation of Gabriel García Márquez's novella *Melancholy Memories of My Whores*. You won't find it here.

It's the story of an elderly gentleman, a lifetime john of leisure, who decides that, on the occasion of his ninetieth birthday, he will spend the night at his favorite brothel with a pubescent virgin.

Our man has every intention of bedding her, but upon entering the small room for their date, he discovers the child fast asleep on the bed. Not wishing to disturb her slumber, he sits beside her to wait, his own mind awash with *memorias melancólicas*.

The witching hours fall upon us once again, when those closest to death are the most conscious.

Márquez declined to be part of this collection—a disappointment to me, forty-plus years his junior. His reason was that the nature of his material was too delicate. I, of course, had a reply that was just as sheer.

Everything in this book is "delicate." Erotic reality is not for the clichéd. I don't publish pulp about Mr. And Mrs. HappyPants waltzing down the shore to an ending you can see a mile away.

The more that public life discourages sexual maturity and honesty, the further truth retreats to fiction, to poetry. The lyric of dissent is delicate indeed.

Every author I publish who "crosses a line" does so not because they have a prescription, or a solution, but because they are compelled to spell something out, and to spill something just as plain.

It's hard to be blunt, to take a risk, to endure misunderstanding. If you are acclaimed as the finest writer of your time in the same breath that they damn you as a lewd pornographer, you'll know you've unraveled something worthwhile. Take your fine lace from Bruges and toss it; what we have here is aroused, conflicted—and very, very wide awake.

On the Eighth Day

Vanesa Baggott

THERE ONCE WAS AN all-powerful superbeing called God. He spent his time wandering around the universe creating life and imposing order. One day he happened across a planet he had created a few million years earlier. He sat astride its pockmarked moon, gazed down at the blue surface, and wondered how it had survived without him. As his head breached the outer atmosphere, he was astounded by what he saw; the oceans were teeming with life. He flew down for a closer look. In the southern ocean he caught up with a wandering albatross that told him a flame-haired woman was responsible for creating everything in the sea. God headed north and found a vast rain forest crawling with life. He lay down in the canopy and breathed in great lungfuls of the sweet damp air. He meticulously examined all the flora and fauna. He interrogated the wriggling insects and the fabulously colored birds, the scaly crocodiles and the leaping monkeys. Everything he spoke to gave him the same answer. He learned that the flame-haired woman was called Mother Nature and that she had a twin sister called Mother Earth.

The more God heard, the angrier he got. Who were these females who dared to challenge his authority? Why had they presumed to usurp his power over his creation? He circled the globe looking for them. He caught sight of a dark-haired woman climbing into a crater, so he flew after her. Down and down he fell, deep into the heart of the planet. But all he saw were molten iron and bubbling magma. He followed a lava tube back to the surface and came out in a crack at the bottom of the ocean. He searched the seven seas and the five continents and still he couldn't find them. It was nearing the end of the day. Tired from his travels, God bathed in a thunderstorm. He whipped up a tornado to dry off and noticed two figures, their bare arms outstretched to the wind. One was tall but round-bellied, with auburn hair that flew around her head like a circle of flames. The other had purple-black skin and a body like an athlete. She wore gold chains about her waist; emeralds, rubies, and diamonds twinkled on her fingers and toes. God gazed at the sisters and started to burn. His mouth dropped open and his breath quickened. His very core throbbed with a heat that overwhelmed him. He took a deep breath and the swirling winds grew quiet. He was revealed in all his glory. The sisters stared at him. They seemed neither surprised nor afraid. A little unsettled by their level gaze, God said, "I am God, the Creator." The women smiled. "My lord," they said, and bowed low before him. His chest swelled with contentment.

The women showed him the bounty of the planet, and God saw that it was good. Mother Nature reached up and peeled off a strip of blue sky. Smiling, she wrapped it lovingly around his shoulders. She smelled of lilacs carried on a summer breeze. Her eyes were as green as a freshly opened leaf, and her skin was as golden as a field of ripe corn. Mother Earth's features were as hard as a chiseled rock face, but her lips were full and smooth like pebbles. Her skin shone like polished stone. God felt the gaze of her glittering black eyes probing his body. The three superbeings spent the day frolicking like children, chasing the sunrise and playing hide-and-seek with the moon.

At sunset the sisters led God to a grove of fruit trees. There they lay him down laughing and fed him peaches, plums, and apricots. Mother Nature squashed oranges into his chest and sucked off the flesh, clamping his chest hairs between her teeth. Mother Earth pushed berries into his mouth and then scooped them out with her tongue. Then to God's delight they squirmed down to his belly and flicked their sticky tongues between his legs. They gathered armfuls of mangoes and squeezed them into a pulp. They smoothed the pulp all over his engorged flesh and slowly licked it off. When the sisters had swallowed the last mouthful and felt God's giant frame shudder beneath them, they sat astride God's face and rubbed against him until his skin shone and his beard dripped. He gulped down their juices. They tasted sweeter than nectar and hotter than lava. All through the night the sisters made love to him. They rubbed his whole body with their scent. His beard grew sticky and his face glowed. They smothered his mouth and his sex at the same time, laughing and sucking on each other's breasts. When he entered one sister, she fed off the other. When he entered the second sister, she lapped up the first. Then they plucked a smooth moonbeam from the sky and pleasured him together. As the rosy-fingered dawn clung to the horizon, the three lovers lay down on the shore with their feet resting on a coral reef and let the brightly colored fishes play between their toes.

Later that day, God awoke and sat up. The beach was empty. Marram grass sprouted where Mother Nature had lain. God walked along the shore calling them, but there was no answer. He sat heavily on a sand dune, feeling weighed down as if there were a stone lodged in his huge heart. He flew across the ocean and asked a basking shark if it had seen them. The shark told God the sisters were on the farthest shore giving birth to two sets of twins.

When God arrived, Mother Nature was still in the throes of childbirth. He stood around feeling awkward. Two baby girls plopped into the waves. Where the birth fluid touched the water it was transformed into a thousand golden elvers. Soon a glistening shoal wriggled at Mother Nature's feet. Her sister leaned against a dune nursing two infant boys. God surveyed his new family and seethed. He had not meant for this to happen. He felt used. He suspected the sisters of somehow luring him to the planet to satisfy their own ends. He vowed not to fall into their tender trap again. It was the end of the second day.

The third day dawned. The Father was missing. The sisters nursed their children and looked up at the sky uneasily. God was venting his fury on the solar system. He whisked the clouds of Jupiter into a frenzy, creating a giant red spot the color of his anger. He threw asteroids at Saturn's icy moons and shoved Uranus off its orbit, leaving it tilted on its side. He sucked the atmosphere from Mercury and spat it at Venus. His energies spent, God returned to Earth resolved to confront the sisters. Mother Nature waved to him from the top of a snowy mountain range. Snow tumbled from the hem of her gown, and a frozen mist hung around her head like a halo. She was flanked by two young women; Eve had pale creamy skin and flaxen hair, while Lilith's skin was white like snow, but her hair was as black as night. Eve shyly averted her gaze. Lilith stared at her father and smiled coquettishly. God acknowledged his daughters with a nod and drew his cloak around himself to hide his engorged flesh. He took Mother Nature by the hand and led her to a continent in the southern ocean.

There he paced up and down a beach, roaring like a wounded lion. How dare she usurp him, how dare she seduce him and bring new life onto this, his planet, he complained. Mother Nature stood in the shallows listening, and at her feet a million silver fishes played. She went to him and stroked his long blond hair. She told him that her sister was to blame and reassured him that she would never do anything against his wishes. She laid his head on her shoulder and plaited white flowers into his beard. She kindled a fire, roasted a wild beast, and fed him its succulent flesh. Then they raised a toast with sparkling wine and strolled along the sands. Crimson flowers sprouted at Mother Nature's every footfall. Her beauty bewitched God. She whispered in his ear, but the roar of desire so filled his head he heard only the suck and fizz of the sea across the sand. Two chocolate-colored nipples as big as his fists rubbed their hardness against his chest, and as the sun set they clung to each other, their bodies steaming in the cooling air. Mother Nature's belly was rounded like the bend in a river. God rubbed his beard over its curves and slid down to the warm nigrescence at the top of her thighs. She wrapped her legs around his head, and the sand beneath them boiled and turned to glass. A great blast of steam rose into the air as they tumbled into the sea.

Cradled by the water, the lovers coupled. Their rhythmic movements created a tsunami that swept across the southern ocean and generated a hot current that circled the planet. They swam as one throughout the seven seas, a trail of phytoplankton and zooplankton blossoming in their wake. Twisted together, they plunged to the seafloor and lit up the pale creatures swimming there. As the third day ended they floated in the shallows of a warm sea. Mother Nature swam under God's legs and pushed herself against him. Silver fishes nipped her breasts as they dipped in and out of the water. As God reached his climax he pulled himself free. Mother Nature cupped him and lapped up his seed, but some dripped from her lips and fell into the sea. A host of strange animals sprang from the waves. Scorpions and poisonous snakes, huge hairy spiders and luminous frogs hopped and wriggled over the sand and disappeared into the bush. A shuddering jellyfish with long tentacles floated out to sea, and a shoal of fish with sharp pointed teeth migrated up a river estuary.

On the fourth day, God awoke to find himself deep in the belly of the Earth. Close by, Mother Earth stirred a bubbling lava lake with a spear of lightning. She dipped a golden goblet into the lake and beckoned to him, but God was wary and did not budge.

Two handsome young men appeared from a cave. God recognized his grown-up sons; Adam had dark hair and looked identical to his father, whereas Lucifer had olive-colored skin and hair like strands of gold. A light shone from Lucifer's skin and, dressed as he was in pure white, to God he looked like an angel. The boys dipped two goblets into the lake and drank the bubbling lava. Instantly they appeared invigorated. Adam offered a cup to his father; this time God took it, and the three men shot out of the volcano and high into the sky.

God, anxious to impress, took his sons on a tour of the solar system. Together they did a slingshot of the sun. Lucifer flew into the center of the star and came out trailing clouds of light. Adam stayed by his father's side. They explored Mercury's craters and the extinct volcanoes on Venus. Adam remained silent, in awe of all he saw, but Lucifer scoffed. He lifted a fistful of Mars's red dust and laughed. "This is nothing but a barren wilderness," he said. God's face reddened, but he said nothing. On Jupiter their father stirred the atmosphere until it spun like a tornado. Laughing, Adam flew straight through the gas giant. Lucifer yawned. God plucked a ring from Saturn and gave it to Adam, who threw it spinning into the Milky Way. Adam explored Uranus on its strange tilted orbit while God rolled ice, gas, and rock together to create moons. Lucifer took a run at the planet and kicked it hard. They all watched as it reversed its spin. God was furious. He seized a passing comet and flung it at his son. Lucifer dodged out of the way, and the comet careered off into space. Adam was bringing a bundle of bright blue methane from Neptune to show his brother. The comet struck, the methane exploded, and Adam's body was petrified inside a ball of ice and rock. God fell to his knees. The aura of white light surrounding Lucifer faded and turned green. He spat at his father and fled. God gently lifted the new moon and set it in orbit around Pluto. It was the end of the fourth day.

The next day, Mother Earth found God curled around a sand dune;

he reminded her of an immense fetus. His tears had created a trail of salt that meandered down to the sea like a stream of crystallized moonlight. She dipped her fingers into a flaming goblet and coaxed him to taste. Tentatively, he licked her finger. The lava sizzled on his tongue. Beneath the burning was a delicious tang. God licked his lips. He snatched the goblet and drained its contents. As the lava flowed into his belly it rekindled the fire inside him. An insane longing surged through his body. Mother Earth's eyes flickered with a green light, and she began to laugh. She loosened her golden bodice, allowing her breasts to peep out. Her skirts billowed apart, and God fell on his hands and knees, panting like a dog. She seized his beard and dragged him after her. The vast white wastelands of Antarctica stretched below them as Mother Nature hauled God into a cave dug into the side of a mountain. She filled her mouth with crushed ice, dribbled it over his thighs, and swallowed him up. She took a draft of lava and licked his buttocks until they sizzled. Her mouth probed his perineum, then settled into a strong rhythmic suck. God shuddered. His hot breath formed a shimmering layer of melting ice over the walls of the cave. Mother Earth poured more lava down his throat and continued to suck. She broke off an icicle, fashioned it into a smooth nub, and pleasured him with it. God reached a crescendo but lost none of his vigor. He lifted Mother Earth's thighs and pushed his face between them. She wriggled and twisted as he drank deeply. The juices made his blood roar for more. He flipped her over and slowly, deliberately, pushed himself inside. Mother Nature reached between her legs and cupped him with her hand. The heat from their bodies melted all the ice around them. They slid out through the mouth of the cave and down to the sea. Penguins and seals swam past, brushing themselves against the couple, infected by the warm currents that swelled around them. At the bottom of the ocean Mother Nature sat astride God while he sucked on her breasts. Attracted by the heat, great clouds of plankton swirled around them. As he reached his climax, he withdrew and pleasured her with a smooth piece of whalebone. His seed touched the water, and instantly the swirling plankton was transformed into bacteria, viruses, and microscopic parasites.

The noxious clouds bubbled up to the surface and out into the cold, clear air. The trade winds sucked them up and distributed them across the planet. Mother Earth was furious. She roared, and the noise was like a million tons of rock falling down a mountain. She opened a crack in the ocean floor and dived in. It was the end of the fifth day.

The sixth day dawned. God lay on a bed of snowy owl feathers looking out at blue glaciers. He felt elated. His plan not to father any more children had worked. Instead he would clone himself, create another Adam. So he split himself in half and clothed his new self in robes of silver and gold. Together God and his son flew across the oceans to find the sisters. Mother Nature sat on the floor of the now-silent rain forest, rocking back and forth. She was holding the flaccid body of a dead jaguar. God sat down beside her and asked her what had happened. She could not answer. Mother Earth appeared and raised her arm to strike God. Adam blocked the blow, and she glared at him with undisguised malice. "Help us!" cried Mother Nature. "Only you have the power to save them." God shrugged and shook his head. "Every creature on this planet is *your* creation," he said. "I can do nothing." Mother Earth spat in his face and dragged her weeping sister away.

God introduced Adam to Eve. Adam was humbled before her beauty. Their father promised they would be immune to the diseases sweeping the Earth. They would have dominion over the fowl of the air and over all the Earth and every creeping thing upon it. But they had to worship him alone. "Forasmuch as it pleases me, being an almighty God of great mercy," he said, "you may go forth and multiply in the sure and certain knowledge that you will be saved from all the ills and misfortunes of this world." Adam and Eve kissed their father's hand and bowed low before him. God fashioned them an arbor and surrounded it with a lush garden filled with fruit trees and freshwater springs. So ended the sixth day.

On the seventh day, Mother Earth raised a storm. Thunder pounded through the skies, and lightning smote the Earth, slicing the tops off trees and mountains alike. God chided Mother Nature for allowing her sister to destroy the world. But she wept and turned away. Lilith and Lucifer stood on a mountaintop and taunted God. Could his power match a tempest raised by Mother Earth? "Show us your strength," they said. "If you are truly a God as you profess to be, then calm the storm and populate this planet with *your* creations," cried Lucifer.

"Save us from that unhappy occasion, brother." Lilith smiled. "If puny Adam is evidence of his creative power, I would rather have another lifeless desert." Lucifer roared with laughter. God drew himself up to his full height, and he towered above the highest mountain. "Get thee hence, Lucifer!" he shouted, and struck him a mighty blow that sent him falling headlong, flaming from the ethereal sky. With a hideous screech, Lilith flew at her father. God silenced her with a sweep of his hand, and she too fell.

The floodwaters rose higher and higher. Adam and Eve cried out in terror.

God built a wooden ark and installed his children safely inside. Then he blessed them and repeated his promise to make them rulers over all the creatures of the Earth. Perched on the ark's roof was Lilith in the form of a great black bird. When God disappeared over the watery horizon, she tore at the roof with her talons. Adam and Eve tried to beat her off, but she burst into flames. Fires erupted all over the ark, then all went out with a hiss. A huge red serpent rose from the ashes and slipped into the ocean. It was the end of the seventh day.

The eighth day dawned to a blue washed sky. Mother Earth lay asleep. Mother Nature swam with herds of sea creatures: whales, dolphins, sharks, and swordfish swimming alongside tuna, cod, and salmon. Jellyfish, octopuses, and squid curled around her fingers and toes. A string of eels slithered in her wake. She sang a whale song and dreamed of all the new things she could create.

The ark settled on a mountain. Adam flew out to find shelter. Eve fell asleep. She dreamed of Adam in a cave. He had lit a fire and spread animal skins around it. She could feel the softness of the fur and the heat from the fire. Adam offered her a cup, and she drank. The liquid was hot and burned her throat. She screamed in pain, and a fire kindled deep inside her. Adam watched. He took her by the hand, and together they dived to the bottom of the sea to a bed of hydrothermal vents. Giant tubeworms wriggled in the heat, and blind white crabs scrabbled for food. Adam removed his robes. Eve was mesmerized by the sleek curve of his thighs and the broad sweep of his shoulders. He stepped into the pillar of hot water and beckoned to Eve. She stood beside him, feeling the heat from without and the heat from within, rising, rising. Adam kissed her gently, and she fell upon him. Her ardor took him by surprise—she opened like a flower and pushed him inside. She slid to her knees and swallowed him up. She pushed her fingers inside him tight and hot. Together they bucked and writhed in the hot current that lifted them finally to the surface. Adam took them to a desert. He whispered to a snake and a lizard that flicked their forked tongues between her thighs while he plucked the spines from a cactus. He licked the succulent and pleasured her with it. A she-wolf trotted up and nuzzled Eve's face. The animal's female parts were human. Eve licked till her tongue bled.

She awoke. The sun was rising above the dunes. Her thighs throbbed and her mouth felt sticky. She lay on a beach, as if she had been washed up by the sea. Adam stood over her. Eve examined his face, searching for answers to the riddle, but Adam shied away from her gaze. He walked off down the beach, kicking sand.

Adam too had dreamed. He had found a cave and lit a fire but had fallen asleep beside it. He dreamed of Eve. She was stirring a cooking pot and offered him a taste of broth. The liquid was hot and burned his throat. He cried out in pain and felt a fire kindle deep inside him. Eve watched him. She took his hand and together they flew over the sea to a great forest of birch, oak, and beech. Moss and fern carpeted the forest floor. Eve unfastened her robe. Her skin was as white as apple blossom. She kissed Adam gently and he fell upon her. He sank to his knees and devoured her. They coupled against the smooth bark of a birch tree, then in the soft, dank leaf mold, and again amid the reeds and the bulrushes on the shore of a freshwater lake. He woke up in a forest clearing, naked and shivering.

Adam and Eve never spoke of their dreams. They lost their ability to fly, and when Eve fell ill it became clear that they were no longer immune to God's accursed diseases. The dreams had robbed them of more than their virginity. Lucifer and Lilith rolled about the heavens laughing. At the end of the eighth day Adam and Eve sat in the cave and prayed for God's swift return.

And they're waiting still.

Dangerous Games with Competent People

Kim Wright

T HE LAST THING YOU want when you're going to see your boyfriend's
hooker is a helpful man. But this man is determined to help you. He
has the look—you know the look—he has the look of a helpful man. It's
three o'clock in the afternoon. You're standing in the lobby of a surprisingly nice high-rise in a suburb of D.C., typing numbers into a security
pad, waiting for a woman to come on the line and tell you her apartment number. Her instructions were quite specific. In her e-mail, she attached a Zip file with directions to this building, the sort of painfully
clear directions that make you understand this is a woman who is accus-
tomed to telling people how to find her.

The money is in a plain white envelope inside your purse. She has in-
cluded instructions about this in the Zip file too: "I never discuss pay-
ment in person, nor do I wish to see cash. Please place the envelope
discreetly on the table as you enter." It strikes you as strange that a
woman with such delicate sensibilities that she cannot bear the sight of
money would be prepared to repeatedly bury her face in the genitals of
strangers, but your boyfriend has described her as "nice" and perhaps
this is what he means.

You key in the numbers she has given you and wait for her voice.
You get a busy signal, and when you try it a few minutes later, you get
the busy signal again. The man sitting behind the marble desk calls out
pleasantly, "Who are you here to see?" That's the problem. You don't
know her name or her apartment number, you know only that she calls

herself alexandriaandrea and that your boyfriend is sleeping fitfully somewhere in Paris. I'll be fine, you tell the man. My friend must be on the phone. I'll give her a minute and try again.

But he wants to help. He waves you over to the desk and says that if you give him her code, he can go into the computer and find her apartment number and ring you in himself. Which seems somewhat the opposite of what a security guard's job should be, but you know that everything about you—your age, your gender, the way you move, and the way you dress—makes you seem unthreatening to other people. Makes you seem like a bastion of respectability. You don't have to wonder how this man sees you. The wall behind him is mirrored, and you can see yourself, your long knit dress with the slits up the side to the knee, your strap sandals, the knockoff Gucci sunglasses pushed back on your head, your real Dooney and Bourke purse over your arm. There is no good reason why a man like him shouldn't help a woman like you enter this building.

But her instructions said nothing about conversations with security men, nothing about struggling to think of a plausible explanation for why you are visiting a woman whose name you do not know. You smile at him, mutter something, go back to the intercom system, type in her code again, and this time she answers. She gives you her apartment number, and, shooting another smile at the security guard, you head toward the elevator.

When she opens the door, she is prettier than you expect. Your age, close to fifty. Her hair is blonde, cropped in a stylish manner, longer in the front than the back, slightly damp from a shower. Andy has said she's a jock, so you're a bit surprised she has on full makeup, that you smell perfume, that she's teetering on bronze sling-back heels. She is wearing a very tight slip, burgundy in color, some combination of lace and Lycra. She is about your height, she has a quick laugh, and she further surprises you by saying that you are pretty.

"Your coloring," she says. "You have beautiful coloring. He didn't tell me you were pretty. He said you were smart."

And although you are happy to see that she is pretty too, and pretty in a way that means she might be a friend to you, happy that no one would take notice if the two of you walked into a restaurant, even though you are relieved to see that she is much as he described her, something about it all throws you, and you forget to leave the white envelope on her table. She has dressed to seduce you as if you were a man. The cups of her slip thrust her breasts forward. When she raises her arms to brush back her hair, the slip slides up her thighs. Her legs are muscular, an athlete's legs, and indeed ropes and climbing shoes are all over her small apartment, as well as oars and a racing bike, partially dismantled and lying on its side. Perhaps you tell her that she's beautiful. You think it. Perhaps you say it aloud.

Then there is nothing to do but to go on through the den into her bedroom and to lie down on her bed to prop yourself up casually on one elbow and watch her as if you were a friend come over to help her get ready for a date. There is a bookcase beside the bed, and it has any number of travel guides . . . Tibet and Peru and Turkey. "Were you scared," she asks, "were you nervous about coming?" "No," you say, "not until a man down in the lobby tried to help me." She laughs. She laughs easily. She has laughed now a half-dozen times since you entered her door.

You say something about how she has so many travel books, but she isn't in the mood to chat. You've hired her for only an hour, and she knows you didn't drive all this way to talk about Peru. She begins to stroke your leg, stopping her hand just above your knee. She notes that you are not wearing any panties. This is not an affectation—you rarely wear panties—but she runs her hand farther up your thigh and whispers, "Bad girl." It's a bit like the high heels and the perfume, vaguely off in some way you can't define. She has undoubtedly called any number of D.C. lawyers and politicians and bankers "Bad boy": she has undoubtedly said this to your own boyfriend. You reach down and slip off her shoe, you cup the instep of her foot. You catch her eye, and you both laugh for no particular reason. When you slide your hand up, you find that she is pantyless too, and you say, "You've got a lot of nerve calling me a bad girl." It's easy to roll around with her on the bed. It's easy to nuzzle her neck and breathe in the perfume and ruffle the slightly wet hair. "I was a little nervous," she tells you. "This is the first time I've had a woman by herself. But you, you're so pretty. I didn't expect you to be pretty."

Truth be told, you're not all that pretty, but these things she says seem to be part of the deal, and you're willing to go along with it. You run your index finger along her pussy lips and find she's wet, and you push your finger into her, feeling the slight sucking quality of a woman, something half forgotten that pulls you in. "But you've been with women?" "Sure," she says, "but only in threesomes." "Have you ever done a threesome?" You shake your head. Her breasts, you decide, are incredible, better than yours, and you reach into the burgundy Lycra slip and lift out one and then the other. It's all quite nasty, the way the Lycra pushes them forward and you bend forward to suck her left nipple, feeling the puckered roughness on the flat of your tongue. She moans. You almost laugh. The moans are like the sling-back shoes and the compliments—a little excessive. She wants to make sure you're getting Andy's money's worth.

This thing about the threesome. It's why you're here, isn't it? Or at least part of the reason. Andy found you, eight years ago, on an airplane between Tucson and Dallas, and now he's found this girl, the only woman in his mountain-climbing club, a group so demanding that she is the only woman who has met the criteria to join. It's been almost a year since he first mentioned her, since he lay across your own bed, five hundred miles from here, and wondered idly what she did for a living, how this woman found so much time to train.

And then he asked her. Asked her one day as they were loading up after a climb what in the world she did for a living that would allow her to train every day. She said she had men, a few men, male friends who sponsored her athletic career. Just a few close male friends who were happy to help her. He didn't totally understand what she meant. Andy is an attorney, well aware of the myriad and costly penalties that can be levied when one person fails to totally understand another. Was she a hooker? He knew only one person to ask. He finished loading up his equipment and retreated to his car and dialed as he drove home to his house in the Maryland suburbs. "Yeah," you said, "she's probably a hooker. Nothing else makes any sense."

You push your face into her breasts, feeling the softness as they separate on either side of your cheeks. She moans and you say, "You don't have to," meaning that you are a woman too, you understand that it is too early in the process for such ostentatious moaning. Sex is a long drive, it's Maine to Florida, and there is no sense in her carrying on like she's in Georgia when you know damn well this is Connecticut at best.

Don't treat me like a man, you want to tell her. I'm not that dumb, and it's only two hundred dollars and Andy's paying for it, after all. He wants us to like each other. She pulls away, as if she's read your mind, and you roll onto your back.

Here's the deal. He went to see her, he liked her, he fucked her and told her about you. She was very open to the idea of seeing a couple. She liked to do women—the only trouble was the women she saw were always dragged there by their husbands. They weren't really into it, and things could get awkward. Two women putting on a show for the benefit of a man, who needed that? When he told you this, you said maybe it would make more sense for you to go see her first by yourself. There needed to be a spark between the two of you; otherwise, she was right, it was just a show. You'd go by yourself? Your offer clearly surprises him. He'd like to be there, of course he would, but you know he's out of town all that week. "Did you forget that's the week he's in Europe?" She is going down on you now; she has pushed your legs apart, and she's very direct. She doesn't do it like he does it, no moseying around, no circling, no lifting of the head to talk. She is very direct, her tongue pointed and focused, and involuntarily you glance at her bedside clock. You have been here ten minutes.

There are ropes around her bedroom, ropes and a pickax, the accoutrements of her sport, and as she pushes through the layers and goes deeper you close your eyes. Your hands find a rope stretched across the headboard behind you, a rope she has probably tied there for just this purpose or one very like it, and you reach back and grasp it. She's good, she knows what she's doing, and people need something to hang on to. Next week Andy will be back from France, and he will fly down to see you. Over dinner the two of you will discuss his last climb. He has this friend Mike whom he adores. Mike is older, balding and chubby and unassuming, but a hell of a climber. Andy likes to lead the climbs. He feels nervous when someone else goes first, and he has described the risks of the sport to you many times. How the lead man finds a ledge or a little toehold, drives a spike, threads through the rope; how the lead man is responsible for everyone below. He told you this the first time you met him, on the plane, told you how catastrophic it would be for the lead to fall. You sat in the slightly vibrating airplane seat somewhere in the air between Tucson and Dallas and listened to him describe how the chain of people are attached—attached to each other for reasons of safety or maybe just for the promise that they won't, come the worst, die alone. This, he said, this is what matters. If the leader fell, everyone else would follow suit behind him, ripped from the rock one by one.

But on this particular climb Mike was leading, and that's okay. Andy trusts Mike. They were right on that edge where things are starting to get interesting. There were some shadows; they knew time was limited until nightfall. Mike had hoisted himself over a ledge, secured his rope, and was watching as Andy followed, as he eased his way past that point where just for a moment you dangle. They were very high and very far from home. Mike had grinned down at him and said, "God, I love doing dangerous things with competent people."

You're loud when you come. You make a noise—you suspect it is not a pretty noise—and your body goes rigid, pushing you away from her like a swimmer pushes off from a wall. You hold it for a minute, you say My God, more to yourself than to her. It was so sharp, so fast, it was on you without warning. She is crouched between your legs, resting her head against your knee. Her hair is still damp. "But wasn't that a great thing for him to say—doing dangerous things with competent people?" Andy will ask you, and he will nudge the last piece of calamari toward you, as if you were in a scene from Lady and the Tramp. You run your hands under her slip. "You don't have to," she says. What is it about this that she's not getting? "I want to do this," you tell her. "Let me."

He said she smelled good. She does. Your face falls forward, and you're momentarily dizzy. You slide your elbows under her thighs and settle into a rhythm. She shudders—it seems real—and your mind wanders. Your mind always wanders when you're going down on someone, it's the only time in your life when you could honestly be called contemplative. It's easy to fall into women, you think; it's easy to let go and fall into them. Women, you think, we are gravity personified. You flash on an island where you once vacationed, a teacher you had in college, how much time is left in the parking meter downstairs. Once, at a Halloween fair at your kids' school, a psychic told you that you'd been male in a past lifetime. A silly psychic—somebody's mother in a scarf—but she leaned toward you and whispered, "Last time through, you were a man. You still remember, don't you?" Silly as hell, but it would explain a lot. It would explain why you're willing to forgive them so much.

She doesn't come. This bothers you. You got the impression from Andy she was an easy come. Hell, got the impression from him she was coming all over the place. "Do you like men better than women?" Your mouth is between her legs as you're asking; you mumble the question into her crotch, and suddenly the two of you are shrinking with laughter.

"A funny time to ask," she says.

"But no," you say, rising up, giving up. "I'm absolutely dead serious. What makes you come?"

"I came a little bit when you did," she says.

"Oh come on. Please. Don't give me that shit. Don't talk to me like I'm a man. Show me. Show me what you do when you're alone."

She shakes her head. You've embarrassed her. She asks what she can do for you. She asks this over and over. You keep forgetting. There is $240 dollars—for you have insisted that Andy tip her—in an envelope in your purse. There's no need to make it reciprocal. Show me, you say again, more sharply, and she opens the top drawer of her bedside table and pulls out a small white vibrator, the cheap kind that takes AA batteries, and she clamps it between her legs.

What exactly does he want? He has a wife and girlfriend and a hooker, as well as some hunchback secretary from another floor who once blew him in the office parking deck and an Asian lady who jerks him off in a massage parlor out by the airport. He calls her the happy-ending lady and he does a funny imitation of her voice. She rubs him the normal way, and then she giggles and snorts and asks him. "You want happy ending?" Andrea has pulled herself into a fetal position, her eyes are clamped shut. She does not move or make a noise. Surely between the five of you he would be sated, and yet you know people are never sated, neither women nor men, and your mind shifts briefly to your other boyfriend, this one in New York. You wonder what he would think of this, but it's not really his sort of thing, is it? No, he wants something else. A simple convulsion, one single spasm, and she's done.

"I liked watching," you tell her, and she says, "yeah, I like watching too. "She likes everything about sex. That's all she wants is sex and time to climb and enough money for an apartment where she can see the river." I don't want many things, "she tells you," but the things I want, I want a lot. "She glances at the clock and offers to fuck you." "No," you say, "I'm fine. I like to come once hard, and then just roll around. This is perfect for me."

"He wants to see me fuck you," she says. "That's part of what he wants, but I guess he told you that."

"Don't worry about it. When the time comes, he'll do whatever we say."

She shrugs. "I guess so. He seems like a nice enough guy."

You're stunned by how quickly she's dismissed him. It's the last thing you expected her to say. This man has been the best lover you've ever had. You expected—what did you expect? You expected that she would congratulate you for having left no stone unturned, for having found this man among all the men who don't know what to do and who don't care that they don't know what to do. That fluttery thing with his tongue. My God, there are times even after eight years that you think your heart will stop. How can she say he seems like a nice guy?

You have a strange and sudden urge to weep. You're from a small town. Your mother was a second-grade teacher. The truth of the matter is you've been over your head for some time now. "I'm not used to all this," you tell her. "But God," she says, "who is?" She opens her arms, you roll toward her. Who among us was raised for this? She was born in Nebraska.

The next week you will confront him, in a restaurant miles from here, in an Asian restaurant in your hometown where you like the calamari. He will hand you that line about dangerous games with competent people, and you will snap back at him, "You didn't give her the full treatment." The minute she said that he was a nice guy you knew it, that he'd gone down on her but he hadn't given her the full treatment. He didn't do the flutter thing.

"I only do the flutter thing with you," he says.

You will walk back from the restaurant to your house holding hands. You'll talk about your jobs, your children. His daughter's volleyball team went to the state finals. She is fifteen, beautiful but very tall, and he thinks the boys will stay away for several more years because of this. You call him sweetie and rub his head. He is a good father, in his way. When his girls leave home, it will break his heart.

And so, she says, "We'll all get together?"

Of course, you say, "We'll get together." You've already put the envelope on her table while she was peeing. She is barefoot now as she walks you to the door, slightly shorter than you as she hugs you good-bye.

On the drive back through northern Virginia you dig through your purse for your cell phone. You call your friend, the one you're staying with tonight, the one you always stay with when you come to D.C. She's married; she says it's good but a lot of work, and she told you, just this morning over cereal, that she thinks you use sex to avoid intimacy. Her husband has hit on you, just as he has hit on every woman in your group of friends, but you do not tell her this. She answers on the first ring. You tell her the Monet exhibit was incredible and offer to stop at the grocery. "Do you need anything, a bottle of wine perhaps?"

"No," she says, "I have enough." She's doing tuna out on the grill because you liked it that way the last time. She is sweet like this. Whenever you come up, she puts a terry-cloth robe on your bed, she gets your favorite green tea, even though it means driving to a second grocery. It is nice that you have called to offer to pick up something on the way in, and it is nice that she already has everything she needs. The rituals of domesticity are so soothing. Men probably do this, you think; they probably call their wives on the way home from hookers.

You sing with the radio. An oldies station. Abba, Joni Mitchell, and then the Mamas and the Papas. You roll your neck from side to side, getting out the kinks. Your tongue is sore from licking her. Sore, right in the root, and it will be sore all the next day. You're lifted, in the way that only sex can lift you. Chemicals have poured into your system—the adrenaline, the endorphins, the alcohol from the beer wedged between your thighs—and colors seem brighter, and you know every word of every song that comes onto this radio station. You see, just for a moment, the interconnectedness of everything, the delicate way we're all webbed, and you send up a quick wordless prayer for your boyfriend's wife. Maybe you'll stop and get another bottle of wine after all, for who can say what is enough?

The traffic has come to a standstill as it often does on I-95 just south of D.C. in the late afternoon. There is a man in a convertible beside you. He smiles, you smile. If you break down right here, if you have a flat tire or an overheated engine, this man and perhaps others will stop and offer to help you. Men like you. Men are nice to you. They will always stop and help; they will give you the last bite of calamari and pay other women to go down on you. That's your karma for this particular lifetime. It's very beautiful here, very safe. You're a safe woman; men can see that at a glance. They will let you into buildings where you have no business being. The man in the convertible edges slightly past you. It's hard to say what will happen next.

from Fledgling

OCTAVIA BUTLER

I T WAS RAINING AGAIN—a steady, gentle rain that had been coming down for some time.

I had discovered a paved road that led away from the burned houses. I had walked on it for some time before I remembered the word "road," and that led to my remembering cars and trucks, although I hadn't yet seen either. The road I was on led to a metal gate, which I climbed over, then to another, slightly wider road, and I had to choose a direction. I chose the downslope direction and walked along for a while in contentment until I came to a third still wider road. Again, I chose to go downhill. It was easier to walk along the road than to pick my way through the rocks, trees, underbrush, and creeks, although the pavement was hard against my bare feet.

A blue car came along the road behind me, and I walked well to one side so that I could look at it, and it would pass me without hitting me. It couldn't have been first car I had ever seen. I knew that because I recognized it as a car and found nothing surprising about it. But it was the first car I could remember seeing.

I was surprised when the car stopped alongside me.

The person inside was, at first, just a face, shoulders, a pair of hands. Then I understood that I was seeing a young man, pale-skinned, brown-haired, broad, and tall. His hair brushed against the top of the inside of his car. His shoulders were so broad that even alone in the car, he looked crowded. His car seemed to fit him almost as badly as my clothing fitted me. He lowered his window, looked out at me, and asked, "Are you all right?"

I heard the words, but at first, they meant nothing at all. They were noise. After a moment, though, they seemed to click into place as language. I understood them. It took me a moment longer before I realized that I should answer. I couldn't remember ever speaking to another person, and at first, I wasn't sure I could do it.

I opened my mouth, cleared my throat, coughed, then finally managed to say, "I . . . am. Yes, I am all right." My voice sounded strange and hoarse to my own ears. It wasn't only that I couldn't recall speaking to anyone else. I couldn't remember ever speaking at all. Yet it seemed that I knew how.

"No, you're not," the man said. "You're soaking wet and filthy, and . . . God, how old are you?"

I opened my mouth, then closed it again. I didn't have any idea how old I was or why my age should matter.

"Is that blood on your shirt?" he asked.

I looked down. "I killed a deer," I said. In all, I had killed two deer. And I did have their blood on my clothing. The rain hadn't washed it away.

He stared at me for several seconds. "Look, is there someplace I can take you? Do you have family or friends somewhere around here?"

I shook my head. "I don't know. I don't think so."

"You shouldn't be out here in the middle of the night in the rain!" he said. "You can't be any more than ten or eleven. Where are you going?"

"Just walking," I said, because I didn't know what else to say. Where was I going? Where would he think I should be going? Home, perhaps. "Home," I lied. "I'm going home." Then I wondered why I had lied. Was it important for this stranger to think that I had a home and was going there? Or was it only that I didn't want him to realize how little I knew about myself, about anything?

"I'll take you home," he said. "Get in."

I surprised myself completely by instantly wanting to go with him. I went around to the passenger side of his car and opened the door. Then I stopped, confused. "I don't really have a home," I said. I closed the door and stepped back.

He leaned over and opened the door. "Look," he said, "I can't leave you out here. You're a kid, for godsake. Come on, I'll at least take you someplace dry." He reached into the backseat and picked up a big piece of thick cloth. "Here's a blanket. Get in and wrap up."

I wasn't uncomfortable. Being wet didn't bother me, and I wasn't cold. Yet I wanted to get into the car with him. I didn't want him to drive away without me. Now that I'd had a few more moments to absorb his scent I realized he smelled . . . really interesting. Also, I didn't want to stop talking to him. I felt almost as hungry for conversation as I was for food. A taste of it had only whetted my appetite.

I wrapped the blanket around me and got into the car.

"Did someone hurt you?" he asked when he had gotten the car moving again. "Were you in someone's car?"

"I was hurt," I said. "I'm all right now."

He glanced at me. "Are you sure? I can take you to a hospital."

"I don't need a hospital," I said quickly, even though, at first, I wasn't sure what a hospital was. Then I knew that it was a place where the sick and injured were taken for care. There would be a lot of people all around me at a hospital. That was enough to make it frightening. "No hospital."

Another glance. "Okay," he said. "What's your name?"

I opened my mouth to answer, then closed it. After a while, I admitted, "I don't know what my name is. I don't remember."

He glanced at me several times before saying anything about that. After a while he said, "Okay, you don't want to tell me, then. Did you run away? Get tired of home and strike out on your own?"

"I don't think so." I frowned. "I don't think I would do that. I don't remember, really, but that doesn't feel like something I would do."

There was another long silence. "You really don't remember? You're not kidding?"

"I'm not. My . . . my injuries are healed now, but I still don't remember things."

He didn't say anything for a while. Then, "You really don't know what your own name is?"

"That's right."

"Then you do need a hospital."

"No, I don't. No!"

"Why? The doctors there might be able to help you."

Might they? Then why did the idea of going among them scare me so? I knew absolutely that I didn't want to put myself into the hands of strangers. I didn't want to be even near large numbers of strangers. "No hospital," I repeated.

Again, he didn't say anything, but this time, there was something different about his silence. I looked at him and suddenly believed that he meant to deliver me to a hospital anyway, and I panicked. I unfastened the seat belt that he had insisted I buckle and pushed aside the blanket. I turned to open the car door. He grabbed my arm before I could figure out how to get it open. He had huge hands that wrapped completely around my arm. He pulled me back, pulled me hard against the little low wall that divided his legs from mine.

He scared me. I was less than half his size, and he meant to force me to go where I didn't want to go. I pulled away from him, dodged his hand as he grasped at me, tried again to open the door, only to be caught again.

I caught his wrist, squeezed it, and yanked it away from my arm. He yelped, said "Shit!" and managed to rub his wrist with the hand still holding the steering wheel. "What the hell's wrong with you?" he demanded.

I put my back against the door that I had been trying to open. "Are you going to take me to the hospital even though I don't want to go?" I asked.

He nodded, still rubbing his wrist. "The hospital or the police station. Your choice."

"Neither!" Being turned over to the police scared me even more than the idea of going to the hospital did. I turned to try again to get the door open.

And again, he grasped my left upper arm, pulling me back from the door. His fingers wrapped all the way around my upper arm and held me tightly, pulling me away from the door. I understood him a little better now that I'd had my hands on him. I thought I could break his wrist if I wanted to. He was big but not that strong. Or, at least, I was stronger. But I didn't want to break his bones. He seemed to want to help me, although he didn't know how. And he did smell good. I didn't have the words to say how good he smelled. Breaking his bones would be wrong.

I bit him—just a quick bite and release on the meaty part of his hand where his thumb was.

"Goddamn it!" he shouted, jerking his hand away. Then he made another grab for me before I could get the door open. There were several buttons on the door, and I didn't know which of them would make it open. None of them seemed to work. That gave him a chance to get his hand on me a third time.

"Be still!" he ordered and gave me a hard shake. "You'll kill yourself! If you're crazy enough to try to jump out of a moving car, you should be in mental hospital."

I stared down at the bleeding marks I'd made on his hand, and suddenly I was unable to think about anything else. I ducked my head and licked away the blood, licked the wound I had made. He tensed, almost pulling his hand away. Then he stopped, seemed to relax. He let me take his hand between my own. I looked at him, saw him glancing at me, felt the car zigzag a little on the road.

He frowned and pulled away from me, all the while looking uncertain, unhappy. I caught his hand again between mine and held it. I felt him try to pull away. He shook me, actually lifting me into the air a little, trying to get away from me, but I didn't let go. I licked at the blood welling up where my teeth had cut him.

He made a noise, a kind of gasp. Abruptly, he drove completely across the road to a spot where there was room to stop the car without blocking other cars—the few other cars that came along. He made a huge fist of the hand that was no longer needed to steer the car. I watched him draw it back to hit me. I thought I should be afraid, should try to stop him, but I was calm. Somehow, I couldn't believe he would hit me.

He frowned, shook his head. After a while he dropped his hand to his lap and glared at me. "What are you doing?" he demanded, watching me, not pulling away at all now, but looking as though he wanted to—or as though he thought he should want to.

I didn't answer. I wasn't getting enough blood from his hand. I wanted to bite him again, but I didn't want him afraid or angry. I didn't know why I cared about that, but it seemed important. Also, I knew hands weren't as good for getting blood as wrists and throats were. I looked at him and saw that he was looking intently at me.

"It doesn't hurt anymore," he said. "It feels good. Which is weird. How do you do that?"

"I don't know," I told him. "You taste good."

"Do I?" He lifted me, squeezed past the division between the seats to my side of the car, and put me on his lap.

"Let me bite you again," I whispered.

He smiled. "If I do, what will you let me do?"

I heard consent in his voice, and I hauled myself up and kissed the side of his neck, searching with my tongue and my nose for the largest blood source there. A moment later, I bit hard into the side of his neck. He convulsed and I held on to him. He writhed under me, not struggling, but holding me as I took more of his blood. I took enough blood to satisfy a hunger I hadn't realized I had until a few moments before. I could have taken more, but I didn't want to hurt him. He tasted wonderful, and he had fed me without trying to escape or to hurt me. I licked the bite until it stopped bleeding. I wished I could make it heal, wished I could repay him by healing him.

He sighed and held me, leaning back in his seat and letting me lean against him. "So what was that?" he asked after a while. "How did you do that? And why the hell did it feel so fantastic?"

He had enjoyed it—maybe as much as I had. I felt pleased, felt myself smile. That was right somehow. I'd done it right. That meant I'd done it before, even though I couldn't remember.

"Keep me with you," I said, and I knew I meant it the moment I said it. He would have a place to live. If I could go there with him, maybe the things I saw there would help me begin to get my memory back—and I would have a home.

"Do you really not have anywhere to go or anyone looking for you?" he asked.

"I don't think I have anyone," I said. "I don't remember. I need to find out who I am and what happened to me and . . . and everything."

"Do you always bite?"

I leaned back against him. "I don't know."

"You're a vampire, you know."

I thought about that. The word stirred no memories. "What's a vampire?"

He laughed. "You. You bite. You drink blood." He grimaced and shook his head. "My God, you drink blood."

"I guess I do." I licked at his neck.

"And you're way too young," he said. "Jailbait. Super jailbait."

Since I didn't know what "jailbait" was, and I had no idea how old I was, I didn't say anything.

"Do you remember how you got that blood on your clothes? Who else have you been chewing on?"

"I killed a deer. In fact, I killed two deer."

"Sure you did."

"Keep me with you."

I was watching his face as I said it. He looked confused again, worried, but he held me against his body and nodded. "Yeah," he said. "I'm not sure how I'm going to do that, but yeah. I want you with me. I don't think I should keep you. Hell, I know I shouldn't. But I'll do it anyway."

"I don't think I'm supposed to be alone," I said. "I don't know who I should be with, though, because I can't remember ever having been with anyone."

"So you'll be with me." He smiled and his confusion seemed to be gone. "I'll need to call you something. What do you want to be called?"

"I don't know."

"Do you want me to give you a name?"

I smiled, liking him, feeling completely at ease with him. "Give me a name," I said. I licked at his neck a little more.

"Renee," he said. "A friend of mine told me it meant 'reborn.' That's sort of what's happened to you. You've been reborn into a new life. You'll probably remember your old life pretty soon, but for now, you're Renee." He shivered against me as I licked his neck. "Damn that feels good," he said. Then, "I rent a cabin from my uncle. If I take you there, you'll have to stay inside during the day. If he and my aunt see you, they'll probably throw us both out."

"I can sleep during the day. I won't go out until dark."

"Just right for a vampire," he said. "How did you kill those deer?"

I shrugged. "Ran them down and broke their necks."

"Uh-huh. Then what?"

"Ate some of their meat. Hid the rest in a tree until I was hungry again. Ate it until the parts I wanted were gone."

"How did you cook it? It's been raining like hell for the past few days. How did you find dry wood for your fire?"

"No fire. I didn't need a fire."

"You ate the deer raw?"

"Yes."

"Oh God, no you didn't." Something seemed to occur to him suddenly. "Show me your knife."

I hesitated. "Knife?"

"To clean and skin the deer."

"A thing? A tool?"

"A tool for cutting, yes."

"I don't have a knife."

He held me away from him and stared at me. "Show me your teeth," he said.

I bared my teeth for him.

"Good God," he said. "Are those what you bit me with?" He put his hand to his neck. "You *are* a damned vampire."

"Didn't hurt you," I said. He looked afraid. He started to push me away, then got that confused look again and pulled me back to him. "Do vampires eat deer?" I asked. I licked at his neck again.

He raised a hand to stop me, then dropped the hand to his side. "What are you, then?" he whispered.

And I said the only thing I could: "I don't know." I drew back, held his face between my hands, liking him, glad that I had found him. "Help me find out."

I LOOKED UP AT him, saw that I had scared him, and took one of his huge hands between mine. "I don't know what I am. I don't know why I remembered just now about flesh and blood. But you helped me do it. You asked me questions and you made me look into the mirror. Maybe now, with you to help me, I'll remember more and more."

"If you're right about what you've remembered so far, you're not human," he said.

"What if I'm not?" I asked. "What would that mean?"

"I don't know." He reached down and tugged at my jeans: "Take these off," he said.

I undid the shirt that I had twisted and tied around me to keep the jeans up, then I took them off.

He first seemed frozen with surprise that I had done as he said. Then, slowly, he walked around me, looking. "Well, you're a girl, all right," he whispered. At last, he took me by the hand and led me back to the main room of the cabin.

He led me to the chest of drawers next to the bed. There, in the top drawer, he found a white T-shirt. "Put this on," he said, handing it to me.

I put it on. It fell past my knees, and I looked up at him.

"You tired?" he asked. "You want to go to sleep?"

"Not sleepy," I said. "Can I wash?" I hadn't minded being dirty until the clean shirt made me think about just how dirty I was.

"Sure," he said. "Go take a shower. Then come keep me company while I eat."

I went into the bathroom, recognized the shower head over the bathtub, and figured out how to turn the shower on. Then I took off the T-shirt and stepped in. It was a hot, controlled rain, wonderful for getting clean and feeling better. I stayed under the shower longer than necessary just because it felt so good. Then, finally, I dried myself on the big blue towel that was there and that smelled of Wright.

I put the T-shirt back on and went out to Wright, who was sitting at his table, eating things that I recognized first by scent then by sight. He was eating scrambled eggs and chunks of ham together between thick slices of bread.

"Can you eat any of this?" Wright asked as he enjoyed the food and drank from a brown bottle of beer.

I smiled. "No, but I think I must have known people who ate things like that because I recognize them. Right now, I'll get some water. That's all I want."

"Until you want to chew on me again, eh?"

I got up to get the water and touched his shoulder as I passed him. It was good to see him eat, to know that he was well. It made me feel relieved. I hadn't hurt him. That was more important to me than I'd realized.

I sat down with a glass of water and sipped it.

"Why'd you do that?" he asked after a long silence. "Why'd you let me undress you like that?"

"You wanted to," I said.

"You would let anyone who wanted to, do that?"

I frowned, then shook my head. "I bit you—twice."

"So?"

"Taking my clothes off with you is all right."

"Is it?"

I frowned, remembering how badly I had wanted to cover myself when I was naked in the woods. I must have been used to wearing clothes in my life before the cave. I had wanted to be dressed as soon as I knew I was naked. Yet when Wright had taken my shirts, I hadn't minded. And I hadn't minded taking off the jeans when he asked me to. It had felt like what I should do.

"I don't think I'm as young as you believe," I said. "I mean, I may be, but I don't think so."

"You don't have any body hair at all," he told me.

"Should I?" I asked.

"Most people over eleven or twelve do."

I thought about that. "I don't know," I said finally. "I don't know enough about myself to say what my age might be or even whether I'm human. But I'm old enough to have sex with you if you want to."

He choked on his sandwich and spent time coughing and taking swallows of beer.

"I think you're supposed to," I continued, then frowned. "No, that's not right. I mean, I think you're supposed to be free to, if you want to."

"Because I let you bite me?"

"I don't know. Maybe."

"A reward for my suffering."

I leaned back, looking at him.

"You know damn well it doesn't."

He drank a couple of swallows more, then stood up, took my hand, and led me to his bed. I sat on the bed, and he started to pull the T-shirt over my head.

"No," I said, and he stopped and stood looking at me, waiting. "Let me see you." I pulled at his shirt and unbuttoned one of the buttons. "You've seen me."

He nodded, finished unbuttoning his shirt, and pulled his undershirt over his head.

His broad chest was covered with a mat of brown hair so thick that it was almost like fur, and I stroked it and felt him shiver.

He kicked off his shoes and stripped off his pants and underwear. There was a great deal more fur on him everywhere, and he was already erect and eager.

I had seen a man this way before. I could not remember who he had been, could not recall a specific face or body. But all this was familiar and good to me, and I felt my own eagerness and growing excitement. I pulled the T-shirt over my head and let him push me back onto the bed, let him touch me while I petted and played with his fur and explored his body until, gasping, he caught my hands and held them. He covered me with his huge, furry blanket of a body. He was so tall that he took care to hold himself up on his elbows so that my face was not crushed into his chest.

He was very careful at first, afraid of hurting me, still afraid that I might be too young for this, too small. Then, when it was clear that I was not being hurt at all, when I had wrapped my arms and legs around him, he forgot his fears, forgot everything.

I forgot myself, too. I bit him again just beneath his left nipple and took a little more blood. He shouted and squeezed the breath from me. Then he collapsed on me, empty, spent.

It bothered me later, as he lay sleeping beside me, that I had taken more blood. If I didn't find another source of blood soon, I would weaken him too much.

I got up quietly, washed, and put on his T-shirt. I would not let myself be seen, but I had to go out and look around. I had to see who and what else might be nearby.

ENTRY POINT

Shanna Germain

'VE NEVER DONE THIS before: the warm wooden paddle gripped in my fists, the canoe that shivers and thrusts beneath me every time I shift in the seat, my husband behind me, guiding us. From the canoe ahead of us, our daughter turns, lifts one hand off her paddle, and waves. She is watching out for us; it was her idea to bring us here, hers and her friend's, to the middle of the Adirondacks, where we will paddle and camp our way down this miles-wide river.

Susan lifts her head beneath her ball cap. The cap, brown with blue lettering, reads "Kiss My Bush." A few years ago, I would have asked her to take it off. For her father's sake more than mine. He's no supporter of Bush, of course, but he's no supporter of "sportin' your business everywhere" either. It makes me laugh, the pun of it all, but I can't imagine wearing something like that. I didn't even get one of those "Women Against the War" pins, although I'd wanted one. I knew I would have just put it in my drawer, and what was the sense of that?

Now, I just smile and take my own wet, cool hand off the paddle and wave back. If he wants Susan to take the hat off, he'll have to tell her himself. Susan smiles—it still knocks my heart back when she smiles, three dimples—cheek, cheek, and chin—like a perfect right triangle, like a constellation in a day sky.

Susan gives me a thumbs-up, a "you're being a real trooper, Mom," sign, and then turns back around. Her friend, no, her partner—partner, I still have to get used to saying that word, to thinking that thought—paddles with long, efficient strokes. Reese. She is tall and thin and pale, the muscles in her bare shoulders moving like miniature pistons with each sweep of the paddle.

They are efficient together—paddling on one side and then the other, switching at some rhythm known only to them, Susan sometimes holding the paddle in the water against the boat, bringing the front of the canoe to one side or the other. They could outrun us, with our halting strokes and fat canoe, with the way Harry steers by waiting until we're close enough to the bank to push off on something. But they don't, they stay nearby as though it is only their inability to go faster and not their fear for the old folks that keep them here. It makes me grateful in my heart for them, for both of them, for Susan, for Reese being the one she chose.

"What you doing, Lese?" Harry's voice at my back, his paddle, swish swish into water. "You plan on making me do all the work back here?"

I take the paddle off of my knees, dip it into the water. "I was thinking about it," I say. I like the way my voice sounds, the smooth sharp youth that has come into it since we got here. My comeback sounds like the crunch and snap of a green twig.

Harry nudges my back with the end of his paddle. I can barely feel it through the thick life vest. "Watch it up there," he says. "I've got a mind to make you steer."

We both know that he would do no such thing. He is a gentleman, Harry, through and through. He holds doors and buys flowers and doesn't say "damn" in mixed company. This is what I fell in love with forty years ago. The first time I went out with him, we were walking to the movies and the rain started falling down around us. He didn't wait one second before he was out of his coat and laying it across my shoulders to keep my dress dry. It wasn't the coat I remember so much as the way he put his arm there too, keeping the coat on my shoulders, giving me the warmth of his skin, never once trying to touch me wrong. He left his coat, and his arm, there all day, all through the movie and the way home. When he left me on the porch, saying good night, and taking back the things that were rightfully his—his coat, his arm—it was the first time I'd felt naked in my whole life.

Of course the something that makes you fall in love with someone can be the same thing you come to hate. This gentleman thing of Harry's, the way he would never say a bad word to anyone. The way he wouldn't get his dander up, not even when he should have. Like when Susan was a teenager, running wild and rampant in the streets, and all he could do was offer her a cup of tea and a towel when she came home. But I'm used to it all over again now, I guess. Now that we're old, I like that arm around my shoulder, the way he does it without thinking.

When the only sounds are water and birds and the slow steady stream of air going past, there's not much else to do but paddle and breathe. Up ahead, Susan and Reese move in their special rhythm. Geese create a V overhead; fall is coming. I don't know how they know—you can't feel it in the air yet. Down here on the river, it's still summer, with the lilies and the water skimmers and the trout that raise their big mouths up to the sky. I can't believe in all our forty years, Harry and I have never done this. Sure, we've done lots of things, broader, wider things. Moved to the West Coast once for about six months, while Harry worked and Susan toddled around the new house, pulling herself from box to box. And we took that trip to France a few years back, cute hotels and food so rich you could just feel it giving your heart a workout. But we've never done this, such an easy thing: drive on up to the most beautiful area in the state, rent a canoe, fit your palm around a wooden oar. Never thought to do it, I guess.

Susan and Reese slow down until they're alongside us. "Put your paddles up," Susan says. Then she reaches out to grab the side of the canoe with wet fingers. A diamond flashes on her middle finger, a gift from Reese. Susan called it a commitment ring. Like a cross between engagement and marriage.

We float that way a while, listening. Dark is falling somewhere nearby. You can see it in the way the shadows lengthen on the river, the way the trees darken and reach.

Susan takes her hand off the boat, points to shore. "We're going to try and camp over there," she says. "Should be an easy landing."

It's not easy, but it's okay. Reese jumps into the river at midthigh, a little splash and sigh, and then she grabs the front of our canoe and pulls us ashore. Harry doesn't like that, being pulled to the sandy banks while he's sitting in the back with his oar on his lap, but he doesn't say anything. And by the time I've got the salmon and corn steaming over the campfire, he's helping the girls raise the tents. One on this side of the clearing, one on the other.

We eat around the campfire, gobbling in the near dark. I'm so hungry I eat the salmon with my fingers, pulling the greasy pink flesh off the bone and sticking it in my mouth.

Susan does the same. "Jesus, Ma, this is the best thing I've ever tasted."

"I agree," Reese says, her mouth so full of fish the words barely come out. I feel a quick surge of warmth toward her.

After dinner, Harry goes off into the woods to do his business somewhere quiet, and I sit on the picnic table, away from the campfire. The dark makes soft edges out of my fingers. Harry's footsteps are light across pine needles. He gives my shoulders a quick squeeze. "I'm gonna hit the hay," he says. His kiss is mint and river water and, somewhere beneath that, a hint of salty, sweet fish.

" 'Night." I sit, watching the trees darken against the sky until I hear the zipper of the tent, the rustle of sleeping bag as Harry settles himself in like a dog. We didn't bring air mattresses or even good pillows—the canoe space was reserved for food and water and tents—and I imagine tomorrow we'll both be bent over and stiff from work and wear.

Across the campground, Susan and Reese are still sitting by the campfire, their backs to the picnic table. Together, near the flame, they are dark and light. Together, they should blot each other out. But they don't. Instead they make each other darker and lighter, luminescent, alive.

I watch as Susan leans into Reese, holding out a piece of fish between her fingers. Reese opens her mouth, takes the fish and Susan's fingers inside, holds everything there, her eyes on Susan's. Susan pulls her fingers out slowly, then she puts her fingers into her own mouth, sucks them the way she used to when she was a child. She'd get so excited by something—the tiger at the zoo, riding in the car, Daddy coming home—that she'd stick her fingers in her mouth and suck on them, just to calm herself.

I don't believe they are being exhibitionists. They are just in their own world, not even aware that I'm watching.

Reese puts her palm against Susan's cheek, runs it up into Susan's ponytail. She pulls my daughter's face to her own. It is not gentle, and for one moment, I want to stand up, I want to slap this woman's face, tear her hand from my child's cheek. But then Susan closes her eyes, leans sideways into Reese's palm. Between their lips, the orange fire sparks and crackles.

When Susan opens her mouth against Reese's chin, I know I should turn away, but I cannot. There is something here that I am coming to understand. Something that is burning its way through my stomach, something that I am afraid of, something that I want. I am afraid that if I step back into the darkness now, that if I close my eyes without seeing my daughter's joy, if I unzip the tent and slide in beside Harry, that this everything will disappear. I want to capture this thing like a firefly, to bring it to Harry and say, here, look. To say, please, yes. But I am afraid that it will die between my cupped palms, that I will arrive at Harry's side with nothing more than a husk of something that was bright and shining.

Reese puts her palm against Susan's breast. Susan lets go of Reese's chin, lets her head fall back. In the darkness above the firelight, the exhale of her breath is clear and white. Reese leans forward, one thumb against Susan's breast, one hand against Susan's back, steadying her.

The thread of warmth inside me climbs up through my thighs into the bottom of my belly. When Reese ducks her head into the hollow space beneath Susan's chin, I force myself to get off the picnic table slowly, quiet. I will go to the tent. I will lie down beside Harry and put my arm across his belly and force myself to sleep. In the morning, I will get up and boil water for coffee and oatmeal over the campfire. Tomorrow, I will paddle with all my heart.

Still, Susan hears me. Her eyes, suddenly open, focus on my face. Reese, too, watching me, watching Susan, waiting to see what we will do. My cheeks flood with heat. I am an old woman in sweats, watching my daughter make love to another woman, living off her desires instead of my own.

Susan stares at me a moment longer. And then she smiles. Dimple, dimple, dimple. A constellation against the night sky. Stars to guide the way. "Sweet dreams, Ma," Susan says, and there is no shame in her voice, no humiliation. There is only my daughter, doing something she loves, wanting to share with me something that she loves. Pushing me, as she always has, to be something better, larger than myself. For her, this thing is no different than taking me canoeing. She is teaching me, watching out for me, taking me only as far as I can go. Then, she will let loose her hand, she will let me float. It is my job to do the rest.

"You too," I whisper. But she is already back in her own space, her mouth at Reese's ear, her hand on Reese's leg.

I make my way back to the tent by feel. The zipper sounds loud in the darkness. When I slide myself in, Harry is awake, waiting. "You okay?" he asks.

I nod, even though I know he can't see it. I slide into the double sleeping bag beside him and try not to shiver. He lays his arm across me, the same way he laid his arm across me when we were twenty. He doesn't even realize he's doing it, I don't think.

I start to say, "Harry, let's try something new." I start to say, "Harry, there's something I'd like to talk about." But I imagine his response, his patient listening, his arm across my shoulder, his gentlemanly ways, and I can't stand it.

Instead, I take his chin in my fingers and turn his head toward me. I am not gentle or kind. I am ravenous. I open my mouth over Harry's chin the way I'd seen Susan do with Reese. Harry's whiskers scrape my tongue, the sides of my gums. I taste his stubble, the spot in the middle of his bottom lip that always peels. My tongue is a fish inside him, entering new dark caverns, swimming to depths that I had forgotten existed. He tastes like Harry, but like something else, too—sweat and sea and salmon. I wonder what he tastes in me, what new flavors I might reveal.

There are too many layers between us—my sweats and his, the soft underskin of the sleeping bag. I slip my hands beneath his shirt, run them up the soft fur and flesh of his chest. My palm hits his nipple, and Harry grunts, something like a porpoise, something like a wild animal.

"Shh," I say, but my shushing is louder than his noise. I run my thumb over his nipple again, the hardening point of it. Forty years, and I'm not sure if I've ever really felt his nipple before, the way its edges pucker like a berry, the way its peak rises beneath my skin. I circle my thumb again, and Harry moans inside my mouth.

I slide my hand out from his shirt, grip the waistband of his sweats. "Take these off," I say. I've never said this before, told him to undress, and the words taste strange in my mouth. I am not sure how he will react, but he does what I say, and fast, lifting his hips off the ground to get the sweats down. Then he sits up and pulls his T-shirt over his head.

"You too," Harry says, but his hands are already at my waistband, pulling my sweats down over my thighs. He only gets them down as far as my knees.

"Leave them," I say. I kick my legs until the sweatpants are in a pile at the bottom of the sleeping bag. I bring his head back toward me, enter his mouth with my tongue. Harry moans again, breath and noise against my tongue, the press and release of tides inside my body. I didn't know how much I loved the sound of him. I didn't know this sound *was* him—do I hear him now because we're in the quiet of the wilderness, or because I am listening hard here in the woods? I want to hear the sound again, feel that tide inside my body, so I run my thumb over his nipples, hard and fast, first one, then the other.

Harry pulls his mouth away from mine. Then he reaches for me, his fingers around my shoulder with some kind of force. He moves fast, faster than I remember, faster than I would have believed possible, and then he is above me, kissing me. Hard. He is not gentle. There is nothing gentlemanly about the way his tongue is in my mouth, hot and hard, the way his tongue runs across my teeth, the way his cock is pressing, insistent and wet as a dog's nose, against my thigh.

I wrap my hands around his cock, the long, sturdy, warm, living length of it. I roll it between my palms until his cock tightens and lengthens beneath my skin. Until Harry sighs, quiet as the woods, above me. If I had more courage, I would use all my strength to roll him over on his back, to press his shoulders down on the canvas floor of the tent and, beneath that, the rocks and sticks of the forest. I would raise myself above him, cup his cock in my hands. I would put my knees on either side of him and ride him. I would whisper *damn cock fuck* over and over in his ear.

But I am too old, too tired for that much courage. The light between my hands, between my thighs, is already waning. Instead, I take hold of his ass, the cool and wrinkled skin. I guide him between my thighs. Normally, I would let Harry take his time, let him take the time that he thought I wanted, needed. But not tonight, not here in the dark with my daughter out there. I am wet already with what I have seen, what I have grasped. The inside of my belly trembles like it's filled with fish and stream. I pull Harry into me, fast, sharp. He slides inside me so quickly that he gasps and falters. He opens his mouth. I am afraid he will apologize. He will ask if he's hurt me, and then all of this—this light, this heat, the hunger—will fall away.

Instead, he opens his mouth again to mine. He thrusts his tongue into me even as he thrusts his cock between my legs. And even as he does this, even as his cock enters me again and again, hard and hard, harder than I had hoped, than I had dreamed, even as the heat rises through my insides, I am grateful for this thing, this small precious gift that I have been given. For this heat, for this heated living thing between my legs.

"Yes," he says, and I'm not sure what he's saying yes to, if he even knows he's saying it, but I say yes too and then I am whispering it over and over, yes and yes and yes each time his cock sinks inside me. Even now his arm is over my shoulder, holding his body above me. I lean forward and open my mouth over the meat of his shoulder, let my teeth sink in a little. My mouth against his flesh still says yes and yes and yes, even as something drops through my middle, sending shivers out in all directions, leaving nothing but liquid and shine.

In the morning, I slip out of the tent while Harry sleeps, quiet, on his side. There is only our canoe waiting at the water's edge and a note scrawled in Susan's handwriting tucked beneath my oar. "Enjoy breakfast. Then get your butts in gear and catch up with us." I think of Susan and Reese, ahead of us, leading the way, believing in our ability to follow, to learn, to grow. I pick my oar up, think of the day opening ahead of us, the water and the woods. The oar reminds me of Harry's cock, the warmth and roll of it, the way it fits perfectly between my palms. I think today I will sit in the back. I think today I will learn how to steer.

from A Mouth Like Yours

DANIEL DUANE

FOR MEN, THE FUNDAMENTAL wrong is an active infringement on the rights of another: by punching me, you violate my right not to get punched. For women, torts have more to do with the failure to fulfill responsibilities. Which was why men never knew what the hell they'd done so wrong when their girlfriends were mad. But of course this hadn't been much help, and the more relevant example was really the Big Dysfunctional Love Number One, with Vicky Freelon, clear back in the tenth grade. That time, too, I'd been betwixt and between, off my game—having only just transferred to the big public high school. When I met Vicky, she became my clique and my world and my sense of self. No matter how bad things got with Vicky, she was all I had, so my attachment only deepened. Even when she declared us "only friends" and then fooled around with a popular water polo player and then "got back together" with me the next day, I'd been right back at her place, watching *Hogan's Heroes* while her wiry-haired father, a straight-toothed, genuinely nice, recently cuckolded deal maker, fried steaks in the kitchen. And when Vicky sensed that I might be indignant enough to make her pay, and Hogan plotted yet another escape from Stalag 13, and Mr. Freelon chatted with me through the doorless passageway, she undid my specially tapered peg-legged Levi's.

"So, what grade are you in, Mr. Harper?"

"Ah . . ."

Vicky's deft, expert fingers fiddled through the zipper.

"What's that, son?"

"Tenth. I'm in tenth grade."

Blue TV screen light bathed my little pinkness, while Vicky leaned over and held back her crucifix and treated my little pecker like the very joystick of my self-control, as if whatever resistance I had bottled up inside, whatever judgment of her or glimmering of pride, could be worked and worked like the cursor in a video game, until all the fire poured out and the guns went empty.

"And did Vicky say you guys have a class together?"

Oh dear God.

And if Vicky's father had walked into that room and seen what no father should ever see—well, goddamn it. Because by the time I'd watched little Vicky pause to call out, "Hey, can Harper stay for dinner?" I was a goner. I had discovered that, yes, erotic gratification was indeed an immutable force in my inner life. And so I stopped even trying to fight, and struggled instead to prove my trustworthiness, but because I was incapable of understanding all the ways in which I was a loser, I had no means of triumphing in the contest that I'd set for myself, the one in which I could finally stop sucking and start feeling good inside. So I started playing an awful lot of electric guitar with the lights out, writing heavy metal songs with titles like "Genocide," and contemplating killing myself, enslaved as I was by my own lameness and by the fickle and vindictive drug of her love and her lips. And then came the afternoon that I lay fully clothed atop Vicky's bed, on my back, with Vicky astride me. She wore a long skirt that day, and she had a new Devo album on the tape deck. A knock at the bedroom door: Mr. Freelon, home early.

Vicky said calmly, "Wait a sec, Daddy."

I began to sit up, expecting her to hop off me.

"Stay still," she whispered, somehow choosing that of all moments to give me what I wanted most of all. Pulling her plaid skirt so that it draped entirely over my clothed stomach and lap, she reached under to unzip my Levi's, pulled aside her pink Hello Kitty panties, and slipped me at long last into the moist heat of her life-affirming creation, the greatest sensation of my short life and quite clearly the whole reason for my existence. Putting her skirt back in place to hide all evidence of our coupling, she called out, in her very best good-girl voice, "Okay, Daddy, you can come in now."

The door opened and there stood miserable Mr. Freelon, having already changed out of his three-piece Realtor's suit and into his candy-striped nylon running shorts, Nike trainers, and tank top. A real adult who'd been jogging a lot, replacing alcohol with endorphins, he was stopped for a moment by wondering what was going on beneath that skirt, and doubtless also by the chaos of expressions flitting across my young face. But then Mr. Freelon chose to ignore his instincts and pretend that he suspected nothing. Breaking into a weird smile, he strode into the room. I can't even guess what my eyes were doing, but I do know that I had zero space in the brain for anything but the ecstatic miracle that was happening and the bewildering circumstances in which it was taking place, Vicky's boiling hot ocean enveloping the happy little fish that was me, while her half-oblivious father pulled up the little-girl desk chair, crossed his hairy legs, folded his ropy arms, and looked directly into my eyes. Who knew why, but Mr. Freelon then calmly asked about my newest skateboard and chuckled with a perverse, unconscious giddiness, while Vicky rocked faintly to bring me closer to that easy little boy's ejaculation, and the very face of her father's impotence loosened every muscle in my body.

Blackberries

Nalo Hopkinson

"YOU WANT SOME BLACKBERRIES?" I asked Tad. "They grow wild all along here."

In fact, blackberry bushes lined the narrow winding road as far as the eye could see. I walked over to the nearest one, where there was a clump of fat, ripe fruit hanging just about level with my mouth.

"You crazy, Shuck?" asked Jamal. "Those things are growing by the roadside with all this pollution! You gonna make him eat those?"

As if to prove Jamal's point, a semi came hurtling down the road, careening around the curves, belching blue smoke. It was huge and it stank, but there were still three cyclists riding in its wake. They had serious gear on and straddled serious racing bikes. One of them looked sure to overtake the truck at the next bend. I shook my head. Vancouver. Gotta love this city. I'd only been living in her three years, but already she had my heart, with her tree-hugging, latte-sipping, bike-riding ways. Some girls are just like that. I waved a wasp away from the bunch of blackberries I was eyeing and pulled the ripest ones off. They just fell into my hand, staining it a little with juice.

"Here," said Tad. "Lemme try 'em."

Jamal sighed and rolled his eyes at his boyfriend. "Your funeral, sweetie."

Tad smiled and made a kissy face at him. "And I know you'll look hot at the wake, so cute in your tux."

I put one of the blackberries into Tad's mouth, enjoying the warmth and slight dampness of his tongue against my fingers. Tad had the kind of plump, ripe brown lips I liked. I imagined crushing the berries against them and licking the juice off. Shit, the things I was thinking about my oldest friend.

Tad bit into the berry. He raised his eyebrows in surprise. I grinned. "The blacker the berry," I told him. He responded with that flirty grin I remembered so well. Oh, gay boys could make me so randy. Gay boys and mouthy femmes.

"Come on, Jamal," Tad said. "You really need to taste one of these. Here." He took a berry from me and waved it in front of Jamal's face. Jamal looked skeptical.

"Just smell it." Tad put the berry under Jamal's nose and winked at me. "You know how they say the way to a man's heart is through his belly?"

"That's no belly," I pointed out.

"You know it," Jamal said. "I don't spend all that time in the gym for nothing." Jamal was wearing denim shorts that looked like they'd been sewn right on him, and a sinfully tight white tank top. Like many black men, he didn't have much body hair to obscure the view. The white cotton made his skin gleam. His chest was a map of every workout he'd ever done. He was long and lean to Tad's short, rotund muscularity. Ah, so what? I bet my arms were bigger than his. I bet I could take him. I felt the warm pulse come and go in my clit and smiled. That was the thing with me and some guys: this balled-up heat, this combination of competitiveness and good, hard wanting. A lot would satisfy it. Wrestling, maybe. Or . . . no. Shut it, girl. I didn't know if I could flip these boys. Even if I could make them, just for a little while, hard for someone with girl bits, would it be someone like me? Every fag I knew was fascinated with breasts, and I was a little deficient in that department.

Jamal got a good whiff of the blackberry, and his face changed. He practically sucked it out of Tad's fingers. Tad laughed.

Two lanky white guys in surfer shorts and skateboarding T-shirts scrambled around us on the narrow verge, trying not to stare at the tableau of three black folks together in the same space. Not a sight you saw a lot in Vancouver. They headed toward the entrance to Wreck Beach, the smell of weed tailing them.

I slurped down the rest of the berries. "C'mon," I said. "Let's go." We continued along the roadside.

Jamal and Tad were up visiting me from Seattle. Tad and I had been buddies when I still lived there. We'd known each other since school days. Sometime near the end of high school, Tad had come out to me; like I hadn't guessed! With his example to follow, I'd come out myself—a good obedient black girl from a fine Christian family, engaged to a minister in training—and fled into the arms of outcast women like myself with no plan of ever looking back. Tad and I had stayed fast friends, but we'd stopped the outrageous flirting with each other that we used to do. No need, right? Now that we'd each shown our true colors and didn't need the other as a shield anymore. Except when Tad contacted me a few weeks ago, we'd fallen right back into the sexual innuendo, the teasing. It felt familiar. Tad was my home. I'd invited him and Jamal to visit me and Sula, and I was thrilled when they accepted. The guys had landed at Vancouver airport a scant two hours ago. I'd whisked them off immediately to show them Wreck Beach.

We were at Trail Number Six, the path that led to the beach. "Nearly there," I told them. I took the first few steps down. Tad and Jamal followed me, then stopped to look around. We were in a forest—dark, damp, and cool. Lean old maples stretched forever to reach the sky. The footpath angled sharply down in steps hewn out of the earth and shored up with planks. A deep ravine dipped down beside the footpath. It was overgrown with saplings, tangled blackberries, and undergrowth. Here and there, a few giant rotted tree trunks jutted up out of it, looking like a giant's caber toss. "*This* leads to a beach?" said Jamal.

"Yup," I replied. "It's about twenty minutes straight down, ten if you're fit."

"Lawd a mercy," muttered Tad. "The child still has a taste for hard labor."

I smirked at him. "Ready to hike?" I asked.

Shot through with bars of precious sunlight from above, a yellowed maple leaf drifted slowly down into the ravine. The leaf was the size of a turkey platter.

Jamal looked at me, a gleam in his eye. "Ten minutes?"

"For me, anyway," I said. The gauntlet had been laid down. Would he pick it up?

"Betcha I can do it in seven."

"You're on!" I burst past him. He yelled and ran to catch up. I knew this path well, could do it in the dark. I had, one night, with my girl-friend, Sula. And when we'd made it to the beach—well, mosquitoes bit me that night in places no mosquito had any right being.

I grabbed a sapling for purchase, slid around that little dogleg you get to about a third of the way down. I shouted for the joy of it.

"Please be careful, both of you!" yelled Tad.

I stopped, looked up at Tad a few yards above me. He was skating and slipping on the pebbles. He skidded to one knee, grimaced as he skinned it. He'd stopped about an inch from the edge. Jamal looked down. It was a steep drop over the side.

"He's right," I said. "I'll race you, but let's not do anything stupid, okay?"

Jamal measured me with his eyes. I let him look. My sawn-off jeans showed the bulges in my thighs, and my arms strained at the sleeves of my T-shirt. I was a fair match for him, and we both knew it.

"All right," he replied. "Nothing stupid. We take it easy. But I bet you I'll be the one to make it down there without breaking a sweat."

"In your dreams." I turned and kept climbing down, Jamal neck and neck beside me.

"Tad, you okay up there?" called Jamal.

"You bitches better slow down!" he shouted back.

"Yeah?" I said to him. "You gonna come down here and make us?"

Tad chuckled. "I bet you'd like that."

I could hear him puffing, his feet landing heavily on the steep stairs, but Tad didn't ruffle easily. Like when he'd come and pulled me out of my parents' house, where my dad had me under house arrest for the crime of being a bulldagger. Dad had reached for the baseball bat he kept behind the couch, but Tad just grabbed it away from him and calmly told me to pack a bag, he'd wait for me. Been too long since Tad and I hung out.

"I can smell the sea," Jamal said.

"Yeah," I told him. "I love this part. The forest belongs to the land, but as you come farther and farther down, the sea starts to peek through. You smell it first, then you begin to see it. A few more steps, and . . . ah. There she is."

We were at the landing, just a few yards above the beach. The sand stretched out on either side with the water just beyond it, its gentle waves licking at the beach. The sea smelled like sex. Off in the distance, the Coast Mountains marched away from us, range upon range, disappearing into the mist.

Jamal stood tall, but he was breathing hard, and I could see the beads of sweat on his face. I bet they tasted like the sea. "Little winded, there, Jamal?" I teased him.

He sucked his teeth. "Don't give me that, girl child. Look at you."

He was right. I was puffing a bit myself, and my T-shirt was soaked. I pulled it over my head. I never wore a bra. Jamal literally jumped. I calmly tucked the end of the T-shirt into my belt. "What?" I asked him. "I told you it was a nude beach." You weren't supposed to get naked until you were actually on the beach, but I was feeling the devil rising in me. Wanted to see how Jamal and Tad would deal.

Tad had caught up with us. He burst out laughing when he saw me. "Susanna Paulette Avery, you're still flat as an ironing board!"

"Don't talk shit, Tad. This a thirty-eight-inch chest. I work out hard to get this chest."

"Chest, yes. But where are the titties, girl?"

"On your momma."

Now Jamal was laughing, too. He looked relieved. Probably 'cause he didn't have to look at bouncing boobies on me. Even with my shirt off, lots of people still mistake me for a man. Nipples a little thicker than on most guys is all.

I pointed to the Johnny on the spot off to one side on the landing. "You guys want to use the facilities before we go down?"

"Nah," said Jamal. "We can piss in the bushes if we have to . . . oh. Excuse me, Susanna. Unless you want to." He gestured toward the toilet. Damn. Show a little bit of girl parts, and he goes all gentleman on me.

"No." I moved past him and headed for the stairs. "And shut it with the Susanna crap. Everybody calls me Shuck."

"Except your daddy!" Tad sang out. Giggling, he brushed past me on the stairs and raced down to the beach. "He calls you—"

"Don't start, Tad!" I ran, caught up with him, tackled him to the sand.

"Ow! Big meanie." Laughing, Tad got me in a choke hold, pinned my back to the sand, one arm behind me. The buttons of his shirt were plucking at my nipples. They swelled. I got my legs around Tad's body.

Men have the upper-body advantage; women have the lower. I twisted, flipping Tad like a turtle. I sat astride him. Jamal ran up and stood there, watching us both with a shit-eating grin on his face.

"Now," I said to Tad, "*what* does my dad call me? Tell me." And I started tickling him.

Tad wriggled helplessly under me. "Bitch! Stop it! No!" He giggled, tried to slap my hands away, but I kept moving them, kept digging my fingers into his tummy, his sides, the bit along the bottom of his belly.

"Here, let me help," said Jamal. He knelt at Tad's head, grabbed his arms. Laughing, Tad struggled, but Jamal held him fast. I kept tickling. Tad started to squeal.

"I think you men need to go to the other part of the beach," said a firm woman's voice.

I looked up. She was pointing to where the gay men usually hung out. She looked part Asian, part something I couldn't identify. She was completely naked, all soft curves, about fifteen years older than me, with a relaxed, amused grin. Just the way I like 'em. I stood up off Tad.

"Yes, ma'am!"

"Oh," she said, hearing my voice. "Maybe not." She'd pegged me for a woman.

"Where is it?" Jamal asked her.

She pointed, but I said, "I can show you." I took Tad's hand, pulled him up off the sand. The woman raised an eyebrow at me, but said only, "I'm sure you can," and sauntered off.

I watched her departing behind: chubby and round, like two oranges. I bet that ass felt good in the hands. It was bouncy, too. "Gotta be jelly," I muttered.

"'Cause jam don't shake like that!" Jamal finished. We laughed, punched each other's shoulders.

I led the boys farther out onto the beach, to a nice patch of sunlight. Sunlight, like black people, was a rare and precious occurrence in Vancouver. Tad and Jamal stared around them. Even in early fall, some people still came down to the water. There was a mound of sand, human height, with a sand sculpture of a naked woman carved into its side. Over to our right, someone had stuck bleached fallen logs into the sand, angling them together into the shape of a teepee. Over to our left an elderly Asian woman and man, nude, sat on towels with their chess game on the sand between them. Three ruddy children and their dog played with a bright green ball. The children's laughter and shouting and the barking of the dog ascended into the cool autumn air and were thrown back from the forest behind us.

"Water? Pop? Smokes?" The vendor strolling the beach was male, stocky, white. He swung a bright red cooler from either hand. He wore sturdy rubber sandals, a money pouch around his waist, a sun visor on his head, and a bow tie around his neck, all in the same red as the coolers. Nothing else. Tad's face as he spied him was a picture.

"We don't have anything like this in Seattle," he murmured.

"Hey, Philip," I called out.

The vendor smiled when he saw me, and came over. "Hey, Shuck," he said. "Nice day, eh?"

"Beauty," I agreed.

Tad quirked an eyebrow at me. "Beauty?"

I shrugged. "Been here three years. Starting to talk like the locals." Philip snickered.

"You guys thirsty?" I asked them. They nodded. So I bought some pop off Philip.

"Smokes?" Philip asked again. "I got tobacco and, um, herbal."

"Reefer?" asked Tad. "You selling reefer out in the open like this?" Philip just grinned.

"Shuck," said Tad, "we're the only black people as far as the eye can see. You know that if some shit goes down with the cops, we'll be the ones doing jail time, not him."

"Just chill, man," Philip told him. The borrowed black phrase sounded odd in a white Vancouverite's mouth. But hell, probably no odder than me saying *beauty*.

"This is Vancouver," I told Tad. "*And* it's Wreck Beach. If the cops start picking people up here for smoking weed, the jail'll be overflowing in an hour."

Tad shook his head. "'S all right anyway, man," he told Philip. "Thank you."

"You guys have a good day, then," Philip replied. He nodded at me and continued down the beach.

I turned to hand a can of pop to Jamal, and my mouth went dry. He'd kicked off his sandals. As I watched, he stripped off his tank top and shorts and slipped out of the skimpy black jock he was wearing underneath. When he bent down, the hollow that muscle made at the side of his butt cheek was deep enough that I could have laid my fist inside it. Graceful as a dancer, he flicked the jock off, tossed it on the pile of his clothing, rolled it all up into a cylinder, and stood. Tad gave his lover's body an admiring gaze. Jamal took the can of pop I held out to him, somehow managing to do so without looking directly at me.

For a while we all just stood, uncomfortably silent. Sucking on the drinks gave us something to do with our hands. I led them to a pile of flat rocks, comfortable as armchairs. We sat and looked at the people around us, looked out to sea—anywhere but at each other.

Not too many people out today; it was early fall and a little bit chilly for the beach. Two more nudists were playing Frisbee not too far from us; both appeared to be in their sixties. He was tanned with a fall of long white hair tied into a ponytail, and elaborate mustachios. Both forearms a rainbow of tattoos. He carried his firm potbelly on his sturdy thighs like a treasure chest. She had long blonde hair, a beautiful and weathered face, a toughness and pride to her movements. She had knotted a burgundy lace shawl around her hips, not that it hid anything. It seemed to be just for pretty. And she was pretty. Her breasts bounced and jiggled as she leaped, laughing, for the Frisbee. She caught it, went and took the man by the hand. Together they walked over to a group of three children frolicking by the rocks. They had a family picnic over there, spread out on towels.

"There's kids here," said Tad.

"Yeah. Everybody comes."

"Doesn't it get a little racy for them to be out here?"

"No. Anybody starts to make out in public, people will stop them."

"Oh." He looked a little disappointed.

"Of course, what happens in the bushes isn't exactly public . . ."

Jamal snickered.

"I'm sure there's a lot that goes on that we don't see." Hell, I'd played my own reindeer games here. That night with Sula and the mosquitoes, for example. No one was allowed down here at night, but we'd managed.

Over to our right, a young woman sat fully clothed on the sand, her knapsack beside her. She had a sketchbook. She seemed to be drawing the mountains in the distance. The two surfer dudes we'd seen earlier were skimming wakeboards in the shallowest part of the water, hopping onto them and riding parallel with the shore.

"There's nobody in the water," Jamal said.

"Nah, not much. It's cold and there aren't any waves. That's not the attraction of this beach."

"No?" Jamal replied, a teasing tone to his voice. "Then what is?"

Tad gasped and grabbed my arm. "What's that?" he hissed. He pointed toward the water.

Jamal looked where Tad had pointed. "Shit. Is it a dog?"

I smiled. "Seal. Harbor seal."

"For real? A live seal?"

"For real."

The seal had surfaced not twenty feet offshore, only its head visible. Its fur was black and shiny, its eyes large and curious in its big round head. It was staring at the surfer dudes.

"It's just curious," I said. "Don't make eye contact with it . . ."

Too late. The seal had turned to look at us and had seen us staring. Shy and cautious, it disappeared back into the water.

"Fuck, that's wonderful," whispered Tad.

"Yeah," Jamal replied. He leaned back against Tad's chest with a happy sigh. He leaned over and patted my hand. "Shuck, thank you for letting us visit. Really."

"No problem." They were gorgeous, sitting in a love knot like that. I think that was the moment I decided to see if I could turn them both on to me, just for the afternoon.

"Hold this for me, will you, baby?" Tad handed Jamal his empty pop can and whipped his shirt off. He'd gotten a belly since I saw him last, and his arms and thighs were heavier.

"Being in love suits you, sweetie," I told him. "You look good."

He looked embarrassed. "Fat, you mean."

"No, I mean good. Like you'd be good to hold."

Tad raised an eyebrow at me. Jamal chuckled. "Oh, yeah. I just wrap my arms and legs around him and ride all night."

I gave them both a measuring stare. "Yeah, I can imagine." Jamal stared me back down. Tad just looked uncomfortable. Shit. Had I pushed too far? Maybe this was a bad idea. Tad was my friend, had stood by me all these years. I didn't want to ruin that over a fuck. Better ease up a little, figure myself out. I stood up and said, "Okay. Let me take you to where the boys are."

NEVER MIND THE COOLER weather; gay Wreck Beach was hopping. A large man in a small, frilly apron circulated through the crowd, selling martinis right off the tray he balanced on one hand. There was a volleyball game going on farther down the beach, a serious game. I recognized those four guys; they came down here a lot, but I never saw them cruising. They really just enjoyed being naked in the sun. One of them jumped and spiked the ball hard, sending his opponent sprawling when he tried to stop it. A few people watching them applauded.

Down by the water, some diehards were trying to swim. Better them than me. They had little triangular purple flags stuck in the sand near their towels. A nudists' club, then. Three women and a dog lolled on the sand. They nodded and smiled at me. I nodded back. A man lay on a towel on his stomach, his perfect bottom upturned invitingly to the sun, and to the eye. A few guys just strolled the beach, alone, their eyes alert for opportunity. And there was plenty. The twinks were twinkling, the bears were bare, and the bushes were shaking. Before winter, certain of the manhandling men of Vancouver seemed determined to get in every last bit of naked cruising on the beach.

It was rockier here. Back at my and Sula's apartment, my shrine had a collection of rocks I'd collected from Wreck Beach, all colors. All worn smooth by the water. We picked our way across the rocks and sand.

The three of us had drawn instant attention the second we crossed the invisible dividing line between the straight part of the beach and this one. No surprise; we had us some permanent tans. Up in the city, being black could get you followed by security guards when you went into stores. But down here, it was a different matter. Most of the guys who scoped me for a girl immediately switched their attention to Tad and Jamal; those greedy two were loving every instant of it. A hairy man with a tall, thin body gave Tad a melting smile. "Hello," he said as he walked by.

Tad dipped his chin in response. " 'S'sup," he growled, all serious and street, but when the man had passed, Tad grinned and gave himself a thumbs-up.

Jamal was likely to get whiplash, he was working so hard at seeing everything there was to see. "It's hog heaven up in here!" he hissed at us. He was getting his fair share of appreciation, too.

My shoulders were getting warm from the sun. It wasn't too bright, but it could still burn. I fished the flat plastic bottle of sunscreen out of the back pocket of my shorts and smeared some all over my upper body. Better protect the nips. Then I flipped the bottle at Jamal. "Here," I said. "Put some sunscreen on that pretty behind."

He caught the bottle, looked at the label, sneered at me. "Girl, what you think I need this for? Got me more melanin than alla these mother-fuckers out here!"

"All right, but don't come crying to me when your hide gets hard and leathery like somebody's old wallet." I held out my hand for the bottle. Jamal cut his eyes at me, but he put the sunscreen on.

An older man came walking past us. He looked white, but he was tanned a deep brick red. His skin had settled into soft folds on his body, and he clanked when he moved. I spotted a pinkie-thick rod through each nipple, plugs and multiple rings through his ears, and a bunch more rings and rods through his dick. There were probably more I wasn't seeing. Tad shuddered, but I thought he looked really interesting. Had to admire his dedication.

Then I got a better look at one of the men coming out of the water. Could it be? I wasn't sure. He saw us, altered his trajectory so that his path would cross ours. Dragonfly tattooed on his left thigh. Yes, it was him!

As he passed by, he looked Jamal up and down, slowly. "Mmm," he said, "chocolate." He walked on, gazing back at Jamal now and again. He flagged down the martini seller.

"What the fuck was that?" said Jamal.

I chuckled. "He didn't recognize me."

"Where you know him from?" Tad asked.

"Shuck," said Jamal, "can we find somewhere to sit that's a little bit private? All of a sudden, I'm not digging these guys so much anymore."

Perfect. Just my chance. "They're not all like that, you know," I said. But I led them to the place I had in mind, a private little patch of sand surrounded by scrubby trees. Good, no one was using it just now.

"Where do you know him from?" asked Tad again.

I pointed to a large flat-topped rock. "You can sit there," I told them. "It's almost like an armchair."

"Susanna . . . I know you when you get like this," Tad said. "What's the story with that guy?"

I grinned. "You gonna take those clothes off? It's warm down here."

Jamal put his clothing down on the rock and went to undo the fly on Tad's jeans. Tad made a show of slapping his hands away, then submitted. I sat on the boulder that was conveniently near the flat rock and watched. Triumphantly, Jamal yanked the zipper down.

"Wait, sweetie, wait," Tad said. "Gotta take the shoes off first." With a shy glance at me, he sat on the rock, put his balled-up shirt next to Jamal's clothing, and started taking off his runners. To keep him company, I took off my sandals, put them on the boulder beside me. Tad got his shoes and socks off, snuck me a glance again, rocked his jeans off his hips, and pulled his legs out of them. He was wearing black cotton shorts underneath. So modest. He rolled the jeans up beside the other clothing.

"Stand up," I said. "Let me see you."

Slowly, he did. His thighs were thick, his calves full and muscled. "Well, look at you," I told him. Jamal was smiling at me thoughtfully. Was he egging me on?

"Lover," he said to Tad, "turn all the way around for your friend. Let her look at you."

He *was* egging me on.

"The two of you are shameless," muttered Tad, but to my surprise, he did what Jamal asked. I took my time admiring his butt, the fullness of his belly. He turned to face me, but I'd barely glanced at his package in his shorts when he sat down. "So," he said, faking nonchalance, "you gonna tell me about that guy?"

"You wanna know what happened, you have to take the shorts off."

He cocked his hand on his hip. "Is the story worth it?"

"Worth seeing you in the full, glorious flesh? It's a high price, baby, but I think I can meet it."

He made a face at me. But he looked pleased, too. This felt good. This felt like the way we used to tease each other. I just wanted to push it up a notch, that's all.

Maybe Tad was thinking the same thing because all of a sudden he pulled his shorts down, stepped out of them, grabbed them up off the sand, and sat down. He tossed the shorts onto the pile of clothing and turned back to me. "There," he said. He crossed his hands in his lap, conveniently hiding his crotch. "So, tell me the story." Jamal sat on the warm sand beside Tad's knee.

"All right," I said. "You asked for it."

I settled comfortably on my boulder, leaned forward. "Well, Sula and I have this game, right? Every so often, one of us dares the other one to do something outrageous. If you chicken out from doing whatever it is, you lose, and you have to be the other person's sex toy for a night; do everything they say."

"Ooh," said Jamal. "Kinky." He stroked Tad's calf.

I snickered. "You don't know the half of it. One time I lost on purpose. Could barely stand the next day, after Sula got done with me." The memory of that night was making my nipples crinkle up. All those girly panty hose that Sula owned had made the most fiendish restraints. I didn't know I could bend in some of those positions.

"You're stalling, Shuck," said Tad.

"No, just setting the story up. 'Cause this one time, I took her up on her dare. There's this gay bar called Pump Jack's, a men's bar. I'll take you there on Friday. Sula said she wanted me to go in there and get one of the guys to let me jerk him off."

"No!" said Tad.

"Yes. And I did it."

"With that guy we just saw?"

"With that guy."

"How?"

"I went to the bar in drag . . ."

"In a dress?" asked Tad.

Jamal chuckled. "No, silly. She went in guy drag."

Though, come to think of it, I pretty much look like I'm in drag when I wear a dress, too. "Yeah," I said. "Little goatee, little bit of extra swagger in the walk. Wore my regular clothes. Walked right in. I mean, I go in there as a chick, so I thought the bouncer would recognize me. He got this look like he almost did, but then you could see he didn't make the connection. I didn't speak the whole time. Ordered a beer at the bar by pointing at the draft spigot. When I started drinking it, I knew I'd have to do something soon, before I needed to go and piss."

Tad was shaking his head. "Susanna, you are something else."

"Susanna left home. I'm Shuck."

"What happened then?"

"I saw this guy looking at me. That guy. The one on the beach. I started staring him down, looking him up and down. If I did that to a woman, she'd probably run a mile. But this guy, he came and sat next to me. Said hi. I didn't answer; just pointed with my chin over to the bathroom. Shit, I didn't think it would work! Figured he'd see I was a woman, and I'd have to pass it all off as a joke.

"But that didn't happen. He just gave me this rude, slow smile. Leaned over and whispered that he'd see me in there. And off he headed, to the john.

"My heart was fucking hammering in my chest, I tell you. But I put down my beer, followed him. He slipped into a stall, and I slipped in behind him. He reached for me, but I didn't want him touching me too much. Women's skin has this soft feeling, you know? Even mine. Didn't want that to give me away. So I pushed his back against the stall door. I sat on the toilet, unzipped him. . . ."

"Shit, that's hot," said Jamal. He was leaning forward, his mouth a little open. His cock was firming up. I was getting a tingle in my shorts, too, telling this story.

"He was hard the second I got his dick out of his pants. I slid my hands up under his shirt, grazed his nipples, pulled on them a little."

Tad swallowed.

"I ran my tongue around the head of his dick. He moaned, kinda low. I held on to his dick, gave it a good squeeze. It jumped in my hand."

Tad got this odd look. He squeezed his knees together and said, "You know, you better stop talking like that; else you might see something you don't wanna see."

Oh yes. Now we were getting somewhere. Jamal looked up at his lover, gave him an evil grin.

I stared right into Tad's eyes. "What you covering up there, Tad?" I said. Jamal snickered, but I held Tad's gaze like the headlights hold the deer's. "Something I'm saying getting you horny? Something about the way I pinched that man's nipples and took his dick in my fist and slid up and down, squeezing whenever my fingers went past the head?"

Tad gulped. He cupped his hands tighter around himself, but he wasn't fooling me; those hands were rubbing up and down, ever so slightly.

"You didn't know I did guys, did you? Only sometimes, Thaddeus. Only when the man is as gay as I am, and there's no hope in hell of pretending that the sex we're having is straight sex."

Jamal shot me a look. Was that admiration? I set my focus back on Tad. Jamal could match anything I could dish out, throw the challenge back in my face. We understood each other. Tad was the one I'd have to convince, if this was going to happen.

"Tad," I said.

"Yeah." His voice was raspy.

"You know what I did next?"

"No."

"I had my fist around that dick, feeling the little surging swells as he got more turned on. I took the other hand away from his nipples—"

"Aww!" protested Jamal.

"Hush, you," I told him. "I took my hand and slid it flat down his belly, toward his cock. Held the head in one hand, just pumping a little, back and forth . . ."

"Oh God," whispered Tad. He was openly stroking himself now, hiding the view from me with one hand, sliding the other up and down over his cock and balls.

"Held that head and drew my nails, very lightly, up the underside of his cock."

Tad's mouth opened.

"He moaned again, louder this time. He leaned back against the door. He had his hands at the top of the cubicle, hanging on to either side. I could see the muscles straining in his arms."

Tad made a little breathy noise.

"He got a drop of pre-come at the tip of his dick, just twinkling in the eye. I rubbed my thumb in it and used it to moisten the head of his dick."

Jamal moved in closer to Tad, laid his head on Tad's knee. Tad jumped and Jamal stroked Tad's inner thigh. "Shh, baby, it's okay," he said. Tad's eyes flicked from Jamal to me—a desperate, needy glance.

Jamal chuckled. He ran his tongue along the outside of Tad's thigh, licked his lips, and said to me, "So, did you suck him off?"

"Jamal!" Tad sat up straight. His hands slipped a little, and I could see his cock—compact, dark like the rest of him, with a pretty pink tip. Nice. "Jesus Christ, Shuck. You're my friend. We shouldn't—"

Jamal pressed Tad back against the rock, stroked his tummy. "Don't fret, Daddy. This is fun." Bless the boy, I thought. He looked back at me. "So, did you?"

I shook my head. "Suck him off? Not my thing. You know what I did instead?"

"What?" whispered Tad. Jamal gave him an encouraging smile.

"I spat on the place where my hand and his dick met, got it nice and wet. I started pumping him really slow."

Jamal ducked under Tad's leg, moved Tad's hands away from his cock and balls, held them out, away from his body. "Like this?" he said. He spat on Tad's erect cock. Tad gasped. His hands made clutching motions. Jamal let them go. Tad held on to Jamal's shoulders, threw his head back. "Like this?" Jamal asked again, and started sliding Tad's cock in his fist. Fuck, they were lovely together.

"Kinda like that," I told Jamal. "Keep going." I opened my own knees, thumbed my shorts open, and yanked the zipper down. I could smell my own musk. I slid my hand between my belly and the spread-open zipper. No underwear; I mostly don't bother with it. The crisp curls of my pubic hair were damp. Jamal dipped his mouth down to Tad's cock, ran his tongue slowly around the head of it. Now both Tad and I were moaning. I splayed my legs wider. My fingers found the folds of my pussy. They were hot and slick. My clit was puffy between them. It jumped at my touch, at the sight of Tad, eyes closed, mouth open, his hand around the back of Jamal's neck. Tad was bucking his hips now, slowly, popping his cock in and out of Jamal's mouth. Jamal, greedy Jamal, kept reaching for more.

"Jamal," I said hoarsely. "Can you get to your knees?"

Jamal made a garbled sound of assent around Tad's cock in his mouth. Tad reacted to the vibration with a slight shudder. Somehow Jamal managed to get into position. He spread his knees for traction, released Tad's cock from his mouth, and started tonguing Tad's balls. His perfect ass was displayed to my view, firm and dark as a cherry; two halves with the split between. With my three middle fingers I started rubbing my pussy, fast and flat against my clit, fingertips dipping into my cunt with each push. I was creaming inside my shorts.

There was sweat running down Tad's chest and heavy belly. More of it beaded in his tight, short hair and the beautifully groomed goatee. "God, you two are hot," I muttered. Tad opened his eyes, saw me looking, squeezed them shut again. He slowed his incursions into Jamal's mouth. I got a flash image of a black-furred head disappearing shyly beneath the water. Oh no you don't, Tad. I wasn't going to let this scene end here.

"So that guy in the bathroom?" I said to them.

"Mm?" mumbled Jamal, around a mouthful of Tad's cock and balls.

"I'm working him up with one hand. I hold the other hand up to his mouth. I'm still not talking, but he gets the idea. He starts licking my hand. Gets it good and wet."

"Shit," whispered Tad. But the rhythm of his hips had sped up again.

"I took that hand, cupped his balls with it. But just for a second." Remembering that forbidden night got me even wetter. I kept working my clit, slipped a couple of fingers on the other hand into my cunt, just at the entrance, beckoning against the front wall. Shit, shit, yeah. "Then," I said, "I slipped my hand past his balls, back, until I touched his asshole. He jumped a little."

So had Jamal. The motion pushed his ass out even farther into relief. His little pink rosebud of an asshole winked at me. I could see the curling black hairs that ran from the small of his back down toward it, like an arrow. *Here's the honey. Here.* Jamal had one hand on his own dick, stroking hard.

"I slipped one fingertip in . . ." I said.

Tad started to pant. His eyes were wide open now, fixed on Jamal's busy mouth.

"His asshole squeezed tight around my finger, like a little kiss. Then it opened up for me."

Jamal was making little groaning noises around Tad's cock. I pushed off from my rock, dropped to my knees beside them. Knees would pay for that later. My clit under my strumming fingers felt like a marble in syrup. The fingers of my other hand stroked hard against the spongy ridge just inside my cunt. It pushed back. Soon. "I . . ." My body was shaking, my crotch jutting toward Jamal and Tad. My thigh muscles knotted. It felt good. "I pushed one finger inside him. Then two. He took them both."

"Shuck," muttered Tad, "it's . . . I'm . . ." Jamal had his fist clamped tight around the base of Tad's cock, his mouth working the head. His hand between his own legs was almost a blur. He was screwing his ass around in the air. He looked so nasty.

"I plunged those fingers in and out of him, feeling him clasp them with each push. His dick was hard as iron in my hands."

The letting-down feeling started inside me, muscles starting to push down and forward. It was like I needed to piss.

"He slammed his shoulders back against the door. His crotch was arched way out. He was calling out for Jesus. He started to come. It spurted . . ."

Tad made this low, deep growl. His body began to spasm. Jamal pulled his mouth away so we could watch the gouts of juice rhythmically pumping out of Tad's cock. He stared, intent, at his lover's crotch, then came himself, hard and roaring.

That put me over the edge. My hand was flying at my clit, my forearms like cables. My own body pushed my fingers out of me, and I let go, and I was flying. I howl and laugh when I come, and I squirt. Lots. When I was done, the front of my shorts was sopping, and Tad's foot and Jamal's knee were in a puddle of girl-juice-soaked sand. I collapsed onto my side, breathing hard. It was going to be hell getting the sand out of my dreads.

I heard a noise behind us. I pulled my hands out of my pants and rolled over. Two eager heads had just pushed through the bushes to see what all the commotion was about. "Oh, excuse us," said the two men. They tromped away, giggling. I heard one of them say, "Was that a *woman* with them?"

Jamal started laughing, a low, slow roll. He put his head on Tad's knee and said to me, "Girl, you are some dirty bitch." He reached out and high-fived me. Our hands made a wet noise as they slapped together.

Tad still looked a little sheepish, but his whole body was more relaxed now. He leaned back against the rock, stroked Jamal's head. "Is this Canadian hospitality, Shuck?" he teased me.

I put my head against the warm sand, reached out a foot, and slid it along first Tad's leg, then Jamal's. I was going to have quite the story to tell Sula tonight. I admired our skins, the three shades of brown against the pale sand. "Look at us," I said.

"Three black sheep," Jamal joked.

"Three blackberries," I replied.

Tad gave a happy sigh. "And such sweet juice."

from The Sluts

DENNIS COOPER

SITE 1

Review #1

Escort's name: Brad

Location: Long Beach

Age: 18?

Month and year of your date: June 2001

Where did you find him? Street

Internet address: no

Escort's e-mail address: none

Escort's advertised phone number: not advertised, but try
  310-837-6112

Rates: I gave him $200

Did he live up to his physical description?

Did he live up to what he promised?

Height: 5'11"?

Weight: 150 lbs.?

Facial hair: no

Body hair: pubes only

Hair color: blond (dyed)

Eye color: hazel

Dick size: 6 inches?

Cut or uncut: cut

Thickness: couldn't tell

Does he smoke? yes

Top, bottom, versatile: bottom

In calls/out calls/not sure: not sure

Kisser: yes

Has he been reviewed before? no

Rating: recommended (see review)

Hire again: no (see review)

Handle: bigman60

Submissions: this is my seventh review

URL for pics: no

Experience: There are usually a few street hustlers working the blocks around a local bar here in Long Beach called Pumpers. That's where they like to hang out and play pool between tricks. It's a pretty sad scene, so I couldn't believe my eyes when I saw this beautiful, skinny kid with a backpack who told me his name was Brad. He didn't look a day over fourteen, but his ID said 18 so I'll let it stand at that.

I took him back to my place. He was very quiet and didn't seem to want to talk. He wouldn't give me a price or say what he was into. He also had a slight twitch where he'd crane his neck and open his mouth. I took that to be a drug reaction since he was obviously on something. There were warning signs everywhere, but Brad was so hot that I just ignored them. I'm glad I did, but keep reading.

He asked if I had any alcohol. I thought he was high enough already, but he said he had to be fucked up to do it. So I gave him some whiskey and he proceeded to get quite drunk but not loud and obnoxious. If anything he got even quieter. He still wouldn't talk money or specifics. He gave me the impression that whatever I wanted to do and pay him was fine. After about thirty minutes of steady drinking, I decided to make a move.

Here's the thing. The sex was unbelievable. Brad will do anything as far I can tell, but he's definitely a bottom. He never got hard, but he sure acted like he was into it. He has the hottest, sweetest little ass, especially if you like them a little used like I do. I must have eaten out his hole for an hour. I got four fingers inside him. I couldn't fuck him hard and deep enough. I spanked him, and not softly either. I pinched and twisted the hell out of his nipples. Nothing fazed him. All the time his cute boy face looked at me with his mouth wide open and made these sounds like he was scared to death and turned on at the same time. I came twice, first in his mouth and then up his ass. I should say that I never practice unsafe sex, but I just couldn't help it. I'm HIV–, however.

Here's where the problems started. He didn't want to stop. It's like he couldn't get himself out of whatever zone he was in. I was afraid he'd lost his mind. It was very spooky. I didn't know what to do with him. I let him sleep over because he didn't seem dangerous, but I fell asleep to the sound of him whimpering and thrashing around. I left $200 for him on the dresser, and when I woke up, he and the money were gone. There was a note from him with his phone number on it, saying to please call him or tell my friends about him. Overall, it was great, but once is enough for me.

You: I'm a middle-aged, overweight top into teenaged street trade, the cuter and skinnier the better.

Review #2

Escort's name: Brad
Location: Long Beach
Age: 18 (LOL)
Month and year of your date: June 2001
Where did you find him? on this site
Escort's advertised phone number: 310-837-6112
Rates: whatever you want to pay him. I gave him $150
Did he live up to his physical description: yes!
Did he live up to what he promised: fuck, yes

Height: 5'9''?

Weight: 145 lbs?

Facial hair: no

Body hair: no

Hair color: blond

Eye color: green

Dick size: don't care

Cut or uncut: don't care

Thickness: don't care

Does he smoke? yes

Top, bottom, versatile: bottom

In calls/out calls/not sure: out

Kisser? don't care

Rating: what do you think?

Hire again? fuck, yes

Handle: llbean

Submissions: this is my first review

Experience: The earlier review of Brad seemed too good to be true, but I called him anyway. It turned out to be the phone number of a homeless shelter in Long Beach. I left a message for Brad not expecting to hear back, but he called me a few hours later. He sounded unfriendly and bored on the phone, but I told him what I was into and he said that was fine. I offered to call him a taxi, but he said he wanted to walk. It must have been a good ten-mile walk to my house from that location, so I figured right then that he was a little strange. He arrived maybe two and a half hours later. I opened the door and couldn't believe my eyes. He seriously looks about fourteen, and they don't get any cuter.

Brad looked and smelled like he hadn't showered for a while, but from the earlier review I'd expected as much. I personally like my boys a little lived in. I met him at the door with a bottle of Jack Daniels, and he just took off the cap, and chugged about half of it down while I stripped him. He has a very tight, adolescent-looking body with long, skinny arms and legs, and the smallest ass and about twelve pubic hairs. The earlier review stated Brad was spooky, and he has some mental problems for sure, but I'm not into being some kid's father, so I could care less.

I don't have the space to go into everything we did, so I'll cut to the chase. Brad let me handcuff him to my bed and I went to work on his ass. I gave him a good finger stretching then started burying bigger and bigger dildos in his ass. I got a fat, two-foot-long dildo all the way inside and he let me churn and pound that ass like I was making butter. The whole time, he screamed like he was dying, but his dick was always rock hard. When I finally got around to fisting him, his hole was so hot that I came within a minute, then sucked the sweetest, biggest load of come out of him that I've ever tasted.

It was clear that he could have gone on all night if I'd wanted. I did have to order him to leave, and he was very out of it and acting pretty strange. But let me tell you, he's worth it. I'll be hiring him again for sure.

You: Leather daddy type, mid-50s, into restraints and heavy anal sex with young-looking bottoms.

Review #3

Escort's name: Brad
Location: Long Beach
Age: 18?
Month and year of date: July 2001
Where did you find him: on this site
Rates: not applicable
Height: 5'9"
Weight: 130 lbs.
Facial hair: no
Body hair: no
Hair color: brown
Eye color: blue
Dick size: don't know

Cut or uncut: don't know

Thickness: don't know

Does he smoke? yes

Top, bottom, versatile? don't know

Rating: not applicable

Hire again: not applicable

Handle: JoseR72

Submissions: This is my seventeenth review

Experience: Call me a caretaker if you want, but after reading Brad's reviews, I couldn't help but feel concerned about this troubled young man, and angered by the callousness with which the previous reviewers have treated him. I work in the mental heath industry in Orange County, not far from Long Beach. I made an appointment with Brad in order to encourage him to seek treatment, although he didn't know my intentions until we met.

Regular visitors to this site know that I'm not against hiring escorts. I will even admit that Brad is my type and that meeting him involved a high degree of self-control on my part. Something the previous reviewers are right about is that he's extraordinarily cute. Brad is one of the cutest twinks I've ever seen in fact. I don't know how a boy as cute and young as Brad ended up in the low end of his profession, but it's wrong to exploit him. He deserves better.

I had a long talk with Brad. It took him a while to open up to me, but he did. My knee-jerk diagnosis is that Brad is probably schizophrenic with an untreated chemical imbalance. He might also be suffering from a mild neurological disorder, as evidenced by the physical tics that the first reviewer mentioned. He allowed me to drive him to the facility where I work and enroll him in an outpatient program. I set him up to live at the home of a female acquaintance of mine. He is no longer at the phone number posted here and with any luck, you have heard the last of him. Shame on you.

You: Hispanic male in my late 30s.

Brad responds: Don't believe this guy. He's a prick. I have a new number. It's 310-666-9876. Call me if you're a generous man. I'm up for anything. I need a place to live too. This guy's a fucking prick. I don't need help. He's a liar. I'm writing this on his computer. What does that tell you? Guys like him are the worst. They promise you shit and they don't mean it. Don't call me if you're like him.

Webmaster's message: My repeated attempts to contact JoseR72 and have him confirm this review have been unsuccessful. Until further notice, I strongly advise all of you to stay clear of Brad.

Review #4

Escort's name: Brad
Location: Los Angeles
Age: 18
Month and year of your date: July 2001
Where did you find him: this site
Escort's advertised phone number: pager 310-666-9876
Rates: $500 overnight
Did he live up to his physical description: yes
Did he live up to what he promised: no
Height: 5'10"
Weight: 130 lbs
Facial hair: no
Body hair: pubes
Hair color: dirty blond
Eye color: hazel
Dick size: 6 inches
Cut or uncut: cut
Thickness: less than medium
Does he smoke? not with me
Top, bottom, versatile? total bottom

In calls/out calls/not sure: Out with me
Kisser: yes
Rating: not recommended
Hire again: no
Handle: bizeeb7

Experience: I read the warning on Brad, but I was in the LA area on business and decided to take a chance. I called the number expecting a pager but Brad answered. Despite what has been said about him, he was quite talkative, too talkative if anything. I suspected he was on drugs at the time, but in retrospect I think he was in the manic phase of whatever mental illness he is suffering from. I offered to pay for his taxi ride to my hotel near the LAX airport, and he said he wasn't far away and would leave immediately. I waited for him in front of the hotel for more than two hours, then gave up and went to sleep after trying to reach him by phone with no luck.

At about 3:30 in the morning I was woken up by a call from the lobby saying a young man was here to see me. I asked the concierge if there was a taxi waiting, and he told me there was. I asked him to pay the driver and charge it to my bill and send the young man up to my room. Big mistake. When I let Brad in, he was in a very agitated state. He wanted alcohol but I told him there was none in the room, and that room service was closed. He seemed extremely upset by this and sat on the bed and began crying. I was half-asleep, naked, frightened, and wondering what the hell I'd gotten myself into. I suggested that we go try to find an open liquor store, but he said no. I offered to call him a taxi and even pay him the full, agreed-upon amount if he wanted to leave, but that just made him even more upset. He started saying, "Don't you like me," and things like that, which I have to admit I found rather heartbreaking.

I didn't know what to do, but I told Brad that he could go ahead and get undressed and that we'd give sex a shot. I really wasn't in the mood, but I thought he might be carrying a knife or something, so it was more of a safety precaution at that point. When I said that, he calmed right down, and took his clothes off, and even made a few jokes about how crazy he'd been acting. Like the other viewers said, Brad is an extremely cute boy. Without his clothes on, he took my breath away, if it weren't for his height, I'd guess from his body he was no older than thirteen or fourteen. He has a slim, slight build with tiny nipples and the most precious little ass. It was just too arousing, and I decided that I had to indulge myself a little.

Brad didn't so much suck my cock as open his mouth and let me pound his throat as deep and hard as I wanted. Previous reviewers mentioned Brad's poor hygiene, and while he certainly wasn't the cleanest escort I've ever been with, he smelled and tasted like a boy should. Rimming him seemed to drive both of us out of our minds. As soon as I started eating his hole, he had almost what seemed like a seizure. His whole body spasmed violently, and his mouth opened wide, and his eyes rolled back in his head. It sounds frightening, and it was, but it was also incredibly hot to see a boy that cute lose control. I knew from the earlier reviews that Brad could be barebacked, and that's a huge fantasy of mine, so I fucked him condom-free and had two orgasms inside him before I felt too exhausted to continue. Still, I was dying to taste his come. He was still seizing and shaking all over, so I jerked him off and felched his hole until he shot, then licked up his delicious load.

As soon as Brad came, his seizure seemed to come to an end. He was drenched in sweat, and looked disoriented and exhausted. I suggested we get some sleep, as I was very spent by that point. That's when things suddenly went bad very fast. Brad started yelling and screaming at the top of his lungs that I was a sicko who'd had unsafe sex with him against his will. He was out of control, and soon enough there was a loud knock at my door. It was the hotel's manager and a couple of employees. He took one look at us and told me to either get the boy out of the hotel immediately or I would have to leave. I asked him to call Brad a taxi and that I would have the boy downstairs ready to leave in a minute, and he agreed and left. (God knows what would have happened if the manager hadn't been gay!) Brad continued to scream at me, one minute saying he was sorry and to please let him stay, and the next minute telling me he was going to tell the police I raped and tried to kill him. I just kept begging him to get dressed and leave, and he finally did, but not before calling me every terrible name in the book.

The nightmare didn't end there. About a half an hour later he started calling my cell phone, begging me to come get him, and that he didn't know where he was, and that he was scared. I tried to reason with him, but he got more and more upset, threatening to kill himself. He told me there was someone who wanted to kill him, and that if I didn't come get him, he was going to go over to this person's house and let himself be killed, and that he didn't want to die, but he was afraid he would do that if I didn't stop him. After about five calls from Brad, I turned my phone off. I don't know if he's alive or dead, or if he was just trying to fuck with my head. I've never had anything like this happen to me in all my years of hiring escorts, and I thought I should warn others interested in Brad that, as cute as he is, he is definitely not worth it.

You: Asian-American man in my early 30s, like to try new things, into young guys, generally a top.

Review #5

Escort's name: Brad

Location: Los Angeles

Age: let's just say 18

Month and year of your date: ongoing

Where did you find him: here

Internet address: bdax@hotmail.com

Escort's e-mail address: bridax@hotmail.com

Escort's advertised phone number: 310-655-0033

Rates: Available on request

Did he live up to his physical description? if you hurry

Did he live up what he promised? and more

Height: 5'10 1\2"

Weight: currently 150 lbs.

Facial hair: no

Body hair: no

Hair color: dishwater blond

Eye color: aquamarine

Dick size: 6 inches

Cut or uncut: cut

Thickness: medium

Does he smoke? not anymore

Top, bottom, versatile? bottom

In calls/out calls/not sure: in or out

Kisser: depends

Rating: highest

Hire again: ongoing

Handle: brian

Submissions: This is my first

URL for pics: no

Experience: I read with great interest the most recent review on Brad. I believe I'm the man Brad mentioned who "wants to kill him." Let me explain something to you all. Both of my parents died of brain tumors. After reading the first three reviews of Brad, I was convinced that his physical and behavioral problems were the result of an undiagnosed brain tumor. I arranged a date with him, but instead of bringing him back to my place for sex, I took him to a hospital and paid for him to have a series of tests to see if I was right. It turns out that Brad does have an advanced, inoperable brain tumor and will die from complications resulting from the tumor within the next six months. That night I moved him into my house and he has been living here off and on for the past few weeks. I am paying for all of his medical bills, as well as his day-to-day expenses. He is on a medication that greatly reduces the severity and frequency of his seizures, although the side effects cause him to be very fatigued and irritable. For two days earlier this week, Brad went off his medication and disappeared, and this is when and how the previous reviewer had the date with Brad that he described. Brad is now home and on his medication again and doing as well as could be expected.

Before you decide that I'm a saint, I should explain that my all-time fantasy is to murder a boy during the sex act. I've had sex with a number of boys who were perfectly willing to be killed, but something always stopped me from going all the way. Brad provides me with the ideal situation, and, except for our disagreement earlier this week, he is also sexually aroused by what we both have agreed will happen. If all of this seems hard to believe, maybe it would help to know that in addition to his fatal condition, Brad suffers from severe bipolar disorder. He grew up in foster homes and has been emotionally, physically, and sexually abused his entire life. He will tell you himself that since he moved in with me, he has felt security and contentment for the first time.

When the day comes that he is so disabled that sex with him is no longer exciting to either one of us, I am going to end his suffering. In the meantime, I will allow him to do escort work on a limited basis. Anyone interested in seeing Brad can e-mail or phone me, and arrangements will be made.

You: none of your business

Webmaster's comments: On July 16, reviewer JoseR72 was found severely beaten in his apartment. He remains in a coma. While there is no evidence to suggest that Brad is responsible, I nonetheless urge you to stay away from Brad. However, due to your overwhelming interest in the Brad saga, I will continue to post any reviews and updates that come in. Let me also say that because "Brian" has never posted on this site before, and because a new review of Brad that I will post in the morning throws the veracity of "Brian's" post into question, his claims should be taken with a grain of salt.

Review #6

Escort's name: Brad aka Steve
Location: Long Beach
Age: 20?
Months and year of your date: July, 2001
Where did you find him? Pumpers

Rates: $400

Did he live up to his physical description?

Did he live up to what he promised? yes

Height: roughly 6 feet

Weight: maybe 165 lbs.

Facial hair: no

Body hair: pubes, ass crack

Hair color: brown

Eye color: blue

Dick size: 7 inches

Cut or uncut: cut

Thickness: medium thick

Does he smoke? like a chimney

Top, bottom, versatile: top for rimming only

In calls/out calls/not sure: out

Kisser: no

Rating: overpriced

Hire again: maybe

Handle: baglover

Submissions: This is my third review

Experience: Not that the Brad story needs another wrinkle, but here's mine. I hired "Brad" about three weeks ago. I question how much of what the two previous reviewers wrote is true. I suspect the reviews were written by Brad/Steve himself. I went looking for Brad at Pumpers in Long Beach after reading the first review. It turns out that I'd seen him there a number of times drinking and sometimes playing pool or pinball. I had been told by the bartender that his name was Steve. He stood out because of how young he looks, but apart from being cuter than your usual street trade, I wouldn't say there was anything supernatural about his appearance. He had a reputation among the regulars at the bar as an arrogant creep who charged a ridiculously large fee ($350) to sit on men's faces and masturbate. That was the extent of his services, and even getting him to agree to that meant buying him many drinks and waiting until he was in the mood, which could take hours. Need I say that this "Brad" is a very different character from the boy described in the recent reviews? The only things that match are his young appearance and the facial tics and body twitching that everyone describes.

I had a couple of drinks and decided to ask this character if he was Brad. He looked shocked but he said he used that name sometimes. I explained that I'd seen a review of him on this site. He said he knew nothing about the site, and had never even used a computer much less surfed the web. I used his curiosity to get him to agree to go home with me, telling him I'd show him the review on my computer. Maybe I caught him off guard because he seemed like a nice enough boy at the time and even agreed to let me top him. But after a few more drinks, he started acting in what I would call a bizarre and aggressive manner. He changed his mind about coming to my place and insisted we go back to his place instead, which I agreed to. It was hardly a homeless shelter. It was quite a pricey, upscale apartment an hour north in Los Angeles. Let me say for the record that there was no sign that anyone else lived there, so it wasn't the home of the self-styled murderer Brian. (He also had a very expensive G4 computer in full view, but he didn't seem to care that I'd caught him in a lie.)

As soon as we arrived, he became very cold and matter-of-fact. He told me to sit on the couch then pulled his pants down and sat on my face. I rimmed him for a few minutes until he came. I hadn't come yet, since I was expecting to top him, but he refused to continue, although for an additional $50 he did agree to sit on my face for another couple of minutes. I will say that if your fantasy is to rim a decent-looking piece of jailbait, he's quite satisfactory. He has a delicious, baby-soft ass with a talented hole that he genuinely seems to enjoy having eaten, but whether it's worth the money is up to you. Clearly what the previous reviewers wrote about Brad is a bunch of lies and nonsense. BTW, he still hangs out at Pumpers. I saw him there two nights ago.

Blue Star

SERA GAMBLE

S HE WANTS A DIAMOND with a blue star in the center. She's drawn a sketch of what she envisions on the blank side of a Coffee Bean napkin. When she hands it to Ari, he sees that her cheap metal ring has haloed her thumb green. Her hands are strong. She bites her cuticles.

Ari asks how big she wants it. "Big," she says. She pulls off her wife beater, revealing a frayed peach bikini top, and turns around. "Right between my wings." She reaches back, pats herself between her flexed shoulder blades.

Ari says, "That'll take maybe two and a half hours. Two hundred bucks." He's giving her a low quote, because she's pretty. The star is full of intricate swirls. It's going to be at least three hours. He could be charging her a hundred fifty an hour, easy.

Outside, the beach is gray and sunless. A row of stoic surfers clutch their boards and watch the water. Too calm right now; maybe too choppy later. It looks like rain. Summer's over.

"I've got . . ." She fishes in the pockets of her denim shorts, pulling them down past her hips. More peach bikini, and a fine web of stretch marks standing out white against her tan. She's not a little girl. Her legs are thick, her hips solid. She seems to know where his eyes are resting, because she takes a long time to find her money. She pulls out a wad and counts. "One-twenty and change."

"Fine," Ari says quickly. It's not enough, but he doesn't care. He wants to tattoo her. It's a slow afternoon, but this morning, when the sun was still out, he tattooed kanji on a large group of German tourists and made plenty of money for the shop. Kanji are simple, small, only take minutes. He takes his time with them, then way overcharges. The Germans seemed happy. Ari thinks kanji are silly: getting a word in a language you don't even know, a symbol that could mean anything, that you trust means what the flash poster on the wall says it means. He gets that writing your message in Chinese makes it secret—except that everyone is just going to ask you what it stands for anyway.

Ari pulls out his sketch pad. He freehands a large rendering of her sketch. "What's your name?" He asks as he draws, not looking up.

"Cam," she says. "You draw really straight lines."

"You better hope so," he says.

She smiles. Her sun-blonde hair is damp and stiff around her face. She smells of ocean. She watches as he fills the star with swirls and loops.

Ari invites Cam behind the counter. He explains that he is going to make a stencil and transfer it onto her skin. She nods, watching him closely. She makes him nervous. Pretty girls always make him nervous. He'd rather tattoo ugly people only—less pressure. Also, lately his work has been so-so. He's the only one who notices. Customers always seem thrilled, but he knows the difference between a decent tattoo and a great one. When he started, when he was sixteen, every piece he did had life to it, an energy under the skin. Lately the tattoos are just there.

Cam leans against the wall by the stencil machine. "How old are you?" she asks.

"Thirty-three," he says.

"That's about what I was gonna guess."

Ari is twenty-one. People have always guessed him older. He got his apprenticeship here when he was a few days shy of fourteen, on a fake ID that made him twenty. No one's ever called him on it. Either they all buy it or they don't care. He leads Cam to the chair and asks her to untie her bikini top. "What about you," he asks.

She tugs the string and catches the cups of the bikini in her hands, holding them over her breasts. The strap has left a ghost of untanned skin. "I'm twenty-five," Cam says. This close to her, he can see that her shoulders are freckled. A fine white down covers the back of her neck where her home-cut hair ends. A few tiny braids tangle in the hair. Boredombraids. There's a scent under the salt water dried onto her skin, a hint of sunscreen long washed off, clean sweat, something green like tea.

Ari explains he must shave her before he transfers the stencil.

"I'm hairy?" she asks.

"No," he says quickly. "Just, any hair gets in the way of the ink." He wets a cloth and eases it down her back, then smoothes on shaving cream.

"Why a diamond?" He asks her as he runs the disposable razor between her shoulders.

"It's instinctual," she says, after a moment. "It seems like the right thing to get. I've been doodling diamonds since I was a kid, then filling up all the empty space in the middle."

Ari dries her skin and centers the stencil. She checks the placement in the mirror, nods okay. "This your first?" he asks as he lays out his inks: black, titanium white, three shades of blue, silver, and a golden yellow for the glint of the jewel.

She nods.

When Ari tattoos, the skin in front of him becomes his whole world. Skin only looks smooth from a distance. Up close it's porous, shifty, alive tricky terrain. Some people bleed more than others. Many jerk back from the first sting. Some inch away from the pain. Some lean into it.

He cups his hand over her stenciled skin. She's warm. Her back is almost as muscular as a man's. A surfer's back. She pulls the bikini off over her head, then leans forward into the chair, now topless. Ari realizes he hasn't seen breasts in months, and the last were those of a fifty year-old woman who was getting a turtle tattooed between them. Cam's breasts are full, pressed into the vinyl of the chair, the outer roundness of them just visible. Ari realizes he hasn't even jacked off in days. He feels that dead feeling, the one that's been following him around, the one that comes up behind him sometimes and throws a black sack over his head. His dick is getting hard now, which only makes it worse. Body waking up, reminding him of his life: coffee-ink-sandwich-TV-bed, his apartment up the block with its big rooms and practically no furniture.

Ari takes his hand away and snaps on latex gloves, loads ink for the outline. "Ready?"

She presses her face into the back of the chair, hugs it with both arms. Ready.

He adjusts himself in his pants. Holding the tattoo gun instantly calms him. "First line's gonna hurt," he warns.

She sits still, waiting.

He turns on his gun and presses it lightly to the point of the diamond, then moves his hand away, anticipating her flinch. But she doesn't move. She exhales softly. He stretches the skin with his right hand, inks with the left. "Not a flincher, huh," he says.

"I have a high tolerance for pain," she murmurs.

He wipes the blood away with a tissue. "But you're a bleeder," he tells her.

"Huh. Must be the aspirin."

"Did you take some today?"

"I take it all the time," she says, just loud enough to be heard over the buzz of the needle. "I have a headache every fucking day. I thought I had a tumor, but I don't."

"Does it work?"

"Does what work?"

"The aspirin," he says, whipping a quick upward line, then catching the blooming blood in a tissue. She bleeds as much as anyone he's tattooed. The tips of his gloves are red and sticky already.

"Yeah, just taking it feels good. I chew them. I like the taste, now. Oh, that part hurts," she says when he runs over her spine. Then, "But not like a bad hurt."

"People get addicted." He thinks about how stupid he sounds, spouting the great cliché of tattooing.

"I'm not surprised," she replies. "I shoulda taken more aspirin, maybe?"

"It wouldn't help. You'd just bleed even more."

"I have this monster bottle. My dad bought like twenty of them. His doctor told him to take one every day after he had a heart attack. It's supposed to prevent another one."

"Did it?"

"No," she says. "Last year." She holds her voice as steady as her body, but last year is not long ago. Ari knows. When someone is dead, last year is yesterday.

"I'm sorry."

"It's okay. I like taking his aspirin, you know?"

And then they don't say anything else.

Ari was six when his mother got sick. His mother is dead, and his girlfriend is dead. Women pull apart in his fingers like wax. They blow away like dust. After his girlfriend he couldn't see how to get close to a girl again. The last four years, every one he met seemed accompanied by an invisible twin: her own death. The car crash to come, the drunken plummet, the disease, the OD. After his girlfriend he felt himself incapable of being surprised. People go the way they are going. His mother worked with chemicals, got cancer from the chemicals, died from the cancer. His girlfriend rode a motorcycle, died in a crash. This girl smells like the ocean. Her invisible twin has already drowned.

Ari welcomes this train of thought. It takes his attention away from Cam's hips. They're full—gypsy hips. His boss would call her "old school." His girlfriend was a slip, a sylph, weightless in his arms. He used to toss her up and down like a child. After she died his dreams were full of her slow-motion cartwheel in the air above the bike, a rag doll made of air and cotton candy.

He finishes the outline and switches needles for the color. Her skin is starting to swell up around the lines, tighten. Her breathing has deepened, dropped lower in her body. He's breathing with her as he paints the star blue. She's sweating a little. Her odor intensifies, sea and earth mingling with the antiseptic, the latex of his gloves, the ink and blood. He has the sudden, strong desire to lay her down on the floor and rest his head against her back.

"You know you won't be able to swim till it's healed," he warns. His voice crackles.

"Yup. Saw the sign on my way in. No hot tub?"

"Chlorine makes the color fall right out."

"I don't have a hot tub anyway." More silence, as he adds wisps of white to make the color stand out. This tattoo is going to be good. Actually good, not just competent. Pressing his gun into her skin he feels a little of what he did when he started at the shop, that desire to change someone, improve a body, add meaning.

But the tattoos didn't do what they promised. They didn't make love last. They didn't make independence easy or fun. So Ari's art became just a job, all about keeping the lines straight and blending the colors.

When Ari reaches over to switch to yellow, his elbow grazes Cam's back and catches a smear of inky blood. Her blood is hot. It stops his arm midair. His dick's screaming now; he wants to turn her around and pull her right into his lap. Instead he cracks the yellow open and dips. I will make this tattoo beautiful for you, he thinks. But it won't change anything. She'll still be pretty and curvy till she gets old and fat. She'll still chew aspirin that doesn't bring her dad back. She'll catch waves till she drowns, or she'll die another way. What he hopes is that she catches glimpses of it in her morning mirror. That when she cranes her neck to look at it, it makes her smile in a moment she wouldn't otherwise be happy. If it does that a couple times, that would be plenty.

He wishes he could tell her this. His customers talk to him all day. They want to tell him all about the significance of the tattoo. Last week a linebacker of a cop wept while Ari tattooed the fineline image of his recently dead beagle onto his meaty bicep. Two hours of stories about this dog, the way he fetched, the sweet look in his eyes. Just yesterday, a stoned couple got matching tattoos of their new daughter's name and, in the time it took for Ari to write "Jessica" twice, gave him an education in raising a vegan baby.

He clears his throat again, but when he opens his mouth, what comes out is, "Do you have a boyfriend?"

She thinks for a moment. "Not really. I have a guy I fuck. Why do you ask?"

He inks and blots. "Curious."

"What makes you curious?"

"I don't know."

"Is it weird to you to do this permanent thing on total strangers? I mean, it's kind of intimate."

No one's ever asked him that before. "Usually not." He examines the intersection of lines at the edge of the diamond—once the color and blood well up, he'll be shading blind. He works carefully. "Right now it's weird."

"Why?"

He can't bring himself to say, Because you're pretty. "Because you don't talk that much."

"People usually talk?"

"People usually can't shut up. It's like I'm their shrink."

"Huh," she says, and they say nothing for the rest of the tattoo.

◆   ◆   ◆

WHEN HE'S FINISHED, ARI cleans her up and leads her to the full-length mirror. He turns her back to it and gives her a hand mirror so she can examine his work. The skin around the tattoo is bright red and puffy, making the diamond stand out in three dimensions, vivid silver and yellow gold. The star within is alive, the blue swirls like perfect waves, capped white. He didn't realize he'd turned the curls into waves. It just turned out that way.

"You put the ocean inside the star," she breathes.

"They look more like waves than I thought they would," he admits. "Do you like it?"

Cam stares into the mirror for a long, tense moment. Ari's stomach knots up. Finally, she nods. She looks at him in wonder. "It's amazing," she says. "It's so amazing. It's like you read my mind. I'm not paying you enough."

Ari exhales. "It was a dead afternoon. It was my pleasure. Let me bandage you up."

He coats her raw skin with antibiotic and covers it with Saran Wrap and cloth tape.

"At least let me . . . let me buy you an ice cream," she says.

Ari checks the clock. It's four-thirty. His boss won't be back for another hour. His boss is an old, sour binge drinker. He would probably fire Ari if he came back to the shop and found it closed.

"Sure," Ari says. "You can buy me an ice cream. Let me just close up."

THE NIGHT ARI'S GIRLFRIEND crashed, he was supposed to pick her up from work. She worked at a pizza place. They had been together for eight months, almost to the day. Other than the lie about his age, everything he told his girlfriend was real. He only bent the truth the first time they made love. He said he had never felt sex like that, when the whole truth was that he had never felt any sex—it was his first time.

Ari's girlfriend was tiny and caffeinated and liked to dye her hair. She barely slept. She wrote songs and poems and played guitar all night. There was something in her voice that made Ari come up from his own depths to meet her. A teasing quality, something that said, If you don't come here, you'll miss something great. She didn't know how much she was teaching him—how to hear music, how to cook eggs, how to hold a crying girl, how to make her come with his tongue, how to have a fight, how to make up after a fight. In the eight months they were together, she slept in his bed every night. He tattooed a sleeve on her skinny arm, koi fish and bubbles and phosphorescent seaweed, a mermaid hiding in her armpit. She squealed when it hurt, chain-smoked through it, her cigarette trembling from the pain.

He was supposed to pick her up to take her to Griffith Park Observatory to see some kind of meteor shower. Instead he worked late. He called her to say he couldn't go, he had customers. She was disappointed, but it wasn't anything dramatic. "Too bad for you," she said. "This only happens once every three thousand years. I'm going to see something tonight that you'll never see."

Ari knows that if she hadn't died that night, she would have died another night. People who ride motorcycles die. Just like Ari knows that if his mom hadn't died when he was nine, she would have died when he was ten, or eleven, or twenty.

Cam notices the lack of furniture in his apartment immediately. She holds up her ice cream wrapper and pointedly asks if he owns a trash can. He follows her to the kitchen and finds her standing at the fridge, staring at the postcard he's tacked on there, of the Tattooed Lady from an old Ringling Brothers promotional poster. "Jesus," she says, "that's a lot of tattoos."

Ari's heart is pounding against his ribs. He hasn't had a girl in his apartment forever, and he doesn't quite understand how she ended up here. She just sort of invited herself.

"Do you have a lot of tattoos?" She steps closer and peels off Ari's long-sleeved shirt. His arms are covered in tribal designs; most of the skin is inked black. "Wow," she says. She traces the designs over his muscles to the ones on his chest and stops. "Your heart," she says.

Should he apologize for his heart? "It's beating," he says. "Fast, I guess."

"Are you nervous?"

"You're gorgeous," he manages to say, hoping that explains it. She laughs. He asks if he can get her anything. "I have water, beer."

"I wasn't gonna get it done today. I went into the shop because I saw you there. I like guys who shave their head." She runs her hand over his black stubble. Her fingers skip down to his ears. She notices the tiny mark behind his ear, a black ink sun. "You have little surprises everywhere, don't you?" she says.

"Are you really surprised?" he counters. "I do this for a living."

"Well, kind of not. But kind of, yes." She pulls off her shirt, moves her shoulders experimentally, feeling the fresh tattoo. "It hurts, like a bad sunburn, just like you said."

He turns her around so that she's leaning against his sink, her eyes level with the little uncurtained window. He kneels behind her and puts his lips to her skin, right at the edge of the bandage. He kisses a circle around it. She sees the expression on his face, and for reasons that are a mystery to him, she looks pleased. She takes his hand. "I am taking you into that room behind the closed door hoping there's an actual bed of some kind there," she explains.

They land together on his futon. She hisses when her tattooed skin hits the mattress, sits right back up again. "I can't lie down," she says. She reaches for his buckle, her eyes holding his, sea green with flecks of brown like sand, even the eyelashes sunbleached. She's the mermaid he tattooed onto his girlfriend's arm all those years ago, voluptuous and brown. A woman. I've never been with a woman, he thinks suddenly. His girlfriend was a girl, nineteen. He wraps Cam's hair around his hands and pulls her onto him, buries his face in her neck, inhales, finds the ocean there, the garden.

She wrestles his pants off his hips and pulls them free of his legs, uncovering more ink, two Japanese masks and a tiger, two koi fish swimming below his navel, more tribal marks on his thighs. "Jesus," she says again. "How many hours did all this take?"

He has no idea. Hundreds.

"That's so much pain. You almost have to have something wrong with you to go through that." She doesn't sound judgmental, just thoughtful.

"I like the art," he says. "It stays, the pain's just for the time it takes to get it down. You get so used to it you barely feel it."

She gives him such an odd look that he asks what she's thinking, but instead of answering she reaches up the leg of his boxer shorts and finds him, cups his balls softly, then firmly in her hands, then slides up to his cock and encircles it. "Is this tattooed too?" she asks, her voice teasing.

She yanks off his shorts to check. Finding it naked, she says, "It looks ordinary."

This makes him smile, makes him brave enough to joke. "I could go tattoo it, but then I probably couldn't use it for a few days. If that's what you want—" But she cuts him off by capturing it in her mouth. He lies back, stunned by how good it feels, wanting to push her off him so he can look at her more, put his hands on her breasts like he wanted to the second she walked into the shop, sit up and pull her into his lap so he can kiss her and find her with his fingers, feel her breathing change as he coaxes her toward orgasm. But he's paralyzed by her tongue, his nerves singing, blood pounding in his ears.

At the last minute he manages to lift her off him. "Take your shorts off," he tells her.

She shakes her head no. "I can't," she whispers.

"Why not?" he asks. She lays her head on his thigh, not answering quickly enough. "You don't want to? That guy you're fucking?"

"I've got my period," she says.

He stares at her.

"What?" she demands.

"You've been bleeding on me for hours," he points out.

"That's different." She unbuttons her shorts, unzips, slides them down her long thick legs. She's wearing only those peach bikini bottoms now. They land just below the curve of her belly. She pulls her knees up to her chest, wraps her arms around them, rests her chin atop one scraped knee.

Her feet leave grains of sand on his comforter. She is staring hard at a spot on his forearm. When he looks down, he sees that it is the only untattooed space on his arms.

She strokes one warm hand over the naked spot. She asks, "Do you fuck a lot of your customers?"

"I don't fuck anybody."

Cam puts her hands on his shoulders and leans into him, pushing him back into the futon. She covers his mouth with hers. She tastes of peppermint ice cream. He knows he tastes of chocolate, and of the cigarette he smoked on the walk to his apartment. His mouth remembers kissing, the ways of kissing, right away. They move together like that, her hands on his face, his tracing her waist, weighing her ass, riding her spine, avoiding the sticky plastic bandage. He tugs the strings of her bikini and they give, she's on him naked now, all that skin speaking to skin, the most direct communication. He snakes a hand between their bodies and down, finding her wet. She starts to pull away, but he holds her there with his other arm around her neck. Holds her mouth on his as his fingers slick over her, find the string between her lips, and pull.

"Wait, let me," she starts, her fingers finding his in her wetness, but he shushes her. He drops the tampon onto the floor. Reaches blind under the corner of the mattress, where he stashed a strip of condoms a long time ago. His fingers close on a wrapper. He tears it open with his teeth. They unroll it together onto his cock, their hands slick with her blood and desire, and now they're in a hurry. He lifts her onto him. She's slippery and hot, and she has him completely.

"You feel good," she whispers, and then they don't say anything. His fingers leave prints on her skin in her own blood. Her smell washes over him in waves: earth, salt, sun.

AFTERWARD, HE BRINGS WARM, soapy towels and washes the fluids from her skin. She lies on her stomach as he runs the cloth over her. He peels the sweaty bandage off her tattoo, gently cleanses it and smooths on fresh Neosporin. She's drowsy, sweet, like a kid. She curls up under his comforter. She looks completely new to him, miles and miles to explore. He could take his time with her. He could learn her. He wants to. He wants to fuck her every day for a year, like memorizing an epic poem. He wants to know her birthday, where she's ticklish. He wants to watch her surf. He wants to tell her things. He doesn't know where to start.

Ari's cell phone vibrates in the pocket of his discarded jeans. It's his boss, wanting to know where the hell he is. Why did he leave early? It's only nine P.M., and a bunch of walk-ins just arrived. Would Ari rather get his ass back to work or be fired? Ari thinks Cam is asleep, so he says he'll be right there.

"Do you have to go back to work?" Cam mumbles, lifting her head, watching him gather his clothes.

He nods, stepping into his jeans, throwing on his shirt. "You can stay here if you want."

She bites her lip, considering, then shakes her head. "I gotta go." She's dressed in seconds.

They stand at the door. She doesn't offer her number. He gets the strong feeling she doesn't want him to ask for it. He asks for it anyway.

"Let's let this just be this," she says, and goes.

Ari walks back to the tattoo shop in the dark. His chest hurts. He asks himself: didn't he believe, somewhere deep down, that she would go? No, he really didn't. Surprised again. Maybe this is what it's like to actually be twenty-one, Ari thinks, the way the spring-break kids who get tribal armbands and geckos and rainbow kanji are twenty-one. Wanting to drink, and cry, and fuck, and wail. Hoping and being crushed.

At work, he tattoos a butterfly anklet on a skinny teen girl with blue hair. He sits on a low stool, her foot on his knee. He becomes aware of the scent of Cam coming up through his clothes. The sex smells, and the rich odor of her blood, like ocean and metal and wood.

He thinks of how he might run into her one day on the boardwalk. How that will be awkward, because she ran. How she shouldn't have run. How if she stayed he could love her.

So she ran. People run. For as long as they're alive, there are things they run from. It's a luxury of being alive, running.

Ari realizes he's been thinking instead of focusing on the tattoo. He's been on autopilot. He lifts his gun hand away from the girl's ankle. He looks up at her; she's staring at her tattoo, mesmerized. He looks down. He's almost finished it, and it's beautiful.

The girl grins. "You're really good," she says.

If You Love Something, Set It Free

P. S. HAVEN

IT FEELS LIKE THE DAY after Christmas when I wake up. I can't believe it's come and gone already. March 5 was like Christmas that way. We'd talked about it and planned and anticipated (and dreaded) for so long. And now it's over and I'm sad and relieved at the same time. And it's like Christmas that way, too.

When we wake up the next day, we're quiet for a long time. Everything seems the same. The sheets on our bed, the stuff on our nightstand, the way Dwight rubs his eyes with his wrists. Everything seems the same. But I know it never will be.

I want to ask Dwight if I've cheated on him.

When Dwight finally speaks, he asks me if I regret it. I tell him I don't, and it's the truth. I honestly expected to, but I don't. All I feel is relief. Not relief that we've finally done it, but relief that maybe we can get on with our lives now. Move on.

I almost can't remember a point in our relationship that Dwight wasn't obsessed with it. At first it was just talk, I'm still convinced of that. We'd talk about our fantasies. Sex with strangers. Sex in public places. All the usual clichés. We'd talk about what celebrities we'd fuck. And it turned him on so bad when I'd talk about how I've always had a weird thing for the Six Million Dollar Man, and how if I could fuck anybody, it would be him. And I would talk about how much I wanted to have a threesome, or how badly I wanted to fuck a black guy; whatever would excite Dwight the most. I would say anything, and I would say it believably.

And when it was Dwight's turn to talk he would describe (and I would imagine) me, half naked, pinned helplessly between, say, Marco and Chris, or maybe Marco and that cousin of his who came over last Fourth of July. They would take me, with varying degrees of reciprocity and complicity on my part, one at a time, one right after another, or all at once, depending on the fantasy. Dwight would tell me how, even though I'd plead with them not to, they would fuck me until I lay breathless, trembling and spent, begging them to stop and then begging them not to, begging for more. Desperate for more.

At first I thought he didn't mean those things he'd say. And maybe back then, he didn't. Even though he swore he did. They were fantasies. What we'd do if only we could. It was simply something said in the heat the moment, partly because he was excited, partly to excite me. And it worked.

And then Dwight started to talk it about outside the bedroom. He'd e-mail me at work about it. He'd quote interviews with sex therapists and psychologists who said that it was perfectly normal. Healthy, even. He'd ask me if I had any idea how many men would love to be with me, and he'd tell me I could choose whomever I wanted to, he didn't care. He'd talk about the contradictions of monogamy, and how we'd still love each other afterward. Even more so. He'd tell me that love and sex could be two totally isolated things, and that it almost went against human nature to deny myself this. To deny pleasure. To resist lust. And he made so much sense.

And still I thought he didn't mean it. I thought it was part of our game, and if it ever got too close to really happening, he'd probably be too afraid to let it. Probably.

We'd go out and he'd point out a guy he'd like to see me with. And soon I started to agree. And then I started to point out others I liked better than his guy. And he loved that. I'd tell him who I figured had the biggest dick, or who'd be the best kisser. He'd tell me that there wasn't a man there who wouldn't kill to go home with me, to spend the night with me, and he'd tell me that they were all looking at me. And I loved that.

"What are you afraid of?" Dwight had finally asked me one night. Not mockingly or hatefully. His question was genuine. Really, truly, what is it I'm afraid will happen? And I didn't know.

We laid down ground rules. Set boundaries and made promises.

Rule #1: Do not kiss him. Under any circumstances.

Rule #2: Make him wear a condom.

Rule #3: Don't ever ask me to do it again.

Simple rules, really. Rules we had conceived of jointly. Rules we had both agreed to. Rules #1 and #2 were his. Rule #3 was mine.

We spent two months trying to decide on someone, even though I know he had Justin in mind the whole time.

"What if he doesn't want to?" I asked when Dwight finally made the suggestion.

"Trust me. He'll want to."

And we fucked. And Dwight promised me that Justin was hung like a fucking horse, and that he'd be every bit the stud I imagined he was, and how he'd have a foot of hard, young cock that he would ravage me with over and over again before finally making slow, sweet love to me all night long, giving me orgasm after wracking orgasm. All while Dwight watched. And I wanted him to.

Justin said March 5 would work for him.

We're quiet for a long time before Dwight speaks again. He tells me that if I don't regret it by now, I won't ever. He talks for a long time about how it will be something we can look back on when we're too old to care about such things, and be proud that we were once young and brave and adventuresome. And I realize, suddenly, in a way I hadn't last night, that from now on we have a marriage in which I've had sex with someone other than my husband.

For some reason I think of that stupid crocheted thing that hangs in my mom's kitchen. The one that says, "If you love something, set it free." And I want to ask Dwight if I felt more like *his* now.

He thanks me for the hundredth time, and I tell him that I wanted to do it, he doesn't have to thank me. And he makes me promise that I had wanted to do it, and that I didn't do it just because he had wanted me to, or because I was drunk, or so he'd finally shut up about it. And I promise.

After another long silence he asks me what I remember most, what my favorite parts were, what sticks out in my mind. I remember:

Our conversation in the car on the way to dinner. Me saying something like, "If we were smart, we'd just forget this whole thing. These things never end well, you know that. Expectations don't get met. Or expectations get exceeded and someone likes it too much. Then someone gets jealous. Feelings get hurt. Bad things." I was right. But it didn't matter.

I remember saying the day before, "Let's say we go through with it. Let's say Justin is still okay with it. And we all agree and he's willing to play by our rules. And we go through with it." Dwight had nodded to it all. "What if it's the worst experience of our entire lives? What if we hate ourselves for doing it? What if we hate each other?" Dwight promised me that wouldn't happen. "Or worse. What if we love it? I mean fucking *love* it. What if it's everything both of us have dreamed it will be? What then?" I waited for the answer, even though I knew neither one of us had it. "What if it's the fucking pinnacle, the very apex of sexual experience, and we can never again recapture this thrill? What if you could know, going in, that would be the case? Would you still do it? Knowing full well it's all downhill from here? Could you live the rest of your life knowing that every time you made love to me I was comparing it to that one time?" I let what I had said sink in. "Or is it better that it's a fantasy? Could it be that the anticipation is always sweeter than the fulfillment, that the fantasy is always better than the real thing?" It was a good point. They were all good points. But it didn't matter.

I remembered Justin telling me he's always had a thing for redheads, and I wanted to tell him about freckles and sunburns and a childhood of Raggedy Ann jokes. But March 5 was about fantasies, not realities. So instead, I told him how rare I am. I told him the gene for red hair is recessive. Not just to dark hair, but to blonde hair, too. And that since neither of my parents were redheads, they only had a one-in-four shot at having a redhead kid. I started to tell him the same thing about green eyes, but Justin's a moron and he didn't have a clue what recessive means, so I saved it.

I remember Justin being a lot better looking than I remembered.

I remember Justin saying to Dwight at dinner, "Tell me something. Why are you doing this? I mean, fuck, that's your wife, man. Do you seriously get off on watching other guys fuck her? Don't get me wrong, I don't give a fuck. I really don't. I'm the last person to judge. I'm just curious. It's got to be more than simply liking the way she looks when she's fucking. A video of the two of you would do that. Is it some kind of possession thing? Like, maybe, you want to be the one who takes her home at the end of the night? You want to be the one she chooses? But she has to have a choice. Is that it?" I remember it sounding right. "Or do you just like the idea of her being dirty? That's it, isn't it? You like the idea that your wife is dirty. That your wife is this sexy, kinky slut willing to do anything with anyone. But you're the one she married. That's it. Right?" Justin looking at me. "Right?"

I remember none of us said anything in the elevator up to Justin's room. I was watching Dwight and he seemed nervous in a way he hadn't before, and I felt a strange, wonderful fear. And I thought about how rare it is to experience something so truly new, and it felt like the first time I had ever been on an airplane, the time I flew to Italy to see my brother. I was excited about where I was going, but sad to be leaving home. And how, even though I couldn't wait to see a different country, I couldn't wait to be home again. And even though I was pretty sure that nothing was going to go wrong with the plane, I knew there was a chance. And how happy I'd be to be back with Dwight after having taken such an amazing trip.

I had turned to kiss Justin, and while I kissed his mouth, Dwight was kissing my shoulders, my arms. And four hands were all over me, pulling up my skirt, pulling down my panties, feeling my thighs. I could feel both erections pressing against me through their pants.

"Are you sure you want to do this?" Dwight asked me, quietly, before we stepped into Justin's apartment. I nodded, watching Justin as he unlocked the door, but Dwight turned me toward him and asked again. "We don't have to do this." I looked into Dwight's face and understood he wanted me to say it. And now he was the one who was unsure. He wanted me to somehow answer all his questions. He told me again, "You don't have to."

"Do you want me to?"

"I . . . yes."

"Then I have to."

But I don't tell Dwight about any of that. Instead I tell him I remember:

Breaking Rule #1.

Liking the sound of "cocksucker."

The taste of Justin's pillow.

I remember breaking Rule #2 in the backseat of our car on the way to Justin's apartment. I tell Dwight I remember that Justin had a little tattoo of Mighty Mouse tucked in the crook of his left hip. Justin brushing the hair away from my face so Dwight could see. Justin's begging me not to stop and me promising him I wouldn't.

I remember wondering suddenly if Justin had a girlfriend. Or a wife.

Bending me over the bureau in the foyer before we even got the door closed.

I tell Dwight I remember when I was a kid we would vacation at Pamlico Sound every summer. There were two radio towers on the other side of the sound. I would lie awake at night and watch the red beacons on top of them, one flashing just slightly slower than the other. And how the fast one got closer and closer to the slow one until finally they flashed at the exact same time, and then they'd get further and further apart until they were as far apart as they could get. And then they'd start getting closer again. "I remember thinking last night," I tell Dwight, "when you were both in me at the same time, how this was exactly like that. Justin's rhythm was always just a little faster than yours, sometimes entering just as you'd pull out, sometimes entering at the same time, making me feel so full I thought I might burst open."

It was so weird, Dwight tells me, to see me do the things I do, the things he never gets to see when I'm doing them to him. He says he's never seen how I lock my ankles when I'm getting fucked on my hands and knees; how the muscles in my neck stand out when I'm giving head.

I remember both of their hearts beating on me.

I remember I was the only thing in the entire world either one of them cared about right then. The only thing. The center of attention. I was the absolute center of their universe.

I remember the idea of getting pregnant turning me on really bad, and then getting over it.

I remember Justin's neighbor calling and asking if everything was all right because she had heard a girl screaming.

I remember that afterward, for a long time, all I could do was sob and sniffle.

Driving home. Talking about dinner. Talking about Justin's place.

Like nothing out of the ordinary had happened. Like our marriage hadn't just been irrevocably altered.

Neither one of us say anything for a while until I ask Dwight, "Was it what you wanted?"

"I think so. Yes." Then Dwight says, "What was it like?"

"What do you mean?"

"Fucking him."

"I don't know. I guess—" I begin, but then, "I don't know."

"Tell me. Tell me what it was like."

"It was like fucking. I don't know."

"Was it different?"

"Of course it was different."

"How?" he asks, and before I can say anything, he asks, "Do you like being called a whore?"

"I don't . . . no."

"You liked it last night."

"Last night, I didn't— I wanted to be something else. Something different. I wanted to be something dirty. Isn't that what you wanted? Didn't you want that, too?"

Dwight is quiet after I say that, and I allow myself to think, if only briefly, that we've reached some sort of closure. Then Dwight asks, "How was it different?"

"How was what different?"

"Fucking him. You said it was different."

"I don't know, baby."

"Tell me. Please."

"He was," I begin and then pause to think about what to say. Or what not to say. "*Everything* was different," I finally say. "The way he smelled. The way he tasted. He was just more . . . I don't know."

"More what?"

"More . . . I don't know . . . aggressive, maybe."

"Do you like that?"

"Sometimes, yeah, I guess," I say, and then immediately wish I hadn't. "But I like they way we do it, too. We don't always just fuck. We do that too, you know? But it can also be sweet. Gentle. I don't think Justin could do that, even if he tried. Justin just fucks."

"Do you like the way Justin fucks?"

"Baby, don't."

"Just tell me. Did you like the way Justin fucked you?"

"Yes, okay? I liked the way he fucked me. I fucking *loved* the way he fucked me, okay? Wasn't that the whole point? This was your idea, don't fucking forget that. You were the one who—"

"Was he better?"

"It's not like that."

"Tell me."

"I'm not going to compare the two of you. You promised."

"That's not what I want."

"What, then?"

"Just say it."

"What, that he was better? Is that what you want me to say? That he has a huge fucking cock and I loved getting fucked by it? Does that turn you on?"

"Yes."

"Fuck you."

And Dwight breaks Rule #3.

from The Washingtonienne

JESSICA CUTLER

WEDNESDAY WAS MY FAVORITE night of the week for going out. You might think that nobody in Washington would want to party hard on a weeknight, but there was always a line to get in to Saki on Wednesdays. Not many Hill people showed up, which was a good thing: we could get crazy and not have to worry about it coming up at work. The crowd was a good mix of rich kids who didn't have to work for a living, and party people who didn't give a fuck about their jobs and planned to call in sick the next day.

Laura met us just in time for "White Lines (Don't Do It)." The deejay played the Grandmaster Flash and Melle Mel song at approximately the same time every night. It was a good song to writhe around and look sexy to.

A boy who looked like Ad-Rock from the Beastie Boys circa 1985 put a glass in my hand and filled it with Grey Goose. He and his friends had bottle service at a nearby table, so we gravitated in that direction.

Seconds later, we each had a drink in our hands and a boy's lap to sit on. I had really come here just to dance tonight, but the Ad-Rock boy kept asking me questions like "Where are you from?" and "What do you do?" The crowd and the music were far too loud to carry on a conversation, so I was forced to lean closer to him so I could hear what he was saying. Then I caught a whiff of his breath, jumped up, and started dancing away from the table.

Just my luck. I found the cutest boy in the club and he smelled like he'd been smoking weed and eating Doritos all day long. Damnit.

Laura followed me to the ladies' room, while April made out with one of Ad-Rock's friends, some dude in a suit who had a bodyguard.

"What time is it?" Laura asked, blotting the sweat from her face.

"It's almost three in the morning," I told her, checking my phone for messages.

"Did you get any calls?"

I shook my head no.

"Loser," she said, snorting a line off the mirror in her Chanel compact.

She had pried out the pressed powder that came inside of it for this sole purpose.

"Are you going to the office tomorrow?" I asked.

"Shit no," she said, chopping out a line for me with her Senate debit card. "Do you think anyone here is going to work tomorrow?"

Apparently, the opening of Saki had heralded a huge drop in productivity among the twenty-something workforce in Washington.

"Do you have any more?" I asked when I finished my line. "I can't do one line and just stop like this."

"Is anybody carrying in here?" Laura shouted at the people in the other stalls.

"No!" they all shouted back.

"Goddamn liars," Laura muttered.

"It's, like, *impossible* to get drugs in this town," I complained. "April and I were forced to do Robo last week."

"A bottle of Robitussin costs what, eight dollars? I should quit doing all this coke and start drinking cough syrup to save money."

Suddenly, we heard April's voice in the bathroom.

"Jackie? Laura? Where are you guys?"

I opened the door to our stall, and we stepped out to meet her.

"Should I go home with that guy I was making out with?" she asked us. "He's a vice president of a bank or something."

"Do you know how many vice presidents you're going to meet?" I asked her.

She shook her head.

"More than you'll know what to do with."

"What about Tom?" Laura asked.

"Until I get a ring," April said, wiggling her left ring finger, "I can do whatever the fuck I want."

April was obviously drunk, but she deserved a fun night out, too.

We heard the deejay put on "Relax" by Frankie Goes to Hollywood, and we all ran back out to the dance floor. April and Laura disappeared, so I started dancing with some fool who was wearing a tuxedo.

Suddenly, Laura grabbed me by the arm and pulled me over to the bar. She had a boy with her.

"Sean has coke back at his place!" she told me excitedly.

By then, it was three in the morning, and Saki was about to close.

"Sidebar, Laura," I took her aside. "Who the fuck is Sean?"

"I don't know." She shrugged. "Does it matter? He's a guy with coke!"

Laura and I followed our new best friend Sean up the stairs to the exit. We saw April climb into a limo with the vice president she had met.

"A thousand points for April!" Laura yelled after her. "Leaving the club in a fucking limo!"

"Who the fuck takes a limo to *Saki*?" I asked as it sped off to some-place fabulous.

Sean took Laura and me to his duplex on nearby Euclid Street. He had a big glass coffee table in the living room, perfect for doing coke on. We gathered around it, watching Sean chop out some big, fat lines for us.

"Dude, we like you already," Laura said, taking a seat next to him on a black leather couch.

"How *much* do you like me?" Sean asked suggestively. "Because I have some more stuff upstairs, if you want it."

Laura and I looked at each other, not sure if we should be offended or turned on.

The coke was making us frisky, so she asked me, "Hey, Jackie, do you *want it*?"

I nodded.

"Do *you*?" I asked.

We started giggling as we followed Sean up the stairs.

SO TYPICAL. HE MADE us snort the coke off his dick. I always felt kind of stupid doing this, but decided it was worth it: it never hurts to make friends with someone who has a lot of drugs.

"So what do you do, Sean?" I asked while Laura did a line.

"Like, tell us about yourself," she said, coming up for air.

Sean climbed on top of me as I assumed the position. "I'll tell you as soon as I finish."

"I'm a bike messenger," he said about two minutes later.

No wonder he didn't want to tell us before. Girls like Laura turned their noses up at guys like Sean. But I *adored* bike messengers. They looked like rock stars to us girls trapped in offices all day, with those big chains around their waists, and the one pant leg rolled up. I creamed my pants whenever one rode by me on the street. The D.C. bike messengers were that hot.

Unfortunately, sex on coke wasn't. It was fast and vigorous, but the technique went out the window when you were high. And the more people involved, the sloppier it got. Laura kept shunting me aside and climbing on top of Sean, forcing all of his attention on her.

Why did girls have to make everything a competition like this? I assumed it was just the coke that made her act so greedy, but few people were having more fun than us that night, naked, in bed with a hot guy with a tight ass, and high out of our minds.

Then the sun came up.

"I want to get the fuck out of here," Laura whispered when Sean left the room to pee. "Where is my bra?"

"I don't know," I said, shielding my eyes from the daylight with the very bra she was looking for.

"They should make a chick flick called *Dude, Where's My Bra?*" I said, laughing.

Laura snatched her bra away from me, and I pulled the bedsheet over my head.

"I'm serious. I want to get out of here," she said, scrambling to get up. "Are you coming or not?"

"Not," I grunted.

I didn't have to be anywhere until Monday. I rolled over, turning my back to her.

Laura crept out of the room and down the stairs before Sean came out of the bathroom.

"Did your friend go home?" he asked, pulling down the shades to block out the sunlight.

"Yeah," I answered, sitting up.

"Don't get up, pretty girl," he said, climbing back into the bed with me. "I want you to stay."

Again, the sex wasn't very good, but his body made up for it. The boy had *back* from riding his bike all day. And he had tattoos on his arms, on his neck, and on his calves. I hadn't fucked a guy with tats in years, but it was fun to go slumming every once in a while.

"You know, you were the primary interest," he told me afterward. "I didn't really like your friend that much."

Of course he liked me more than my friend: that's what guys were supposed to say to the girl who ended up staying when the threesome was over.

I gave him my number, and he promised to call, but whatever: call me, don't call me. Sean was hot, but I could never bring him home to Mother. . . .

APRIL CAME HOME SHORTLY after I did, her hair disheveled and her eyeliner smudged.

"Why does my makeup always look better the morning *after* I put it on?" she asked, dousing a cotton ball with my Caswell-Massey Sweet Almond Oil. "Do you know if Laura is going to work today?"

"I doubt it," I told her.

"Shit! That means it's my turn to go into the office."

"You're going to work today?"

"Well, we *both* can't call in sick on the same day, and I called in *last* Thursday."

"Do you need any of this?" I asked, showing her the nice parting gift that Sean had given me: a vial of coke, street value of $300.

"Where did you get that?" she wanted to know.

"Laura and I had a threesome with a drug dealer-slash-bike messenger."

April's green eyes widened.

"Are you serious?" she asked. "Did she eat you out?"

"No! We didn't do anything with each other," I explained. "Laura is really pretty bad at threesomes—don't tell her I said that."

"Don't worry, I won't," April said, doing a bump of coke off her finger.

"So what happened with the vice president?" I asked her.

It turned out the guy who April left the club with was the vice president of a small *country,* not a bank—which explained the limousine and the bodyguard.

"He was such a freak. Do you know what he wanted to do?" she asked. "I'm warning you, it's totally sick."

Of course I wanted to know. I lived for this stuff.

"He wanted to put M&Ms in my butt," she whispered, even though she was telling me this in her own bedroom.

"What?"

"And then he wanted to eat them!"

"Ugh!"

I fell on the floor, laughing.

"Plain or peanut?" I asked her.

"He had plain ones."

"Did he keep them in a candy dish next to the bed?"

"Oh, shut up, Jackie! It was seriously the scariest thing that ever happened to me. I couldn't understand half the stuff he was saying, but he implied that he could do whatever he wanted with me because he had diplomatic immunity or something."

"But that doesn't give him the right to make you his human Pez dispenser! You didn't let him do it, did you?"

She wouldn't answer.

"Ha," I laughed. "You can never tell me anything ever again!"

"I was scared, okay?" April admitted. "For all I knew, the guy could have kidnapped me, pumped me full of drugs, and dumped my body into the ocean from a helicopter when he got tired of raping me. And he would get away with it because he's a Very Important Person."

"I don't know, April. That seems pretty far-fetched."

"Oh, whatever! Didn't you once say that you had a boyfriend who liked to strangle you during sex?" she reminded me. "There are a lot of weirdos out there."

"It's actually pretty common. I used to think that I was the only one who did this freaky stuff, like there was something wrong with me, that I was attracting all these sickos. But the more people you talk to, the more you realize that *everyone* has stories like these."

April shook her head.

"No, that's not true," she said after doing another bump. "Most people have really boring lives. I really think that we have a tendency to attract weirdos."

"No," I argued. "We just have a tendency to find strange ways to entertain ourselves."

I took off the Heatherette Hello Kitty minidress that I had worn out the night before. My eyeballs hurt, and I could feel a headache coming on.

"I think I'm coming down," I said, pulling my Donovan McNabb jersey over my head.

"Then I'm out of here," April said, throwing her Coach bag over her shoulder. "If I talk to Laura, I'll let you know what she had to say about last night. I hope things don't get weird between the two of you."

On her way out the door, I didn't want to burden April with the regrettable truth that it was too late.

Laura came by the apartment that afternoon to discuss.

"I think we need to talk," she said, sunglasses clamped to her face. We were both fighting coke hangovers, and I wasn't in the mood.

"There's nothing to talk about," I offered. "We were both high as kites, and we got carried away. It's no biggie."

"Speak for yourself," Laura said. "I don't want you to get the wrong idea about me. I'm really not the threesome type."

"Well, who is?" I laughed. "Everyone has at least *one* threesome at some point in their lives."

"Maybe where you come from, they do," she snorted, "but where I come from, people don't do things like that."

"Not true! Haven't you ever watched Jerry Springer? Apparently, poor white trash have threesomes all the time."

I knew that it was a mean thing to say, but someone needed to knock Laura off her high horse. No wonder I didn't have many female friends: girls were such goddamn bitches.

"How dare you make yourself out to be the innocent Southern Belle," I told her. "What does that make me? The Big City whore? Give me a break! We both know what happened last night, so just cut the shit."

Laura smirked.

"Well, I'm glad we finally got it all out into the open," she said. "Now I can go home and get some sleep."

"Good for you," I retorted. "Now get out of here and take your ugly Vera Bradley bag with you."

She walked toward the door, then turned around.

"Jackie, I would really like for us to be friends," she said, taking off her sunglasses. "I hope we can keep what happened between you and me."

"I don't really give a damn if people know shit about me, and I hope that you don't think that having a threesome is anything to be ashamed of, because if you do, then you shouldn't have done it in the first place. Besides, I already told April."

"I assumed that you would. We girls love to share secrets, just not with the world, okay?"

Her pleading eyes filled with tears, and I couldn't help but feel bad for the girl: crying in front of a bitch like me was not a fun thing to do. As much as I would have liked to be, I wasn't made of stone.

"I'd really like to be friends with you, too," I admitted. "I promise not to tell anyone else."

We kissed each other good-bye (on the cheek), but there was something about this girl that I didn't trust. Despite whatever label we put on our relationship, she was no friend of mine. Like I had said, I hardly knew her, and I didn't owe her a thing. I could go out and get drunk with her, but that was about it. Such was the nature of most friendships in D.C., I supposed.

Comeback

NICHOLAS KAUFMANN

THE BIG SHINDIG WAS at Bruce Glasser's house in Tarzana, the only part of the Valley I don't consider a shithole. It's the same house where we shot a lot of my movies when it belonged to Ricky Samson, owner of Luscious Video back in the '80s. The *Virgin High* series had turned Bruce into one of the biggest adult-film producers in the country, making him rich enough to buy it when Ricky died from screwing the wrong junkie. (Ricky always liked it bareback, and everyone knew it would get him in trouble one day, either dead or a daddy.) It was weird being there for a party instead of a shoot. I kept expecting the doorbell to ring and the late, great Johnny Calzone to come in dressed like that fucking pizza delivery boy from *Who Ordered Sausage?* I still can't believe that's the role that got him famous. Though I guess I'm still best known for playing a high school girl who fucks her gym teacher on the parallel bars, so maybe I shouldn't talk.

Bruce only invited me to the party because he was giving me a role in his newest film, mostly out of pity, I suppose, but I wasn't about to say no. It's hard being a former starlet who's crossed to the other side of forty. Everyone thinks you're too ancient to be in their movies anymore, or you're only good for the granny-porn sites, so I'd mostly been doing dub work on Japanese anime, the ones where girls get fucked by demons or whatever. The money's all right, but the job's kind of limiting. There are only so many ways to make that surprised gasping noise when the tentacles come out of nowhere and Little Miss Wide Eyes gets one in every hole.

I felt like a visitor from another planet standing there in Bruce's crowded living room. Everyone knew everyone else—they all had their arms around each other and were laughing at private jokes—but I didn't recognize anyone. A whole new generation of filmmakers had sprung up since the last time I was there. I guess I'd expected to sign at least a few cocktail napkins—"Stay tight! Love, Amber Fox," just like in the old days when everyone asked me to sign video boxes—but no one seemed to remember me, or if they did, they didn't give a shit. I was just some old lady to them, not worth their attention when there were so many young hotties in the room.

I flashed for a moment on Jay, my ex-boyfriend, the night he packed his bags and took off, our two-year relationship dead all of a sudden because he'd found someone else. Someone younger. Standing at my door, confused and hurt, I caught a glimpse of her as Jay tossed his suitcases in the back of his Ford Expedition. Just a slim, tanned arm poking out of the passenger's-side window, the tattoo of a daisy on her shoulder, her fingers decorated with silver rings. Not a wrinkle or an ounce of fat on that arm, just the smooth, golden skin of a twenty-something beach bunny. Inside the car, the round tip of a cigarette glowed, briefly revealing an orange-tinted hint of a button nose and curly hair before it faded.

A high-pitched squeal pulled me out of my memories. "Amber?" A girl I'd never seen before ran up to me. She was a skinny, tiny thing with big blonde hair, tight bell-bottom jeans, and a cropped T-shirt that barely covered her melon chest. She didn't look more than eighteen.

"The one and only," I said, perking up a bit. It's an old joke. Half the women in the biz call themselves Amber.

"Oh my God!" she shrieked, giving me a peek at the metal stud through her tongue. "Amber Fox, I can't believe it!"

"In the flesh," I said. I was relieved someone had finally recognized me, even if she was probably one of the younger stars I'd been losing roles to for the past six years. I tried not to look at how toned and tight her stomach was, but the glittery string of diamonds dangling from her pierced belly button kept drawing my eye back. I felt like a whale all of a sudden, so I sucked in my gut and made a mental note to avoid the hors d'oeuvres table for the rest of the night.

"You have no idea how big a fan I am!" she cried, her eyes wide and crazy-looking.

"You'll just have to tell me then," I said, laughing my party laugh. Behind her, someone spread lines of coke on the coffee table. Suddenly it felt like no time had passed—it was still 1986, and I was the hottest adult-film actress this side of Seka.

"I'm Krystal Lynn," she said, extending one remarkably tiny hand. Her nails, though, were enormous and had green dollar signs stenciled onto the white polish. I winced in sympathy for any guy unlucky enough to get a hand job from her. "Maybe you saw me in *Ready, Willing, and Anal 5*? I won an AVN Award for that. Best Ass to Mouth."

"Congratulations," I said, shaking her hand. "I have an AVN myself."

"I know, Lifetime Achievement!" Krystal squealed. "I know, like, everything about you. You're my hero. You're totally why I got into the business."

I grinned. "Really?"

"Totally! My father had, like, all your videos. I found them under the sink in his bathroom, and this one time when he was out of town I invited over all my friends from school, and we had an Amber Fox marathon. You were so cool."

Her father? She might as well have stabbed me in the heart. Sometimes I forget how long ago the '80s were.

She turned around and shouted into the crowd, "Hey, Terry, get your ass over here! You gotta meet someone!" A tall, chunky man closer to my age than hers, with a fuzzy handlebar mustache, a ponytail sticking out the back of his trucker cap, and a big blue knapsack slung over one shoulder, made his way over to us. "This is Amber Fox."

"Yeah?" he said. Not hi, not pleased to meet you, just yeah. "Terry Left. I own Sunset Auto Parts." He said it like I ought to be impressed, then shook my hand with an overly strong grip. I knew his type immediately: the small-time, loudmouth loser who'd managed to catch a hot, young porn-star girlfriend with daddy issues and thought it made him big shit. I knew the type because that was every boyfriend I'd ever had. They drove me crazy, but sometimes you need to come home to someone who still wants to be with you after you bitch about how a costar got jizz in your eye when he came on your face.

Every boyfriend except Jay, that is. He was the only one I ever really cared about. But he'd been disappointing in a different way. Like the car enthusiast he was, he couldn't resist trading in his old ride for a shiny new one.

"You remember those *Virgin High* videos I told you about?" Krystal asked Terry.

"What, with the chick on the balance beam?"

"Parallel bars," I said.

"This is her!"

"No shit," Terry said. He put his arm around Krystal's shoulders and crushed her to him. "I bet you could fuck on the balance beam no problem, right, baby? Maybe you should do a remake."

I kept the smile on my face, but inside I cringed. There's a superstition in movies, in all entertainment probably, that once an idea is put out there, even as a joke, it will inevitably become a reality, as if somebody could pluck it right out of the air. If a remake of *Virgin High* happened with some new starlet in my signature role, I would personally hunt Terry down and kill him for bringing it up. Not that I'm a superstitious woman, but *Virgin High* was all the cred I had left.

"You still got that marker in your bag, hon?" Krystal asked. Terry swung the knapsack off his shoulder, rummaged through it, and pulled out a black Sharpie. She snatched it out of his hand and put it in mine. "Do you mind?"

"No, sure, do you have something for me to sign?"

I expected her to produce a cocktail napkin or even one of her father's old video boxes, but instead she lifted her T-shirt up to her neck with both hands. "To Krystal," she said, "with a K."

Her breasts were enormous, way out of proportion with her tiny body. I was afraid the Sharpie might accidentally pop her implant when I pressed it to her left breast, but the opposite happened. As the felt tip of the marker squeaked over the skin just above her stretched nipple, it didn't even indent the flesh. I've signed a lot of tits in my time, but I'd never seen anything like that. It was like writing on a bowling ball. She should sue her plastic surgeon.

"Get the camera," she told Terry. He nodded and pulled out a sleek, silver digital number. "Can I get a shot of this?" she asked me.

"Sure," I said, "but I finished signing my name."

"Pretend you're still writing."

I held my hand over her breast, keeping the Sharpie's tip just above my signature. My arm began shaking with fatigue. As I watched my wrist tremble, I wondered what had happened to me. Time was, I could maintain a split on the parallel bars for fifteen minutes without so much as breaking a sweat, but now I was shaking like an old junkie just from holding a pen above some girl's tit while her mongoloid idiot boyfriend tried to figure out how to press a fucking button.

Finally, the flash went off. Krystal thanked me, and she and Terry wandered over to the coke table. She kept her shirt up to show off my signature. I needed to get away for a minute, so I went out into the backyard. No stars came through the smoggy night sky, and the moon was just a bright smear on the clouds. Bruce had set up tiki torches on the lawn, but that was more for effect than anything else, since the muggy night was keeping everyone inside with the air-conditioning. I was alone in the orange glow of the flames.

I reached into my bag, fumbled for my pack of Newports, and lit up. My hand was still trembling. After being accosted by Little Miss Rock-Hard Abs, I felt old as dust and about as sexy. Maybe there was no place for me in the industry anymore. Part of me wanted to walk away and leave it all behind, forget Bruce's new movie, forget all hope of a come-back. How could I compete with the Krystal Lynns of the world?

But porn was all I knew and, frankly, all I wanted to know. The job only asked you to fuck some broad-shouldered hunk you'd probably want to fuck anyway, and by the end of the day you had enough money to make two months' rent. Everyone always said I was too smart for this business, but what else was I qualified to do? Waitress? Run day care? Hey, kids, did I ever tell you about the time Ron Jeremy shot his load on my tits and couldn't stop giggling?

More than that, I didn't want to be just some grande dame with a Lifetime Achievement Award. I wanted to be the fantasy of pubescent boys everywhere, I wanted guys on their commutes to think of me and have no choice but to pull their cars over and jerk off. I wanted to be wanted again. Dubbing hard-core anime wasn't going to make that hap-pen. Being back in front of the camera would.

I stamped out my cigarette and started toward the sliding-glass door that led to the kitchen. But before I reached it, I caught sight of shapes moving in the darkness of the yard, and I stopped. A couple I hadn't noticed before stood just beyond the glow of the tiki torches and the light spilling out from the house. The man was tall, slender, and stood as straight as a board. He wore a finely pressed suit and a tieless dress shirt, with one arm around the shoulders of the petite woman in a dark, slinky dress next to him. They were both looking at me. I felt uncomfortable, strangely embarrassed by their attention. Normally I want people's eyes on me—nobody gets into adult films because they're shy—but this was different. They were staring at me so intensely, like they were trying to see the bones beneath my skin. I hurried inside. I wanted to find Bruce, get the script from him, and pour as much Cristal down my throat as I could before going home to my empty little apartment with its reminders of Jay everywhere.

Rounding the corner from the kitchen to the living room, I found him. Bruce was leaning against the wall with a glass of white wine in one hand, some rolled-up papers in the other. He was surrounded by a gaggle of starlets who laughed at everything he said and touched his arms and chest every chance they got. Bruce was never a handsome man, not even back when he didn't have to dye the gray out of his hair. He's got one of those noses that looks like it's been broken a few too many times, and a bushy mustache that looks like a fat caterpillar died on his lip. Still, money is money and power is power, and these girls could smell both on him. They would do anything for him, and he knew it.

When he saw me, he shouted over their heads, "Amber!" He waved me over. The girls reluctantly parted to let me through. A few of them looked me up and down with one of those who's-this-bitch? expressions that comes with being cock-blocked. Bruce handed me the papers. "Here's the script," he said. "We start shooting tomorrow night."

As with most scripts for adult films, it was really just an outline. The movie would probably run an hour, but the script was only six pages long. I sat down on one of the Italian leather chairs in the living room, blocked out the laughter and clinking glasses, and read it. It was called *The Big Cumback,* about three slutty female gangsters, Sabrina, Katie, and Jess, who escape from jail and fuck their way to the top of the male-dominated criminal underground. I had to flip through it three times before the part Bruce had in mind for me even registered.

I jumped out of the chair and stormed all over the house looking for him. No one knew where he was. That meant he was in the bedroom with someone and didn't want to be disturbed. I didn't care, I threw open the bedroom door and marched right in. Bruce was sitting naked on the king-size bed, his back against the cushioned headboard. Some starlet's head was between his legs, a cloud of blonde hair bobbing over his hairy gut like a poodle dancing for scraps. I couldn't see her face, just her bare ass in the air and, beneath it, the snake eye slit of her shaved pussy.

A momentary pang of jealousy hit me—I used to be the one he took to the bedroom at parties—but I shrugged it off and shook the script in the air. "What the fuck, Bruce?"

He didn't flinch or yell or even tell the girl to stop. He only sighed and played with her hair when he said, "What's the matter now?" His unfazed reaction only infuriated me further.

"I'm playing Sabrina's mother?" I shouted. Bruce's cock slid out of the girl's mouth with a wet pop, and she glanced at me over her shoulder. It was Krystal Lynn. Why wasn't I surprised?

"Oh my God," Krystal said, "you're playing my mother? How awesome is that? We're going to be in a movie together!"

I glared at Bruce. "She's Sabrina?"

Bruce put a hand on Krystal's head and pushed her face down again. "Did I say you could stop?" Then he turned to me. "Relax, babe; it's a part, isn't it? You'll be on camera again like you wanted."

"I don't even have a goddamn sex scene, Bruce. I just come out of a shower and walk in on her and a guy—"

"It's not sex, but you'll still be naked. Everyone will see your tits, everyone will see your bush, I promise you. That gets you back in the public eye. And it's a funny scene, too. You do comedy well, I've seen it."

I shook the script at him again. "This is bullshit, and you know it. I can do more than this. You owe me, Bruce. I put *Virgin High* on the fucking map; I made you who you are today."

He sat up, and Krystal made a little gagging sound as she readjusted. "I'm the one sticking his neck out even putting you in the movie at all! The real bullshit here is thinking our audience wants to watch a forty-year-old woman fuck. Have you seen the new movies Marilyn Chambers is doing? They're shit and they do shit business, but even she knows she's better off hosting them than having any sex scenes."

"I'm not Marilyn Chambers, I'm Amber fucking Fox! Do you know how much fan mail I still get?" It was a lie—I didn't get much at all, maybe a letter every couple of months—but I was hoping Bruce didn't know that.

"The audience has moved on, Amber. Your DVD reissues aren't even selling. They don't care about you, they want new girls like Krystal here. She's going to be huge. Bigger than Chasey Lain, bigger than Tera Patrick, she's the next Jenna Jameson, and I'm not going to fuck up her big break by putting anything in the movie the fans don't want to see."

"The next Jenna?" Krystal asked. "You really think so?"

"You know it, babe." He guided her head down again.

"Bruce," I said, "just give me a chance—"

"Enough, Amber. Get this straight. Most of our customer base is in their teens and twenties. It's not that they don't remember you; they've never heard of you. You might as well be their mother, and no one wants to watch their mother fuck. The script is what it is; there won't be any changes. If you don't like it, find someone else to put you in a movie. Oh, that's right, I forgot. No one else will."

I turned on my heel and stomped toward the door.

"One more thing," Bruce called after me. I half expected him to say, I've decided to remake *Virgin High* and give Krystal your role—I plucked the idea right out of the air, but instead he motioned toward my crotch and said, "Be sure to trim your pussy before we start shooting. Or better yet, shave the whole thing clean. This isn't the '80s anymore; no one wants to see a jungle down there."

I slammed the bedroom door behind me. I could hear the party raging, laughter and popping champagne corks and a loud, arrogant voice somewhere announcing, "I own Sunset Auto Parts," but I didn't want to deal with the crowd. I ducked into the bathroom, locked the door, and ran the faucet into the shell-shaped marble sink. I splashed bracing cold water on my face, then scrutinized myself in the mirror. I looked myself up and down, turned to the side to check my stomach, turned around to check my ass. I'd taken care of myself over the years. I hadn't turned into a cow like Marilyn Chambers, or gone craggy and gray like Georgina Spelvin. I looked good. So what the fuck was Bruce's problem?

"Keep your eye on the goal," I muttered to my reflection. I was going to be in front of the camera again. Bruce might have cast me thinking it was a kitschy cameo, but for me it was a whole lot more. It was the start of my comeback. I wouldn't let it be anything less. I'd do whatever it took to stand out, to be noticed in this role so people would say, Holy shit, Amber Fox is back? I can't wait to see that!

But first I had to get the hell out of this party. If I had to look at Bruce or Krystal Lynn one more time tonight, I'd go ballistic. I opened the bathroom door, stepped out into the hall—

And nearly bumped into the couple I'd seen outside. They were standing in the middle of the hallway, blocking my path. In the light, I could better see the olive complexion of their skin, the pitch blackness of their hair.

"You are Amber?" the man said. He had a slight accent I couldn't place.

"The one and only." I was nervous because they were staring at me with the same intensity as before, so the old joke came out of my mouth automatically. I tried to move past them, but they wouldn't get out of my way.

"Allow me to introduce myself," he said. "I am Ashraf Hammad, and this is my wife, Raha." The woman nodded, her dark eyes glistening, but didn't say a word. "We enjoy your movies."

"That's great," I said. I felt bad for blowing off fans, but I was so desperate to get out of that house I'd stampede over them if I had to. "Excuse me—"

Raha raised one small tan hand, her palm an inch from my face. I froze, thinking the crazy bitch was going to slap me, but then something happened. The space between her hand and my skin suddenly felt like it was inhabited by a thousand tongues, a thousand caressing lips. She moved her hand over my face and down my neck.

"No, I . . ." But I couldn't finish protesting. Instead, I closed my eyes and gave in to the sensation. I couldn't help myself.

"We were hoping to find you here tonight," Ashraf said softly. "You are more experienced than the others. You have what we need."

Raha moved her hand over my breasts, and though she never actually touched me, the sensation coaxed a loud moan from my throat. I leaned back against the wall and put my hands in my hair. Raha moved her hand lower.

"She likes you," Ashraf told me. "You should be honored."

"I . . . really have to go," I managed to say.

Raha cupped her hand at my groin. I gasped as those thousand invisible tongues stroked between my legs. I felt myself getting wet.

"No," I said, pushing her away. There was something unnatural about this. Who were these people? How was she doing that with her hand?

"Why do you resist?" Ashraf asked. He sounded genuinely confused.

"I don't understand what's happening to me," I said, trying to catch my breath. I still had to lean against the wall for support.

"You do not need to understand," he said. He started unbuttoning his dress shirt. "All you need to know is that you have been chosen." He pulled the shirt open, and there on his chest, hanging from a thin chain around his neck, was a gold medallion. At first I thought it was an eye like the kind you see in Egyptian hieroglyphics, but as I looked closer I saw it was made up of smaller geometric shapes, triangles and circles. The center seemed to be moving, swirling, as if an entire galaxy of stars were hidden inside it.

"Your necklace," I said. I felt warm, feverish, dizzy. "Moving . . ."

"It is not the necklace that moves," he said. "It is the Eye."

Raha smiled. It was the most beautiful smile I'd ever seen. The desire to kiss her came over me without warning. I wanted to see what was under that dress, run my hands through her thick black hair, my lips over her bare skin, kiss every inch of her. And when I looked at Ashraf, I wanted more than anything to please him. I would do whatever he wanted. The need for them both burned inside me like an unquenchable fire.

I went with them to their car. I let Raha run her hands all over my body in the backseat while Ashraf drove. I didn't care where we were going. I never wanted the ride to end. When it did, we were in an enormous house in the Hollywood Hills. I didn't remember leaving the car or walking inside, I simply found myself lying on a luxurious bed in the middle of a room with big stone walls. My dress and underwear were on the floor, but I had no memory of taking them off. Raha appeared above me, nude, straddling me on her hands and knees. Her midnight hair cascaded around my head. When I reached up for her, my hands cupped soft, pointed breasts with hard, dark nipples.

Ashraf walked around the bed, still fully clothed. He looked at the stone walls and the symbols etched into them. I didn't recognize any of the carvings, except the same eye that was on his medallion was also on each wall.

Raha bent down and kissed my breasts, suckling the nipples until they stood almost painfully erect. I arched my back in ecstasy and wrapped my legs around her. I was so wet I thought a flood would pour out of me.

Ashraf's voice floated through the room, echoing off the stone. "It is said that in the time of the ancients, Ra, the greatest of all the gods, grew disgusted at man's disregard for his laws. In his anger, he created Sekhmet, the Eye of Ra, the goddess of destruction, a bare-breasted woman with the head of a lioness, and unleashed her upon man to reap vengeance."

Raha moved lower, kissing my belly. I squirmed and moaned on the bed. The inferno raging between my legs could only be extinguished by her tongue.

"The Nile turned crimson from all the blood she shed. When Ra saw the horror he had created, he regretted his actions. He laid a trap for her, hundreds of barrels of beer stained red with pomegranate juice to resemble the blood she enjoyed drinking."

Raha ran her tongue lightly over my pussy, from bottom to top. I shivered and arched my back again. It wouldn't take much more to make me come. I could feel it building already, dancing on the cusp of onset.

Ashraf appeared behind Raha. He removed his shirt and let it drop to the floor. I couldn't take my eyes off the medallion hanging over his chest.

"Ra's plan worked," he continued, undoing his belt. "Sekhmet grew drunk and fell asleep."

I ran my fingers through Raha's thick hair. "Oh God, don't stop."

Ashraf bent to remove his shoes. I watched the well-defined muscles move under the skin of his torso. I wanted him inside me so badly. Raha's lips on my clit made me gasp.

"While she slept, Ra made it so Sekhmet forgot who she was, and the destruction she spread across the kingdom." Ashraf hooked his thumbs inside his pants and pushed them down. He wasn't wearing anything underneath. "Ra changed her name to Hathor so she would never have to remember her deeds. Her nature was changed also, to the sweetness of love and the strength of desire." He stepped toward the bed, his heavy cock growing bigger, stiffer, as he approached. "And henceforth Hathor laid low men and women only with the great power of love."

I looked at Raha between my legs again, but my vision blurred, and for a moment I didn't see her, only what looked like the shaggy pyramid ears and tawny pelt of a lioness, black-and-yellow eyes hovering over my pubic hair like twin moons. I closed my eyes, letting the feel of her tongue take me to the very edge of climax.

And then she stopped.

Panting for breath, I opened my eyes again. Raha crawled up the bed to lay down beside me. She kissed me, her mouth flavored with the vinegar tang of my pussy, and her fingertips played lightly over my nipples.

"That is the story they tell," Ashraf said. He grabbed my ankles and pulled me down until my ass was at the bottom edge of the bed. Raha turned, kissing me upside down. "But it is not the whole story." He pushed my legs up and apart. "How is it, do you think, that Ra really tamed a woman as wild as Sekhmet?"

I started coming the moment he slid his cock inside me, wave after crashing wave of intense orgasms. I thrashed on the bed, made noises I'd never made before, as he slowly pulled out, almost to the point of exit, then rammed it back in. Every time he did, I shuddered with a new climax.

"What incentive do you think Ra promised her to keep the goddess of desire from turning back into the goddess of destruction?" he asked.

Raha crawled on top of me, still upside down, spreading her thighs over my face. Between Ashraf's slow and steady thrusts and Raha's tongue on my clit again, I came so hard I thought I might pass out. Little white dots exploded behind my eyelids. I wrapped my hands around the smooth skin of her ass and eagerly pulled her cunt down to my mouth. She didn't make a sound, only ground her hips above my head and continued licking me.

"It was Isis and Osiris who valued virgins, not Hathor. Hathor had little patience for teaching them the way of pleasure. She treasured experience above all else."

Raha shuddered hard, pushing her cunt right up against my face as she came. Now, finally, a sound escaped her throat as the orgasm steam-rolled through her, a low, guttural cry that echoed off the stone walls like a roar. Hearing her come made me so hot I thought my skin would burst into flames.

"Ra promised her lovers of exceptional experience. He fashioned the Eye of Hathor, a powerful symbol that awakens in all who see it an irresistible desire, in order to procure lovers for her."

Raha lifted one leg and swung herself off of me. Ashraf pulled out, his cock dripping wet. I moaned in disappointment, but Raha silenced me with a deep kiss, our tongues dancing around each other like frisky cubs. Ashraf took hold of each of my legs and pushed them up until my knees were against my chest. Then, effortlessly, he thrust his cock into my ass.

I've done a lot in my career, girl on girl, two guys at once, bukkake trains, you name it, but the one thing I never did was anal. It'd always been off limits, even in my private life. But I was so hot, so willing to do anything he wanted, that I didn't care. It didn't hurt like I thought it would, either. His cock slid right in on the natural lubricant from my sopping pussy. It was the most incredible feeling. Raha kept kissing me, working my clit with her finger until I was on the brink of orgasm again. Then she stuck her finger inside me, and I came harder than I had all night.

Ashraf's breath caught in his throat. He tilted his head back, his mouth hanging open. I felt his cock stiffen in my ass, then pull out. He climbed onto the bed, holding his prick in one hand, and positioned himself on his knees above Raha and me. The first hot spurt of semen hit my face, cooling immediately as it rolled down my chin. Raha opened her mouth to receive the second, and I did the same. A few moments later, his cock drooped, spent, and our lips, chins, and cheeks were coated in a thick white goo. Raha kissed me once more, her mouth slippery and salty.

I looked at Ashraf above me, the golden Eye of Hathor glittering on his heaving, sweaty chest. I stretched out on the bed, a satisfied hum buzzing through my body. I'd almost forgotten what it's like to be so wanted.

My eyelids drooped as the afterglow pulled me toward sleep. I saw Ashraf bend over me, the medallion flashing, then there was only a warm darkness. And yet, I could still see the medallion burning brightly in my mind, in perfect detail. I felt arms around me, as if I was being carried, and when I opened my eyes we were in the car again. My clothes had reappeared on my body. I shut my eyes, wanting to sink back into the comfortable blackness, and saw the medallion once more behind my eyelids.

"The Eye," I managed to say, little more than a whisper. "It's in my head . . ."

"Our gift to you, in thanks," Ashraf's voice replied. "Any who gazes upon it will be yours. Choose wisely."

I opened my eyes once more and saw Raha sitting next to me. I put my hand to her cheek. "Will I see you again?"

She shook her head, and from the front seat, Ashraf said, "We will not meet again, nor will we be here if you come looking for us. It is the way."

I nodded sadly, closing my eyes only for a moment. When I opened them again I was slumped in the driver's seat of my car on the empty street outside Bruce's house. The sun was coming up, tinting everything gray. I shook the cobwebs out of my head and drove home. The Eye of Hathor burned in my mind the whole way there. It was there when I collapsed onto my bed and when I woke up a few hours later with Bruce's words circling my brain like song lyrics that get stuck in your head: "Everyone will see your tits, everyone will see your bush, I promise you."

If he wanted me to trim my pubes before the shoot, there was only one man in all of L.A. for the job. He called himself The Gardener, and everyone who was anyone used him when it was grooming time. After calling to make an appointment, I drove to his home office in Orange County.

"Amber!" he exclaimed, greeting me at the door in an orange polo shirt that almost matched the color of his Irish hair. "How long has it been?"

"Too long," I said, hugging him. He invited me into his living room, where big glossy photos of his work adorned the walls, women's nude crotches with all manner of shaved pubic hair: the standard landing strip, a Valentine's heart, a jack-o'-lantern, a Christmas tree, a lightning bolt, even the Gucci symbol. When I told him what I wanted and asked if he could do it, he spread his hands and said, "Hey, I'm The Gardener, aren't I?"

He brought me into the brightly lit, white-walled room in back, where there were two tables of shaving equipment and, in the center, a large barber-style chair tilted back with two silver stirrups protruding from the seat. I dropped my skirt, my panties, and sat, nude from the waist down, on the chair. I stuck my heels in the stirrups and rolled my blouse up a bit.

The Gardener knelt down on the floor between my legs, first trimming the hair with electric clippers, then dipping his fingertips in a jar of petroleum jelly and gently smearing a thin layer over the fine fuzz in slow circles. Finally, he picked up his trusty straight–edge. I painstakingly guided him through the process, describing everything down to the minutest detail. Two hours in, my cell phone rang. I fished it out of my purse and looked at the caller ID. It was Bruce.

"So," he said, "are you all set for tonight?"

"You bet. I'm at the Gardener's now, getting a shave just like you said." I felt the blade clear away the last of the extra hair. He was finished.

"How's it look?" Bruce asked.

"Hold on, I'll find out. How's it look?" I asked the Gardener. He didn't answer. He stared at my crotch, transfixed. Under his belt buckle, I could see his cock stiffening, straining against his fly. "I'd say it looks pretty damn good," I said into the phone.

"Great," Bruce said. "The camera is going to love you, babe."

The Gardener couldn't control himself anymore. He leaned forward, put his hands on my thighs, and started eating me out, his tongue disappearing beneath the Eye of Hathor shaved into my pubic hair.

"Bruce," I said, "once this movie comes out, everyone is going to love me."

from Towelhead

ALICIA ERIAN

AT LUNCH THE NEXT day, Thomas said, "I thought of something you could do to impress me."

"What?" I asked. It was Hamburger Day and I was tearing open a plastic packet of mustard.

"Have sex with me."

"Okay," I said.

"Really?" he said. For the first time in a long while, he sounded kind of friendly.

"Yes."

"Great," he said. "When?"

"Whenever you want."

"Well," he said, "I guess we need to figure out a place first."

"We can't do it at my house," I said. I couldn't risk Mr. Vuoso and Zack telling on me again.

Thomas nodded. "We can do it at my house."

"What about your parents?" I asked.

"They'll be at work."

"What if they come home?"

"They won't. They never come home early."

"I'll have to walk home," I said.

"You can take a taxi," Thomas said. "I'll pay for it."

I thought about this, then said, "All right."

"Can we do it today?" he asked.

"Do you have a condom?"

"No."

"Then we'll have to wait until tomorrow. I have one at home I can bring."

"Where'd you get it?"

"From Mr. Vuoso's duffel bag."

"I don't want to use that racist's condom."

"You have to," I said. "It's the only one we have."

He said okay, even though he seemed kind of bothered.

When I met Denise at her locker later and told her about my deal with Thomas, she said, "No way! He's using you!"

"No, he's not," I said.

"He's totally using you. You can't have sex with him in exchange for not being a racist. That's ridiculous."

"But I want to have sex with him."

She looked at me. "You never told me that. You told me you were in love with that guy next door."

"I am," I said, "but I want to have sex with Thomas, too."

"Then you won't be a virgin anymore."

"So?" I said.

"So?" she said. "It's important that the first person you have sex with is someone special. Not someone who's using you."

"Well," I said, "I'm probably going to do it."

"I can't believe you," she said, and she closed her locker and walked away. I thought about chasing after her and telling her not to worry, that I already wasn't a virgin, that the person I had done it with was special, even if he had only become that way later on. But I didn't, of course. Besides the fact that I didn't want to get Mr. Vuoso in trouble, I didn't think Denise would understand. If I couldn't explain to her why Daddy was bad, then I probably couldn't explain why Mr. Vuoso was good.

All the way home, I thought about having sex with Thomas. I disagreed with Denise. I didn't think he was using me. I thought he was making a fair trade. Plus, I missed him. I wanted to be his girlfriend again.

After getting off the bus, I went to Melina's house. "Can I read my book for a while?" I asked.

"Sure," she said.

I followed her inside, noticing how skinny she always looked from behind. It was nice because for a couple of seconds, I could pretend she wasn't pregnant.

In the living room, Melina sat down on the couch beside a ball of yellow yarn and a tiny sweater, stuck on knitting needles. "That looks like doll clothes," I said.

"Yup," she said.

"Maybe when your baby gets older, you could give her those clothes for her dolls."

Melina shrugged. "If she plays with them."

My book was on the coffee table, where I'd left it last time. I wondered if Melina and Gil ever had company over, and if they ever wondered what it was doing there. "Shouldn't you keep this someplace else?" I asked, reaching for it.

Melina looked up from her knitting. "Why?"

"I don't know."

"There's nothing wrong with that book," she said. "I'm happy for anyone who comes into my house to see it."

She went back to her knitting, and I looked around for a place to sit. There was a chair, but I decided to take the floor. I wanted to be far enough away from Melina that she couldn't see what I was reading. Plus, I liked being lower than her. It made me feel young.

The book said that if I decided to have sex, I could get a lot of diseases, and that I needed to use a condom. It said that the part of me where the orgasms came from would feel a vibration when Thomas's penis was inside me. There was a section, too, where it said that virginity was seen as something that made a girl pure, but that really, a girl could do whatever she wanted and that she wasn't anyone's property. In a way I liked that, but in a way I thought it seemed very sad. Most of the time, I really wanted to belong to somebody.

"Jasira," Melina said.

I looked up. "Yes?"

"I have something for you."

"What?"

"Hold on a sec." She set her knitting down on the couch and went into the kitchen. When she came back, she handed me a key. "Here."

"What's it for?" I asked.

"My house. This way, if you ever needed to come over here, at any time, for any reason, you can just let yourself in."

"Really?" I said.

"Yes. And you don't even have to tell me why. You can just come over, watch TV, read your book—whatever."

"What if you're not home and it's just Gil?" I asked.

"It doesn't matter," she said. "He knows I'm giving you a key and that you might use it."

I thought about walking into Melina's house with only Gil there and how I wouldn't know what to say. It would be embarrassing. "Well," I said, "thank you."

"You're welcome," she said, sitting back down on the couch.

"I probably won't need it," I said.

She picked up her knitting. "You never know."

I tried to start reading again, but I couldn't pay attention. I kept thinking about coming into Melina's house and never leaving.

That night before bed, I told Daddy I was taking a shower, but really I shaved my pubic hair. I used one of the razors Thomas had given me, and I did it just like he liked, with the thin strip down the middle. When I was finished, I collected all the black hairs from the drain, wrapped them in a piece of toilet paper, and threw them away.

In the morning when I woke up, I dressed in my nicest bra and underwear. For the first time, I noticed that they didn't match. The bra was one of the gray ones Daddy had bought me, and the underwear was white cotton. I put my jeans and sweater on, then took my backpack in the bathroom and slipped Mr. Vuoso's condom in the small zip pocket.

When I got to school, Denise was waiting for me at my locker. "You're not going to do it, are you?" she said.

"Yes," I said. "I am."

"But why?"

"Virginity doesn't make me pure," I said.

"What?"

"I'm not anyone's property."

"I never said you were," she said. "I just don't think it's fair for Thomas to make you trade your virginity for his forgiveness."

"It's not like that," I said.

"Then what's it like?"

"I already told you," I said. "I want to have sex with Thomas. If it also helps him to forgive me, then that's good, not bad."

"This is stupid," Denise said. "I hate that I know anything about this." She walked away, and I watched the back of her hair bounce from how heavy she was stepping.

At lunch, Thomas wanted to know if I had remembered the condom, and I said I had. "Just one?" he asked, and I nodded.

After school, I walked past my bus and met Thomas in front of his. We got on together and took a seat toward the back. He held my hand all the way, like he used to in the halls at school. Every once in a while he would lean over and whisper in my ear, "I'm going to have sex with you." I wasn't sure what to say back to him, so I just nodded.

When we got to Thomas's house, he reached inside his shirt for a key he wore on a chain around his neck. He didn't take the chain off, just lowered his neck to the level of the doorknob and leaned forward a little until the key reached the lock.

The first thing I noticed when we got inside was how much bigger the living room looked without the Christmas tree. There was still a pine smell in the air, though. Thomas set the mail he'd collected from outside on a table beside the door. "Do you want something to eat first?" he asked.

"Okay," I said. I was a little nervous.

I followed him into the kitchen, with its clean counters and dirty breakfast dishes in the sink. Daddy always said we could never, ever leave dishes in the sink or the roaches would come, but I didn't see any bugs at Thomas's.

"What do you want?" he asked, opening the fridge and leaning slightly into it.

I pulled out a chair at the table and sat down. "What are you going to have?" I asked.

He shrugged. "I'm not really hungry." Then he knelt down and opened the crisper. "How about an apple?"

"Sure."

He got two of them and bit into his without washing it. I did the same, even though Daddy had always warned me about pesticides on fruits and vegetables.

"I'm getting really turned on," Thomas said after a few bites.

"You are?"

He got up from his chair and came and stood in front of me. He took my hand and put it on his pants. "See?"

I nodded, feeling his erection.

"Are you ready?" he asked.

"Can't I finish my apple?"

"Sure," he said, and he went back to his seat.

Thomas finished his apple first and ate the core and the seeds, too. It was like Daddy with his chicken bones. "Why do you eat the core?" I asked.

"It's just roughage."

"You want mine?" I said, offering it to him. Daddy liked me to pass him my chicken bones when I was done so he could crunch on the cartilage.

"No thanks," Thomas said, but he did take my core and toss it in the trash under the sink. Then he came back and said, "Let's go to my room."

We walked up the stairs. I went first, and Thomas squeezed my butt while I climbed. On the way to his room, he stopped at a hall closet, opened it, and took out a towel. "We'll probably need this," he told me. "There's going to be blood."

When we got to his room, he said, "I'm taking my clothes off," and in a few seconds he was naked. He had nice broad shoulders, from swimming, I guessed, and his stomach had a couple of ripples in it. His penis stuck straight up, nearly hugging his stomach. He unfolded the towel and laid it out on the bed. Then he lay down on top of it. "Now you take your clothes off," he said.

It took me longer than it had taken Thomas. I had never played strip poker before, but I undressed as if that was what we were doing now. Where you only took off your bra and underwear at the very, very end.

"You shaved." Thomas said when I was finally naked.

I nodded.

"That looks good," he said. "C'mere."

I walked over to the side of the bed where he lay. He reached out and put a hand on the little bit of hair I had left. "Lie down," he said, scooting over to make room for me.

I lay down on the towel on my back. I was worried about how there wasn't going to be any blood at all, and what Thomas would think about it.

He rolled onto his side, then reached out and ran a hand over my stomach. "Your skin is soft," he said.

"Thank you."

He moved his hand up to my breasts and pinched one of my nipples. "Ow," I said.

"Really?" he said. "That doesn't feel good?"

"No."

He looked confused. "It's supposed to feel good."

"It doesn't," I told him.

He touched my nipple in a softer way and said, "How's that?"

"Better."

I wasn't sure what to do with my legs—whether I should open them or keep them closed. Soon, though, Thomas was moving in front of me, opening them himself. I thought we were going to do it then, but instead, he bent my legs at the knees then pushed them apart as wide as they would go. After he did that, he just stared. He stared and stared and stared. He wouldn't stop. Even though he wasn't touching me, it was exciting. It was like the girls in *Playboy,* having their picture taken by men photographers who wouldn't hurt them.

Soon, he put his head between my legs. He started to lick me there, or kiss me—I couldn't tell. It felt good, though. Warm. He did it for a long time before he finally pulled his head up and said, "I think you're ready."

"Okay," I said.

"Where's the rubber?"

"In my pocket."

He reached for my jeans, which I had hung over his desk chair, and took the foil packet out. I watched him tear it open and roll the condom on. It looked a little tight. "These are for guys with little dicks," Thomas said.

I wondered about Mr. Vuoso then, if he had a little dick. "Does it hurt?" I asked Thomas.

"It's okay," he said. "Don't worry about it."

I had closed my legs while he put the condom on, and now he opened them again. He lay down between them, this time with his face up by mine. I could smell myself around his mouth. The smell that was on my hands every time I had an orgasm alone.

"Listen," Thomas said, "I promise to be careful. I won't hurt you."

"I know," I said.

"Just tell me if you want me to stop and I will."

"But then you'll think I'm still a racist."

"What?" he said.

"You said if I had sex with you, I would impress you and you wouldn't think I was a racist anymore."

This seemed to bother him. "Forget about that, would you?"

"All right," I said.

He reached for his penis then and started to put it inside me. "Just try to relax," he said.

"Okay."

He pushed a little harder now. "It'll only hurt for a few seconds."

I nodded. It was true. It did hurt. Not from anything tearing, like with Mr. Vuoso, but from the feeling that there wasn't enough room. But Thomas kept pushing anyway. "Oh my God," he whispered.

"What?" I whispered back.

"Nothing," he said. "It just feels so good."

"Oh."

"I'm sorry if it hurts," he said.

"It's okay."

"The first time is always painful for girls."

"Yes," I said.

He had an orgasm pretty quickly after that. I wasn't exactly sure what I was supposed to do to have one myself, so I just lay there. When he was finished, he rolled off of me and onto his side of the bed. We lay there for a long time, not talking. Finally he looked over at me and said, "Is there a lot of blood?"

I rolled to one side of the towel so he could see. There was no blood.

"Where is it?" he asked.

"I don't know," I said. "Maybe some girls don't have it."

He was quiet for a minute, then said, "It *was* painful, right?"

"Yes," I said.

"You just didn't look like it was bothering you that much."

"It was."

"I mean, it's not like I have a small dick or anything."

"No," I said, "you don't."

"Huh."

"Maybe you were just really careful," I said.

"I guess."

"Anyway," I said, "I'm glad it wasn't that bad."

"Yeah," Thomas said, "that's good."

"So you don't think I'm a racist now?" I asked him.

"Stop saying that," he said. "I already told you to forget about that."

"Sorry."

"It definitely should've hurt more," he said.

I didn't say anything.

"Why didn't it?" he asked. He rolled onto his side and looked at me. "Who'd you do it with before me?"

"No one."

"You never did it with anyone?"

"No."

"But what about the blood?"

"I don't know, Thomas." I got up off the bed and started to get dressed.

"I'm not going to be mad if you had sex with someone else," he said. "I'm just curious."

"I didn't," I said, pulling on my underwear.

"Was it back in Syracuse?"

"It was nowhere."

"Nothing popped," he said. "It's supposed to pop."

"Can you please call me a taxi?"

He sighed and went in the bathroom, the rubber hanging loosely off the end of his penis. When he came back, it was gone. After putting his clothes on, he walked out of the bedroom and thumped down the stairs. I followed him shortly afterward. He was standing at the kitchen counter, opening a jar of peanut butter. "The cab'll be here in fifteen minutes," he told me.

"Thanks," I said.

"Do you feel like a woman?"

"Uh-huh."

"I feel like a man," he said, spooning peanut butter into his mouth.

When the cab beeped, Thomas walked me outside and opened the car door. He gave the driver ten dollars and told him my address. After he shut the door, the driver kept looking back at me through his rearview mirror. He did this all the way home. He had dark brown eyes and hair the same color. I thought he was probably Mexican.

At first I tried to stare back at him, but then I started to feel bad and looked away. It seemed like he was mad at me even though he didn't know me. When we got to my house and I opened the door to get out, he said something in Spanish. I didn't know what it meant, except for one word: *negro*.

The Rock Wall

Peggy Munson

Stone

WE ARE LEANING AGAINST the rock wall by the high school where I have taken him because it's deserted. He has that board-splitting butch gaze. He's worn his letter jacket, the one he earned back in high school, and today he delicately wraps it around my shoulders and says, "Do you want to be my girl? Do you want me to be your Daddy boyfriend?" And I nod shyly and say, "Yeah, okay." He holds my hand and we walk.

This is how it begins. It begins with something made from stone.

The bed he has me in is firm. Daddy's calloused hands are hard. Daddy's face looks like it was chiseled off Mount Rushmore. The wind is parting the curtains the way he brushes my hair back from my eyes. He gets serious. "Do you want to play a game, little girl?" he asks me. I know Daddy's games: rock beats scissors, scissors beat paper, paper beats rock. Hands equal power. Sometimes I am a paper doll and my clothes fold on with paper tabs, and Daddy undresses me absently, like he's opening mail. Sometimes I am a stone tablet, the stone on which commandments are carved. Sometimes, my legs are safety scissors, lying like dull blades, waiting to be crushed by rock. And Daddy spreads them open and they pull reflexively shut. He kisses to relax me. He curls his hand into a fist, into a stone. He slides that power into me. This simple game of hands.

But this is not just a game, Daddy-Girl. This is not just a game, Paper-Scissors-Rock. These are the scissors that cut up paper guises. This is the crane that breaks buildings. This is the fist that destroys orderly origami. This is the red paper of my cunt unfolding. This is me coming. This is how real. "Take it, bitch," says Daddy's voice into my ear. "Be a good girl. Take my fist." This is me pressed against surfaces. This is the stone that does not acquiesce. This is the statue becoming a Girl.

Quarry

SOME DAYS, I HATE everything about Daddy. I hate how orphaned I feel when Daddy goes to work. I hate how Daddy can choose the simplest onomatopoeia and roll it off the tongue so that *cock* sounds as hard as it is. How I sit all day with that word jammed in my head, cock, Daddy's cock, Daddy's hard cock, spreading out with acres of modifiers, until it becomes Daddy's hard cock that isn't fucking me. I hate it that I am so Electra. I hate it that Freud is on my shoulder and that he told me so. I hate it that I need a Daddy. I hate it that words never add up to cocks.

I lie on my back all day waiting and watching TV. I like watching teenage rock stars almost as much as anorexic figure skaters. I used to read about anorexia and about gymnasts and I would think about their discipline when the dentist was drilling pain into my smile. And I would read about how the girls didn't want to grow up and I would walk around for days with the pain in my smile and it was such good pain. And with my fading numb lip I thought of how benevolent the dentist was when he told me I was brave, and such a good girl. I hate Daddy for not being a dentist. I watch the Britney Spears video where she sings "Hit me baby, one more time" and dances around in a Catholic-schoolgirl outfit. I want to pull up my pleated skirt and show Daddy that we can end biblical racism right here, because the devil is made of white cotton. That's what little girls are made of. This exquisite, pretty rage.

I go to therapy and I want to talk about Daddy, but I don't even want to get into it with my shrink. I can't explain how my girlfriend is a boyfriend who makes me call him Daddy. Sometimes when my shrink listens to me talk, he thinks about other things. I can see the ViewMaster clicking in front of his eyes. Sometimes he thinks about what I would look like naked, and how he finds the professional boundary titillating. I sit in the waiting room and think about Daddy's cock and my pussy is all wet and I decide to go wipe myself before going into therapy but the bathroom lock has been ripped off the wall. My shrink might walk in on me, or smell me. He might see what a bad girl I really am. I return to the waiting room, still wet.

I don't talk about Daddy's cock, but every word I say in therapy sounds like cock and I know my shrink can see right through me. I know he has linguistic X-ray vision and that he knows I am really saying cock, cock, cock and he wants me to sit on his lap but I am thinking about Daddy. How I want the day to go faster so that Daddy will get home from work. My shrink tells me to have a good week, but he is really saying cock. The double doors shut behind me, cock, cock. And far away somewhere, in San Francisco, lesbians are pouring silicone into dildo molds and not thinking cock at all. Happily distracted, they are chattering and squeezing cock after cock out of molds and thinking business. I hate Daddy for thinking business. I wish he would think about my pleasure.

I hate how without Daddy I am a book with one bookend, so I just fall and my words get crushed. I hate it how Daddy is a petty thief. Because if he steals what's petty, then what am I when he takes me? I hate how Daddy makes me sputter inarticulate phrases so that I choke out sounds that have nothing to do with theory. I hate how Daddy makes me write him stories, because I cannot sculpt a sentence out of cock. I hate it how that word becomes so eloquent inside of me, pushing through me and out of my mouth.

I hate how Daddy's cock knows the way to hidden quarries, the watery places that were mined. How Daddy sees the drunken dives that kill sixteen, euphoric girls kissed to epiphanies on their mossy knees. Sophomoric girls getting their nipples touched on their mossy knees. And the skin scraped against sharp things, and the rustle of cops approaching, and the second before the kids run, and the hastily abandoned trunks. How he knows what to do about each truncated fuck. Of each lifetime. Daddy takes care of things.

I hate it how Daddy makes me need his cock. Because then I am a place that once held diamonds, sitting home yearning for him, waiting for a girl's new best friend. Because then I am always too ready for him. So hungry every time his key turns in the lock. So hungry for that handcuff sound of his key in the lock. So hungry for that four o'clock, drowsy, sharp sound. I hate it how Daddy walks in and feels me to see if

I'm wet, and wonders what I anticipate, and then ignores me while removing his jacket. I hate it how those fingers on my pussy make me whimper like a little dog.

I hate how seconds turn to hours before Daddy leads me into the bedroom, and his belt buckle glints like it's submerged. How sweetly Daddy takes my hand and says, "Baby girl," and then pulls me to his denim lap. And how the things to be filled must be emptied, must be stripped. Daddy grips me and undoes me and lowers me to the bed. And I shiver because I need it. I give when Daddy pushes. Daddy pulls on my hair.

I hate how good and raw he strips me. How good it feels to be this bare.

The Rock Wall

EVERY NIGHT I GO back to the rock wall. It is covered in moss and the rain is drizzling and I search for grips. I am ripped and mud-covered and hungry. My grasp is tenuous, and my fingers are slipping. I'm tired of being a wide-eyed waif always scrambling over walls where there are more walls and more slippery rocks and more places to bruise and nowhere good to land. The rain is so irritating, the noise, the noise that's always a soft fuck when you need it hard, that's always a drizzle when you need a thunderstorm to break the air and shock the animals so they run frenzied—wild—crazed—scattershot—into spaces they never dared to go. The wall is unforgiving and I begin to slide. I land on my knees in a muddy pool and my dress is ripped and I'm old and there is no Daddy. The landing is soft. Nothing impaling me. Nothing tearing me and ripping me. No fairy-tale wolves, though I always thought they would be there, their dripping incisors and hunger, waiting for me to fall. There is nothing to wound me, no imaginary battles to reenact. No hole in the earth to open up and swallow me there.

Maybe I am already in the hole. Maybe I am the hole. This dark and damp place that feels like the inside and not the outside and my dress is ripped and I start crying. I hold my face in my muddy hands and my tears clean my hands and my hands smear the mud into my tears. Everything undoes everything. Nothing undoes me. Nothing does me.

Then suddenly, so dark and quick and I can't even scream, something reaches from behind and grabs me with its arm under my throat and drags me backward, and drags me while whispering things. "Daddy's here now, little girl. Daddy's got you." He's not comforting and not scary, just unsettling, just the kind of thing that makes me all animal, all animal splitting from the pack the way the wolves want it to be, all animal-confused and asking for it. I try to flail around and pull away. I try to break the grip, the wall is waiting. Doesn't Daddy understand the wall? How I need to climb it always, climb and climb and climb it? Daddy pulls my muddy body so that I'm sitting on his lap and I still can't see him but I feel his hard cock. "Daddy's got you," he says again.

I want not to want it. I want not to feel how my thighs are smeared with mud and my pussy feels smeared, but it's not, it's just mine. There is nothing between my pussy and his cock but a thin layer of fabric. And he is rubbing his cock against my panties and I squirm. I want to squirm away, but he rubs me so hard and I start to want to push down onto him. I start to push down as if the fabric will just dissolve. He pushes the tip of his cock against the fabric, and the fabric goes into me. And the elastic of my panties follows the fabric and pulls me, pulls my legs, into me. I'm going to fall into me. I have to fight. I try to struggle, but Daddy holds me against his moving, pushing cock.

"Daddy, wait," I say, but I keep pushing to make the fabric go away, and I want him. "Daddy, stop!" Daddy grabs under my arms and pushes me slowly forward so that my face is down but he pulls my hips back.

"Daddy wants you to take his cock," he says. "All of it. Can you be a good girl and do that?"

I want to taste the mud. The mud smells oddly like Daddy. Daddy slides my panties down my legs so I'm just there in the night air and my pussy and my ass are high up behind me. "Daddy, no," I say, but this time weakly. This time it's all reverse psychology. This time I'm not sure at all.

"Daddy can just leave you here in the mud if you want, little girl. Is that what you want?" He snarls this.

"Daddy . . . no," I say. "No, please, no."

"Beg for what you want."

"I want you, Daddy."

"Beg me."

"I want Daddy. I want Daddy to fill me up."

"Daddy's very hard for you. Is this what you want?" He slides the tip of his cock into me. "Is this what you want?"

"Yes, Daddy. *Please*."

"Beg me."

"I want you inside of me. Please."

"What?"

"I want you, Daddy, please." I say it with the urgency I use to climb the walls.

Daddy starts sliding his cock into my pussy, and I push back onto him, but he holds my hips and makes me wait for him. And the rain gets harder, the drops batter my cheeks, the rain turns everything to mud while Daddy fills me up and my hands slide in front of me for something to hang on to, but there is nothing, nothing there, nothing but my hips pushing back and Daddy's hard cock and my need. And I need to hold something. I need to hold on because I am used to holding and I need the wall, and Daddy pushes in so hard and I want to scream, it feels so good. My hands are fumbling forward for any handhold, but there is nothing there . . .

"Daddy's got you, baby," he says soothingly. "Fall back into me."

Gravel

THE GRAVEL REMINDS ME of old roads cutting between fields to deserted places, the way it clatters and then hums, keeps me unsteady. Once I cut my chin on the gravel in the Dairy Queen parking lot, holding on to my Dilly Bar all the way to the ground. I remember losing my footing, bleeding on the car upholstery, wondering if kids found reddened chunks of rock where I landed. I think about all of these things now, now that I'm old being young, riding next to Daddy in the truck. The big wheels slide over the gravel. The dark moves from beneath trees to the sides of buildings. We are near a warehouse with broken windows. And the gravel is not the kind you buy in bags at Home Depot, but stained. I get out and stumble like a tipsy slut. I straighten my skirt and start to walk, but Daddy is there already, and he grabs my arm. "No," he says, pointing. "You little whore. Right here."

I look down distastefully, then up at Daddy. "Here?" I sneer. I can't believe he means it. The rock is soaked dark with things dying, bled oil and shoe rubber. I look at him again, his stern expression, then kneel down. The rocks are sharp against my knees. Daddy gives a little push on my back so I fall forward and my palms slide through the rocks. Then, when I'm on all fours, he pulls up my skirt from behind, just flips the material so that it lands on my back and I feel the breeze trying to go into me. I've got no panties on.

"Such a pretty little ass," he says. "Untainted lily-white ass. Not dirty like the rest of you." The breeze seems to follow the current of his voice and rubs the goose bumps on my ass. "Are you afraid to have Daddy's big cock in your pretty ass?"

"Maybe," I say. I feel defiant. I feel the way the rocks are cutting me, and I don't move my hands.

Daddy's hands fondle my ass cheeks, spread them open, press against them so I slide forward more. He's so much stronger than I am. I let myself fall and feel the rocks against my cheek. I think of how I fell that time, when I was young, and tried to taste my blood. And how I always tried to taste my blood when I got cut. But what I liked to taste was not just mine, but also that which made me bleed. It was the thing that made the cut, the flavor mixed into the blood. It was the combination of the two, the grit that touched the cutter and the flesh. It was the generosity of both, and how my bleeding made the two combine. I think of all of this while Daddy moves his cock against the hole, and pushes hard because it's tight.

He pushes hard because it's tight, and pulls my hips against him. My face gets scraped against the gravel. My lip begins to bleed. I taste the blood and salt and earth and pain and fear and trampling. I taste the blood and all that has been done to it and lick and give it back to me. I give me back to me. And Daddy gives me, too.

"Who gives you what you need?" he asks. The natural light has fled. A streetlight shines behind his hair. I smell the tires. I smell the dew. I feel the walls that crumble into gravel. I feel the girls who must undo.

"Daddy," I say. He looks like a monument. "You do."

Best Friendster Date Ever

ALEXANDER CHEE

I N HIS PROFILE PICTURES, he looks like a dirty-minded angel, blond hair sticking up, electric blue eyes, and a pink mouth that pouted beautifully. He was biting his finger, teeth bared, in one. It reminded me of an incident a long time ago, a day when I ran into an old boyfriend's old trick with said boyfriend, and while we were talking the boyfriend turned his back on us. The trick smiled at me and slid a finger up the leg of the boyfriend's very short shorts, pushing in visibly past his ring. I could see the finger slow and then slip forward. When he pulled it out, he looked at me and ran it under his nose with a grin.

The old boyfriend whipped his head around, uncertain which of us had just defiled him there on the street. I was upset for a moment, but also completely turned on.

It was, after all, a championship piece of ass.

This boy, he reminded me of both of them that day.

I FOUND HIM ON Friendster, the giant electronic yearbook for the never-ending high school that is life in the United States. On the outside chance you've no idea what I'm talking about, you join the site, link your page to your friends' pages, and soon you can follow a network out to, in my case, 156,550 people.

I was living in Los Angeles in a sublet with friends in a four-thousand-square-foot, four-bedroom apartment, where we could be home and never see each other, in a building that looked so much like a New York building it was constantly used for location shots. In L.A., people took the Internet really seriously, and my first summer there was the first time

I was ever getting hit on over the Net. I decided to hit back. It hadn't been a very romantic summer. The best I'd done live and in person was get blind drunk on vodka and Red Bull at a West Hollywood bar, like a sorority girl, and I bought someone a rose off one of those people who wander through bars with buckets of roses. Said recipient was said to be charmed, a friend of friends, and represented as such on Friendster, with some fairly amazing naked pictures of himself on his Friendster page. My birthday was coming up, I was single again, and while it was too gruesome to contemplate writing to the man from my blackout, I began paging through the pages and pages of strangers with their brightly colored snapshots and their witty or not so witty profile one-liners, until I saw this one. I sent a very casual note and said something stupid and low-key, like, *This is just a fan letter to say, You're hot.*

A friend of mine has a theory about corny lines from guys. You see it in movies all the time, guys saying, *Hey baby, show me your tits,* or something really beautiful like that. And the girl gets all mad, etc. But we figured out the reason it doesn't work on girls is because guys like it. It works on *guys*.

Sure enough, the guy with the pout, the guy this story is about, wrote back. He was completely inappropriate: twelve years younger than me, just out of college in New York, but he was smart. A California Rimbaud, skinny and perhaps tall in the photos.

He ended up agreeing to meet me while I was celebrating my birthday at the Silverlake summer street fair. *Sounds like my kind of tragedy,* he said.

Fair enough, I thought.

We exchanged numbers for meeting up that weekend, but he became a little hard to find. We kept missing each other. By the time I met him I was annoyed by the seven calls exchanged, and no longer particularly interested. I found him across from an enormous inflatable ride, the kind kids get inside of and bounce around, a moonwalk.

In person, he looked like another kind of boy altogether. He was a little taller than me, probably about 6'1", and had glasses, and was dressed like the sort of boys I used to meet back in New York. From his appearance I was fairly sure there was an ex he wasn't over, that he read the *Economist,* and that he had intimacy issues, especially after I saw the rock-climbing shorts. I was about to give him the brush-off, but a flash of something in his eye caught me—a fishhook notion. And his skin was a miracle of smoothness. He had the kind of perfect, slightly golden skin of some blonds. It was a bit Nordic, but he looked like a child of Great Britain, the bastard of a Viking and the one the Viking found when he got off his Viking ship.

I had friends with me; he had friends with him. It was my birthday, after all. *Let's get a beer,* I said, and we walked. The street fair had seemed like a good idea in theory, but now that I was there I found the bands dull, the people uninteresting, and the goods for sale unappealing. It was like the ugly stepchild of a really cool street fair somewhere else in time and place, just not here. His friend group vanished, at which point he admitted one of them was an ex-boyfriend who wasn't over him (check, I thought). My friend group said they were going off to look for a present for me.

We were alone. The beer was almost good enough to stay.

We ran out of things to talk about fairly quickly. He mentioned a pilot show he was writing. I listened, the idea was pretty good. He seemed nervous and a bit abrupt.

My friends returned. With wicked smiles they tossed a paper bag onto the table.

The friends in question were my three roommates, and the subject of how I'd not gotten laid that summer had come up a few times. As had the last, most inappropriate relationship I'd just gotten out of. In a kind of emergency conference, we'd decided *appropriate* would have meant twenty-eight or older, and this date didn't qualify on that score. Wouldn't for about three years. I pulled out the contents.

Lube, single-portion size. Rubbers. Restraints, made of nylon, clasps from a backpack, and Velcro. A few porno mags. Absurd enough to make it sexy. I laughed. It was a fairly direct editorial comment.

Thanks, I said.

The roommates laughed and removed themselves to another table.

The date reached over for the restraints. He tentatively put one on his wrist. *Hunh,* he said. He seemed blankly quizzical, and I wondered what was going through his mind. I didn't know him well enough to know if he was hard to read.

All I was thinking was, *The real bottoms, you don't actually have to tie them up.*

I looked at the Velcro snaps and plastic hooks. Perfect for hiking and tying up vegetarians. Waterproof.

THE NIGHT DRAGGED AFTER that. The fair mercifully came to an end, a nearby party was suggested, and we went. There was a liquor store stop, where it seemed one of my roommates was about to make a move on my date. I let it go, wanting to see how it would play out in the gray-white light of the store. There wasn't anything he wouldn't hit on if it was young and smooth, and he could likely sense I was almost abject about the state of the conversation. It wasn't that my date was stupid; we just were interested in very different things. And there were the climbing shorts.

When I really think about it, several things were in play. I was on a date I knew had no future. I had just gotten out of a relationship with a closeted man so frustratingly asexual in its nature, and so tortured, I was a bit like a man on a fast, who didn't know how to start eating again. I was uncertain, but the terms of things around me were not. At the party I watched the boy come in and out of view. I drank a bit, he got more interesting, but noticing this, and remembering the earlier disaster of the summer, I watched myself. He eventually vanished into a crowd of men doing blow in the other room, which wasn't even as interesting to me as a pizza. People were boring on drugs. At least in L.A.

And then when I least expected it, in the light of the garden, he sat down near me and we each smoked a cigarette, he offering that he didn't normally smoke. *Check,* I thought. *A copy of* The Economist, *climbing shorts, ex-boyfriend, in denial about smoking.*

If this wasn't boring enough, he was nervous again, or perhaps it was the blow. I had thought him indifferent to me by now, as I was to him. I think we both knew enough to know it wasn't a love match. He was sexy, and I was thinking right at that moment how in order to have sex with him I was probably going to have to endure weeks of dull conversations. I was probably going to have to know everything I didn't want to know about him before we got there. I dreaded the ex-boyfriend story.

I really wanted you to have a good impression of me, he said.

What are you talking about, I said.

Well, he said. *I just. I just did a bump.*

Hunh, I said. I shrugged.

I just . . . he said. *I do this.* And he made some kind of sound, like a child makes, and shrugged into himself. It was sweetly awkward.

What, I said. *Don't worry about it,* I said. *Whatever it is, just say it.*

You just got restraints for your birthday. Do you want to just go home and have a lot of sex?

I laughed. *Let's go,* I said.

As I said, only guys like lines like that.

THE FIRST PERSON I ever tied up was my old boyfriend from the beginning of this story, who asked for it. He was wanting me to be someone dirtier and more aggressive than I was then. He wanted me to be the person I felt myself to be in relationship now to my birthday date, who was about to be the second person I was going to tie up.

Twelve years had passed since that first time. The exact age difference between him and me.

My hideously large apartment's layout matters to the story. For this to really work you have to understand that my three roommates and I had taken rooms all on one side of our four-bedroom apartment, while on the other side off the kitchen were former servants' quarters: two smaller bedrooms that doubled as offices. We had a library, a dining room, a living room, a butler kitchen, and pantry. Each bedroom had walk-in closets, and the West Wing, as we jokingly called it, had its own bathroom. We could easily have had a guest there and not known. We usually never heard each other, even with our rooms, which were technically suites, I guess, right next to each other. It was an incredible apartment, and I don't know if I'll ever live in another as odd and amazing in sheer spectacle.

I showed him around. The roommates were still at the party. I took him into the West Wing last, and in the room at the end of the hall, which I used as an office, we realized the tour was over.

We stood for a moment in the dark room. A futon was on the right, a desk on the left, books stacked on the walls where bookshelves should be.

I understood something there in the dark: I realized he was waiting for me to take control. That there was someone each of us didn't normally give ourselves permission to *be.* And that here was where they'd meet.

Take off your clothes, I said.

He blinked and began immediately in a way that was touching, for how quickly it happened.

Turn around, I said. He had a slim body, angular but athletic, almost completely hairless. His skin glowed blue in the sodium-vapor light from outside the room.

I fastened restraints to his wrists behind his back and raised his arms lightly, to make sure they were loose enough to allow him to move. I turned him back around to face me.

His dick was already hard. I tapped it with my finger and watched it bounce. His breathing was already rapid, from the calm of a moment before.

Close your eyes, I said.

He did. He stood there, chest moving, eyes closed.

I'm not going to fuck you down in my bedroom, I said. *Just in case there's shouting.*

Okay, he said.

I turned and closed the door and went back to him. It was incredibly moving to see him like that. For all that the restraints were ridiculous, they did work. I stood close to him, close enough to feel the heat coming off him, and his breath. I leaned in and ran one fingernail across his nipple. He jumped and gave a huffing kind of cry, and I slid the nail down along his skin to just above his pubic hairline, where I pressed in again. *Hu-uh,* he let out. And then I pulled him in against me, reaching around to hold on where his wrists were joined. I hadn't taken off my clothes.

I'm not going to take off my clothes, I said. *At least, I don't think I'm going to. But I don't think that's what you get this time. This time, I'm not sure you even get to touch my dick. We'll see.*

Okay, he said.

I put my face near his, and ran the tip of my tongue gently along his lower lip. His mouth opened with another gasp. His tongue met mine, and I pulled the cool wetness of it into my mouth, sucking for a moment. I pulled back slightly so that just our mouths touched. He lunged forward to keep the contact.

I pulled back again and his mouth fishmouthed open. I spat into his open mouth. It was halfway down his throat before he knew. He gasped and gulped on it, and his dick banged up harder. He opened his eyes to catch his balance, and I said, *Eyes closed,* and knocked him backward onto the futon couch.

I pushed his mouth open and leaned down and licked the lower lip again. The magenta pout of him. I bit on it, lightly. It was the only part of me touching him. He was breathing hard still. I let the lip go, sat back, and from above let the spit drizzle out of my mouth, like a fishing line seen by the light of the streetlamp coming in. He gasped again, *hu-uh,* opened his mouth wider, and I just let it fall for a moment in a straight line, him gulping on it. Drinking me.

He was now completely fascinating. I leaned down and kissed him, and he reached back hungrily, noisy. *Uhmmm,* he hummed into my mouth. I sat back and opened a condom, pulled it over two of my fingers, lubed it. He opened his eyes.

I'm sorry, he said.

What, I said.

I'm not usually this turned on, he said.

He was apparently embarrassed of his emotions and responses. It made it fun to play him, then. *Can I have a drink of water,* he asked.

Sure, I said.

I went to the kitchen and looked at the lubed condom on my fingers. I filled a glass in the fridge dispenser and went back to the dark room.

Stand up, I said, as I entered, and he struggled to his feet. He looked expectantly at the glass of water. I held it waist high, so it wasn't too hard to stick his dick into it.

It was cold. He jumped in place. *Fuck,* he said. He almost lost his balance, and I steadied him as I thrust his dick deeper into water. He was panting again. I held the glass to his mouth, letting him drink from it. When he was done, I put it on the desk. I kissed him hard again, and as I did, reached underneath his balls and slid my finger back and forth gently across his hole, getting it slick. He was breathing as hard as a runner. I slid my wet hand over his dick, down the shaft, and over the knob of it, running the rubber on my fingers across the crown in circles before going back down the underside of the shaft and then continuing, under his balls and back toward his hole. I did this a few more times, luxuriating in the way he shook and shuddered and yelped. I kept him close, my teeth on his underlip, his breath fast against my cheek, and when I had established the back-and-forth rhythm, as I went back under his balls one more time, this time I pushed in.

Aaa-aa-aah. I let his lip go as his head flew back and I thrust inside him, his arms tight against the restraints. I slid out and felt him croon a little, disappointed. I made like I was headed back to his dick and instead returned inside him. He was slick and wet there, and it went easily.

He crooned again. It was like feeding him, sticking something in there.

I got him on his back on the futon couch, his legs in the air, arms behind his back, and as I kissed him I worked his hole open with those two fingers, gently, feeling it push back against me like his mouth did as I kissed him and gently fucked his mouth with my tongue.

His face was wet and his eyes drunk on just plain lust. His face was flushed, I could tell, even in just the blue lights from the street, and his skin had the sheen of his exertions on it. He was the most beautiful thing I'd seen right then, arms behind his back and yet also out of control. I tapped the crown of his dick lightly and he winced, his pouty mouth closing slightly and then hanging open again, his lips the larger from the bruising kisses. We'd been at it now for a while.

It would ruin it if he saw anything coming. I unzipped and his eyes focused. I drew out my dick.

I want to see it, he said.

No, I said. *You don't get to.*

I drew the condom on and lubed it and covered his eyes with my hands, tipping his head back and up as I pushed inside him. The warmth of him slid over my dick, and as I slid down into him I spat hard again into his open mouth and he gasped. He swallowed and made a kind of low hum as I slid in. I slapped his face with my other hand, his legs falling down around my thighs. *Unnh,* he said. *Hunnnh,* I slid my stubble down over his right nipple as I shoved even farther, rubbing against it, and his head slammed back and down. *Oh fuck,* he said. I grabbed his dick, letting the crown circle freehand in my palm as I fucked him and ground on that nipple and he used his head to hold himself in place, pushing it into the couch. *Fuck, fuck, fuck,* he said. And then *Hrnnnh,* like he was in a hard cry, his arms thrashing underneath me, stuck under the weight of him and lashed together by the stupid Velcro and nylon, somehow still holding. *Ah fuck,* he said. *Ahhh.*

I sat back and pulled him onto the floor, onto me, turning him on my dick so that he lay full on top of me, unsnapped his arms into a new position and snapped them back again so they were over his head, arms straight. He lay naked and wet, me underneath him in my T-shirt and jeans still, my fly open, and I thrust up into him. He was groaning now, his hard dick bobbing on his stomach as I shook him. I bent my knees, forcing him into place so his legs fell out to the side in a V. His head tipped back beside mine and he reached for me to kiss him and I spat again, this time not caring if I hit his mouth, and it ran wet down our faces so he could slide his mouth over to mine as I ground into him and he ground back.

I made him cum with me inside him, which he hated once he was done. And so I pulled out and put him over my knee, his cum seeping down my jeans leg. I spanked him and when I started to get bored I pushed him over onto the bed and stared down at him. He stared back.

It had to be ugly like this. I wondered if he'd ever let me do this again. Whenever I treated people like this, they loved it but hated me for doing it and also for knowing it about them afterward, and it wasn't always true there'd be a next time. There was the rich shame and defiance, and it wasn't clear which would win.

I shucked off the rubber and beat off over him like that, letting it splash down his leg when I came. The spell was off after that. I bent down, gave him one last short kiss, but I could tell we both didn't care by now. By now it was just a little more than boys done wrestling. I wondered if he'd mind sleeping in there.

Do you mind if I sleep in here, he said.

I was going to ask you to, I said.

Whatever we were to each other, it was mutual from start to finish, I saw then. We'd been at this for four hours. When I got to the kitchen, I was shaking my head with a smile, headed through the vast apartment to my own cool clean bed.

THE NEXT MORNING I went in to find him awake. I sat down on the bed. He seemed gently friendly. He'd been reading something.

We went to Starbucks, had coffee, talked a bit. He was meeting friends to continue drinking, asked me to maybe come along. *No,* I said.

I get so crazy, he said. *The first time I did that I went home with some guy who had me in a sling.*

Do you like it, I said.

I do, he said. *But I don't let myself, most of the time. None of my friends know me like this. I freak out, I can't admit it, or something. I run away.*

It was my second time tying someone up, I said, *and I want to do it again.*

The Starbucks we were at was in a corporate center in Koreatown. We sat outside, the traffic on Wilshire on our right, the corporate park in front of us. It was like we'd wandered into the set of *Office Space* or something and made what he was saying more surreal, like the sunlight hitting his blue eyes.

I knew we would probably try to have sex again, as it had been that good, and that we also probably wouldn't. When someone says *I freak out and run away,* what they are saying is *I am freaking out and about to run away.* Life is easier when you take people at their word.

Also, it's good to be wary of people who are afraid of what they desire.

See you later, I said.

I WENT IN TO DO the sheets. He had left his pot pipe and an empty ciga- rette box. As I took the sheets off the futon I noticed the stains from the lube and cum. I saw broken wood strings hanging down from under the couch's front edge.

We'd broken the two-by-four that ran the length of the frame.

The memories and images of that night strobed through my days for a week. I'd be somewhere and see the blue silk image of him, bound and heaving, hard, sobbing. I sent him an e-mail, he sent one back, we ran into each other at the gym. It was hard to speak. We were listless now, like prisoners who'd used each other to break out, and now that we were in the wide world, there was nothing more to say to each other. I knew who I was now, or what I was. I suspected he did too.

At the party that night, after he pulled his face off a plate of blow, I remember how he said to me *This is the best Friendster date ever.* I'd grinned at him then and thought, *Well, maybe for you.* But, yeah. It was.

from Envy

KATHRYN HARRISON

W ILL BUZZES IN HIS three o'clock—that is, he buzzes in someone he thinks is his three o'clock, but, as announced by her
distinctive, staccato ascension of the uncarpeted stairs, it's the girl.
It's been three weeks since he terminated treatment with her—since
he told her what she has not accepted. Instead she's hounded him
with messages and voice mails, some polite and beseeching, a few
bordering on abusive. She's even called his home number, spoken
with Carole.

"You have to leave," he tells her now. "I'm expecting a patient."

"I have to talk to you."

Will inhales deeply, lets the breath out through his nose. "My— we
don't have anything to talk about. We are no longer engaged in—"

"No," she says. "You don't understand. I need to talk to you.
Please." The look on her face is one of what appears to be genuine desperation.

"Have you contacted either of the people to whom I referred you?"
he asks her.

"No. No, I—"

The buzzer buzzes, and Will pushes a button by the light switch to
release the lock downstairs. "My three o'clock," he says. "You have to
leave now."

"I'll wait," she says.

His patient starts up the stairs; the girl starts down; as they pass each
other, the patient averts her face in the usual manner of an encounter at
the analyst's office: deferential, blind. As Will closes the door behind

her, he sees that the girl is sitting on the landing downstairs, rummaging in her backpack.

When he looks out his door at 3:50, she's reading.

"What can I say to help you understand that we cannot continue to work together?" he says as soon as his patient has left the building.

"Please," she says, coming up the stairs. "Give me another chance. I don't know why I pulled that shit. I know I behaved badly, but I promise nothing like that will ever happen again." Will watches her face as she speaks. Either she's sincere, or she's an actress with genuine talent.

"It's best—best for you—to begin over again, with someone else."

"I don't want to! I can't. I swear I can't Please!" Will doesn't answer. If only she'd stop saying "please" like that. Mitch could always get him to do anything if he just said "please" enough times. Will's impulse—his determination—was always to even things up between the two of them.

"Please forgive me," the girl says, striking at this vulnerability with the accuracy of a mind reader. "We can start over."

"Our professional relationship has been compromised. Compromised in a way that would lessen my effectiveness in treating you."

"But why can't what happened be part of what we talk about? Wouldn't that be, like, useful? Useful in figuring out what makes me do these things?" Will doesn't answer her, and she throws herself onto the couch. She's wearing a pair of trousers that are, he guesses, a kind of commentary, or protest. Made of camouflage material in which the army greens and browns have been replaced with bright pinks and purples, their legs are absurdly wide, each one sewn from enough fabric to upholster a chair. "I don't get why you're making such a big deal about this," she says. "You act like I stabbed you or something."

Sitting cross-legged, the girl takes off her pullover the way a little boy might, by grabbing the scruff of its neck and dragging it over her head, making her hair crackle with static. Underneath is one of those sleeveless undershirts commonly known as wife beaters. Her bra, visible through the sheer fabric, looks like the top of a bikini; it's striped blue and white. She reclines, arms behind her head.

"Please do not lie on my couch."

"Because I'm not your patient?"

"Yes." Will turns his back on her, and on the little surge of panic he feels, dismissing it as claustrophobia. Across from his office, someone turns on the light in the dance studio. A few students enter and begin stretching. Will twists the Lucite wand that adjusts the blind; he turns around to tell her once and for all to go, good-bye, good luck, but what he sees stuns him into silence.

"Put on your clothes," he says as soon as he's recovered his voice. "Put them on now."

"No."

"Yes," he says. "Or you'll have to leave without them."

"What are you going to do? Drag me out into the street? That doesn't seem like such a great idea, actually. I mean, all I have to do is start kicking and screaming, right?"

Will opens his mouth, then closes it. If she screams, if she accuses him of assaulting her, then what? He has no witness to prove otherwise. She takes a compact from her backpack and consults the mirror within, considering her reflection. Paralyzed, he watches her. She's still young enough to be caught instantly by her own reflection, caught and consumed. She stares into her own face, licking her finger and rubbing at the makeup smudged under one eye; and Will, as is his tendency when threatened, responds by hyperanalyzing the situation, sure that in the moment she's forgotten him.

Wouldn't that be the appeal of an affair with a much younger woman? All those times she didn't understand or even notice you, and the attendant freedom from having to work constantly at interpreting pregnant silences and meaningful glances, all the weary, oft-traversed terrain of marital responsibility. And it's not just Will. It's the same with every patient, every marriage: an unlimited number of dialectics leading to the same disagreement. To each couple its own insoluble, often inarticulable conflict. If you discounted lust—which would, of course, be a mistake—the key motivation for infidelity might be the chance to bed a woman who didn't engage reflexively in the fight you'd fought so often before, the Rome of every conjugal union, the one to which all quarrels lead. . . .

WILL LOOKS AT THE girl looking at herself. She may not be drop-dead beautiful, but her body comes close, very close. She snaps her compact closed and tosses it onto the pile of her discarded clothes. "What's the matter, Dr. Moreland?" she says, taking a step toward him. "Pussy got your tongue?" She's close enough now to put her hand on his crotch. "See?" she says. "I told you you liked me." Deftly, she unbuckles his belt, unbuttons and unzips his fly, and puts her hand against his cock, feeling how hard he is through his shorts before pushing and pulling his trousers down, underwear along with them.

Will stares at her breasts, at what strikes him as their almost impertinent defiance of gravity, the delicate color of her small, flattish nipples. Carole, by contrast, has big, ruddy nipples, sexy but in a very different way. She's nursed two children for a total of more than four years and in doing so reformed her breasts into flesh that is deferential, not pert but self-sacrificing, at once modest and unself-conscious. They're mammalian, he supposes; their attraction rests in the fulfillment of nature rather than in the conceit of beauty for a beholder. Although, in the end, isn't it just that the girl is young, Carole not so young, a simple animal fact that he has convoluted into a thesis?

Her legs look even longer unclothed, and her pubic hair has been barbered into a narrow strip. "Brazilian," she says, seeing him look there.

"Brazilian?" he repeats. He hears his own voice as if it's been brought to him long-distance, in the days before fiber-optic cable, delayed as if it were an echo.

"Yeah. A Brazilian wax. You know? As in J sisters?"

"Jay sisters?" Maybe he really can't talk anymore, only parrot one or two words.

"Yeah. J as in the letter *J*. I thought everyone in this city knew about the J sisters. Where the bikini wax was, like, invented? At least for Norteamericanas." She lifts an eyebrow at him.

"Skip Brazil," she says when he still hasn't replied or moved so much as an inch from where he's standing. "Think of it as your landing strip." She sits and pats the couch next to her. "Why don't you take a step closer because . . . well, your cock's big, but no one's is that big." She takes him in her hand, guiding him forward. "Cold hands, warm mouth," she says, and then he's on his back on the narrow, black leather couch not even seeing the ceiling, not even seeing, eyes open and blind because of what she's doing. Between his legs, with her teeth, gently—gently enough—she's nibbling along the shaft of his cock, her tongue hot and slippery and all over the glans, the root of it in a tightening ring of thumb and forefinger and—"You just have to . . . you have to stop," he forces himself to say. "Just—stop. Please. Don't move your mouth. I . . ." But instead, she picks up speed, tightens her grip, and he comes fast, feeling it up to his neck, those last strokes or licks or sucks or whatever it is that she did, every atom of him concentrated into one accelerating charge. "Oh God, oh Jesus, oh—" and Christ, she doesn't break stride, doesn't even flinch. She's a swallower, heaven help him. Different, not better, just different from Carole. His wife's less predatory, but that's just a—

"Okay, now we fuck." Will picks his head up to look at her, back at work lest he get soft. She's keeping the blood in his cock with some twenty-first-century tantric vacuum trick. Not a little-girl pout, after all, he—

"Check," he pants. "Check—"

"Check what?" She sounds irritated by the interruption.

"Door."

She stands to let him up from the couch. "I think we better get down on the rug, anyway," she says after he's ascertained that the door is, in fact, locked. She points at the couch. "Too narrow," she says.

As soon as he lowers himself to the floor she takes his cock in one hand and plants the other in the middle of his chest and pushes until he's flat on his back. Less than a minute in her feverish mouth and he's hard again, as hard as before. She straddles him and starts moving, back arched so that her pelvis is tilted into the shaft of his cock and going at it hard enough to make him ache. "Do I have the right tempo?" she asks, clearly uninterested in his response to a question that's just knee-jerk sexual etiquette, no more personal than saying bless you to a sneezing stranger. He watches her face, her eyes open and glassy, preoccupied by what she's doing to herself with her fingers.

She comes again and then once more, each time arching her back to pump him until it hurts. He searches her eyes, finds them empty. Not that he'd expected affection, or any other emotion, just some indication of pleasure. But she looks businesslike.

"Your turn on top," she says, "but only if you promise not to come. Not yet. I might want to go back to this. And I don't want to skip all fours." She lies on her back and slowly guides him into her. She's unbelievably wet and tight and impossibly, almost unnaturally, slippery.

"Astroglide," she says, reading his expression.

He stops moving. "What?"

"I used some—a lot, actually—while your attention was, let's say, elsewhere."

"A lot of what?"

"Astroglide?" She lifts the last syllable into a question: You're so last season / last year / last century that you've never heard of Astroglide?

"What's that?"

"Some super-poly something. Poly-propyl-glycerin-glyco-blah-blah-whatever. Lubricant, but different from that old K-Y junk. This stuff's for real. Better than spit. A triumph of science over nature."

What happens when she's through with him? Will she move on, according to habit? That's what he's counting on, he realizes, that's what he's decided will happen. Having collected him, she'll lose him, lose interest, refocus on the next in her series of old guys. Maybe she'll leave afterward, and tell no one, and he'll get away with it, this transgression that's been forced upon him. Hasn't it? Already he's trying to figure out just how culpable he is in this. Whether he communicated his lust to her unconsciously but still intentionally. Whether the fact that he's as turned on as he is makes him guilty, no matter who initiated the sex. Whether his fear of being exposed and accused of attempted rape makes him dishonorable. Well, of course it does. She reaches over her head to where a little bottle with a white cap is lying on her camouflage pants, almost invisible.

"Check this out," she says. Before he can protest she has a finger in his asshole, all the way in. "Hey, relax, will you? This'll be good. I know how to make this feel good."

Will closes his eyes. The only other finger that's ever been up there is the internist's, a quick rubber-glove (and, yes, K-Y) check of his prostate, neither man looking at each other and neither, he's quite sure, with an erection. But with her space-age product she's doing some kind of inside-out hand job—finger job, he guesses he'd have to call it—and it's . . . it is good. It's really, really good.

"Oh no," she says, "no no," just as he's wondering shamefully (meaning he's ashamed but he's still thinking what he's thinking) how suspicious Carole would be were he to introduce her to a little bottle of—

Out goes the finger, and she pulls away on the back stroke, rolls right out from under him. "Getting a little too close to the finale." Will doesn't answer, jerked back from the precipice so suddenly that he's dizzy with teased lust; but it doesn't matter, she goes on talking regardless of his regression into a state of mute passivity.

"Here's the deal," she says. "First you go down on me. I want to get off at least three times. Then I'm still bottom, you're top, but this time it's from the back, hands and knees, and I want it in the ass with plenty of this." She holds up the bottle. "Don't worry. I'm clean. I always make sure. After that, when I tell you, we do vaginal but still on all fours and you fuck me, and you go deep—you're in as far as you can possibly get, until I come, which might take a little while, or it could be fast. We'll just have to see. The good news is then you're rewarded for all your hard work. You don't have to hold back any longer."

It's accurate to say that a lot of him feels good while somewhere on the periphery of himself he's aware of a slight, shivery sort of nausea, like the distant approach of a migraine or fever, that first warning of infection. "My God," he hears himself say to Daniel, "do you know what I've done?"

She tastes like no other woman he's encountered. Of course, he hasn't had his tongue between anyone's legs besides Carole's for seventeen years, and it's not as if he was some junior Casanova before, but something about this girl, maybe it's the Astroglide, reminds him of a low-calorie sweetener, sucralose or aspartame, a slightly puckery, syrupy savor like those old fluoride treatments he'd get at the dentist's office when he was a kid, anticavity gel leaking from the mold into his mouth, a gaggy trickle going down the back of his throat.

Her first orgasm is demure compared with the bucking and howling he expected; the second, after an intermission of less than a minute, a carbon copy of the first. The third he has to work for, resorting to a failsafe, tongue-punishing technique that leaves his mouth ringing with exertion. She curls up so abruptly that it's a challenge to hang on to her, to keep his tongue in the spot he's found, the right spot, the one that makes her writhe and howl, a freaky, unfeminine noise, the kind of noise, frankly, he would have thought a woman couldn't make, but so sexy: throaty and wet, a low growl that rises octave by octave into a wail. As long as it takes for her to arrive at this climax, and as long as it is that she manages to ride it, there's no denouement: one minute she's curled up, spine lifted from the floor and her face twisted in a knot of concentration; the next she pops up and flips right over, pushing the Astro stuff into his hand before she settles into position on her hands and knees.

"Slather it all over," she says. "Enough so you're, you know, really slick, and put some on me, too. You don't have to put your finger in or anything. I mean you don't if you're squeamish. If you're not, it's okay by me."

Will squirts the clear, colorless stuff on himself, a line of mustard on a hot dog, more than enough, it turns out. He uses his shirttail to wipe some away, otherwise he'll never achieve any friction at all. He holds his breath and pushes in. The girl gasps, very softly, a whispered gasp, if there is such a thing, and he pauses, a bit too long, evidently, because she twitches in obvious irritation.

"Hey," she says. "How about, you know? Moving? It is supposed to be a form of, like, sex."

Will pulls back and pushes in, feeling the rush of blood summoned by the heat of her. She's tight, tighter than anything he's ever felt before, and beyond that close grip, the rest of him is in a hot, soft place, encountering no resistance, none at all. Hands on her hips, he's got the two of them in a slow back-and-forth, guiding her along the shaft of his cock as much as thrusting himself in, afraid to hurt her.

She's sweating; tiny glittery beads form on her shoulders and spine, and she shivers; he feels the tremor under his hands. "Am I—I'm not hurting you, am I?" he asks, but all the response he gets is a huffing uh-uh. Or is it *uh-huh?*

"Keep moving," she says, and they go on until, as before, she takes the opportunity to pull away on his back stroke, sliding off him and onto her stomach.

"Are you clean?" she asks after a minute, sitting on her heels, her back to him, breathing hard enough that he sees her ribs rise and fall. "Just look all over yourself, will you? On the underside, too. Because you have to be, like, totally clean." She walks forward on her hands, back in position.

"All right," he says. "I'm . . . I am."

"Go on, then. Use more glide if you want."

After so many and so deliberate a sequence of preludes, intercourse itself seems an afterthought if not, by definition, an anticlimax. As with all that preceded it, Will has no sense of any choice, and when she says "Deeper!" he thrusts deeper. Ditto faster, ditto slower.

He's stupid with sex, or maybe the right word is *stuporous*. When she comes, moaning, the noise startles him, as if he's forgotten what they've been doing. His own orgasm, produced dutifully, is silent, second-class, undeserving of sound effects.

They both lie on the carpeted floor, saying nothing, she on her stomach, he on his back. He closes his eyes and is instantly asleep.

What Happened to That Girl

BY MARIE LYN BERNARD

CHRISTY, MY FOURTH AND final foster sister, disappeared from our home on the morning of her eighteenth birthday, three weeks before both Jason and I left for college in Santa Barbara. Now apparently Christy's a porn star. Jason called me this morning at nine to break the news.

We're grown-ups now, the kind who don't talk about things like Christy or things like porn. We have grown-up lives—I'm working on my master's in biology; Jay's a computer programmer. I still masturbate to those '80s videos we'd buy at the smut shop out by the airport; I still salivate for the women in leg warmers, their bangs as fluffy as whipped cream. But when we talk about sex now, it's a lot like talking about football.

I remember the afternoon of Christy's departure vividly, even though Jason and I never speak of it. She shared a room with our other foster sister, Rochelle, but Rochelle was at tap class that afternoon, and so we were free to lie on Christy's bed and bask in the air she left behind: the lingering scent of drugstore Vanilla Musk and weed. We held her abandoned panties to our faces and inhaled. We closed our eyes and remembered her, mutually avoiding the fact of each other's hard-on, those nasty flags in our track pants.

I often reminded myself: Jason wasn't my real brother and Christy wasn't my real sister. Our family played host to a number of foster kids over the years, and our house felt, at times, like some sort of privatized orphanage. My mother liked it that way. Perhaps she felt the guilt of the newly and unfortunately wealthy—my father was killed in a car accident while I was still a baby—or perhaps she was just restless without her husband. My mother has a heart like the Tupperware she hawked at neighborhood barbecues: sturdy, durable, long lasting. She has a fierce ability to endure heartbreak. I, her only biological son, do not.

Jason, the son of a Dominican teenager, was the closest thing I had to a permanent sibling. He moved in when I was eight and stayed. He was the kind of guy who never looked back, and I'm the guy who misses things even before they go, who clings to worthless relationships, dead-end jobs. Even when Jason reminded me that Christy would surely flee upon becoming legal, I imagined she'd change her mind, that our lives of varsity athletics and chicken dinners would quell her thirst for fast cars and drugs and the dark corners of the human psyche that enabled her to live so easily without love, and without family.

That afternoon was a mess of taboo. Resigned to unrequited lust in Christy's bed, we pumped our hands around our own shafts, simultaneously, the air dense with the potential of our love. I worked my clean-cut dick and saw that it was smaller than Jason's, which was uncircumcised and thick, the kind of dick I imagined girls wanted inside them, the dick that still makes me tentative to unveil my own.

A strange kind of dance, that mutual masturbation: our synchronized movements, my fingers rubbing the rim of the head, our exhalations swimming in a fog of long-deferred desire.

I still think of Christy every day, of how she was then: a year older than us, with the reading skills of a grade-schooler and the coy wit of someone who didn't need something so trivial as reading skills. She streaked her short black hair with skunk lines of red and white, wore pigtails and stocking caps and bandanas during all the wrong seasons. I remember her slight body; her handful-size breasts, her skinny pale limbs, her irresistibly full mouth lined with shoplifted Glamazon lipstick. She hung out in punk bars, and hung out on my favorite couch, legs sprawled everywhere, playing Chutes and Ladders with Rochelle and yelling at the adulterers on television talk shows. When I dream of her, it's those legs, wrapping around my back like some kind of giant, earth-shattering hug.

"Seth, you aren't gonna believe this," Jason tells me on the phone. "You're gonna bust a nut. I was like—I don't even know. All I know is, you gotta see this. You gotta see it, like, now."

"Bring it over," I say. "I was gonna study, but I mean, this is, like, a special occasion or some shit—"

"Dude, I'll be there in twenty minutes."

I feel my chest. Hot. My forehead. Hot. "All right, man, I'll see ya." Hot. Hot.

By the time Christy moved in we were grown. Mom was always out—taking yoga, flitting around with her social circle of estranged housewives—so she didn't care, really, that Christy pranced around the house in men's wife beaters, her nipples visible beneath the flimsy fabric, or that Christy sometimes didn't sleep at home, or that Christy had become Rochelle's mentor, or that Christy played loud music at inappropriate times. Christy went to school—diligently, dressed in my father's old college hoodies—and she was always on time for dinner, so it didn't matter.

And my mother didn't know that Christy liked to bound through the bathroom door when I was washing up, announce: "Shower time!" and strip bare, naked all of a sudden and setting my veins on fire with her callousness, to jump into the shower, pulling the curtain tight just before my erection reached full mast.

The first time, she peeked out only moments later, her smooth skin covered in droplets of water: "I'm sorry—does that bother you? I'm so used to, like, well, living with a bunch of girls." Christy had been in a home. Or rehab. These were the things we didn't know about her, because she never talked about anything but the immediate present.

"Um . . . no," I said, maybe too enthusiastically, and she grinned. "I didn't think you minded."

But that was the closest I got to sex. Instead, I fumbled around with the breasts of my bright girlfriends, trying to get someone into bed before graduation. Even in the throes of high school love, I thought of Christy.

It occurred to me once—maybe she got naked for Jason, too? But I could've thought about that until it split me open, so I chose not to.

An hour later, Jason's here, in sweatpants, grinning.

"Get ready for the best hour of your fucking life, dude," he says, pushing past me to the living room.

"Can I see the cover?" I ask. "Is she on the cover?"

Jason hands it to me as he clears a spot on the couch, fiddling with the remote.

She is on the cover. Christy. Christy-of-the-shower, Christy-of-the-white-tank-top, Christy-of-my-wettest-wet-dreams. *Honor Roll Cocksuckers*. Christy, clad in a plaid skirt and saddle shoes, with suspenders tight across her new boobs. Her face is covered in cum and her hand is down her skirt.

"Hot, right?" Jason asks. "I always wondered what happened to that girl."

All the time, I want to say, I wonder about her all the time. "Yeah, me, too. Kinda makes sense, y'know?"

"Yeah, especially if she's still into drugs."

I brush off his accusation. "You've already seen the whole thing?"

"Nah," he says. "I watched like, the first five minutes. I thought—uh—I should save the rest to see with you."

A silence. We're men now, I think, but weren't we men then? In college, a buddy and I bought blow jobs from the same hooker, and I waited in the room during his and then he saw me get mine, and wasn't this like that, except less so? And why should I feel unsettled anyhow, with the object of our desire so clearly a woman? But I prefer his being here. I'm drawn to that nakedness, that vulnerability that feels like family.

"Cool, cool." I nod.

Honor Roll Cocksuckers is the opposite of seeing a movie star on the street. Christy, in pigtails and a skirt, with breasts straining against her selectively buttoned shirt, is "taught a lesson" by the principal and then the janitor, and then both at once. The film unfolds at a pace that's like your train charging past when it's supposed to stop, like watching a game that you wish would go into a third overtime just to see if he can score like that again—over, and over, and over.

Bend her over, I yell silently. Bend her over and fuck her everywhere. I wanna see that round white ass, the same ass that lazed around the house on Sunday afternoons in boxer shorts, the ass connected to those legs laid absently across my lap as we watched TV.

The janitor bends her over the desk and yanks her panties off. She yelps. He smacks her ass and she yelps again.

A close-up: beneath the thicket of black hair that once coated her pussy lies a shaven, beautiful hole, lips like a canoe around the slippery line of her clit, better than I imagined. The janitor rubs his dick against her and slips in. She yelps again, and he smacks again. Then he fucks her madly, pounding her—it cuts to her face, her intense eyes and her skin still white as soap.

The principal approaches the front of the desk, fitting his body between her arms and shoving his dick into her mouth. She moans and tightens her glossy lips around him.

I look at Jason, but he won't look at me. Maybe this is too much, I think, maybe this isn't right, Jason with a dick like the Hispanic janitor's, and me skinny and white like the principal, me at her front and him at her back, me fucking Christy's throat and him, now, pulling his dick from her cunt to tickle the rim of her asshole, which flexes, eager for penetration.

When he breaks into that tiny hole, cupped by her perfect cheeks, I can't take it anymore. I slowly unbutton my pants and extract my dick . . . and rub. I have no inhibitions now; lust is a kind of drunkenness.

Out of the corner of my eye I see Jason doing the same.

The janitor lies on the floor, and Christy mounts him. The principal takes her from behind while her ass bounces over the janitor's dick.

"Double penetration," Jason says.

I smile too, and feel better everywhere. The moment I pop is bright white, like Christy's spotless ass.

I look at Jason smiling at me, his hand unapologetically smeared. He goes to the bathroom, and I'm limp, rendered half conscious by the power of porn. By Christy and the *Honor Roll Cocksuckers*.

The movie moves on to other girls, other scenes, as Jason and I navigate the tender terrain of our situation. He brings washcloths, and we clean up. He sneaks me another smile, and I feel okay, a safe distance from our frightening adolescent desires.

When Jason speaks, it's like the end of a football game: "Some good shit, man, right? She did good."

"Hell yeah, she did."

Jason nods solemnly.

I zip my pants.

"But dude—I didn't even tell you the best part."

"I don't think I can handle anything else," I say, laughing. I'm in a dark room surrounded by ghosts, and naked girls are fucking on television.

"Okay. I'll call you tomorrow," Jason says. "Get some work done, schoolboy."

Jason takes the movie with him, and I'm back in my apartment feeling like I've just had the best sex of my life. I dream of smacking Christy's ass, of punishing her with her skirt over her head. I wake up wet and alone.

Jason picks me up after the exam. "We're going on a road trip, my man."

"A road trip?" I'm groggy, half awake. "Where?"

Jason grins. "You'll see."

The rocks in my head knock around wearily, too worn out to imagine anything. I fall asleep.

I wake up as we pull up to a nondescript office building. Jason calls someone as we lumber out of the car, and I fix my hair in the window's reflection.

"Where the fuck are we, dude?" I ask. It's painfully sunny. I'm thinking of Christy, of all the bodies that came in and out of our house, no one ever sticking. I feel the emptiness that pounds when I think of her, of Jason, of my mother, of the difference between knowing where you've come from and knowing you've come from nowhere.

My mind is still murky as we ride the elevator up to Untitled Scream Productions. Jason's grinning like a kid on his birthday.

I rub my eyes. Is this real? Will I see her, knowing now what it's like inside that quivering pussy? Will I slide my hand along her taut stomach, tickle the Playboy bunny in her belly button?

There's an empty desk, and Jason buzzes in. We're greeted by the principal. He and Jason are—apparently—friends. I'm dizzy, everything in slow motion like an acid trip. It's one of those moments where life slows down and opens itself up like an orgasm, and everything in you turns into so much air.

I am following Jason, feeling like I'm in a children's book, the kind where you feel three times smaller and follow imaginary friends into strange rooms.

This sparse room, with black leather couches and a view of the Hollywood Hills, is strange. Because Christy is in it.

Right there. There she is. She's wearing gray sweatpants and white tank top, her full breasts peeking out of the sides. I liked her real tits better, but I don't care; being near her is more than I can bear. I don't know if I'm going to get a hard-on or throw up.

"Blast from the past," she says, but it sounds like a come-on. What has Jason set up? "It's my brothers."

She hugs us, and squeezes me as she hugs. I'm already hard.

"Things haven't changed, I see," she whispers in my ear, tapping the head of my dick.

She's still so skinny; but she's a woman now, why is she still so skinny? Still so pale, living in the Valley and still so pale?

But I don't care. I want to bend her over the table, fuck her with the wrath of all my mornings of blue balls, all the times she riled me up and left me dry.

I want to fuck her for not leaving a note. I'd said that to Jason, too, then, that she didn't leave a note, and he'd scowled and said, *It's not like she killed herself, and besides, look, she left all her panties.*

"Sit down, boys," she says, and we sit on either side of her.

She makes small talk, asks us what we're doing, how Mom is, tells us how she dropped out of art school, that she's been doing porn for a year now and she really likes it, that it's her calling, that she lives with Matt, who co-owns the company with Jeff, who's a friend of Jason's from college, and that she was surprised, really, when Jeff told her that we'd called. She thought about us, she said, from time to time, not all the time but sometimes, and felt a little bad about leaving without saying anything, but she was just a kid, not that she was all together now, but that she knew things, some things, like why people leave notes when they leave forever, and why people tell other people where they are going and why they don't.

Then she has her hand on Jason's inner thigh, tickling near his dick. He leans back and closes his eyes.

"I wanted to do this then," she says, getting on her knees in front of Jason. She breathes hot between his legs.

There's something sad lingering in her face, something that makes me angry and mixed up, but then she's pulling Jason's huge cock out of his pants and scratching his balls, wrapping her lips around his dick. Did Jason pay for this? I wonder. Is this why we're here? Or is she just doing this because she wants to—because she wants us?

Is she so good at performing on cue?

She undresses, and I'm wide-eyed at her new breasts. I want to watch all her other movies, over and over again for hours and hours, for as long as I live.

She sucks Jason's dick like a porn star, all the moaning and the moisture, all the upward glances for approval. She doesn't resist when he places his hand on the back of her head, pulling her closer and shoving himself deeper. I watch her lips move up and down the length of his cock, and mine hardens like concrete. Her breasts nudge his knees.

"Seth," she says, popping Jason out of her mouth, "why don't you fuck me while I suck Jason off?"

I look around like there's another Seth in the room.

"You want me to, uh—fuck—to fuck you?"

"You want to, don't you?"

"Uh—um—of course."

She stands up, walks to the desk, and bends over it.

"Jason, wanna break me in first?"

Jason, glee in his eyes, erection in hand, goes over to the table and rubs himself against her ass, like in *Honor Roll*. He gives me a look: isn't this a good movie?

She reaches back and guides him south into the sticky wetness of her hole. She grabs his balls, rolling them in her palm. Then he begins to nail her, and my mouth falls open. He makes sounds I've never heard from him before. He fucks her like a hellhound, like he's drilling into something thick and thorny and he's got to get through to the other side.

Then he whips it out, jerking, and the foam from his dick slides over her ass like soapsuds.

"You ready, Seth?" she says, still bent over. Ready? I want to fuck her up the ass. I want to fuck her in the mouth. I want to cum in her ass, on her tits; I want her to take my cock in her mouth and swallow my cum until she gags. Fuck, I want to be a porn star, too. Fuck fuck fuck fuck.

But I don't.

"Let's uh—" I'm nervous. "Go to the couch?"

Jason's on the other couch, cleaning himself with paper napkins. I try to pretend he isn't there as Christy leaps across the room, obediently, and bends over. I edge closer to her, my dick in my hand, but my stomach flips, and flips again, and I can't.

"No—no—" I say. "Lie on it."

She does, looking confused.

"On your back," I say, watching her pert ass roll over.

I get on top of her, our eyes locked, and I ease myself in like I'm the first one, breaking her open, setting that thing loose in her that got her here in the first place. She gasps but doesn't moan, and I shift, in and out, gently I look into her eyes, and I grab her hair in fists.

I make love. To her. Inside her it feels pure, a million miles away from cameras and lights. It feels utterly private.

We kiss, we suck and pull, our tongues courting and wedding and dancing.

I lie on top of her. I kiss her ear. I want to whisper so many things, but instead I just tickle her earlobe with my tongue. I kiss her nose, which is red and sad. I look at her eyes, and she looks back at mine, and it's almost like I could cry.

She reaches out and grabs my ass with her hands, her finger softly rimming the outside of my asshole, but she doesn't enter it. We roll over, and she's on top of me.

The muscles of her cunt tighten around my cock—she's a pro—and she rides me. Her breasts bounce like tennis balls, her soft hands grip my biceps. She rubs back and forth, her clit grazing the hair above my dick.

"This feels so goood, baby."

"Yeah, it does," I say. There are dirty words we could exchange like endearments, but we don't.

She smiles, clenches her muscles hard around my cock. "Ah—yeah!"

She lowers to me. "Let's go back the other way. I wanna feel you over me, is that okay?"

So we roll back over. We are careful, athletic, on the limited space of the couch.

Jason might still be in the room, and he might not be. But as I continue, thrusting deeply, feeling her clench around me at just the right moments and grind her ass up and down with finesse, I see that she's going to come, and I know that I can, too, and so we do, together, and I come inside her even though I know I shouldn't.

I rest my head between her breasts, which are supple though clearly fake. I feel her breathe. Jason is no longer in the room; I can hear him laughing outside, him and another man laughing.

I feel naked but not empty anymore. Not for just that second, the second that I lie inside her, silent.

"That was nice," she says finally.

"It was," I respond, giving a smile that looks like an apology. "Thank you."

She smiles. "Thank you, Seth."

"For what?"

She shrugs as I slip out of her and stand up. She sits up, thinking. She's naked. With me.

"For loving me, I guess. Even if it's just for"—she looks at the clock—"twenty minutes."

I shake my head and laugh. "Twenty years. At least twenty years."

I watch as she dresses, her eyes still huge and empty. I realize that I've never known someone who needed love as badly as this girl—more than my mother; more than the twelve other kids shuffled in and out of our house like supporting actors; more than Jason when he first arrived on our doorstep, tattered and broken and hardened to the bone. Maybe even more than I do.

"Maybe I'll see you guys again?" she asks.

"Maybe." I smile. "I hope so," I say, even though I don't know if that's true or not.

That's the last thing I say, because then Jason comes in, triumphant and sportsmanlike. "Dude, you ready to bust?"

I nod. In that same dreamlike state I entered with, I leave the office and we get in the car. We pull onto the highway and drive until the building fades into the millions of office buildings around us, recedes under the ominous landscape of the hills.

Jason recites his play-by-play, eager, and then says, "Hey man, what happened after I left?"

I shrug. "Same thing, more or less."

He nods. He keeps talking. The radio plays, the car moves, and we move on, together, in his car, in our strange, beautiful brotherhood, the kind that stands naked in front of itself, unashamed.

Heads-Up Poker

SUSAN DIPLACIDO

D AN DIDN'T SEE THIS coming. In the seven years they've been gather-
ing each month to swig beer and slap around poker chips, there's
been plenty of weirdness, but nothing like this.

Until now.

He can't even figure out how it started. But as Dan looks at his cards
he feels a draft on his exposed ankle and his pocket tens don't seem so
strong. He sighs and folds.

He takes the taunts from Joe and Mickey. Kelly, Joe's wife, grins
at him, but at the other end of the table Lucy is leaning back in her
chair, eyes lowered. Dan notices her tongue peek out between her
lips.

She remains in the hand. He can't decide whether her tongue was a
"tell" betraying the strength of her hand, or a tell of something else. Of
anticipation? Or a deliberate move designed to get into his head? Wasn't
it Lucy who started all this weirdness tonight?

He takes a deep pull on his beer, inspecting her across the table.

Lucy can feel his eyes on her, but she stays focused on her cards.

She did start it. Slyly. She'd laid the groundwork earlier this week
when she made a fuss over Kelly's sweater, told her how much she liked
it. Kelly's susceptible to flattery: naturally she wore it to the game
tonight. Kelly's first tell was a few hands ago, crossing her arms, but
Lucy had a shitty hand herself and couldn't take her on. The second
time, though, was perfect. When Lucy saw those pocket queens in her
hand, it was play time.

Sitting on the short stack, Kelly bit her lip when Lucy pushed all in.

Lucy'd said, "Tell you what, Kel. To even it up, I'd take that sweater you've got on."

Lucy won. She hates the sweater, but the primary objective wasn't the sweater, of course. It was to get Dan in her bed . . . again.

The game took on a life of its own after the sweater swap. The men catcalled when Kelly stripped off the creamy cashmere, and, even though Kelly had a blouse on under it, everyone's eyes glinted with the potential. They aren't prudes, this circle of friends. They skinny-dip together in the summer. Everyone's caught Joe and Kelly screwing at some point, either by walking in on them in a bathroom at a party, or stumbling across them in the woods when they were all camping.

That sort of thing used to happen with Lucy and Dan too, before the breakup.

So it wasn't unexpected when the "innocent" sweater swap turned into full-blown strip poker. Lucy got everyone's shoes in one bold swipe. And then people chipped away, taking socks and accessories. Now, with this hand, Joe's raised the stakes to shirts.

Dan folded. Disappointing, but not a problem. Because Lucy knows that the key to getting Dan back isn't getting his shirt off, but taking hers off.

So she plays the hand out, hoping to lose.

When a king comes on the river, Mickey—their perpetual single guy—flips his cards, and he's got it paired. Lucy fights off a smirk of satisfaction. Kelly stands and makes a playful show of pulling off her shirt while Joe hums the stripper theme, and Mickey applauds and waves a dollar bill. Dan's watching Kelly, smiling.

Lucy stays seated and undoes, first, her top button, and then the second. At the third, she feels Dan's eyes on her, so she again deliberately lets her tongue peek between her lips. She unhooks the fourth and fifth buttons. When she slides the shirt over her shoulders, she raises her eyes and looks Dan in the face.

But Dan's not looking at her face. He saw the tongue action. Now he knows she's trying to get into his head. So he intended to look away, but Lucy was on the fourth button and the satiny cream color of her bra was already peeking through. She pulls the shirt off, shrugging, that smooth skin of hers spilling over the top of that skimpy bra.

Christ. He gulps. It's not cold in here, but it's not a sauna either.

Those nipples of hers, they always were sensitive—and they're starting already. What was smooth, seamless fabric is rising in the center, darkening, letting even the color of her hardening nipples show through. Lucy twists, hanging the shirt over the back of her chair, accentuating the swell of her breast, the jutting nipple interrupting the otherwise perfect contour.

Dan forces his eyes closed. He can't sit here staring at her, and now he's sure that's exactly what she wants.

The slick little minx.

After they broke up, she caved when Dan came on to her that horny night six months ago. But last month, he turned her down when she wanted some action. Clearly, this is her payback.

She wants to play?

Let's play.

Mickey deals another hand, and Dan catches him peeking out of the corner of his eye at Lucy. Mickey's always had a thing for Lucy, even if he won't admit it. But Dan sees Mickey's nervous glances, his smiles at Lucy as he deals.

Fanning his cards, Dan's not sure what he's hoping for. He's trying to win, of course. But what's winning?

Does he want Lucy sitting here naked—in front of everyone? In front of that damned Mickey? Does Dan really want to be looking at her naked himself—in front of everyone?

Christ, why do the words "Lucy naked" send a tingle right to where he doesn't want one? He doesn't know. But he knows he doesn't want to be sitting naked in front of everyone. Leaving his cards facedown, he goes for a new beer, his bare feet slapping the cool linoleum. He gives fresh ones to Kelly and Joe too, and discovers Mickey'd topped off Lucy's wine.

Downing half his beer in one pull, Dan sets his head straight. He doesn't know yet what game Lucy's playing, but he's going to beat her at it.

It doesn't matter how bad he's wanted her lately. Since she put the moves on him and he rejected her, he's had the upper hand.

He'll win.

He doesn't. In just two quick hands, Lucy wins Dan's shirt and then all three men's pants.

Kelly high-fives her as the guys shuck their pants. Joe's not the least bit bothered that his boxers are tented out, laughing as Kelly says, "Hey, baby, you're at half mast."

"That's cause I'm half drunk. Besides, so are you!" Joe nods at her chest. Kelly shrugs. "It's cold in here."

"It is cold," he says, pulling her onto his lap. "Warm me up!"

"You don't need any more warming," she warns, but she doesn't pull away.

Lucy smiles. Dan, she notices, is sitting forward on his seat.

Oh, she watched him strip. She took a sip of wine and was casual about it, but she watched him. She got a nice eyeful of torso when he lost his shirt. But she always loved his legs most. They aren't scrawny chicken legs, and they're not too hairy either, especially for his olive complexion. And his crotch. Ah, his crotch. He's wearing those black boxer briefs that can't conceal his bulge.

It's bulging, but he's not really turned on—yet. He's trying to appear relaxed, but Lucy can tell he's not. Joe and Kelly, they're relaxed. Mickey, he's a little uncomfortable, but hanging in there. But Dan? His shoulders are tight and his jaw's clamped, and he's not moving. He's not moving because he's concentrating so hard on staying calm.

Lucy takes another sip of wine. She's deliberate in her moves, trying to act nonchalant. Because she's thinking about how Dan wasn't excited—yet. And the thought of his getting excited, getting fully aroused, even while he's consciously willing it not to happen, really turns her on. Thinking about his bulge growing and stiffening makes her hard nipples ache and her crotch moisten. And she knows exactly how to get him to that point.

So, let's play.

Kelly deals, still on Joe's lap, slapping his hand away with mock indignation.

Their silliness relaxes Dan. They're comfortable, even Joe with his half boner hanging out. They're mildly drunk, of course. And Joe and Kelly never did have much discretion anyhow. Like that time Kelly went down on Joe at that French restaurant in New York.

Checking his cards, Dan sees he's pulled a monster hand. He could get Lucy's pants off and even the score with his ace/king. But this time she doesn't pull her little tongue trick. When the flop comes, she takes a gulp of wine. Mickey tops her glass off with a smile. The prick.

Dan doesn't pair the ace or the king, but he's victorious anyway when Lucy shows queen/four, unpaired. His ace beats that, and next thing he knows, she's standing, unbuttoning and unzipping. Her underwear matches the bra: satin, creamy, but thin and scant, riding low on curvy hips that match her tits. She turns around to drape her pants over the back of her chair. The panties aren't a thong, but they're riding up the cheeks of her ass, tempting. It sends another tingle to the pit of his stomach; blood starts to flow to his cock. Then he catches Mickey staring at Lucy even as she turns back. The prick is focused not on her ass, but on her crotch. It sends another hot flash through Dan. He clears his throat loudly, and Mickey looks away.

Lucy flashes Mickey a big smile. Taking her seat, she stares at Dan, his face red, one hand tapping the table. He's refusing to look at her.

Joe deals again, and Lucy has a terrible hand, but she stays in. So does Kelly, and so does Dan. Dan wins with a flush draw, and Kelly happily sheds her pants.

Lucy reaches back and unhooks the clasp of her bra, letting the straps glide off her shoulders. She knows Dan's fighting against looking but won't be able to resist. He always loved her tits.

Don't look, Dan tells himself. Just don't look at her.

He looks.

He can't help it. She has great tits. She snakes her arms out of the straps and reaches up and pulls away the front of her bra. Her tits spill out.

Those damn hard nipples of hers, deep burgundy, poking way out. Dan's breath goes shallow. A surge goes to his cock. He closes his eyes, but it's too late. His throat is tight, and his head is humming. He can't resist looking back.

Even Joe, shouting, "Holy shit, Lucy! You got a great rack!" doesn't break the heat for Dan. His cock rises. Mickey dares a long look, and that only worsens matters for Dan. He's hard, a frustrating throb already setting in, and he wants to slap Mickey upside the head.

Lucy knows exactly what's happening to Dan. Flushed face, quick breath: he's trying not to look, and he's failing. She watches him glance at Mick, his jaw set. She knew he still had heat for her.

Dan shifts, and his eyes fall directly on her. Staring, inspecting her naked breasts. She's done it all right, she's set Dan off good. The monkey wrench is that she didn't expect it to get her so hot so quickly. But watching him get hot for her, get jealous for her—it electrifies her. The slight damp between her legs turns to sopping, slick wetness. She wants to squirm, to find a way to relieve the humming insistence in her crotch.

Kelly, bless her, cuts the electricity by answering Joe's comment to Lucy. "Hey. What about my rack?"

Joe gives her breasts a squeeze, still inside her bra, saying, "Yours is the best, baby."

Mickey, he blushes.

They play a couple more hands, but it's a stalemate, with no one willing to risk any more clothing and everyone folding. All the while, Joe's hands snake randily across Kelly's belly and thighs. And Lucy's exaggerated breathing, the hypnotic rise and fall of her exposed breasts, keeps Dan's pulse surging. And Dan's blushing amps up the frustration knotted in Lucy's crotch.

And Mickey, he watches, trying not to let Dan notice.

Finally, Joe pulls a big hand and calls: winner takes the losers' skivvies. Mickey and Kelly fold, and Mickey scrambles for the fridge to grab another beer.

Dan checks his cards, then grits his teeth, trying to think beyond the throb in his dick. He shouldn't touch it. But if he could tame it, for just a minute, he imagines could get back in control. Lucy. He doesn't dare look at her.

He can't touch it.

He touches it. When no one's paying attention, he dips his hand under the table and squeezes his hard-on through his underwear. It gives a little relief, a moment of satisfaction. So he squeezes again, harder, this time with a rub. He licks his lips, eyes sweeping the table to make sure he's in the clear.

That's when he sees Lucy staring at him.

Her mouth slack, her hard-nippled tits rising and falling, her dark eyes boring into him. It's so fucking hot it makes him crazy.

Lucy can't stand it. It's too much, watching Dan grab himself. She crosses her legs, but that sends the slickness flooding her panties. She uncrosses them but still feels the pulsing in her clit, so she crosses them again and scootches to the edge of her seat. She sees Dan's biceps flex and knows he's touching himself again. He's looking at her, ignoring everyone else. Uncrossing her legs, she plants her feet on the cool floor and undulates her hips, grinding against the chair, easing things for a moment but then instantly heightening the frustration. She rocks again, harder, meeting Dan's gaze. Fuck, it almost feels so good.

She rocks, Dan squeezes and rubs . . . and Mickey comes back to the table. Lucy and Dan freeze.

Dan and Lucy both call Joe's bet, their voices husky.

They sit helplessly, Lucy's fists clenched, Dan still holding himself under the table with one hand, the other clutching his beer. Joe flips his hand, showing an ace that got paired. Lucy goes next. Nothing. Biting her lip, she stares at her losing cards.

Dan's got her now. Feisty, isn't she? But she'll never have the guts to do this.

She does it. She wants Dan so bad right now that she doesn't care who knows. She stands and peels off her panties, soaked with her juice and the brine of her scent. She tosses them on the table.

Joe and Kelly cheer. Dan fists his cock and grips his bottle.

Mickey can't tear his eyes away from Lucy. When she takes her seat, Dan releases himself and slams his beer bottle on the table, startling Mickey from his goddamn reverie. Mickey stands and hurries toward the bathroom. Dan glares after him.

Lucy watches Dan. Cocking an eyebrow, she dares him to turn his cards.

He doesn't bother to flip his over. Instead he stands, his arousal plainly evident. He confronts Lucy, a hard edge to his voice. "This what you wanted?"

Lucy stares at Dan, silent.

He strips his underwear off, flips it onto the table. Even the chill air isn't deterring his hard-on.

Kelly, she says, "Oh, my."

Lucy licks her lips.

Joe reaches a hand between Kelly's legs. Kelly grabs Joe's hand and pulls him after her, out of the room. Mickey's not coming out of the bathroom any time soon. Nobody's left but Dan and Lucy.

Dan repeats his question, but this time the heat in his voice isn't anger. "Is this what you wanted?" he asks, and takes hold of himself.

As Lucy watches, he starts rubbing. Asking again, "Is this what you wanted?"

"Almost," she answers.

"We're all out of clothes," he says, and releases himself, then sits back down. He won't give in first. He knows she's throbbing too. "What's left to gamble?"

Lucy knows that the only thing holding him back is that he won't give her the satisfaction of winning. But she's got an idea.

As she reaches for the deck, he tosses her his hand so that she can shuffle them, but they land faceup. Joe, he'd won the hand with an ace/ten kicker. Dan's hand is an ace—with a queen.

He'd won. He didn't have to put on that little show.

Lucy shuffles. She deals, flicking his cards at him, stating the wager. Looking Dan in the eye: "Loser comes last."

He ignores his cards. He lunges up, knocking the table over, sending bottles and glasses crashing to the floor, cards and chips skittering. He stands over her and takes hold of himself. Growling, "Start now."

And he strokes away.

Lucy stares. Dan's legs are spread in a slight crouch, and he's pumping himself directly in front of her chest. He reaches between her legs, wets his hand with her juice, and immediately starts again, stroking furiously now. His mouth is contorted in a snarl.

His hand on her crotch did it. He's working himself to a frenzy in front of her; he's lost control and it's so hot, and if she gets left behind she knows she'll go home the loser. A loser with a screaming clit.

He's pumping and panting. "I'm gonna, I'm gonna beat you. Fuck you, Lucy. Fuck you."

She starts working herself, and she knows right away it's not going to take her long, watching him as he watches her, getting close to the edge already.

He hits another level watching her, her legs spread, her fingers pressing and stroking, getting herself off—on him.

"God," she groans. "I'm, I'm close." Their eyes are locked on each other.

Christ, she's too hot. Dan crouches lower and buries his free hand in her cunt, making her buck, helping her along, pressing and sliding fingers inside her.

His cock is seared with pleasure, her cunt is pulsing. Both of them are strung high, stuttering, "I'm gonna, I'm gonna, I'm gonna . . ."

Lucy grabs Dan's cock. He's got half his hand inside her.

Dan spurts—onto her stomach, and she aims him higher, holding tight, every muscle clenched as she strokes and he spills the rest, shooting it all over one distended nipple, his other hand crushing between her legs as she spasms against him.

Her body shudders with release.

Panting, Dan sinks to his knees between her legs and leans his fevered forehead against her sweaty neck.

High and hazy, Lucy whispers, "Who won?"

"Draw," he rasps. "It's a draw. We're gonna have to go again."

Lucy closes her legs around his torso, puts her arms around his shoulders to keep him warm.

"Yeah?" she asks.

He kisses her neck, wraps his arms around her waist.

"Yeah," he says. "Let's play."

She licks her lips, then smiles.

Taste

SUSAN ST. AUBIN

NOTHING TASTES BETTER THAN illicit love, Evelyn thinks, as she stands with her back against the wall, her mouth around Laurent's tongue, sucking its spongy length, the spatula in her hand dripping cake batter down his back. They're working together at one in the morning, making the day's bread and desserts, a new routine now that Laurent has made her the baker in his small restaurant, and has hired Ed Jones, whom he calls Edouard, to replace her as sous-chef. She likes working when Hal is home, and sleeping while he's at work; and she finds she no longer cares about his life apart from her, almost as if they were divorced. Already she's a single person, tasting her boss's tongue for the first time, rolling it around and under hers, savoring the remains of the cinnamon roll they've just shared while she lets her spatula drop to the floor.

Laurent's hand lifts her short skirt and slides between her thighs, moving in a stirring motion, as though she were a thickening sauce. She wonders how far he's going to take this first kiss. After knowing him for three years, being his employee for one of those years, and craving him from the first sight she had of him, she feels that whatever happens can't happen soon enough. She spreads her legs so he can reach higher. They're alone now, waiting for the bread to rise, the cakes to bake. The restaurant is closed, and Edouard left an hour ago.

Laurent's fingers dip into her underpants, sliding along the elastic to the back, then pulling them down, fondling her ass on the way. After he glides the panties down her legs she steps out of them, leaving them on the floor like a pink-and-white pastry.

Laurent blows in her ear. "Can I?" his breath asks. "Do you do? Do you want to do eet?"

She's not quite sure what she's heard, as is usually the case with Laurent. His self-taught English can be unique, and she doesn't know much French aside from cooking terms, but puree, fricassee, abaisse don't seem to be of any use in this situation.

"Do eet? Do eet?" he murmurs rhythmically, grinding his hips against hers. "I can?"

"Can?" she repeats. A long-forgotten English grammar lesson loops its way to her from the past: can or may. Is he asking permission or asking her to confirm his technique? She giggles, blowing in his ear. "Can you? I don't know."

But he stops, not getting the joke, and looks at her with sad brown eyes.

She melts. "Of course you may," she answers, knowing she really doesn't need to teach him anything because he knows so much more than American men. Did Hal ever ask her permission? Did anyone, ever? "How nice that you ask," she tells Laurent.

"May," he says, triumphant, another concept mastered, as he glides his arms around her waist, burying his lips between her shoulder and neck, then kissing his way up to her ear. "No one is here," he blows in her ear, but what Evelyn hears is "his ear."

No one is his ear. This strikes Evelyn as profound. No one is his cock, either; no one is her cunt. She reaches into his front pocket and glides her hand around the firmness dangling like a baguette along his thigh as her brain slowly translates: No one is here. We are alone. We are so much more than cock and cunt, but for now? She shrugs, a gesture she has picked up from him, communication beyond language. Her movement makes him trail his hand lightly over her shoulder and down her arm until she shivers.

"We do it. *Mais oui. S'il vous plaît,*" she says, tasting his tongue. In his pocket she feels a square of something wrapped in cellophane, which she grasps and runs up and down the length of his penis, listening to the muffled rustle of the packet.

He says something indecipherable: "Tahk eet oot."

French? English? For a moment she's not quite sure. Take it out. She does, and holds it up to the ceiling light, which burns brightly above them. As she suspected, it's a condom, here in his pocket, not even in the wallet in his jacket, which hangs in the small storage pantry off the kitchen, but right here in the pocket of his white chef's pants.

"Do you always carry them on you like this?" she asks.

"Only when I am wanting," he answers. His English comprehension is better than his speech, and better than her grasp of their relationship. He's been wanting, after she'd given up on him?

"Tahk eet oot," he pleads now.

She pretends not to understand. "What?" she asks, sliding her leg along his.

His breathing fills the room. "Tahk eet oot."

"Eat?" she asks. "Eat out?" Her clit is swollen enough for her to know that teasing him is teasing herself. A thread of her moisture is already beginning to trickle down her thigh. She catches her breath and puts one hand on his hip, pulling him closer, stilling his back-and-forth motion. In her other hand is the cellophane packet.

"This?" She draws the wrapped condom under his nose. "Eat this?" He rubs himself up and down against her. "Poot eet on."

"Eat," she giggles. "Eat on what?"

He raises his hand. She almost wants him to slap her, but instead he pulls the hairnet off her head, letting her hair fall over her face.

The scent of baking drifts around them, the sweetness of cakes, the yeastiness of rising bread. She feels her body lifting like dough, alive with the possibility of its future form. She moves her hand off his hip to unzip his pants, sliding her fingers around his moist cock, feeling that he wears nothing beneath the soft white professional trousers, which drop to the floor.

He groans and puts his hand over hers to guide it to the tip. She strokes the slit there, spreading it with her fingers. "Do you want to do?" he asks again.

"Eat, eat?" she answers, kissing his neck while she opens the buttons of his white shirt and blows troughs through his chest hair, winding her tongue along the trails of skin, then sliding to her knees so she can reach his cock, tonguing in slow circles to the head, which she pops into her mouth.

His hips swing back and forth, asking to thrust deeper, and he mutters words she doesn't understand, sounds that almost, but not quite, are musical, like the high school Spanish she has long forgotten. She moves her tongue in time to his alien song, listening to the sharp breaths that punctuate the phrases and words, which get shorter and shorter, broken into syllables by his gasps. She can taste the salt of his pre-cum.

With her fingernails Evelyn breaks the packet she still holds. Laurent pulls away from her mouth and takes several deep breaths, punctuated with his mysterious language, the words flowing together as his breathing slows. She removes the condom, blowing it out like a balloon, then sucking it back into her mouth. She wants to try something she's heard about, mouthing a rubber, putting it on using only her mouth and tongue. She takes his prick in her hand, thinking, What a funny word that is. Will he prick the rubber? Will he prick her mouth, stab her tongue? The sound has an aura of danger: The hard "p," the "ick," would carry meaning in any language.

Prick into mouth, where the rubber (not rubber, she realizes, wondering why that word is used for a narrow plastic baggie)—where the anti-rubber rolls under her tongue. She has to spit out his penis to get the condom into position on her tongue tip before sliding it back in her mouth. Things are getting far too moist. Her spit runs down his shaft, soaking her hand. She swallows the sweetness of plastic and possibly a lubricant, and almost gags. This is not going well. Her tongue positions the rubber onto his prick (prick rubber, she thinks again, dangerously), but it slips off before she can guide it down the shaft.

He sighs as she moves her hands to rescue the baggie, which she holds by its base while unrolling it onto his cock before popping the whole thing, like an encased sausage, into her mouth, moving it back and forth gently over the edges of her teeth. She's on her knees before him, humming deep in her throat as he pushes in and out of her mouth, both of them rocking hypnotically back and forth until he pulls away with a cascade of unintelligible syllables and stands panting before her. She wonders what he means.

"I don't, I don't want to," he says, then pulls her to her feet. "Too soon," he explains. "Too much eeef I go too soon."

She smiles at him, to tell him she's heard, to let him know it's not something she's heard often.

"For you," he says, sliding his hand between her legs again.

How French, she thinks, all the stories of considerate, knowledgeable, courteous French lovers spilling from her memory. He's doing this for me.

He fingers the rim of her vagina, then inserts one finger, two fingers, swirling them around inside, but somehow off center, tantalizing her, teasing, but never delivering the touch that will make her come. When she moves her body, his fingers back away, frustrating her. This is considerate? He has a half smile on his face, and his eyes are closed. If she didn't think she might, maybe, almost come, she'd pull away.

He stops. "Ah, how I play you," he says, and then reminds her, "Time for bread."

With a sigh of annoyance, she lifts the loaves of bread that have been rising on the counter into the oven next to the one where the cakes are.

Laurent is behind her, hands on her shoulders, and after she closes the oven door, he turns her around and backs her into the opposite wall, where he unbuttons the front of her dress, pulling it over her head. She feels the cotton catch against the rough concrete of the wall, and leans forward so the dress can drop to the floor, leaving her naked except for the white tennis shoes she bends over to untie.

The ovens make the kitchen so hot that even nude she's sweating. Beads of sweat also mark Laurent's forehead as he watches her. He shrugs his shirt off his shoulders, letting it drop on top of her dress, then moves behind her, squats down, and puts his hand on her hips as she takes off the shoes. When he opens his mouth, his tongue forms soothing sounds, round and flowing like a lullaby. Although she doesn't know the words, she understands their meaning, and she stretches out on the floor, face-down on her dress, while his tongue licks her fleshy buttocks, his teeth nipping lightly all the way across, ending in a swirl against her asshole. He turns her over, his foreign tongue murmuring again as it flicks at her cunt.

How do you say pussy in French? *Gato* comes to her from Spanish, though she doesn't know if this would mean what she wants it to.

"*Gato,*" she whispers, and he laughs, his lips releasing a flow of gentle syllables she thinks might be Spanish, but since she can't separate them into words, she lets the sounds wash over her. She knows one of his grandfathers came from Spain, so maybe he knows that language, too.

He kneels over her now, holding her hips firmly between his knees, and lifts her arms. "Move?" he asks.

She struggles beneath him, but his knees have her firmly pinned.

"There is some place." He looks around. "Ah!"

He stands up, pulling her after him. "There." He points to the table in the middle of the kitchen, the table right under the ceiling light, the table where she kneads the bread and rolls out pie crusts, where the kitchen staff, under the supervision of Edouard, chop mushrooms and onions and chilies for the omelets. He's going to lay her on that table like a slab of meat. His dick still hard, still holding on to that plastic sheath, he leads her across the floor.

"Here," he says, boosting her to the table.

She throws her arms around his neck. "Eat me," she whispers, though there's no one but Laurent to hear. "I'm your midnight snack."

But he's already laying her on her back, murmuring "Pussy" with a long hiss as he spreads her legs, parting her hair with his fingers. His tongue knows what she wants without words; it swirls around her clit, pulls back, flickers at the edge of her cunt, flits to her asshole, then dashes back to her clit, but not quite long enough before moving on to her cunt again. Then he kisses her, injecting her own self into her mouth with his tongue. She eagerly sucks the fishy sweetness off him, savoring the taste, but again he withdraws too soon and stands back, holding her legs apart, smiling at her.

She begs wordlessly with her small, sharp breaths. Inside she quivers, though not quite enough; inside, she's starving, the walls of her cunt undulating, ready to devour him. He pulls her legs until she's at the edge of the table, then moves closer, touching her clit with his sheathed prick, pulling back, touching, until she wails, "In, in, put it in!" with her feet kneading his shoulders.

"Too fast, you Americans. Eeen?" he says. She knows he understands, she knows he's mocking her. She twists away, but he holds her firmly, playing now with her cunt, now with her asshole, sticking the tip in, pulling it out, until finally he pushes deeply into her cunt and gives four strokes, then pulls out and bends over to suck her clit into his mouth, then drops the clit and plunges into her again, and goes on like that, sucking and plunging while she moves her hips side to side and up and down.

They're speaking the same language now, and with her clit in his mouth she comes with a scream she's afraid will be heard and understood for blocks around. He penetrates her cunt again, moving in and out, stirring and mixing, kneading her clit with his thumb, keeping her coming until he comes, too, with an international cry of "Ah!" Afterwards he bends over, looking down at her with the replete smile of a gourmet, as though she were the remains of the evening's special. She lies limp on the table, her legs dangling beside his thighs.

"See? I can," he says, and then asks, "You like?" with the same tone of doubt he has when she tastes one of his new omelets, inventively stuffed with avocado and portobello mushrooms or crab and Gruyère cheese. He licks her juices from his lips and nose with a satisfied sigh. She wants to hand him a napkin, but there's not one in reach. She lifts herself off the table, hands like spoons, legs like forks, the whole plate of her cunt licked clean by him.

"For you," he says, as he kisses her once more, and together they wipe the table clean for the bread and cakes, which, wordlessly and still nude, they take from the ovens, long thin loaves of sweet French bread and two large pans of cake, one carrot and the other apple spice, spreading them across the table to cool. Evelyn and Laurent also cool as they walk around the kitchen, washing pans and bowls, wiping counters, picking up their clothes and getting dressed, until everything is in order again so they can turn out the lights and drive away in their separate cars, leaving the kitchen tidy for Edouard and the morning crew.

The Sex Box

Nikki Sinclair

MRS. BROWN HAD MANY private orgasms. She had private orgasms in her bed, in her closet, in the bathroom, and in the bathtub. Once, while the gutter installer hammered outside the window, she had a very intense private orgasm in her kitchen, one foot raised on a step stool. In her defense the gutter installer was shirtless and exceedingly handsome.

Mrs. Brown didn't tell Mr. Brown about her orgasms. He never questioned her about their sex lives. Mr. Brown thought of sex as a private matter, and he thought it best to respect her privacy.

This should not imply the Browns were poorly matched. They agreed on everything, including Amy Brown's recently deceased Aunt Elaine. The old lady had led a disgraceful life.

"Oh my god, look at this," Amy Brown said to her husband. A ruffled maid's outfit draped from her arm. She wiggled a finger through crotchless undies.

"Don't touch it!" her husband, Bradley, warned.

Amy threw it into a box.

"Don't worry, hon. These things are clean. Aunt Elaine was a tart, not a pig."

Aunt Elaine's life closed on a typically spectacular note. While group skydiving, one of her many arcane hobbies, she failed to open her parachute. The investigation revealed simple negligence, and something not so simple. Aunt Elaine died quite naked. What this meant was open to conjecture, for none of her skydiving group was talking.

The Browns threw the rest of Aunt Elaine's clothes and shoes into boxes, along with her (filthy, in Bradley's estimation) many books. In the closet one thing was left: a large, black box.

"What," Amy Brown wondered, "do you suppose this is?"

Bradley hauled it out. "It's got a padlock," he said. Made of plastic, the lock simply popped open when he broke the latch. Both he and his wife stood back.

Inside was a magnificent, curving dildo.

"Oh, my god," Amy said, her voice hushed.

"Awful," Bradley said. "Just awful."

Amy pulled it from the box. Purple, almost a foot long, the dildo was heavy, clublike, with thick veins on its latex surface and big raised studs near the base.

"Aunt Elaine," she said, "you naughty girl."

"Dirty old maid is more like it." Bradley rummaged through the box. "There's more in here."

Next out of the black box were European skin magazines, a real collection. Most of the pictures featured naked men with oversize pricks and voluptuous women with immense, hairy snatches. Under the magazines were more gadgets—cock rings, clips, doodads, and old-time VCR tapes.

Grabbing a tape, Amy read the label. It was in German.

"Let's take a look." She walked to the TV.

"What are you doing?" her husband demanded.

"I'm curious."

"I don't want to watch her smut."

"C'mon. Don't be a scaredy-cat."

Taking the TV remote, she made herself comfortable on the bed. Aunt Elaine owned a big bed. Settling into the pillows, Amy patted the covers.

"C'mon, hon."

The screen flickered. Porno music played, slow, sultry. Smiling, a naked woman entered. The woman had long legs, a big derriere, short, dark hair, and large breasts. At the ready were two men. None of the actors were especially good-looking, evidently winning their roles based on their disproportional sexual equipment.

The woman lay back on a bed while one of the men performed oral sex on her. Then the man entered her, holding one of her legs high as he pumped away. Reaching over, she found and began sucking the very erect cock of the other man.

The woman had a wide mouth and thick lips, and she put them to good use. Her throat went up and down as all three of them came together.

The next scene began immediately; this time the same large-breasted, short-haired woman was giving another woman, almost a girl, a backrub. Both were naked.

Bradley grabbed the remote. "This is a disgrace."

"Wait!" Amy said. She took back the remote.

"For god's sake, Amy. It's two women!"

"One is just a girl." Her eyes were glued to the screen.

The older woman stroked the younger woman's breasts, gently touching the nipples from behind. She stroked and stroked. The girl took both the woman's hands in hers and turned around. They kissed.

Bradley reached for the remote but saw his wife was transfixed. They watched together.

Slender, blonde, pretty, the girl laid the older woman on her back. Down she kissed, down, down, spreading the woman's legs to reveal a big black pussy. She stuck that pert, innocent nose into it as though it were some great poisonous flower.

Bradley heard Amy gasp.

The young girl started licking, slowly, ever so slowly. Then faster. She inserted a finger, then two. She licked faster. The older woman's back arched. She wasn't faking it. Her breasts shook as she came. You saw her come.

The next scene started with three women and two men. One of the women had a riding crop. Amy turned off the television and unbuttoned her pants. For a big woman Mrs. Brown pulled off her pants very fast.

"What are you doing?" Bradley said, helpless.

"Hurry! Get the dildo!"

"Amy, what's gotten into you?"

"Hurry!" Her breath came fast. She began fingering herself.

Bradley grabbed the dildo the way a fireman grabs an ax. There was no time to think.

As he began to slide it in, his wife's back arched.

"More!" she begged. "More!"

She grabbed the base, and Bradley watched as the dildo gradually disappeared, all the way to the wicked spiked nubs.

She ground away. The lights were never on when the Browns made love. The sight of his wife naked, writhing, insatiable, was magnificent to Bradley. And terrifying.

"Brad! Get up here with your cock!"

"What?"

"Your cock. I want it in my mouth *now*!"

Bradley fumbled with his zipper. He stuck his cock in her mouth, and she went into a frenzy, sucking it and jacking herself, the dildo in to the hilt.

Together the Browns came in messy, loud confusion.

"Oh, my god," Bradley said. "What happened?"

Amy went into the bathroom. Washing her face, humming, she cleaned the dildo and returned it to the box.

"What should we do about the box?" Bradley asked his wife.

She put the VCR tape inside and closed it. "We can't throw it out," she said.

"We can't?"

"Some child might find it."

"I see."

"And we can't just leave it here."

"Why not?"

"There's Aunt Elaine's reputation."

"What's left of it," Bradley said, watching her lift the box.

"We better take it home."

"If you think so," he said to her.

"Filthy thing," Amy said.

"Terrible. Just terrible." Bradley followed her.

She carried the box out to the car and put it on the backseat. Mr. Brown drove home.

The Pancake Circus

TREBOR HEALEY

C LOWN DADDY BUSED DISHES at the Pancake Circus, a tacky breakfast joint on Broadway in Sacramento. I only went there when I was depressed and, in my half-baked noncommittal self-destruction, craving food that would kill me if I ingested enough of it. I wanted a steamy stack of buttermilk pancakes with that whipped butter they use that melts slowly and thoroughly, sort of like my psyche does when it's heading south. (It does not have the same effect on your arteries, however, which slowly harden like dog shit in the sun.) And I wanted that diabetes-inducing syrup, of course. Two or three shots of it—lethal as sour mash—surreptitious, sticky, and sweet as it vanishes into the spongy cake, absorbed like a criminal into the social fabric.

Clown Daddy began as a tattoo of a tiger jumping through a ring of fire—a tiger with a pacifier in his mouth. A tiger caged in a mess of plump blue veins—veins like the roots that buckle sidewalks. Straining as they held the pot poised over my cup; straining like my throat suddenly was; like my cock caged in my drawers.

"Coffee?" It was Josh Hartnett's voice.

In an effort to compose myself, I drew a breath and followed those veins up that forearm, down through the dimple of its elbow, and up across the creamy white bicep, firm and round as a young athlete's buttcheek, before the blood-swollen tubes vanished into his white polyester shirt, reappearing at the neck and passing the Adam's apple, which was nothing less than a mushroom head pushing boy-boisterously out of his neck skin like a go-go dancer in Tommies. *God have mercy,* my soul muttered, as my eyes, having lost his veins somewhere under his chin (and damn, what a beautiful charcoal-shadowed chin), proceeded with anticipation up his clean-shaven cheek, savoring the pheromonal (and I mean "moan"-al) beauty of him, dead set for his eyes like a junkie tightening the belt. And bingo, like apples and oranges lining up in a slot—oh my god, I won!

I'm a homo, and you know where I'd look for the coins. I felt my sphincter dilate, and my buttcheeks were suddenly like open-cupped palms, holding themselves out to him.

I came in my pants. And then, a bit unnerved to say the least, cleared my throat. I'm not sure I would have been able to even answer him if I hadn't relieved the pressure somewhere. Fortunately, God had mercy after all.

I whimpered, "Yes, please." I couldn't even look at him, so I watched the cup as he filled it to the top, and then some. It crested the brim and ran down onto the saucer—and then I watched the pot move away, off to the next table.

Jesus H. go-go-dancing Christ. My drawers were soaked and cooling. I felt like a kid who'd wet his pants. This had happened to me only once before, in junior high, when Greg Vandersee had stretched, lifting up his arms and revealing a divine cunt of undcrarm hair that made me lurch forward as my cock emptied its boy-fresh copious fluids into my little BVDs.

Fortunately, Clown Daddy was a busboy and not my waiter. I could handle *yes* and *no*, but *the buttermilk stack, with sausage and one egg over easy* wouldn't have been pretty—or perhaps even possible.

"Hi, I'm Edna. What'll you have?" She smiled.

A bed, some lube, and an hour with your busboy would have been the honest answer. *Or a fresh pair of undergarments.* But this wasn't about honesty; this was about self-destruction. Wasn't it? I ordered the low-cholesterol Egg Beaters in a vegetable omelet with whole-wheat toast. Say what you will—lust leads to healthy choices. Doesn't it?

What I hadn't realized as I sat back gloating, my penis clammy in my damp, semen-soaked briefs, was that when I'd looked in Clown Daddy's eyes my days as a law-abiding citizen had abruptly ended. Choices? Choices had nothing to do with it.

But ignorance is bliss. While it lasts. And while it lasted, my head wobbled like one of those big-headed spring-loaded dolls that resemble

Nancy Reagan, swinging this way and that, watching for him, rolling up and down and around like an amusement park ride, taking in the Pancake Circus as I did so, its paint-by-number clowns adorning the walls, its circus tent decor, its uncanny ambience of a sick crime waiting to happen.

I watched him move about while my fly tightened like a glove over a fist. A wet fist, sticky and greedy for whatever it had just crushed to a sticky pulp. My mind played the sideshow song as I imagined Clown Daddy behind the curtain, Edna up front barking for him: "Step right up; see the man who makes you cum in your drawers!"

I gulped the coffee down, which drew him back to my table like a shark to wet, red, bleeding bait.

He didn't look at me until I thanked him, and then it was just a shy, straight-boy grin. God, but his features were sharp, angled, and clean. His dark, deep-set eyes, the long lashes, the wide mouth with its full lips, the arresting pale blue-white of his skin and the night-black hair—that goddamn shadowed chin. And his eyes: dark as crude oil, raw out of the ground. He was undeniably, painfully handsome. Prozac handsome because he cheered me up. Wellbutrin handsome because one saw one's sadness disappear like a wisp of smoke—and those pesky sexual side effects? Gone. Every woman in the place blushed when he cleared their plates. I probably wasn't the only one stuck to the vinyl seat in my booth. Thank god my cock has no voice or it would have been barking like a dog.

But I felt the letdown all the same. He's probably straight. Though he ignored the blushing dames. He seemed even a little annoyed by their attention. But we knew who each other were, the girls and I. I eyed them and they me. Did I look as greedy as them? Like there was one Cabbage Patch doll left and they'd kill to wrest it from whatever fellow shopper had his or her eye on it. Fact was, we all had holes we wanted his cock in. Simple as that. It was like there was one tree left in the world and the ditches yelped like graves to be the chosen one.

I gulped my food like a scat queen falling off the wagon. Delirious, my diaper soiled, I paid my check and left, one glance over the shoulder to see him bend to pick up a fallen fork. Damn, Clown Daddy had a butt like a stallion. My dog leaped, knocking over the milk dish again. Jesus H. cock-hungry Christ. I lurched out the door as my piss slit opened like a flume on a dam.

Clown Daddy sent me home in a frenzy, is what he did.

I rushed home, needing to get naked. Onto my back on my bed, my legs kicking like an upended insect as I pulled like a madman, again and again, on my slot handle, hitting jackpot after jackpot until my bed was plain lousy with change.

From then on, he filled my nights and days like a cup, brimming over.

I WENT FOR MORE pancakes two days later, but he wasn't there. On the third day, he was, with a beautiful zit on his cheek. Clown Daddy looked right through me when he recognized me, and then he pulled himself back out.

I lurched. Shit—I came again.

"Coffee?"

"Uh, yeah," I half coughed.

"Cream?"

I nodded. The greed. My shorts were already full of it.

"Sugar?" He's talkative today.

I regained my composure. "No sugar—sugar's for kids," I answered flirtatiously.

I don't know why I said it. I had to say something. I wanted to hold him there, even if for only a few seconds.

He smiled the brightest smile, and walked away.

My head swiveled. What was that? Had he flirted back?

While I waited for my waitress, I read the ads urethaned into the tabletop: vacuum repair, van conversions, derogatory credit, body shops, auto detailing, furniture, appliances, and bail bonds. The clues were everywhere. It occurred to me then that he was the only white busboy in the place. The rest were illegal Latin guys who didn't have a choice. What would a citizen take a job like this for? Maybe he was Romanian or something. But he had no accent. What could he be making—four, five bucks an hour? Hell, his looks alone could get him ten doing nothing for the right boss. He could hustle at two hundred an hour, do porn for a few thousand a feature; he could wait tables and fuck up and they'd still forgive him because the doyennes of Sacramento would return for the way he made them feel against their seat cushions. *What* was he doing here?

Who *cares*. Just let me fuck him. Shoot first, ask questions later.

He was as aloof as ever when he came back with the coffee. Three cups later, I asked for sugar. He smiled again. "Sugar's for kids. You like kids?"

"Sure, kids are all right."

He nodded and raised his brows with just a hint of a grin as he said, sort of stoned-like, "Kids are all right." And he walked away.

Go figure. I scribbled my phone number on the coffee coaster, with a little cartoon kid, waving.

AND HE CALLED. BUT he never left his name.

"This is the guy who likes kids, down at the Circus. I can't leave a number, but meet me at the Circus at three Wednesday."

I jacked off at two-thirty, not wanting to repeat my little Pancake Circus habitual jackpot when I sidled up to shake his hand. My knees might buckle, and then what? Would I hold on to his hand and pull him down with me? Would I beg him to clean up my shorts with his tongue? Would he do it?

I needed to get hold of myself. I turned the key in the deadbolt as I left the house. I pushed the key in hard, my mouth agape. In and out went the key. I reached for the knob. Good God, I've lost it.

I saw him from two blocks away. He sat on the low wall of the planter that had endured, neglected and falling to pieces with its ratty bushes and weeds, between the sidewalk and the parking lot.

He wore black boots, Levi's, and a camouflage winter coat. Not a promising fashion statement for what I had in mind.

He nodded when he saw me coming, but ignored my hand when I put it out to shake. He just said, "What's up?" And then, without waiting for an answer, added, "There's a playground about five blocks from here."

"What?"

"Come on, I'll show you."

I feigned having a clue, but I really didn't have one until it occurred to me he might be suggesting a place to have sex—some doorway maybe, or a clump of trees out of view that school yards were notorious for. But it was three P.M.; school would still be in session.

I could see the school-yard fence from a couple blocks away as we approached. Stepping off a curb, he abruptly grabbed my arm by the bicep, and my cock leaped like a Jack Russell terrier.

"Stop here," he stated flatly.

I looked at him inquisitively, at a loss. He dropped his gaze and I followed it as, with his left hand firmly in his pocket, he lifted his pant leg slowly to reveal a plastic contraption surrounding his ankle. A small green light pulsed intermittently. He studied it, then, backing up three feet, got it to stop pulsing and simply glow a constant green.

"This is as far as I can go," he stated, matter-of-factly.

It took me a minute to realize he was under house arrest. What does it mean? I didn't know anything about law enforcement. Drunk driving? It must be some kind of probation. He's probably a rapist or a killer, a thief or a drug dealer. Nah, too cute to rape. But if he's fucked up enough, what would that matter? Too smart to kill. Thieves are a dime a dozen, and I'm only carrying twenty bucks. Drug dealing? Humbug. So what. But none of these possibilities were in any way convincing. He was just too sexy to fit any criminal stereotype, which shows you what a dumb fuck I was.

I may have misread him, but I wasn't completely foolish. Not completely. I knew he was a criminal, so I figured I'd need to find out about the ankle bracelet before taking him home. Just in case he was going to murder me or steal my stereo. The logic of queers. On top of all that, I assumed he'd tell me the truth, which was preposterous—except that he did. More or less.

He retired to a sloping lawn in front of a house on the corner, offering, "This will be fine." I was getting more and more confused. Sex right here?

Within minutes, we heard them: the cacophony of tykes, who were now streaming down the street in gaggles. They reached the far corner, stopped, looked both ways, and then proceeded across. Group after group of them: little Koreans and Viets with rolling book bags, Mexican kids burdened by overstuffed backpacks, white kids on skateboards, little black kids strutting.

"Aren't they beautiful?" he said.

"Sure they are," I concurred. "Kids are like flowers."

"Flowers?" He looked at me like I was stupid.

"You know, those colorful things? New life? All that?" He wasn't buying my poetry.

"I mean beautiful like meat," and he ran his tongue lasciviously across his full upper lip as it occurred to me, amid my throbbing erection, that he was a pedophile. My cock was like a poised spear now, but not because of what he'd just confessed about his sexual orientation—it was his tongue and what it had just performed. Take me, you beast. I must confess, the moral repugnance was not the first thought that entered my mind, nor the second. The tongue being the first, what followed was my sudden disappointment that not only was I possibly the wrong gender, but I was most definitely not the right age. I hadn't a chance. My cock still reached for him, fighting against the binding of my jeans—not to mention the limits of his orientation—like a child having a tantrum, refusing to let go of a cherished teddy bear. But I felt the sweat on my asshole cool.

HE LAY BACK, a sprig of grass in his teeth, smiling at the kids—a pedophile cad. They smiled back. Jesus Wayne Gacy, we were cruising!

I tried to get a foothold. "Uh, would you like to go grab a coffee?"

"Nah, I'm happy right here."

I said nothing more, paralyzed with ineptitude. We sat there for just fifteen minutes, until the herd had passed.

"Damn, I gotta jack off. Come on."

Speaking of come-ons—was this one? I'm not sure I was interested anymore, but of course my cock still was, throbbing like a felon in chains. I followed.

Back to Broadway, to an ugly stucco motel–looking apartment building streaked with rusty-drain runoff, its windows curtained and unwelcoming. Clown Daddy said nothing. He simply keyed the lock, and I followed him into one of the saddest apartments I'd ever seen. A mattress lay in the middle of the living room, with a single twisted blanket on it. There was an alarm clock on the floor, and in the kitchen, fast food trash in the sink.

The toilet was foul and ringed with dark grime. There were no pictures; no kitchen utensils, plates, or cups; no toaster; no coffee maker; no books; no phone. Other than the bed and the roof and plumbing, there was but one thing that made the place habitable at all: a TV with a VCR.

He pulled a videocassette out of the back lining of his camouflage hunting jacket and placed it in the VCR. He sat down on the bed, suddenly eager and animated. "I just got this from a dude I met. It better be good; it cost me thirty bucks." There were no credits, no title, not even sound. There were a lot of kids though, doing things that got people put away.

"I think I better go," I muttered, when all at once, with his elbows now supporting him on the bed, he leaned back and yanked his jeans down, revealing an enormous marbled manhood that slapped back across his taut belly like a call to prayer. His eyes fixed on the TV, never even acknowledging his handsome cock as he grabbed it full-fisted. *Jesus God,* I muttered to myself, staring at one of the most stunning penises I'd ever seen: nine inches, wired like the backside of a computer with mouth-watering veinage, and nested in the blackest of hair, which right now was casting deep forested shadows as it worked its way under his well-stocked jumbo-size scrotum. I never had a choice. It was in my mouth before I made any decisions or even considered whether he wanted it there. He didn't protest, bucking his hips and driving into my whimpering mouth as he glared at the TV set. I shot in my pants with out so much as touching myself, just moments before my throat filled like a cream pastry, hot gobs of his God-juice leaking from the crust.

I tongued it clean before he quickly grabbed it like a hammer, or anything else I could have been borrowing, to put it away. He didn't even look at me as he hopped to his feet, yanking up his jeans in one fluid motion. It wasn't fear of intimacy like I'd seen with other guys. He was simply done, and more or less emotionless—in his own world. God knows what he'd been thinking as he bucked his manly juices into my craving body, which for him had become just one big hole to propel his antisocial lusts into. I can't call it my mouth; it was just what was available. I'd have torn my skin back like curtains if it were possible and let him drill through whatever part of me got him off.

"That tape sucked," he casually related. I was still sitting on the bed, stunned, not knowing what to do, licking the remnants of his now-cooling semen off my chapped lips. "I gotta go to work," he informed me, pulling the videocassette out and handing it to me, without making eye contact.

"Uh, I don't want this," I said as my hand opened to accept it.

"No? Don't you like kids?"

"Uh, I think you know what I like."

He said nothing. Then: "Keep it for me till next time." And he grinned.

"Next time?" I was in a daze, but hope springs eternal.

"Yeah, next time I see you." I lit up even though I was consumed with dread from what, other than the amazing cock action, was a profoundly depressing social interaction.

"I'll just leave it here," I said, balking.

"No can do, guy. I'm on probation. Can't have that here. Keep it for me."

"Uh, yeah, sure, till next time."

I didn't think myself an accomplice as I walked home. What did I know about such legal machinations? I only knew I was no longer depressed and had just had one of life's peak experiences. Had his cock literally trounced thousands of years of science that had eventually developed selective serotonin reuptake inhibitors? Imagine the clinical trials. I'd seen a lot of cocks, a lot of naked men, like any fag. But Jesus H. Priapus Satyriasis, I had never seen such a beautiful manifestation of the male organ anywhere—in print, on film, in my bed, even in my fantasy life, which was no slacker when it came to cock. I imagined what it must have been like for explorers coming upon Yosemite, Victoria Falls, the Grand Canyon. Unimaginable and sublime beauty. I leaned against a wall at one point on the walk home, needing to catch my breath, my cock once again tenting my jeans. The fact of the matter was: I was strung out on his cock. And I didn't even have a phone number.

No matter. He called, thank god. It was either that or I was in for a lot of pancakes.

"I got some more tapes. Wanna come over and check them out?"

I didn't hear any of it but the come-over part. "When?"

"Now."

"I'm on my way."

The door was cracked when I arrived. When I opened it to step in, I lost my breath. Splayed across the bed was Clown Daddy, his substantial manhood like the clock tower at some university—everything converged toward it.

"Oh baby," was all I could think to say, which was oddly appropriate considering what was happening on the VCR where his gaze was fixed. My brows furrowed. Good god, they can't be more than three.

"Come to poppa," he said with a fatherly grin.

I was like a panting puppy with the promise of a walk. He held the leash. I leaped and was sucking on his teat like a hungry lamb before you could say baahhh, drooling and lapping up and down the hard shaft, savoring the throbbing gristle of his veins, weeping at the sweet softness of the massive velvety helmet. I was aware of what felt like a tear rolling down my inner thigh. My asshole was sweating like a day laborer short on rent: more baskets, more peaches.

I knew I needed to strip but balked at taking a time-out for fear he'd lose interest or lose control. I hopped up and stripped quickly. He didn't even notice, his eyes locked on the romper-room shenanigans stage left like a baby enthralled with a mobile.

I knew all I had to do was get into position, and in no time was on my knees, facing the TV, blocking Clown Daddy's view. He didn't miss a beat as he hopped up on his knees and grabbed my waist, answering my plea for "Lube, Clown Daddy, lube," with a hawk into his palm.

I opened like sunrise, pulled him into me more than he plunged. I heard him as he vanished into my sleeve: "Uuuuuuuuuuuuuuuuhhh." And I matched him like a chorus: "Aaaaaaaaaaaaahhhhhh." I dropped my face into the mattress as he pounded me, knowing I'd be unable to maintain any balance with my arms, which not only were shaking with excitement, but were seriously challenged considering the slams he was delivering and the fact that my body's focus was pretty much solely directed at the contractions of my rectum as it greedily grabbed at what can only be described as the bread of life. A baguette of it, no less.

He sent me onto the floor by thrust ten or so, and then he emitted an enormous Josh Hartnett *"Fuuuuck,"* as my asshole filled with his ambrosia.

He pulled out with a *pop* and wiped his cock with the blanket and fell backward onto his back. "That's a great age," he wistfully concluded, staring at the ceiling.

I felt a momentary sinking feeling as I looked at the video monitor, realizing all at once the makeover I would need if I was to hold on to Clown Daddy past the duration of his probation.

"I gotta go to work," he stated. I nodded; I knew the protocol. He popped out the tape and handed it to me. I staggered down the walk-way of that shitty apartment building, past dried-out cactuses in pots and a pair of roller skates—good God, did his or her parents know who was living next door? What about Megan's Law? I was lost in a strange milieu of overarching lust, revulsion, horror, responsibility, and that unique postfuck feeling of *that was great; everything's gonna be just fine*.

AT HOME, I FUMBLED through my bathroom drawers for the Flowbee and set to work shaving my body clean of hair. While my mind remained a stew of anxiety, and I winced at the razor nicks I was inflicting on my balls, I reveled in how I was going to finally incite his lust as he had mine.

Next, I got out my sewing machine and set to work on a new wardrobe: a sailor suit, a Boy Scout uniform, a large diaper, Teletubbie briefs.

I put on the briefs and sailor suit, looked at myself in the mirror. Ridiculous. *Don't be so negative.* I self-talked back. I did a striptease, attempting to be convincing. I worked on my little-boy shy look. But when I finally dropped my trousers and gazed at my hairless cock, I was sorely dismayed. I had a big dick, huge really, and the shaving had only made it look bigger. How am I gonna convince Clown Daddy I'm a child with this thing? How many grade-schoolers are packing eight inches? Then there was my chest and arms. I worked out, for God's sake; I was a mess of secondary sex characteristics. I needed to gain fifty pounds, maybe take some hormones. *One step at a time*, I calmed my-self.

I'd done what I could and I wanted to see him, to show him how I'd be whatever he wanted me to be. I don't think at that time I was considering saving him and reforming him. I just wanted to please him, make of myself a gift. Woo him.

Chocolate. I bought a box of Le Petite Ecoliers and went for pan-cakes. He smiled big when he saw me. The hostess looked askance. The crowd wondered. It occurred to me I was exposing him. I blushed red as a swollen cockhead. I left as quickly as I'd come, racing back up the street. Whatever happened, I didn't want to hurt Clown Daddy. Good-ness no, I was interested in his pleasure.

There was a message on the machine when I got home: "Nice suit, hee, hee. Eight P.M. Wear it." Click.

The shirt never came off, as Clown Daddy's maleness-hovered over me and he ominously climbed up on top of me, his lead pipe of a cock bobbing like a tank gun, my legs held behind my ears like the spring-loaded pogo stick which I would soon be playing the part of as he bounced me off the mattress.

"You look fucking great." He smiled, and he kissed me this time, full, his tongue like a tapeworm, bent on my intestines, determined to reach all the way down to where his cock was reaching from the other end to meet it in a hot sticky mess of saliva and semen.

"Daddy, Daddy, Daddy," I yelped. We growled; we lost ourselves and rode our dicks like runaway horses. His final thrusts were so divine, my hands digging into his firm white butt cheeks like talons holding their kill. He split me like a piece of wood, and my cum hit his chest so hard it bounced and splattered like blood would if the ax of his cock had buried itself in my forehead.

I'd brought the diaper in my backpack.

"Daddy . . . please . . . diaper me."

He guffawed, and then with an eagerness I'd never seen, yelped, "Yeeeeaaah!"

He diapered me. Patted my ass. Told me to pack up and get out.

My god, I'd done it. I'd seduced Clown Daddy.

He didn't kiss me good-bye, of course, or invite me to brunch. But I walked away without a videocassette this time. Progress.

I GUESS THAT'S WHEN it occurred to me I could save him. And maybe not only him. Maybe I'd just found the treatment for pedophilia. God knows, no one seemed to give a damn about these people. The last sexual minority. I could rehabilitate them all. My shaved asshole, a rehab center.

That's when I saw the squad car. Parked in front of my house. Next to the undercover white Crown Royal. Three men in dark suits. It was *The Matrix,* and I was Neo, standing on a street corner in a sailor suit, my hips bulging from the diaper that swaddled my manhood.

I knew what they'd found. I knew my chances. I ran. It wasn't much of a chase. I had nowhere to go. All I had was a shot at making it back to Broadway, where the great voting public could witness four cops tackling a child—a rather large child, to be sure—in a sailor suit.

I felt the tug as one of them got hold of the back of my shirt just as I reached the intersection of Twenty-third and Broadway. I screamed as high-piercing a preadolescent scream as I could muster.

I was interrogated at length. I assumed they had Clown Daddy somewhere. How else would they have nabbed me? I drank coffee, got knocked around, but through it all I endured by dreaming of meeting Clown Daddy—when I was finally convicted—in some filthy prison cell where we could pursue our love affair in peace—my trading cigarettes and gum for razors to keep my cock and balls soft as a baby's behind for my Clown Daddy and his meat-Eucharist, truly a transubstantiation of all the misery around us into an Elysian Field of bliss.

"Where did you get the tapes?"

I refused to tell. "I found them."

"Where?"

I had to place them as far away from Clown Daddy as possible. "In a trash can in Vacaville."

"What were you doing going through trash in Vacaville?"

"Someone on the Internet told me he'd put them there." I was indicting myself. I thought I was saving Clown Daddy. If I had to lie, even to the point of destroying my own future, I'd do it for Clown Daddy—blinded by love, or myopia for his cock. Same difference. And to think I didn't even know the details of his crime. We'd never discussed it. I didn't want to know.

"Who?" The cop demanded, but in a boring, annoying, nonsexual way. Why couldn't Clown Daddy be my interrogator?

"It was one of those throwaway names."

"What was it?"

"Bob."

"Goddamnit! Bob who?"

"Bob1 at aol-dot-com."

Whack! And he backhanded me across the face.

They threatened me with a stiff sentence if I didn't give them something. I only considered that their sentence could never be as stiff as Clown Daddy's meaty member, so I was unimpressed by their threats.

They gave me five years.

CLOWN DADDY DID NOT appear in my cell block, though I looked and waited and pined. It had been explained in my trial that the videos found in my home had been coded with a tracking device, leading the authorities to my house. Not unlike an ankle bracelet such as Clown Daddy wore. It had even been suggested that Clown Daddy was a narc, or had used me as a patsy. The judge put a stop to those conjectures, admonishing the defense: "Whoever gave him the pornography is not on trial today. Another day. Right now, we're trying this man." And he pointed at me like Clown Daddy's member used to do.

Clown Daddy never appeared. Only Vernon. He was my cell mate, and he informed me, as a skinny white fag, I'd be wise to do his bidding. I've done it, though he lacks both Clown Daddy's girth and length, not to mention all the other characteristics that gods wield over man.

Ah, but the gods are kind for they have blest us with imagination. And so when Vernon slicks his member with Crisco I steal from the commissary and mercilessly impales me, I close my eyes and see a circus tent, and the circus music begins, and all the clowns drop their baggy pants, and then the tigers and lions turn, lifting their tails, and the dwarves and ape men offer up their tight behinds, hands firmly gripped to their ankles—and the crowd cheers, and then goes *Aaahhh* as Clown Daddy in all his naked huge-dicked grinning Josh Hartnett–throated glory comes swinging through on the trapeze spraying his jism all over the clowns and animals, dwarves and freaks, and the whole damn crowd, who bathe in it as in the blessed waters of Lourdes.

And Vernon is proud. He thinks he's made that mess all over my chest and belly. Let him think it. The truth is hardly important at this point. I'm an innocent man doing time for kiddie porn; the police are fools; Vernon's a chump; and my asshole's just a 7-Eleven that he holds up every Saturday night. As for the cash, I hand it right over. In fact, I leave the register open. No way to run a business. But I, unlike Vernon, am not proud. For I have seen God.

I spend all my time with him. Vernon that is, not God. We even eat pancakes together. I stuff my face. I'm fattening up for Clown Daddy, while Vernon goes on and on with his theories.

"The earth is a plate," he tells me. "Mankind sat down and is eating. When he's through, it'll be over."

"Where are we now?" I ask, bored.

"Somewhere deep in the mashed potatoes, maybe halfway through."

"Are you gay, Vernon?" I like to get a rise out of him.

"Not at all," he explains. He tells me men are pigs, and this is why you can't call him a faggot. Vernon says if it were legal most men he knew (and he knew a certain kind, though he always meant every man) would fuck everything in sight, and what's more, they'd never let their sex partners survive to betray them (as they always will, by his reckoning—something to remember when I get out of here). Therefore, he's of the opinion that men "would drill holes in their sex partner's skulls if they could, and fuck their brains out. They'd drill holes in backs and arms, thighs, through the bottoms of feet, right through the front of 'em, core the motherfuckers like apples," he says drolly, "leave them like the dough after all the cookies have been cut out of it. But the screaming would be annoying, so you'd do the brain first."

"Do you like the circus, Vernon?"

He shrugs his shoulders. "I don't like those clowns. Creepy."

"I knew a clown once."

"Shut up and eat."

I pour more syrup on my pancakes and watch it vanish, watch it run away and join the circus.

The Razor

TSAURAH LITZKY

I'M GOING TO TELL you what I want; I always wanted to have someone do this to me," she said. "I've never asked anyone, but I'm asking you."

The bed smelled of her ripe juices. She was a fountain when she wanted me, all her desire rushing out between her legs, wetting the sheets, soaking the hair at the base of my prick. My crotch would dry all matted and stiff, but I didn't care. I liked to listen to her talk, her voice going all high and squeaky when she gets excited about something. I draped my arm across her body like a flag. "Why me?" I asked.

"Because you're the one I want to do this to me," she said.

"But why?" I asked again.

"Well, for one thing, you let me do what I want with you," she answered, "like when you let me tie your ankles up with my bra and then let me climb on top of you. Then remember that night when you let me stick my fingers up your ass, first one, then two, even three. You didn't say no, you fucked me even harder even though by finger three, it must have really hurt."

It did hurt, but now I was glad I hadn't told her.

"You never laughed at me," she went on, "when I got confused trying to operate your microwave or even that time I pissed your bed after Ursula's birthday party. I fell out so drunk with all my clothes on, and during the night I pissed your bed. In the morning you weren't angry with me. You got me up out of the wet and got me into the shower and then you made me French toast. While I was eating, you stripped the sheets."

I moved my hand up along her rib cage. It was thin and delicate like a bird's, yet her breasts were so full they fell over my fingers, warming them. I put my hand over her fat tit. I squeezed it. "But what is it you want me to do exactly?" I said. I squeezed some more, and her little nipple hardened and pressed into my palm like a penny.

"I'm getting there, I'm getting there," she said. "Now, this is what it is: One time, I want to come to see you. When I get here, take me into the bathroom, take off all my clothes. Run me a nice, warm bath. When it's full, pick me up and put me in the tub. Scrub me all over with that green Ayurvedic soap you have. I love how it smells like a pine forest. Use your hands to scrub me, not a cloth; wash me good.

"When I'm real clean, take me out of the tub, and dry me with a big, fluffy towel. Now, this is a very important detail. I want you to get nail polish remover and a decent nail file. Take the polish off my fingernails and my toenails. Then file them. I want you to do a very, very good job; make sure my fingernails are filed down smooth and soft like a baby's. Then you can sit me down on the edge of the tub and run fresh water.

"I want you to get one of those old straight-backed razors, and then shave my body hair all off, every single bit. You can use your Brylcreem. Shave the spiky growth under my arms; shave the down off my arms and legs. Now here's the best part: when all the hair is gone, spread my legs wide open and kneel down between them. Shear all the hair off my delta. I know it's a tough, wiry growth, but keep at it, take your time. While you're shaving me, I'll put my fingers in your mouth so you can suck them if you want."

I was getting hard, just hearing her talk. "I want," I told her.

"Then," she continued, "shave along both sides of my slit, and make sure you clear away this silly, thick tuft on top." She grabbed one of my hands and moved it down to show me the stubborn curl she meant. "Yeah, this one," she said. I tugged it a couple of times. "Then," she instructed, "keep shaving until all you can see is pure white skin. After that, stand me up and turn me around so you can shave my back hole. Shave the little hairs that grow there away so it looks like a baby's mouth opening for its first kiss."

I was breathing heavy, and I could feel my prick rising, jumping up like a frisky goat.

"And when my body is totally, totally hairless," she went on, "I want you to pick me up in your arms, cradle me, and carry me into your bedroom. Put me down on the bed, kiss me all over, and fuck me like it's our first ever."

My prick was standing up like a pole. "I could do that right now," I told her, and I took her hand and placed it around me. "Feel," I said. "I could shave you, but I don't have one of those razors. I have an electric one, a Norelco."

"No," she said, with a little frown, "that won't do. I want one of one of the straight, folding ones, like my grandpa had. He used to let me sit on the toilet and watch him shave. He let me soap his shaving brush up in a little cup he had with soap inside while he got the razor sharp on a big old leather strap. I loved how that strap smelled, like good heavy man sweat and bittersweet chocolate. Maybe that's why I still love the way old leather smells, it gets me hot."

"Do you want to smell my belts?" I asked her.

"No, no silly," she said, "but I would just love it if you would get one of those razors."

"Okay," I said, "I will." She was still holding me. She began to move her little hand slowly on me, gently up and down, up and down.

"Would you, would you really do that?" she asked, turning on her side so that her silky breast touched my arm.

"Sure," I answered, "Why not?"

"Great, that's great," she said, leaning over me, and then she bent her head and took me in her mouth.

THE NEXT DAY JUST before I woke up I had a dream that I was shaving, and she was sitting on the toilet watching me, smiling. Only she wasn't a little girl, she was all grown up and gorgeous like now. I could see the thin strip of black hair above her open knees, her shapely legs, the pink panties resting against her ankles like a garland. With every stroke of the razor she opened her legs wider until I could see, finally, her pretty purple nether lips reaching out to me. I woke up, then, with my rigid prick in both hands. It took only two or three fast stokes till I came like a geyser. That's what she always did to me.

I got up, took a shower, made coffee, and drank two cups trying to distance myself from her enough to write. I tried to work on the article

I was in the middle of about contemporary journalism. Yesterday I enjoyed calling my colleagues yellow-bellied fleas, but today I was too obsessed with her to concentrate. I stared at the computer screen. Instead of the words in front of me I could see only her face, all screwed up like it gets at the moment of orgasm. Her mouth is always pursed together as if she is about to speak, as if to call me "love" or say my name, but she never says anything.

I turned off the computer, grabbed my jacket and wallet, and headed out the door onto Thompson Street. I turned the corner and walked up to Sixth Avenue toward Bleecker. I knew just where to get the kind of razor she wanted.

I headed over to Bleecker Street; between Christopher and Charles Streets, there is a little antique row. I went into the second store from the corner, Born Again Antiques. I liked the name. The proprietor was bald, with a lotus surrounded by a ring of flame tattooed on the top of his head. Perhaps I had come to the right place.

I told him what I wanted. "I got a couple," he said. He led me to a long glass case. From within a jumble of flasks and cigarette lighters, he pulled out two razors and put them on top of the showcase. One had a black handle, the other a white one.

"This," he said, picking up the black one, "is a German make, a Wostenhomer, 1890s. Excellent condition, handle's probably elk bone. The blade is perfect, no rust or nicks." He flicked open the blade to show me. "I keep 'em so sharp they can peel a grape," he said. He put down the Wostenhomer and picked up the other one. "But this, this is a Barlow, made here, right in the U.S.A. There's a hairline crack on one of the pins," he said, and he opened the blade to show me. "And it's seen some wear, but hell, man, it's a Barlow. They never made a better straight-edge razor. The handle's ivory," he told me.

Ivory, I thought, *Ivory, the color of her skin*. "How's it feel?" I asked. He handed it to me. It fit perfectly across the palm of my hand, the blade reaching out between my thumb and forefinger.

"I'll take it." I said. "How much?"

"Ninety bucks," he answered me. I took out my wallet and handed him my credit card.

All the way home I walked beneath the green spring trees holding the razor folded inside my hand like a lodestone that would lead me to her. At home, I put it on my worktable between the computer and the telephone; then I opened the blade. I wanted to look at the long clean line of it, eager and erect. I reached for the phone; she picked up on the third ring.

"I got it," I said.

"Got what?" she asked.

"The razor," I told her. "The straight-back razor; you know, like your grandfather used."

"Oh, you did," she said. I couldn't interpret the tone of her voice.

"Listen, do you want to come over here tonight? I have plenty of Brylcreem, and I'm going to out to buy towels now."

"I don't know," she said. "I guess I'm surprised how quick you just went out and got it; maybe I'm not ready yet in my mind."

I was already disappointed, "Come on, b-b-baby," I stuttered. "I can g-g-get you ready." I was trying to sound like a tough guy, like Bogart in *Casablanca,* but I knew I sounded hesitant, more like Jake in *A Farewell to Arms.*

"I'm tired from the shoot this morning, and I'm still kind of sore from last night," she said. "Let's do it tomorrow."

I wasn't going to fight about it. "Okay, whatever. Tomorrow it is, eight-thirty?"

"Yes," she said.

The next night, I had everything I needed in place by eight. The bathtub was clean, new towels were on the towel rack, and I had fresh sky blue sheets for the bed. I was on the sofa, listening for her footsteps, trying to keep my eyes off the clock on the wall. I was nervous, my palms sweating. Was it ambivalence I sensed on the phone? Had someone else suddenly entered her life, a young stud she met on her job or maybe an older man, a grandfather type? Maybe there was someone else all along?

The razor was still on my worktable. I was aching to show it to her. She was ten minutes late when she knocked. When I opened the door, I couldn't stop myself from grabbing her, hugging her tight.

"Hey," she said, pulling away. "I need to breathe. I can't believe you found one."

I told her I got it in an antique store. "Want to see it?" I asked.

She nodded.

I led her over to the table.

"The way it curves," she said, "reminds me of the raccoon penis bone I saw at the Museum of Natural History."

"The handle is ivory," I told her as I picked it up and handed it to her.

"It's beautiful" she exclaimed, her fingers curling around it. "Now I want you to use it on me," she said. "I want you to slice away all my stubborn hair, all my tangled secrets."

She stood on her toes to kiss me, her pointy tongue leaping into my mouth like a little snake, my little snake. When we finished kissing, we sat together on the couch; her hand, still holding the razor, was resting on my knee.

"I have an idea," she said. "Before we start, I want you to blindfold me. That way, I'll feel the whole thing more; the scrape of the razor, your touch keeping me still. I don't want to look at my body until I am hairless like a baby. But one thing, before you blindfold me, I want you to open the knife, show me the blade."

"All right," I told her, "but first we have to find a blindfold."

We settled on my old blue work shirt. I folded it in such a way that the sleeves hung down. Before I tied it on, I opened the knife to show the blade to her. She ran her finger across it so sharply she drew blood, a thin red line. She wiped her bloody finger across my lips.

I tied the blindfold around her eyes. The razor in one hand, I pushed her into the bathroom. I yanked off my clothes and threw them on top of the hamper. I turned the water on in the tub, then peeled off her things and threw them on top of my own. Blindfolded, she didn't look like herself. Her naked body looked heavier, almost puffy in the strong fluorescent bathroom light. I noticed for the first time the beginnings of cellulite on the backs of her thighs as well as a disturbing small circular scar under her armpit that looked like a cigarette burn.

I scooped her up and put her in the tub. The water covered her legs, her hips, and came partway up her chest. I shut off the tap. She turned her face up to me and smiled blindly. For an instant, she changed, she became a sea creature, my shirt spreading out behind her like the tresses of a siren, her legs spread straight out in front of her to form the glistening opalescent tail of a mermaid.

I soaped her up pretty quick. The open razor resting on the edge of the sink was beckoning me. I lifted her out of the tub and toweled her dry.

"Bet you forgot the nail polish remover and nail clippers," she said.

"Ye of little faith! They are on the sink." I said. I sat her down on the toilet and tended to her nails, taking special care as she requested. Then I emptied out the bathtub, swabbed it clean, and started the water running again. She stood in front of me, one hand on my shoulder to steady herself. I lathered her up with Brylcreem and started to shave. She had so much hair on her pubis. Every few strokes I had to stop and rinse the razor, then lather her up again.

Her whole body started to tremble. She didn't say anything, but as I kept going, I could feel her hand on my shoulder getting hotter, melting into me, as if wave after wave of deep heat were steaming up from her vortex as I shaved. Carefully, painstakingly, I kept at it, revealing more of her ivory vulva and, finally, the rosy curled petals of her cunt. My dick was so heavy between my legs. I wanted to spear her right then and there, but I still had to shear off the hairs around her butt hole.

I put the razor back on the sink and cupped her bare pelvis in my hand. I put my middle finger inside her twat as I turned her. She began to rock on my hand, back and forth. I bent her forward at the waist, guiding her so she could grasp the rim of the tub.

I pulled her crease open, revealing the bosky dell I knew I'd find there. I grasped the razor again. Using more Brylcreem, I worked my way up her perineum and into the tight fleshy crater that topped it. Soon every hair, every wisp, was gone.

What faced me did look like the mouth of a baby, such a sweet pink little mouth. I put the razor down again and grabbed her, pulling her toward me by the hips. I could not resist that baby mouth. I fucked her there with my tongue, in and out, round and round. She started to moan, "Oh, oh, oh." This time she did call out my name.

I was so excited, I was ready to let go, but I didn't want to come, not yet. I stopped, moved back.

"Take off the blindfold, take it off," she cried out. "I'm all shaved now. I want to see."

I stood up, untied the knot at the back, and let the blindfold fall to the floor.

"Wow," she said, looking down, "I'm white as a pearl, and you did it, you did it!"

My prick was aiming straight at her, like an arrow. She reached out and grabbed it, traced a circle with the tip around her new smooth-as-satin vulva.

"I can really feel you on my skin now," she said with a giant smile. "Now pick me up and carry me to bed."

I gathered her up and held her high, rocking her. Her face was against my chest, and she opened her lips to take in my nipple, sucking it hungrily like a newborn sucks. How could I have ever doubted her? My prick jerked against the bottom of her crack, tap, tap, tapping, *Let me in, let me in* . . .

As I carried her out of the bathroom I noticed the razor lying open on the sink, its blade still covered with puffs of foam.

Soon, I was hammering her. She moved in perfect sync beneath me, pulling me deeper and deeper into her heart. Just as I was about to burst, she whispered, "You know why I wanted you to file my nails short?"

"So they'd feel like a baby's?" I gasped.

"There was another reason," she said. I felt her smooth hand on my buttocks, moving toward my ass, and then, her small, sure fingers gliding inside.

Dream Machine

LAURALEIGH FARRELL

I'M NOT SUBMISSIVE AT all, really, but, well . . . I do have this fantasy. I want to be taken by a machine. I want my lover to be mindless, a thing hard, clumsy, inorganic, unsympathetic—and to treat me like an object. This is my romance: I want to be taken by the cold clatter of the impersonal.

I've also been told that if you go to sleep every night visualizing something in your head, you will dream about that something. I don't live by this New Age stuff as a rule, but if it can deliver me good sex, I'll get on board. So I've started a program. Every night before I go to bed, I fantasize about the machine that will take me. It's not just a Fuckingmachine, that one-trick in-out with a motor, all about the drill. No, this is a machine that will fuck all over me. It has little metallic bird claws for grasping breast flesh and nipples and lips. It has perhaps a hundred of these because I want to feel inundated. I want my body to feel like a beach head for an invasion that's out of control. I want it to be as though mindless hoards have converted me, turned my whole pig being into choice cuts, parceled me off into ham and hock, rump and tongue, claimed the bits and carried them away. I want to be sexually disassembled. In my sleep.

So I picture these metallic claw feet clacking and clamping away at the end of thin, steely penciled arms jointed together. The arms are greased, like any good machine would be. So that when they grab and claw me, they leave behind a slick mucus on my skin. It shines; it makes my parts more sensitive. I jump at every cool claw touch. And the machine claims me for a piece of territory with this grease, like a male dog with its pee.

The claws are clumsy. When they stab and grab at my nipples, they miss mostly, clutching a piece of breast here or poking a sensitive patch of areola there. Each random jab makes me jump and my clit tumble till the nipple of that tit goes quivery from breast abuse, which makes the breast even more difficult to grasp. The claws' vicious cycle of clumsiness, of machined insensitivity, wreaks intense nerve twitch all over my body. I like that it doesn't care. The claws snatch the soft flesh under my armpits (my nipples turn to goose bumps), the skin around my jaw, my breasts (which roll from side to side under the sheer number of them snipping and shoving), my thigh meat, the soles of my feet, the sweet plumpness of my pussy mound. Pinch, pinch. Every nerve ending in my pitiful human pelt is on a hair trigger right now. And the hundreds of rude machine insults continue unabated across my body. It does not ask what I want, this machine. It doles out sensations like a god. Insisting, insisting, coming at me, coming at me, it overwhelms me speechless.

My machine has parts other than its claws, of course. Things to probe me. Things to open me. Things to spread my parts, uninvited. It has hard, steely bands that clamp down on my upper arms (imprinting the soft flesh), and pin me to the cold table it has thrown me over. When the time is right, it will clamp hold of my thighs, firm, merciless around the muscle. It will pick them up, open them wide, slam them back down, and fix me there spread so wide my cunt unsticks itself and the lips drop open, fall wider, wider apart. If I squirm, I will go nowhere. If I wrench, this machine will be unyielding. My trunk is held fast with an inhuman certitude. And it feels so right. I want no human touch, no warmth, no flesh that gives, no bones that break, no softness, no aliveness. I want this machine badly. My cunt flips when I say it. "Shhh," I say as my pussy sniggers. "This is a dirty little secret."

I know I'm imagining it. But this machine I see doesn't feel like imagination. It feels like calling something to mind. Something very real. And, well, I know it sounds weird, but I have a crush on this machine. In fact, it gets even worse than that. I want to be its slave. I want it to mock, slap, and humiliate my organic, mushy, squirmy, dribbly parts with its indifference. Meanwhile, it hovers over me, iron cold. Its little bird claws at the ready. It wants to sample me, test me, try me, extract my juices, force my organic autoparts to beat and pulse on demand. It wants to work me like a machine because it is programmed to, no other reason. I do not make this machine hot. It looks at me and sees nothing. I am nothing to it. My forced-open pussy, my unprotected, half-open hole, do not make it breathe heavy, its eyes dilate, its blood rush. It couldn't care less. And that's why I love it so. I love it desperately. I crave its heartless touch. Like pewter, it doesn't shine and gleam—that's too much for show and smells like human pride. No. My machine, my love, is pure, heartless utilitarian. Its face is dull. And because of all this, it makes me love it with a passion that is like lips stuck to dry ice. My machine, I whisper, rule me.

Briefly, I imagine one delightfully soft appendage. A black, round, flat-bottomed suction cup. My machine comes at my wet cunt with this thing, a thwack to the twat and its suction cup is mashed all up in my squisher. It presses hard, squeezing out the air until the lips of my pussy are flattened against it in a suffocating hug, and my juice glues me to its rubber walls, and we are locked together, me and my machine. An embrace I do not want to let go. But I have no say. My swollen cunt has no power to hold it. When it pulls away, it simply takes, and I feel like I'm losing myself through the cunt, losing my vital root. And to what? The withdrawal of a machine.

That's the nature of our relationship. And to punctuate, my machine Master takes its wet suction cup and stamps me with my own wet. It pulls me up by the thighs and stamps my rounded bottom. It stamps my breasts, dabs my own pussy juice all over my nipples. My machine stamps me slut bitch; stamps me its property. All I can say to that is I'm owned! Clamped down tight, marked, fucked, dejuiced, stamped, and packaged, by a machine, and it makes me so hot I want to come with a claw pinching each nipple and two claws snapping their pricky mouths up my vagina, biting at my soft inside walls like piranha. I can't help but mumble filthy sex talk to it. "Let my sloppy, slutty human juice run in rivulets down your impregnable metallic arms. Fuck me, you hard bastard!"

(I get carried away, don't I? It's getting to be a problem.)

Anyway. That's what I picture the first night before I've gotten myself so horny I pinch my nipples and the cunt juice starts running down my leg and I barely touch my chubbied clitoris before it blurts out all over itself, crass and uncontrolled like a rube at the opera.

After I have a splitting orgasm, in the quiet darkness, I think, man, this is going to ruin the charm. Coming off on the visualization before I go to sleep—it will dissipate the tension, and now I won't have the dream. The one that will make my machine come to life, real as rape.

Sure enough, I don't have a machine dream that night. Or any other dream that I can remember. But the next night I try again. I'm determined to make it work, you see. I want my machine to fuck me in my sleep. In the mouth, in the ass, in the cunt. Fuck and pull and squeeze and slap and maul and prick and poke. My need is escalating. My fantasy grows obsessive. It is only a matter of time until all this hot filthy desire leaks into my sleep. This I know. And so the next night . . .

The next night I try again, but I visualize a different world. A machine world to be sure, but now we have an assembly line of machines. I'm a product in a factory; my body stripped, sprayed, flopped, is placed chest up on a moving belt. Hoist, lower. First machine to take me moves like a piston. It holds a wide cylindrical cork in its hands. It treats me like a container. Spread legs, bums up, stuff ass, bums up, stuff ass, spread lips, stuff cunt, spread lips, stuff cunt, stuff cunt. Its jerky motions pound and squeal a beat, a machine beat, arrhythmic but uncompromising. My naked body spread and stuffed, jerked to the next station. Conveyor jerks to a stop, breasts shudder. Another huge robotic packer, stuffs, twists the stuffing in my ass, seals my ass. Stuff, twist, I'm corked. Seats, twists, the wad in my cunt, bevels the protruding stuffing, presses, bevels, presses, into pussy, flush against flesh, seals off cunt. Bam, grind, rock, move, halt, breasts quiver. Next stop, a machine with long arms yanks my bent legs up. Yank, legs up, like a frog electrocuted. Rope straps, loops, knots—I'm trussed like a frozen turkey now. Bam, forward, breasts jiggle, slam, stop, breasts quiver. Metallic arms grab me by the limbs, flip me on my front, yank back my arms. Rope straps, loops, knots. My arms tied back, forearms flat against the small of my back. Now it's like I'm going through a car wash. My plugged ass is up hard and a strop slaps it methodically, *back-slap, back-slap,* as if to strike the road dust off my butt. I am flipped back, dropped, breasts roll, conveyor rolls, two arms like windshield wipers, pass, back and forth and back and forth across breasts that squish and roll, squish and roll, quiver, squish while rubber blades scrape the nipples with each pass. Over and over till I have raw, red breast burn, and the nipples are frozen into points that can't melt.

At the end of this cleaning I am clutched by hooks under my bound knees and slipknot nooses around my breasts and lifted, knots tightening, and lowered into a vat of something hot, brown, thick and viscous, like molasses, and lifted—my breasts stretch to their limits—and hung there, dripping. I can feel the hot liquid cool and the substance harden. Harden and harden. I am stiff. And suddenly swiveled from the hanging place and dropped into a cardboard nest, and slam, forward, slam, stop. I'm a treat. Shaped like a candied frog with two candy cones on its chest. A two-handed arm comes out and places a cherry on each conical breast, right where the nipples used to be.

I do not let myself cum when I visualize this, though I know that once again all I'd have to do is flick my swollen clit, and the waves would roll out of my pelvis and shudder puddles from my pussy. I try to sleep, tossing and turning and squeezing my legs together, cheating a little, because it feels good against my clit, and feeling the wet ooze from my crotch, so I then open my legs to get the air slap, and it's not enough to make me cum, but it keeps my arousal high. Knowing how wet I am, I imagine an army of robotic ants crawling up my leg, instructed to clean the filthy slime out of my pussy. The ants clamor into my pubic hair, they round the curves of my labia. Inside, the folds are soft sticky hills. The robotic ants climb, metallic battalions. As they scuttle up over the fleshy hills of my pussy, their little metallic mandibles bite, pluck, and prick. Soon every nerve ending in my raw cunt is twitching. They're at the hole now nibbling cunt juice. A hoard of them clusters on each naked nipple. Antlike stinging, thousands of infinitesimal bites on the craggy but tender terrain finally force the nipples to surrender a defensive mucus. The creatures nibble and lap and gather and feed. The more juice I give up, the more frenzied they grow, and it's a sharp, maddening ecstacy. There are legions on my clit, forcing on it these low-grade, endless spasms. I cannot cum, but I can cream. That's what they want. They make me cream so they can suck, but they don't let me get off, they just keep me in this frantic, shivering state, waiting with hungry mouths at my cunt hole for the stream to run down. I want to scream "Stop!" but I don't. And they feed and pursue. And it seems endless. Only when every pore of my cunt and my skin is dead dry do the merciless robots cease. It happens suddenly: they fall off me in a little clatter and disappear.

Oh, how I tried not to let myself come after this fine, fine imagining, but I fitted three fingers into my cunt hole (shamelessly sopping cunt hole), oozed my fingers up me, and slid them around—under the guise of trying to assure myself that no robotic ants remained. I rubbed my taut, bug-out nipples, and the fingers inside my pussy started stroking. Stroking, soothing my velvet walls. Warming my hole. Surely the ants were not real because the thick slime that strung from between those pussy lips testified to a backup of horn juice. I can't help imagining one more machine. Big piston, three arms with bird-claw ends. The piston, wide as a baby, its business end rounded as a baby's head, sits at my cunt opening. The bird claws sit open around my nipples and clitoris. Suddenly, with a clank and a whir, the machine is cranked and its piston fucks me deep and wide. The claws pinch. Fuck and pinch, fuck and pinch. It's so machine. It so doesn't care. It so easily enters and opens me, and never gives. Entry is expected. Over and over. Expected. Flesh has no say. As I picture this heartless machine, I can almost feel the insides of me. I'm giving it up, over and over. Ungh. Ungh. Taking it. Taking it. Just thinking about it makes my thumb touch my clitoris—by accident, I swear—ever so barely. I give the swollen nub a light brush. Barely a flick, while deep inside my hole, fingers squeeze against a moist, yielding wall, toward the pubis so soft and spongy, and somehow one firm nipple is gripped between three fingers—I swear they came from nowhere, my fingers, nipple, cunt, clit . . . grip—ahhngh, gasp, groan. And, "oops." And, "shit!"

What can I say? I slept in my own wet spot. And I did not have the machine dream that night, either.

But now, the third night. The sweet third night . . . I think I finally outsmarted it. . . . The third night is not about visualization, but about, well, invocation. I talk to it, my machine, but in a positive way: "Tonight, in my dream, you will come to me. You will take me, fuck me, do unspeakably machinelike things to me, and I will remember you. You will force me to orgasm in my sleep, and I'll wake up dripping between my legs."

After that small prayer, I strip down completely naked, lie on my bed in the dark, and run my hands over my body—up my thighs, over my nipples, down my belly, circling the sensitive navel down my ticklish lower abdomen to my cropped bush. I softly brush the fuzz. I do all this in the dark until the wet wells up between my legs. I open my legs a little. I can smell it. I tell myself that my machine can smell it too. The scent of my pussy calls so powerfully that the machine will have to materialize. And so I add, in a whisper, "Come to me. Take me," over and over. Rubbing my aroused body, thrusting my cunt up in the air, undulating as I whisper "Take me" in the dark, it starts to feel like a powerful ritual. I don't let myself go any further. No opening my cunt and resting my fingers between the warm lips. No touching my clit. No pinching my nipples, fingering my butt hole, pressing on my pubic bone. Uh-uh. I'm wise to the fact that these are invitations to failure, and this night I do not intend to fail. So I keep up with the chanting and touching and thrusting. My intention is to fall asleep that way, so aroused that only a sex dream could release the tension.

But suddenly I hear a sound, clink-slam, like the sound of a wrought-iron gate. I know that everyone else in the house is asleep. I'm still whispering. I'm still touching my naked body, a little titillated by the thought that someone could come in and shed light—see my roving hand, my bare breasts, my exposed pussy. I hear a sound like a freight elevator approaching. But the house has no elevator. The door opens. And there it stands.

I'm surprised that it has an old-machine look, painted green and with rounded edges, like a giant lathe or miller from the early twentieth century. It's got belts and motors. It is made of iron, more solid and heavy than anything I could imagine—and yet, I'm sure that I am visualizing again. Except for the noise. The sound of it is so real. The slapping of the belts, the squeaking of motor shafts. It is colder and more beautiful and merciless and charismatic than anything I could imagine. Could it possibly be a dream? It wheels in. It has arms run by belts. It has endless appendages with strange hands and feet. It pulls my naked body up off the bed by my armpits, hangs me there, facing it.

I feel so helpless with its cold hardness at my skin. My machine is all iron and appendages, motors and belts. It shakes me as I hang there. The shaking opens me up, loosens my sphincter, my pussy, gives me bouncing boobies. Blood rushes into the tips of my breasts. It puts my nipple nerves on red alert, just as the two little tubes shoot out of the machine's middle that attach to my breasts and draw in the nipples and areola. While it sucks them into itself, it rushes air over the stretched skin, a tickling breeze. When I visualize, I never get feelings like this. These are not something I can imagine. I am still hanging in the air by my armpits, and it feels exhilarating. I can feel my clit jumping with excitement. The machine is going to work me like I'm the machine and it's the human. Two pincers dart out, seize my labia, open them like curtains, and, behind the curtains, my horny flesh sparkles. It's a little swollen, too. Something takes hold of the shaft of my clitoris, and suddenly it squirms. It's being pummeled by what feels like a Water Pik. I am penetrated then. Something narrow enough and comfortable at the insertion end. It goes in so easily, I have no time to clench my legs. Not that it would help as this icy, conical arm spreads wider and wider. My cunt hole is stretched to the limits. It pulls and gapes; the skin burns. The sensate mouth of my cunt feels as cold like dry ice where my machine penetrates. The skin around my hole burns from the stretching while it freezes from the cold iron fist. The arm inside my walls is not the least concerned with these schizoid sensations, and it begins pulsing.

I know this sounds strange, but it was like we merged then. I felt the life of the machine inside me. Alive like a dumb beast. How could it be in me, vibrating, beating with a rhythm that spoke to my most private chemistry, and not be alive?

My machine did things to me, processing me efficiently, quickly. It opened my legs and fastened my ankles to grips in its sides, then it seized me by the waist and gripped my arms up in the horizontal so it had access to my armpits and could get under my breasts. It had secured all ports of entry open. It was free to start the sensational deluge: it entered my ass with an object that seemed to breathe, in, out, in, out, turning my anal walls into a great lung. I am spread and spitted and powerless. That's what a machine can do by being so immutable, so itself. It can redefine you, by getting inside because a human makes room, a human adapts. It does not, and so it makes you be machine, take on its rhythm. With multiple arms it had me covered, pulling pressing, pricking—my clit, my cunt, my ass, my nipples. Pick-click, pick-clack. I almost couldn't take its barrage. My every nerve ending was possessed, my every hole was stuffed, and me, I was just a slab of sensation. I came right there and then. On demand. Like its mechanical toy.

But my machine didn't care that I had come. Do you think it stopped driving me with its probes? A machine has its own agenda: a human does not exist. Remember it. You can let it inhabit you and become part of it, and so survive as something bigger than yourself. Or you can resist. And it will systematically disassemble your sense of self, make you a thing ever approaching zero. I chose to surrender to my machine.

Physically I had no choice, however. I could only feel and let it do what it would do next. It kept its hands in my holes, and my tits in its grasp. It sent vibrations through my body, it lifted me, turned, and folded me in humiliating positions. It slapped and polished me with its belts, vibrated me inside and out, tickled, poked, and pressed. It would have me so close to orgasm I could taste it; then it would snatch the good feelings away. It plucked out pussy hairs, tickled armpits, scrambled with rubbery ticklers around the inside of my mouth, forced the ticklers under my tongue, pushed my tongue from side to side, sprayed my mouth, cunt, ears, nose, ass, with burny-tingly liquid, all the while I was impaled and immobile. Oddly, taking its liquid up my nose made my nipples twitch with desire. My machine would flick them right then. Just enough to have me burning hot.

I have to say, I went through so many sensations at once I can't remember them all. I'm sure I've skipped a thousand or two. And don't get me wrong. It did torture me with near-orgasm repeatedly, bringing me closer, then stinging me away. But during the course of this machine takeover of my body, I had orgasm after orgasm all the same. Clit orgasms and cunt orgasms, body orgasms, all helpless orgasms, time after time. How could I not? It knew me! It fed on my spasms, it scrambled around in my juice. I could only succumb. All the while, my machine's hum soothed me—the chirping of the pulleys, the slapping of the belts—like a lullaby.

"I am yours, now," I cooed, dazed and spent. "My Master."

I awake. The reality of the machine, its coldness and hardness begin to drift away. I try to hold on as it becomes more like air. I recite it from memory. But it drifts off still, to a mental figment, to a vague cloud. I come to my senses, weak, shivering. "It worked," I say to myself. "The machine has come to me in a dream, so real! I've done it. And I will continue. Now I can be a human by day, and by night just an orgasm in a machine." As I say all this, my whole body is flush, my crotch feels warm; I dare to hope that my dream machine fucked me until I came, and when I spread my thighs, I realize my cunt is in a pool of hot slime.

Wish Girls

Matthew Addison

MAX OPENED HIS BEDROOM door, and there they were, his wish girls, sitting primly on the bed with their legs crossed, looking up at him through lowered lashes. Allison (the blonde) and Stephanie (the brunette), wearing the modified cheerleader outfits that made him cringe with inward embarrassment now whenever he saw them. The wish girls were fresh and perky and eager as always. "Hi, girls," he said, tossing his coat onto the chair and dropping his bag. He'd had a hard day at the bookstore, and more than anything he wanted someone to listen to his troubles and make him dinner, but those were two things his wish girls wouldn't do, couldn't do, hadn't been made to do, so he'd have to be satisfied with the services they did offer.

Stephanie and Allison were seventeen years old, and had been for the past fifteen years, never changing. They wore yellow-and-red uniforms that resembled the ones worn by cheerleaders at Max's old high school, but altered to titillate the perpetually aroused fourteen-year-old he'd been when he wished them into existence. The tops of the outfits were tight and thin and clinging, and Allison and Stephanie's ever-erect nipples stuck through visibly. There was a round keyhole cutout in each bodice, revealing the full side swells of their firm high breasts, and the skirts were so short they hardly qualified as garments. The wish girls wore no panties, and even with their legs demurely crossed he could see the curling of their pubic hairs, blonde and black. They wore knee socks over their smooth, lithe legs, and Max felt a bit like a dirty old man for admiring them. The wish girls had been older than him when they first appeared, but they hadn't aged as he had.

"Strip," he said. "Then go into the bathroom and shave." He lingered to watch them undress each other, with many shy glances and coquettish looks at him, peeling off each other's tops, shimmying out of their skirts. Their bodies were perfect: fine tits, taut bellies, round firm asses—the fantasy amalgamation of all the girls he'd lusted after as an eighth-grade loser. Their bodies were identical, both the same height, both with pink nipples, breasts the same ample size, and he wished for the thousandth time that he'd given one of them brown nipples, at least, or made one of them 5'9" and the other 5'2" (they were both 5'7"), done something to differentiate them, but he'd only wished for one blonde and one brunette, and that was the full extent of the variation. Even their faces were identical, *Seventeen*-model faces, with full lips, big blue eyes, high cheekbones.

The wish girls were undoubtedly lovely, but they'd been lovely in exactly the same way for a long time.

They finished undressing, and he stepped aside to let them into the living room. His apartment was too small for three people, but the wish girls didn't live with him, exactly—sometimes he fell asleep with them in his bed, but they always disappeared by morning, and they didn't use the bathroom or cook meals or do anything to take up space. There was a time, even a few years ago, when watching them undress each other would have aroused him enough to make one of them kneel and suck him off, but he found that more elaborate steps were required to excite him now.

Max made a microwave pizza while the girls shaved each other in the bathroom, and sat eating on the couch when they emerged, arm in arm, cunts freshly shorn. "Position 16," he said, and the girls knelt before him, facing each other. Each put a hand on the other's hip, and each slipped a hand into the other's always-wet cunt, then they began to finger the other; and they tilted their faces together, eyes closed, and kissed, lips parted, pink tongues moving gently. Max slipped off his pants and his boxers and sat back down, tugging his cock while they made out. "Pinch her nipple, Allison," he said, and the blonde reached out and tweaked, bringing a moan to Stephanie's throat. "Harder," he said, and she twisted, but Stephanie didn't make any sounds of pain. As far as Max could tell, they didn't feel pain, which made his forays into S&M less satisfying than they might have been, and made him wonder if they truly felt anything. "Gasp like it hurts you," he said, and Stephanie did, making high sounds of distress. "Slap her tits, Allison," he ordered, and watched for a while, but even this wasn't doing much for him.

"Position 39, variation b," he said, and the girls turned facing away from him, first getting on all fours, then lowering their heads to the carpet, leaving their asses in the air. They crossed their arms behind their backs at the wrists—that was the "variation b" part—and Max took two silk scarves from the table by the couch and used them to bind their wrists together. He went to the tall red tool chest in the corner, which contained years of accumulated sex toys and supplies, and took out lube and a pair of clear acrylic butt plugs. Returning to the girls, he squirted lube onto their pink rosebud assholes and rubbed with his fingers. They moaned and moved against his touch—he'd taught them to do that— and gasped as he slipped the plugs into them. Once he'd filled their asses, he wiped his lube-slicked hand on a towel and began spanking the girls, alternating between Stephanie and Allison, full-palm swats that made their beautiful asses bounce. Their skin never bruised or reddened, no matter how hard he hit, and he'd never broken their skin. The wish girls were the product of adolescent fantasies that hadn't gone much beyond groping, blow jobs, and vague misconceptions about fucking, and they weren't well equipped for some of the kinks he'd developed since then. Still, they gasped and cried out and begged for mercy, as he'd instructed them to do, until he was sufficiently turned on to slip his cock into Stephanie's tight, welcoming cunt, while fingering Allison with one hand. When he was close to orgasm, he pulled out. "Position eight," he said, and pulled them into upright kneeling positions. They put their faces close together and looked up at him worshipfully, licking their lips, and he tugged his cock until he shot come onto their smiling faces.

Once spent, he sat back on the couch, feeling empty. He liked coming on their faces, but he didn't find it as physically satisfying as coming in their mouths, cunts, or asses. They kept kneeling, attentive, waiting for any further orders, but Max shook his head. "I'm done. I'll call if I need anything." The wish girls unbound their own hands, removed the butt plugs gracefully, and slipped back into the bedroom. They would disappear, now, into whatever place they went when he wasn't using them.

Max sat on the couch, flipping channels, until he got lonely. He called, "Stephanie!" The brunette stepped out of the bedroom, clad in her cheerleader costume and with her full complement of public hair again, reset to her default state. "Put on the nightgown," he said. She stripped off her uniform, dropping the garments to the floor, where they would remain for as long as Max looked at them, though they would vanish the moment he looked elsewhere. She went to the toolbox and took out a sheer silk nightgown that was, relatively speaking, modest. "Position 115," he said, and she sat beside him, one hand resting on his leg, her head leaned against his shoulder, a warm and intimate nuzzle. Sometimes having her act like a girlfriend—like he imagined a girlfriend would act—made him happier, but tonight it just made him sad and even lonelier. "Position 43," he said, sliding down a little in his seat, and she lay sideways on the couch, head resting on his belly, and she sucked slowly, almost meditatively, on the head of his cock until he built toward orgasm again. He grasped her head in his hands and thrust his hips, his cock hitting the back of her throat again and again until he came in her mouth, and all the while she made moans of exquisite pleasure. Letting go of her head, he said, "Okay," and she sat up, swallowing and licking her lips. "Kiss me good night," he said, and she did, sweetly, softly, and then he sent her away for the night.

MAX WORKED IN THE genre fiction section at a big chain bookstore, shelving mysteries, romances, sci-fi, and fantasy. That morning he held a purple trade paperback with a golden Aladdin's lamp on the cover, the second book in some series about a wisecracking genie, and he tried to remember what, exactly, the circumstances of his wish had been. He knew he'd been in the woods behind his childhood home, and found . . . something, a ring, a bottle, a colored stone, and he'd been given a wish, though now he couldn't remember if some spirit or being had spoken to him, or if the knowledge of the wish had simply appeared in his mind. That was part of the wish's defense, he understood, to make the memory of its genesis vague, because then it would be harder for Max to tell other people about it. Whatever the specific circumstances had been, Max had held the wishing object in his hand, or he'd buried it in the dirt, or he'd broken it open, and he'd made his wish, voicing one of the many elaborate fantasies he concocted in his narrow bed each night, and then Allison and Stephanie had come to him. He'd spent the next three years slipping away to the woods every chance he got, on weekends and afternoons, even some days when he cut school, going to a secluded clearing beyond earshot of his house and waiting for Allison and Stephanie to step out of the trees. They'd done everything he wanted, and in those years he did everything a young man could think to do with two girls, and watched as they did everything two young girls could do to each other—at least, without the help of props and accessories and costumes. Max's grades fell, he stopped seeing his friends, he didn't take part in sports or theater or band, and he didn't ask girls out—why should he, with two lithe nude eager wish girls waiting for him in the woods? They'd been like a drug, he understood now, like heroin, and everything in his life became secondary to the pursuit of the pleasure they gave.

Someone tapped him on the shoulder, startling him. He turned to see a woman, about his age, with short copper-colored hair and round-rimmed glasses, and he automatically compared her to Stephanie and Allison, as he did with every woman he saw—her face was round, her eyes were startlingly green; she had a pimple above one of her eyebrows, and her expression seemed amused even at rest. "I'm the new girl," she said. "Just transferred from the downtown branch. What's your name?"

"Uh, Max," he mumbled, looking down at the book in his hand, uncomfortable standing so close to her.

"Nice to meet you, Max, I'm Kira. I used to work in genre at my old bookstore, but they stuck me with photography and art books here. Let me know if you ever want to trade."

"Uh," he said. "No, I, uh—"

"Just kidding, Max, I'm not going to poach your section." She patted his shoulder and said, "See you around."

He turned and watched as she walked away, and he noticed her curves, her hips. She probably weighed fifty pounds more than Allison or Stephanie, and was four inches shorter than them, but it looked right and proportional on her—Kira didn't have their willowy figures. Max turned back to his shelving. Why had she made him so nervous? Spending fifteen years with Allison and Stephanie had rendered him incapable of interacting with women normally. He'd never been on a real date, and didn't have any close friends, didn't go out to bars—and why would he? The other guys at the bookstore went out, drank, and tried to pick up women, but Max didn't need to pick up women. He had the holy grail at home, two hot girls who couldn't get enough of him. His life was perfect. He'd blundered into magic, and his life was magical as a result.

So why didn't he look forward to going home anymore?

Max had expected things to change with the wish girls when he got his own apartment. Once he'd moved in, on his own for the first time, he'd called the girls, and they'd emerged from the bedroom, seeming happy, as always, to be summoned. "This is our place now," he said. "You never have to leave or disappear. No more going to the woods; you can just stay here." Their smiles didn't falter, but they didn't seem to absorb what he said, either. They could talk, and they understood the often-complicated tasks he set for them, but they never truly conversed with him. Beyond a certain basic repertoire of phrases—"Yes, please, God"—he'd had to teach them whatever he wanted them to say.

"Allison, position 1," he said, and she knelt before him, unzipping his pants and pulling out his cock, stroking it to erectness and then licking the shaft slowly, from bottom to top. "What do you think of the apartment, Stephanie?" he asked, while Allison tongued the vein beneath the head of his dick.

"It's so big," she said. "It feels so good inside."

Max frowned. The words made superficial sense, though they weren't exactly accurate, and they were, of course, things he'd taught her to say under other circumstances. He wondered how intelligent they were, really, these wish girls of his, and it was something he would come to wonder again and again in the coming years.

Over the next weeks he tried to make them understand that his home was theirs, but they kept disappearing when he was done with them each night, and he kept running up against the limits of their capabilities. Once he tried to teach Allison to wash dishes—after all, if they were his willing slaves, why shouldn't he use them for something other than fucking? He'd explained everything required to wash dishes, and told Allison the chore was her responsibility from now on. The first night, she emerged from the bedroom and changed into a frilly white apron, four-inch spike heels, and nothing else. She'd filled the sink with soapy water, then leaned over the counter on her elbows, breasts in the suds, ass lifted invitingly, and Max had been so turned on he'd come up behind her and pounded her hard, pulling her hair and squeezing her soapy tits while he thrust into her. It was only later that he realized she hadn't done the dishes at all, even when he was done fucking her, and all his later attempts to get them to do anything nonsexual ended that way—he'd fucked Stephanie from behind while her head hung in the toilet after he tried to teach her to clean the bathroom, and while they were more than willing to let him eat off their bodies, they never prepared food for him. They were happy to dress up in maid uniforms—that was one of the first mildly kinky things he'd done with them once he had his own apartment—but not to act like maids.

He'd had great plans for their life together, but most of them hadn't panned out. Once when he was desperately short of money—car broken down, dental bills overdue—he'd tentatively asked if they were willing to fuck other men, thinking he could pimp them out. They'd shaken their heads in unison, almost sadly. Another time, he'd wanted to go out on the town and impress people with the hot women hanging all over him, intending to strap them into butt-plug harnesses, dress them in tight tops and skirts and stripper heels, and let them follow him around bars and nightclubs, squirming from the plugs in their asses—but they'd refused to cross his threshold. They wouldn't let anyone else see them. That was probably his own fault. Max couldn't remember the precise wording of his wish, but hadn't there been some element of the grasping and the selfish? Some phrase like "only for me, just for me," when he'd wished for Allison and Stephanie? He'd been young, and he hadn't thought through all the ramifications of his wish.

"I wish you would talk to me," he'd said one night that first year out of high school, hungry for conversation, wishing for something more than the endlessly physical.

Allison and Stephanie gazed up at him. "We belong to you," Allison said. "You can do anything you want with us," Stephanie said. "We love you," they both said. Just like he'd taught them to.

MAX LAY IN BED and fondled his cock and balls, thinking of Kira, fantasizing about the softness of her belly against his cheek, the weight of her body upon him, imagining birthmarks and freckles—he'd been with the wish girls for so long that he'd begun to fetishize blemishes. He stroked and tugged himself toward orgasm, the first time in years he'd jerked himself off—why masturbate when at a moment's whim he could have a perfect, sweet-faced cheerleader giving him a hand job or sucking him off? But now he was thinking of Kira, and he imagined her face—those green eyes, that half smile—as he came, spurting hot come over his fingers and onto his stomach.

As he lay in the dark he thought, Maybe it's time I started dating.

A WEEK WENT BY, and before Max could work up the nerve to ask Kira out, she asked him if he wanted to get a bite after work. "Sure," he said, and they went to an Ethiopian place near the bookstore, where they ate spicy and savory food, scooped up with hot soft pieces of *injera*, Ethiopian flatbread. They talked about working for the bookstore, why she'd transferred to his branch (hers got downsized), about books, and Max managed more or less to think of her a person rather than a woman. Gradually his anxiety diminished. She was cute, funny, and interesting, and he did his best to keep her entertained and interested in talking to him. It was surprisingly easy to do so. They liked the same books, hated the same movies, and Max eventually realized she was flirting with him. They started talking about fantasy novels and stories, and without much conscious thought Max steered the dialogue toward wishes. "What would you do with three wishes?" he asked.

Kira sat back against the cushioned booth, hands laced across her stomach, under her breasts. "I always thought three wishes was too many. With three wishes, you can ask for wealth, eternal youth, and top it off with world peace, and feel like a big hero for the last one. I think it's more interesting to ask what you'd do with one wish. That's how you can tell the selfish from the generous. So tell me, Max, if you had one wish, what would it be? World peace, or strippers and blow?"

Max thought it over. He knew what he'd done with his one wish, but he'd been fourteen at the time, and by definition almost sociopathically self-centered. If he had the wish again, now . . . "I'd wish for happiness," he said, and it felt true, like something he wanted very much.

"Selfish, but abstract," Kira said. "I'd probably go for the strippers and blow myself. I've read too many stories to think that even well-meant wishes would turn out the way I wanted."

They finished the meal, and Max walked Kira back to her car. "We should do this again sometime," he said. "Soon."

"We should do more than this sometime," she said, and leaned up to kiss him. Her breath tasted of *timatim fitfit* and after-dinner mint, and his surprise made the kiss awkward, but there was something behind it, a warmth and pressure of a sort he'd never felt with the wish girls. "Soon," she said, and that was good-bye for the night.

MAX WANTED KIRA, WANTED to make love to her, but he couldn't. But he had other means of release. He drove home from dinner and found a package on his doorstep. He took it inside and opened it on the kitchen counter, smiling as he drew out the tangle of leather straps and D rings. It was the strap-on harness he'd ordered from an online erotica catalog, along with a nine-inch black silicon dildo. "Girls!" he called, and after they appeared he directed them to shave, put on red cocksucker lipstick (they appeared fresh-faced and without makeup by default), and be back in the living room on their knees in ten minutes. "We're doing scenario 21, variation c," he said. "Stephanie's top, Allison's bottom."

"You heard him, you little bitch," Stephanie said, and slapped Allison's ass. "Get in there and get your clothes off." Allison hurried away, eyes downcast, hands held behind her back.

Max leaned against the bathroom door frame and watched them get ready, Stephanie cajoling Allison, slapping her tits, and promising her humiliation and violations. For her part, Allison was obedient but frightened, her lower lip quivering as she put on mascara, which she would cry off in act two while Stephanie flogged her.

"Come get dressed, Stephanie," he said, and took her into the bedroom. He laced her into a black leather underbust corset that lifted her tits even higher than normal, and she put on knee-high leather boots. He gave her a wicked riding crop, which she lashed through the air experimentally. "I just got this for you today," he said, and showed her the new strap-on harness. She oohed and aahed appreciatively, the way she always responded to the sex toys he brought home, a sort of automatic erotitropism. He helped her into the harness, taking great pleasure in pulling the leather straps tight around her hips, the black dildo rising impressively erect from her crotch. "You like being top, Steph?" he said, and she nodded. He grabbed both her wrists, wrenched her arms over her head, and forced her down to her knees. He twisted her wrists, and when she gasped he shoved his cock into her mouth, thrusting hard. "Just remember, I'm the one who's really top," he said. "Tell me you love it. Tell me you love the taste of my cock." He adored the way she sounded, trying to speak while he fucked her mouth, and it took all his willpower not to come then. He pulled out and looked down at her where she knelt, breathing hard, breasts heaving prettily, arms still held over her head.

How could she be so perfect, with her teeth never brushing his cock no matter how hard he used her, never sweating, never belching, never having a headache or having her time of the month? Never . . .

Never surprising him. Perfect, and perfectly familiar. She was exactly what he'd wished for, and every night he spent with his wish girls was a night of incredibly sophisticated masturbation. Nothing more.

Well, fuck it. Pleasure was pleasure, and there was something to be said for the familiar. At least Allison and Stephanie didn't make him nervous.

"Get up," he said. "Let's get Allison trussed up. I've got a new mouth harness I want to see her in. I'm thinking, after we whip her, we can lay her out on her back across the dining room table, and you can fuck her ass while I fuck her throat. Sound good?"

"Whatever pleases you, Max," she said.

"I CAN TELL YOU'RE the shy type, Max," Kira said, pouring him another glass of sangria. "And I don't mind being aggressive, but I want to know my advances are welcome. I don't want to make an idiot of myself. Are you interested in me?"

Max sat on Kira's couch, and she passed him his drink, then sat beside him, tucking her legs beneath herself with casual grace. "You move so beautifully," he said, the two glasses of sangria already inside him relaxing him enough to say such things.

She looked at him over the rim of her glass, sipped, and said, "I studied ballet when I was a kid, but I didn't have the body to keep it up—not thin enough, too zaftig by half. I was crushed at the time, but in retrospect, I'm glad I don't live a life of glamorous starvation and crippled feet."

"I think you look wonderful," Max said, but he looked down into his drink, shy. This was nothing like talking to the wish girls. "I'm sorry. I do like you a lot. I just . . . haven't gone out much. I'm nervous. I've only been with a couple of women in my life."

"That's okay," she said. "That just means you won't have as many bad habits to unlearn." She grinned—a twinkling, mischievous look of a sort he'd never seen on the faces of the wish girls—and she plucked the drink from his hand and set it aside. Kira leaned into him, and they began kissing; she took his hand and pressed it against her silk shirt, against her breast, which was large and full and shaped differently from those Max was used to. Her hand touched his thigh, then slid up to squeeze his cock. She kissed his neck, stroked his leg, slipped a finger into the waistband of his pants, her fingernail brushing through his pubic hair, making him shiver and tingle all over. Max's heart hammered, pulse throbbing through him and making his cock twitch, and he felt weightless, unmoored—he didn't know what she was going to do. Kira was an independent operator, an ongoing surprise. Her hair smelled of strawberry shampoo, and there was a hint of sweat, and her skin—the wish girls smelled almost of nothing, a little bit of baby powder, nothing else. This was intoxicating, and for the first time, it occurred to Max that sex could be a collaborative act.

"Bedroom," Kira said, and tugged him by his waistband into her cluttered room, walls decorated with painted kites, a double bed with a white comforter. They fell into bed together, touching each other urgently, and she stripped off her shirt and bra, revealing pale breasts with large brown nipples. Her left breast was slightly larger than the right, and this amazing human variation made Max moan and push her down on the bed, bowing his head to take her nipple in his mouth and suck. She made a sound like a contented cat and lifted her hips against him. He stopped kissing her breast and pulled down her skirt, taking a moment to admire her panties—black lace, hardly there, she must have planned all along to take him to bed—and then he pulled them down, too, and buried his face between her legs. Oh, the smell, sweat, and wetness, and something unmistakably feminine—the wish girls were nothing like this. He'd gone down on them countless times, and they'd never had a scent like this, just that baby-powder neutrality.

What had he been missing all this time?

He tongued her, slipped a finger inside her, was surprised to find she wasn't very wet yet. Another way she differed from the wish girls. He licked her, bottom to top, and she said, "Oh, that's right, warm me up, Max." When she was wetter, he slipped a finger into her and moved it while tonguing her clit, and this went on for a minute or so before she touched the top of his head. "Max, sweetie," she said, "your heart's in the right place, but your finger isn't."

He looked up at her, his hand unmoving, and realized that all the thousands of hours he'd spent fucking the wish girls had taught him nothing at all about women. "Tell me what to do," he said, and she gave him that grin again. She guided him—"There, press your fingers up toward the, yes, right there, now swirl your tongue, to the right, no, my right, yes, there, keep it up." Max did as she said, though his wrist got sore and his tongue got tired. He'd never spent so much time going down on Allison and Stephanie, just enough to satisfy his own urge to taste and finger them, but this was something different, something more worthwhile, and after a while Kira got much wetter and bucked against his hand and tongue. She trembled, almost silently, with none of the theatrical orgasms Max had seen in porn films and had taught the wish girls to emulate.

He kissed her belly, and she stroked his hair, and he said, "Can I fuck you now?"

"You'd better," she said, and he rose up and pushed her legs apart. She said, "Who, Max, not so fast, condom first." She reached to the bedside table and lifted a square foil-wrapped packet.

"Ah, right," Max said, suddenly terrified. He'd never worn a condom in his life.

"I'll put it on you," she said, and rolled him onto his back. She grasped and tugged his cock, then put it briefly in her mouth, and he swelled to full hardness. She tore open the package and deftly rolled the condom—cold, strange—onto his cock, then swung one leg over to straddle him and eased herself down, guiding his cock up into her warm wet cunt. She rocked on top of him, reaching down to tweak his nipples, slipping a finger into his mouth for him to suck. Her weight, her spontaneity, the way she moved, it was all so different, and if not for the condom acting to dull the sensation a bit, he might have come in her right away. A euphoria grew inside him, spread through his body, suffusing his limbs with outrushing lightness. Max had never felt so good.

She lowered herself, breasts against his chest, cheek against his cheek, her breath in his ear, and he reached down to take hold of her ass in both hands, thrusting his hips against her, and her breath quickened as she thrust back, and soon they were rocking together, headboard slamming against the wall, moving faster and faster until he felt himself starting to come. He squeezed her ass harder and thrust away, the two of them moving in wonderful concert, and she gasped in his ear and shuddered, trembling. He couldn't tell whether his orgasm had excited her into her own, or vice versa.

Afterward, she didn't disappear, and he was glad.

"We should do this again sometime," he said, tentatively, afraid she'd turn away.

"Soon," she said. "Take me to your place next time?"

"Of course," he said.

MAX KNEW BETTER THAN to think it was true love. Oh, maybe it was, but Kira could just as easily grow bored with him, or more likely he would fail her in some way, since he had no experience with romantic relationships. But he'd turned a corner. Even if he didn't stay with Kira forever, there would be other women, other relationships. He'd discovered how things could be, now, and there was no going back. He'd finally grown up.

But he hadn't grown up so much that he didn't want one last fling, for old time's sake.

The next morning Max called in sick to work, and summoned Stephanie and Allison. He dressed them in black stiletto heels and knee pads and nothing more. "Stephanie, kneel there, legs spread, and reach behind you and grab your heels. Don't let go of your heels, no matter what." She did as she was told, and he fastened a leather and plastic ring gag around her head, a mouth harness that held her jaws open for constant access. She gripped her heels, breasts jutting out beautifully, and he slipped his cock through the gag into her warm wet mouth, sliding it back and forth. "Keep looking up at me with those wide eyes of yours. And you, Allison, kneel behind me and lick my asshole." He fucked Stephanie's face for a while as Allison tongued him. He could have come on them then—Stephanie had never looked more fetching—but he wanted to run the gamut today. He put collars and leashes on them and led them around the room on all fours, lashing their rumps with a riding crop. He leaned them both over the couch, lubed their asses generously, and pounded first one, then the other. He lay down and had Stephanie straddle his cock while Allison sat on his face, and they kissed and fondled each other while he tongued and fucked them. He had Stephanie put on the new black strap-on, and they double penetrated Allison, who whimpered as Max thrust into her ass, begging him to do it harder, harder. Then he had Allison put on the old strap-on harness and let his wish girls fuck him—he went down on all fours, Allison sliding a smaller dildo in and out of his lubed ass, Stephanie shoving her big black dildo in and out of his mouth. After that he spanked them, whipped them, fondled them, caressed them, and fucked them every way he could think of. By day's end he was exhausted, sweat-soaked, and trembling from the exertion. His cock felt drained dry from the day's several orgasms. The wish girls, of course, seemed as calm and well rested as always.

"I'm letting you go," he said.

Allison and Stephanie looked at him, then looked at each other. They frowned in unison. He'd never seen them frown before, except when they were playing Harsh Mistresses, and even that was a different, more theatrical expression.

"I appreciate all you've done for me," he said. This was harder than he'd expected. "You've made my life wonderful. But . . . I don't think this is good for me anymore. I've met someone . . . well. It doesn't matter."

"You're setting us free?" Stephanie asked.

Had Max ever taught her to say that, as part of some bondage role-play scenario, maybe? He didn't think so. "Yes. You can go."

"Turn your back while we get dressed," Allison said.

Max knew he'd never taught her to say that. He'd seen her in every conceivable state of disarray—even now, his come was drying on her breasts. But modesty, he suddenly understood, was a privilege of the free. He turned his back.

"Okay," Allison said a moment later.

He turned to find them dressed in jeans and gray sweatshirts, not outfits he'd ever have chosen for them, clothes they'd conjured for themselves. They stepped toward him in unison, each kissing one of his cheeks.

"'Bye, Max," Allison said.

"We didn't think you'd ever get to this point," Stephanie said. She patted his cheek.

The wish girls left. They didn't disappear; they just went out the front door. Maybe they'd get to be real people now, and make choices of their own. He didn't know.

Max spent the rest of the evening filling heavy black garbage bags with sex toys, bondage gear, and lingerie, tossing it all into the big Dumpster behind the apartment complex. The garbage men were sure to get a kick out of that. Maybe he and Kira would start playing with toys eventually, but he'd buy new ones for that. Even Max's vestigial sense of gentlemanly conduct told him that was the appropriate thing to do.

TWO DAYS LATER, MAX sat on his couch, and Kira knelt on a pillow between his feet, sucking his cock. He looked down at her closed eyes, the expression of tender concentration on her face, and he was overwhelmed with happiness. She was doing this because she wanted to, because she liked him, because she wanted to make him feel good. And because she knew he'd return the favor.

Kira's teeth brushed against Max's cock. It hurt, a little. He'd never been happier.

CONTRIBUTORS

Matthew Addison hails from the mountains of North Carolina, where cold winters require inventive methods of keeping warm. His stories may be read online at Fishnetmag.com, though he hopes to branch out soon. You can contact him by writing to: addmatt@gmail.com.

Vanesa Baggott lives in the Pennines outside Manchester. In 2005 she graduated from Sheffield Hallam University with a postgraduate diploma in writing; she won an Internet poetry competition at ABC Tales.com, and had her poetry published by Templar Poetry. She is currently completing a novel and training to be an Iyengar yoga teacher.

Octavia E. Butler (1947–2006) was the first black woman to come to international prominence as a science-fiction writer. Her powerful, spare language and rich, well-developed characters gave her work a special legacy as she tackled race, gender, religion, poverty, power, politics—and science—in a way that touched readers of all backgrounds. She received numerous awards, including a MacArthur grant, both the Hugo and Nebula awards, the Langston Hughes Medal, and a PEN Lifetime Achievement Award.

This edition of *The Best American Erotica* is dedicated to her memory. Butler's publishers, colleagues, and the Science Fiction Museum have created in her honor an Octavia E. Butler Memorial Scholarship Fund, which will enable writers of color to attend one of the Clarion writing workshops, where Ms. Butler got her start. During her lifetime Ms. Butler taught several sessions for Clarion West in Seattle, Washington, and for Clarion in East Lansing, Michigan, giving generously of her time to a cause in which she believed.

The scholarship fund will be administered by the Carl Brandon Society. The first scholarship will be awarded in 2007. Please send your tax-deductible contributions made payable to "The Carl Brandon Society," and note that it is for "The Octavia E. Butler Memorial Scholarship Fund." More info at: http://www.carlbrandon.org.

Alexander Chee is the author of the novels *Edinburgh* and *The Queen of the Night*. His stories and essays are anthologized in *Loss Within Loss, Boys Like Us, The M Word*, and *Best Gay Erotica 2002* and *2006*. He is a recipient of the Whiting Award and an NEA fellowship in fiction. He lives in Amherst, Massachusetts.

Dennis Cooper is the author of eight novels: *God Jr., The Sluts, My Loose Thread*, and "The George Miles Cycle"—an interconnected sequence of five novels including *Closer, Frisk, Try, Guide*, and *Period*. His novels have been translated into eighteen languages. He currently lives in Los Angeles and Paris, France.

Voted one of "Washington's Most Loathsome," and one of *Jane* magazine's "30 Under 30," **Jessica Cutler** is best known as the author of *The Washingtonienne: A Novel* and her blog of the same name. She has also written for *The Guardian, Capitol File*, and *The Washington Post*.

Susan DiPlacido is the author of three novels: *24/7, Trattoria*, and *Mutual Holdings*. Her short story "I, Candy" won the 2005 Moondance International Film Festival Spirit Award, and *Trattoria* has been nominated for the Romance Times Reviewers' Choice Award. Visit her at: http://www.susandiplacido.com.

Daniel Duane grew up in Berkeley in the 1970s and '80s and lives now in San Francisco with his wife and two daughters. The author of *Caught Inside: A Surfer's Year on the California Coast*, he has also written the novels *Looking for Mo* and *A Mouth Like Yours*, among other books. Currently a contributing editor for the magazines *Men's Journal* and *National Geographic Adventure*, he has also written for *The New York Times Magazine, Mother Jones*, and *Bon Appétit*.

Alicia Erian is the author of *Towelhead*, a novel, and *The Brutal Language of Love*, a collection of short stories. She received her B.A. in English from Binghamton University, and her M.F.A. in writing from Vermont College. Her short fiction has appeared most recently in *Playboy*, *Zoetrope*, *The Iowa Review*, *Nerve*, *Open City*, and *The Sun*. She is currently the first holder of the Newhouse Visiting professorship of Creative Writing at Wellesley College.

Lauraleigh Farrell is the online editor of three adult magazines plus a local theater reviewer. Ms. Farrell's writing has appeared under various names in *Prometheus*, *Spectator*, *Bitches with Whips*, and the Circlet Press anthology *SexCrime*. In her "spare time" she's a musician and—don't tell the neighbors—beekeeper.

Sera Gamble leads the charmed life of a television writer. Back in middle school, Ms. Gamble and her best friend enjoyed a weekly ritual: walk to library, attack "Romance" section, flip through each book to find sex scenes. She vowed then that when she grew up and wrote her own, she would put the good parts closer to the front. Visit her at: http://www.seragamble.com.

Shanna Germain's poems, short stories, and essays have appeared in places like *The American Journal of Nursing*, *Aqua Erotica 2*, *Best Bondage Erotica 2*, *McSweeney's*, and *Salon*. She is also a fiction editor for CleanSheets. Visit her at: http://www.shannagermain.com.

Kathryn Harrison is the author of the novels *The Seal Wife*, *The Binding Chair*, *Poison*, *Exposure*, and *Thicker Than Water*. She has also written the memoirs *The Kiss* and *The Mother Knot;* a travel memoir, *The Road to Santiago;* a biography, *Saint Therese of Liseiux;* and a collection of essays, *Seeking Rapture*. She lives in New York with her husband, the novelist Colin Harrison, and their children.

P. S. Haven was raised on *Star Wars*, comic books, and his dad's *Playboy* collection, all of which he still enjoys to this day. He has been writing erotica for over fifteen years. Haven peddles his smut from Winston-Salem, North Carolina, where he fights a never-ending battle for truth, justice, and the American way. Visit him at: http://www.pshaven.com.

Trebor Healey is the author of the 2004 Ferro-Grumley and Violet Quill award-winning novel *Through It Came Bright Colors*, as well as a poetry collection, *Sweet Son of Pan*. His short story collection, *Eros and Dust*, is forthcoming in 2007. Mr. Healey lives in Los Angeles. Visit him at: http://www.treborhealey.com.

Nalo Hopkinson is the author of the novels *Brown Girl in the Ring*, *Midnight Robber*, and *The Salt Roads*. Her short story collection *Skin Folk* received the World Fantasy Award. Her fourth novel, *The New Moon's Arms*, comes out in spring 2007.

Nicholas Kaufmann's fiction has appeared in *The Mammoth Book of Best New Erotica Volume 3*, *Shivers 5*, *Fishnet*, *Cemetery Dance*, *City Slab*, and a host of other fine venues. He lives in Brooklyn, New York. Visit him at: http://www.nicholaskaufmann.com.

Tsaurah Litzky writes dirty stories because she wants to put cupcakes in your panties and she believe in making love. This is her seventh appearance in *Best American Erotica*. Her erotic novella, *The Motion of the Ocean*, was published by Simon & Schuster as part of *Three the Hard Way*, a series of erotic novellas edited by Susie Bright. Tsaurah is also a poet and a playwright. She teaches erotic writing at the New School in Manhattan.

Marie Lyn Bernard's erotic work has appeared in *The Best Women's Erotica of 2005*; *The Mammoth Book of Best New Erotica, Volume 5*; *Erotic Interludes 2: Stolen Moments*; *Fresh off the Vine*; *Desdemona.com*; and *CleanSheets*. Her less-sexy but equally fabulous fiction and nonfiction has been published by *Nerve*, *Conversely*, *The Sarah Lawrence Review*, *ElitesTV.com*, and *Xylem*. She's a recent graduate of the University of Michigan and currently lives among all the other aspirational young hipsters in Williamsburg, Brooklyn, and works for the Donald Maass Literary Agency.

Peggy Munson's first novel, *Origami Striptease*, won the Project Queerlit Prize. She has published poetry, fiction, and erotica in such venues as *Best American Erotica 2006*, *Best Lesbian Erotica 1998–2006*, *Best Bisexual Erotica II*, *Tough Girls*, *On Our Backs*, *Hers3*, *Blithe House Quarterly*,

Lodestar Quarterly, Best American Poetry 2003, Margin: Exploring Modern Magical Realism, and elsewhere. Visit her at: www.peggymunson.com.

This is **Susan St. Aubin**'s fourth appearance in *Best American Erotica.* She has stories in *Best American Erotica 1995, 2000,* and *2003.* She's thrilled that "Taste" survived the demise of *Herotica 7* as well as editor Mary Anne Mohanraj's computer crash, to find new life in *Fishnet* and now in *Best American Erotica 2007.* Her recent work can be found in *The Best of Both Worlds: Bisexual Erotica* and *Amazons: Sexy Tales of Strong Women.*

Nikki Sinclair lives and writes in Minneapolis, Minnesota, a city of trench coats, wine bars, brick streets, faded movie houses, old china, stained menu cards, espresso machines, and lovers making it in cold doorways as foot cops in brogans and heavy blue coats with polished buttons look the other way. Visit her at: http//nikkisinclair.blog.com.

Kim Wright is a travel writer who lives in North Carolina with her three children, four cats, and dog. She is presently at work on her first novel.

CREDITS

READER SURVEY

Please return this survey, or any other BAE correspondence to:

SUSIE BRIGHT
BAE—Feedback, P.O. Box 8377,
Santa Cruz, CA 95061. Or, e-mail your reply to:
BAE@susiebright.com.

1. What are your favorite stories in this year's collection?

2. Have you read previous years' editions of *The Best American Erotica*?

3. Do you have any favorite stories or authors from those previous collections?

4. Do you have any recommendations for next year's *The Best American Erotica 2008*? Nominated stories must have been published in North America, in any form—book, periodical, Internet—between March 1, 2006, and March 1, 2007.

5. How old are you?

6. Male or female?

7. Where do you live?

8. Any other suggestions for the series?

Thanks so much. Your comments are truly appreciated. If you send me your e-mail address, I will reply to you when I receive your feedback.

Read the entire collection of Susie Bright's groundbreaking
EROTICA SERIES

0-7432-5852-5   0-7432-5850-9   0-7432-2262-8

0-7432-2261-X   0-684-86915-2   0-684-86914-4   0-684-84396-X

0-684-84395-1   0-684-81823-X   0-684-81830-2   0-684-80163-9

TOUCHSTONE
A Division of Simon & Schuster
A CBS COMPANY
www.simonsays.com